BALAAM'S ERROR

BOOKS BY MICHAEL WEBB

GIANTS IN THE EARTH TRILOGY

Book 1
THE MASTER'S QUILT

Book 2
BALAAM'S ERROR

Book 3
SONG OF THE SERAPHIM
(to come)

BALAAM'S ERROR

Michael Webb

CROSSWAY BOOKS

A DIVISION OF GOOD NEWS PUBLISHERS

WHEATON, ILLINOIS • CAMBRIDGE, ENGLAND

Balaam's Error.

Published by Crossway Books, a division of
Good News Publishers, 1300 Crescent St., Wheaton, Illinois 60187.

Cover illustration: Chuck Gillies

First printing, 1992

Printed in the United States of America

Library of Congress Cataloging-in-Publication Data
Webb, Michael, 1953-
    Balaam's error / Michael Webb
      p.   cm.
    Book 2 in the Giants in the earth trilogy.
    I. Title.
PS3573.E1982B35 1992   813'.54—dc20   91-47635
ISBN 0-89107-641-7

00	99	98	97	96	95	94	93	92
15	14	13	12	11	10	9	8	7	6	5	4	3	2	1

First British Edition 1992

ISBN 1 85684 041 7

Production and Printing in the United States of America for
CROSSWAY BOOKS
Kingfisher House, 7 High Green, Great Shelford, Cambridge CB2 18G

For
Elizabeth Gail Zambrano,
one of the Lord's dedicated
and faithful intercessors
and a true friend
in Christ

ACKNOWLEDGMENTS

My thanks to all those at Crossway Books who have been, and continue to be, involved in bringing the GIANTS IN THE EARTH trilogy to publication. Special thanks to Jan Dennis for taking a chance on an unknown, struggling author whose passion to share with the world the importance of the blood of Christ far exceeds his abilities to communicate it.

Woe to them! For they have gone in the way of Cain and have run greedily into the error of Balaam for profit, and perished in the rebellion of Korah.
These are spots in your love feasts, while they feast with you without fear, serving only themselves. They are clouds without water, carried about by the winds; late autumn trees without fruit, twice dead, pulled up by the roots; raging waves of the sea, foaming up their own shame; wandering stars for whom is reserved the blackness of darkness forever.

(Jude 11-13)

But there were also false prophets among the people, even as there will be false teachers among you, who will secretly bring in destructive heresies, even denying the Lord who bought them, and bring on themselves swift destruction.
And many will follow their destructive ways, because of whom the way of truth will be blasphemed.
By covetousness they will exploit you with deceptive words; for a long time their judgment has not been idle, and their destruction does not slumber.

(2 Peter 2:1-3)

PROLOGUE

Outside the small hut the China sun hung hot and glowing in a cerulean sky. Inside it was dark, and the smell of sweet smoke hung thick in the air like a thin veil. Chi Lin kept her eyes to the floor, bowing as she shuffled toward the old man seated on a mat. She did not look up into his eyes, as was proper for an obedient Chinese girl, but her heart burned. She needed what the old man could give her. Yet she had to be careful, very careful, not to alienate him.

"Come forward, my daughter," the old man said, lighting a candle.

Chi Lin obeyed.

"You may speak," he told her in a raspy voice. "What can this old priest do for you?"

"I have come a long way, revered one." She kept her eyes cast down. "I have come because it is said that you talk to the gods . . . And that the gods hear you."

"Have you brought the sacrifice?"

Chi Lin nodded. "The breeding pig is tied outside." Her heart was hammering, and she was glad she didn't have to meet his gaze, because he might see the truth of how she'd come by the sacred pig.

"And the other?"

Mutely she reached inside her sleeve and withdrew a small jar containing the thick brown powder made from poppies. She'd paid a month's wages for it, but if he could influence the gods on her behalf, it would be worth it.

The aged priest took the ceramic jar, and when his hand brushed hers she noticed that his skin was dry and fragile, like ancient parchment. He caressed the jar as one would a lover's hand, then asked, "And what do you want from the gods, my daughter?"

Even with her head bowed, Chi Lin felt defiance rear. She would have to be careful as to how she asked. Proper Chinese girls never forgot that men were the ones who ruled and who held absolute power over body and soul. She desperately wanted her husband's favor, she'd made up her mind to do whatever it took to get it, and she knew what Franklin wanted above all other things. "I am barren, revered sir."

"You have been with your husband?"

"Many times, but still I do not conceive."

"Where do you live?" the priest asked abruptly.

"Bashan."

The sudden silence in the hut wrapped itself around Chi Lin like a tight-fitting glove, and she felt as if she were suffocating. Fear welled up inside her. Had she said something improper?

"You came far for nothing," rasped the old man. "Your local priest can sacrifice to ensure that your womb be filled."

Chi Lin's fear flared into panic. She couldn't let the priest dismiss her — not until she received that for which she had come. She dropped to her knees and bowed until her forehead touched the edge of the mat. "A male child, holy one. It *must* be a boy."

"You may look at me," the priest directed.

She raised her eyes slowly, forcing herself to keep them wide with humility and gratitude. He was completely bald and older than she'd even imagined, and there was a milky film over his eyes. He was blind! Her disappointment tasted acrid in her mouth. How could this sightless, foolish old man help her? And after all she'd done to gain access to him.

"Your husband is *gwei lo*," the priest continued, using the colloquial term that meant "foreign devil." It wasn't a rebuke, merely a statement of fact. "He lost a wife and unborn child, a daughter, and chose you to take their place. In the night he holds you and weeps . . . and you cannot console him."

Chi Lin's mouth dropped open. How could he possibly know?

"This foreigner came to China to speak about his God . . . To change our ways and fill our land with another Light."

"He is a Christian. But I am not. I still believe in the power of the old gods. That is why I have come." Chi Lin prayed silently that the old man did not know her other secrets. Especially about her father. If he did, he would surely send her away.

"You have chosen wisely." The priest inclined his head, as if he were listening to someone talking.

Chi Lin strained her hearing, but discerned nothing more than the sounds of the village outside. She took a chance and darted her eyes, but saw nothing beyond the meager trappings of the hut. Sweat trickled down her chest.

"You are fortunate," the priest whispered. "The gods want very much to favor you."

Her heart leaped. "Then they will grant me a son?"

"Much more than that, my daughter."

His cryptic message made no sense to her, but she didn't care — the gods would grant her heart's desire. And Franklin would love her. And one day her son would live with his father in America, away from the stink and injustices of China. And when her female babies were thrown into the rivers, in bags weighted with rocks, it would not hurt so much because she had a son in a place where the ancient gods could not touch him. "I will do whatever you ask," she whispered to the priest.

The old man nodded. "Yes, you will. No matter how frightened you become, you must do exactly as I say."

Chi Lin lay on her mat rigid with fear, but wild with anticipation. This was to be the night the gods would visit her and give her a son. It was written in the stars in the moonless sky. And it had shown up in the tea leaves when she'd washed out the teapot that night. Franklin was away, in another village. The god would come to her unnoticed.

In spite of the fact that it was the middle of winter, the hut was hot. Yet she shivered, because she was naked and because she was hours away from fulfillment. She reached for the small teacup next to the mat and finished off the amber-colored liquid in one long gulp. It burned all the way down, making her eyes water. Suddenly she felt light-headed. She smiled and set the teacup down. The drink she distilled from almonds was Franklin's favorite.

She shut her eyes tightly and chanted the words the old priest had taught her. Her litany went on for hours, but she never wearied. Just before 2 A.M. she felt something come into the hut. The flow of words stopped abruptly. What if Franklin had returned?

She opened her eyes and saw a shape, a form like a man's, but not a man's. It was huge. Words of greeting wedged in her throat. The shape that was darker than the night leaned down over her body, and she clenched her eyes shut again, because all she'd seen had been its eyes. They were orange, the color the China sun had been in her dream, when she'd seen the cloud shaped like a mushroom that grew out of the belly of the earth and blotted out the ocher-gray sky.

She heard the being breathe, and her flesh constricted, suddenly taut, along her belly. Her fear was so palpable she almost gagged. What if he ripped her apart, from the inside out? Reason prevailed. She was needed to nurture the baby. There was no need for alarm. Still . . .

She sought to fill her mind with the litany, but all coherence had fled. Other words came instead — words Franklin had taught her. "Jesus loves me, this I know . . ."

The shape above her recoiled. Her face stung, as if it had been slapped, yet no hand had touched her. Chi Lin squeezed her lips tight, so as not to cry out. Slowly sanity returned, and with it resolve. It would be over in minutes, and afterward the boy-child she'd been promised would be hers.

She was wrong. It took hours.

Just before dawn, something rippled along her skin. She was exhausted, but still she shuddered, half in pain, half in joy, like a king about to hold a great treasure. She sensed the being crawl over her, grow large again.

Chi Lin gasped, arching her back. Franklin was gentle, but this being . . . She balled her fists, gripping the edges of the mat, and bit her lip until it bled. The smell of her blood filled the room, and she heard an odd, guttural, wailing sound, like the wind whipping across the desert. She felt the being fleck the drops of blood off her lip, and even though her eyes were closed, she had the sense that he was tasting it.

At last his assault was over, and she felt him withdraw. She gagged because of her pain and because of the acrid smell that had invaded the room. It was as if a thousand matches had been lit, and she couldn't get the stench out of her nostrils. Tears escaped from the corners of her eyelids. She didn't know how long she lay crying, but at some point she realized she was alone again.

Relief washed over her. Yet she didn't move. Gradually the rapid thudding of her heart slowed, and her breathing changed from gasps to sighs. Hours later the fire in her belly still burned like a blacksmith's coals, but she smiled. Slowly she lay her palm across her abdomen, and from far away a wild dog howled. She knew with certainty that her womb was full and that in nine months she would have the son she wanted.

Franklin would never know.

She wondered if his god did.

Far back in my childhood
the struggle began.

(*de Monade*, Giordano Bruno)

I

The Sinai, October 1948.

Benjamin Kingman almost missed the entrance to the cave. But the early-morning sun reflecting off a shiny object half-buried in the pulverized limestone and marl caught his eye. The tall, wiry Jew bent over and, pulling the soft paintbrush he carried for just such a purpose from the rear pocket of his khaki shorts, methodically brushed the parched earth away from the partially oxidized piece of metal.

Once he had it entirely exposed, his heart beat so rapidly he felt the throbbing in his ears. His whole body tingled with the sudden infusion of adrenaline. "Praise God," he muttered as he squatted down in the dust, "I *knew* Qumran revealed only a portion of what this ocean of sand has hidden in her depths."

The object was a sword — the type carried by Roman centurions. Even though he was only twenty-three, he'd been an archaeologist long enough to know a treasure when he saw it.

Carefully, he began to dig some more, and within a few moments he'd uncovered another treasure — a goblet made of pure silver. Holding the sword in his left hand and the silver cup reverently in his right, he put his face close to a small, elongated opening and sniffed. The air was musty but not rank. He decided to probe further. He set the artifacts to the side gently, as if they were objects that could easily be damaged instead of ones that had survived almost two millennia virtually unscathed, and continued digging into the side of the cliff.

At dawn the air had been cool, about 60 degrees, and there had been a thick, vaporous canopy hovering over the Great Salt

Sea, called *Bahr Lût*, the Sea of Lot, by the Arabs. Because of the high concentration of marl in the limestone deposits, and because of the lack of pollutants in the desert air, the yellow-orange rays of sunrise had produced a dramatic and breathtaking scene. A peculiar white mist, striated with ocher and red variegations that made it almost seem *alive*, hung in the air. It was as if the mist were a spectral apparition pulsing with blood pumped through arteries of light.

Now, barely three hours later, the 100-degree heat sucked moisture from his body as he worked, just as a parasite sucks blood from its host.

After an hour of patient digging, Benjamin had cleared away enough debris so he could squeeze through the opening. He paused to take a sip of water from his canteen and rummaged inside his knapsack, then pulled out a flashlight and turned it on to make sure it worked. Satisfied, he glanced around furtively, then crawled headfirst into the cave.

The diffuse light penetrated the cloying darkness only a few feet. He was still sweating profusely, in spite of the fact that the temperature inside the cave was considerably cooler than the air outside. He took a deep breath and looked around, then walked forward a few feet. Suddenly his eyes grew wide, and his hands started to shake.

He stared for several minutes at the bundle of thick linen lying on the floor in front of him, then let out the breath he'd been holding and wiped the sweat from his brow with the back of his hand. He moved closer and fell softly to his knees to avoid stirring up the fine, yellow-white dust that covered the floor. He shifted the flashlight to his left hand, only with difficulty keeping it from trembling as he reached out and gently grasped the bundle in his right hand.

It was heavier than it looked. And as he panned the flashlight over the bundle up close, he realized it was stained a reddish-copper color in several places. Dried blood perhaps?

Elated, Benjamin hugged the bundle to his chest and scrambled out of the darkness into the light. He ignored the implacable heat as he sat cross-legged beside the opening and stared at his discovery. He felt light-headed, almost giddy, and he couldn't stop his hands from shaking. Finally, unable to restrain himself any longer, he unwrapped the linen. "What a find!" he muttered aloud, overcome by his discovery.

Two weeks later Benjamin stared out the window of his hotel room and knew it was time to leave Palestine. Below him sprawled the city of Jerusalem. In the distance he could see the Dome of the Rock, the site of the former magnificent Temples that Solomon, Zerubbabel, and Herod had built. The war had ruined and physically divided much of the once beautiful city. But now, barely six months after the last British ship had sailed out of Haifa, leaving the fledgling state of Israel in the hands of the politicians, new buildings were growing out of the debris like green shoots in a fire-ravaged forest. One day the city would be beautiful again.

He sighed and stepped onto the balcony. The sky was a mosaic of crimson-colored receding light and gauze-like cirrostratus clouds. On the street below merchants were closing their shops for the evening and people were disappearing into doorways, their lingering silhouettes framed by the long shadows of late afternoon. *Time, death, and the desert are unappeasable*, he thought as he watched the sun set over the Mount of Olives.

Dusk in the East was peculiar. It had an almost tangible characteristic about it that he had never experienced in America, as if light were taking on corporeal form for a brief tryst with the physical world.

Benjamin knew that the Romans had expressed their feelings on the matter by associating twilight with the wolf, usually in a negative context. He smiled, thinking how ironic it was that a man nicknamed "The Wolf" had dramatically changed *his* life.

The previous April an itinerant bedouin of the Taamirah tribe, calling himself Muhammad adh-Dhib, "The Wolf," had arrived in Jerusalem with a number of what appeared to be very old, brittle, and badly decomposed leather scrolls wrapped in linen cloth. "The Wolf" and his compatriots had been smuggling goats and various black-market goods from the Trans-Jordan into Palestine, hoping to sell their contraband in Bethlehem. They had stopped along the shores of the Dead Sea in order to stock up with water at the only source of fresh water for miles around—the spring of Ain Feshka. The route Muhammad and his fellow bedouins had followed was approximately the same route that Elimelech, husband of Naomi, and his family had followed traveling from Bethlehem to Moab.

While throwing stones into one of the many limestone caves that had been carved out of the cliffs rising above the arid landscape, he had chanced upon several clay urns that later examination proved had been resting undisturbed in the cave for centuries. Muhammad was sure he had stumbled upon something he could sell; he praised Allah for guiding him to the cave a mile north of the old ruin Kirbet Qumran. Some scholars believed that Qumran — whose Arab pronunciation was very similar to "Gomorrah" — was the site of the ancient city where Lot and his family had resided.

"The Wolf" had packed the leather scrolls safely away with his other "valuable" goods and headed off to Bethlehem. And that was how the "Dead Sea Scrolls," as they were now being referred to, had come to light. Fortunately for Benjamin, he'd been only a stone's throw away when the discovery had been made.

A soft breeze teased his disheveled brown hair and cooled his deeply tanned skin. The dry air absorbed his sweat like an invisible sponge. He licked his chapped lips, and his tongue came away tasting of salt.

He rubbed the back of his neck, then bent forward, trying to loosen some of the tightness that had become a permanent companion during the last three months in Israel. The long hours of solitary work had paid off, but the significance of what he'd found had been overshadowed by the discovery at Qumran of ancient scrolls by others. *It's just as well*, he thought as he massaged the tiredness from his legs.

A tingling shiver danced a momentary promenade up and down his spine. He turned and gazed over his shoulder as his eyes were drawn, almost magnetically, to the bundle of linen. Inside were the parchments that would make him a hunted man if anyone knew he had them. They were rolled up in the corner, beside the sword and goblet, pointing at him like accusatory fingers.

With a sigh, he turned his back on the ancient Canaanite city whose original name meant "foundation of peace" and walked back into the room. Lately his life had been anything but peaceful. When he reached the makeshift desk he'd put together from several old crates and some rough wood planking he stopped and cocked his head, as if straining to hear a barely discernible sound. He stayed that way for several minutes, standing silently in the shadows, as the last light of day suffused itself around his body and outlined his lanky form in an orange-red softness that belied the hard tightness he felt inside his chest.

Finally he sat down wearily and, lost in thought, stared at his journal, which was in many ways his conscience . . . his salvation. He'd started writing it just after his father died, and between its leather covers he'd chronicled his personal war with an enemy older than time. A war between Light and darkness. A battle in — and for — his soul.

He stared at the words he'd scribbled across the yellowed pages with such intensity that an observer might have thought he was trying to decipher some kind of magical revelation hidden between the journal's bindings. And perhaps that was not far from the truth, for the words he had so methodically penned over the past two years were sutures binding him securely to the mast of sanity, like Ulysses, and keeping him safe from Sirens' call to oblivion.

He'd also transcribed key passages from the parchments into the journal with painstaking care. It had not been an easy task. He'd been so overwhelmed by what he'd uncovered that he'd also been compelled to write a detailed analysis of what the parchments said. Perhaps one day the full story could be told.

The author of the scrolls had chosen to write in Hebrew

instead of Greek. Benjamin was not surprised. Greek would not have done justice to the story. Hebrew, *Lashon Ha-Kodesh*, the Holy Speech of Tongue, was necessary. In composition, it is simple, pictorial, and poetic. More importantly, Jews believe Hebrew to be the perfect language of God, given by Him to His "chosen people" so that they might communicate with Him.

Benjamin knew from his college studies that Hebrew was already in spoken and written use when Moses and the Israelites came out of Egypt in approximately 1440 B.C. During the centuries between that time and the time when the parchments were apparently written, the language had become more and more refined, until it was a sophisticated form of communication.

He also knew that in the late thirties a simple alphabetic Semitic script similar to Hebrew had been discovered on tablets found in northern Syria, at Ras Shamra-Ugarit. While he'd been in Damascus, fortune had smiled down upon him. He'd met one of the men who'd worked with Schaeffer and the other Frenchmen who'd uncovered the tablets at the archaeological site from 1935 to 1937. He'd questioned the man extensively over dinner and several bottles of wine one night and had been given some startling information.

"Are you aware," asked the man once they'd finished eating and had begun their second bottle of wine, "that even though Hebrew is the language of the Jewish Scriptures, except for a few passages written in Aramaic, nowhere in Scripture is it referred to as such."

Benjamin nodded. "It's called the 'language of Canaan' in Isaiah, in order to distinguish it from the Egyptian language, and the authors of Second Kings refer to it as the 'Jewish language' in order to distinguish it from Aramaean."

The man smiled and continued, "Very good, my young friend. You have done your homework. But what I'm about to tell you, I'm sure you *don't* know."

"Oh? Why is that?"

"Because it's not written in any textbooks. At least not *yet*." The Frenchman belched loudly, punctuating his statement and signaling his approval of the meal and the wine, then continued. "Not only did we uncover important data that will shed new light on the origins of the alphabet and the Phoenician influence on a variety of languages, including Hebrew, but our excavations of the mound also unearthed an incredible corpus of Canaanite religious epic poetry inscribed on clay tablets . . . in alphabetic cuneiform."

"Go on, tell me the rest," prodded Benjamin as he poured them both more wine.

"The texts are written in Ugaritic and clearly demonstrate the moral depravity and effeteness of the Canaanite culture. They graphically depict the culture's orgiastic nature worship as well as the cults of fertility, replete with serpent symbols and sensuous nudity. Baal, the son of Dagon, an ancient Mesopotamian deity associated with agriculture, and El, son of Baal, were the two great gods. Anath, Ashtoreth, also known as Astarte, and Asherah were the three principal variations of the name of the goddess of sensual love, maternity, and fertility."

"I've heard of her," interrupted Benjamin. "The Babylonians called her Ishtar, the patroness of sex and war. The name Asherah is mentioned over forty times in Scripture, usually in conjunction with a stripped tree, a pillar, or a pole as a phallic symbol."

"That's not the half of it," continued the man, the tenor of his voice suddenly growing somber. "We found tablets in which Asherah/Ashtoreth/Anath is repeatedly depicted as a nude woman sitting astride a lion with a lily in her left hand and a serpent in her right. The lily represents grace and sexual appeal, while the serpent symbolizes fecundity. Her shrines, especially those at Byblos, the ancient Phoenician city twenty-five miles north of what is now Beirut, were temples of legalized vice."

"Wasn't Asherah also the chief goddess of Tyre, over a hundred and fifty years *earlier*?"

Benjamin's newfound source of information suddenly shuddered and grew pale, as if Benjamin had struck a raw nerve, reminding him of something he'd been trying to forget. The man quickly finished off the last of the wine in his glass, then feverishly motioned for the waiter to bring another bottle. He stared at Benjamin with eyes filled with revulsion.

"What's wrong? Are you alright?"

The man waited until the waiter had uncorked a fresh bottle of wine and poured them each a full glass before he answered. "This goddess, Asherah, is an abomination."

"You mean *was*."

"I said what I meant."

"I don't understand."

"Never mind. Forget it."

"Please. I'm sorry if I said anything to offend you. I was only trying —"

"It isn't anything you said," interrupted the man, suddenly back in control of himself. "It's what's inside here . . . the things I saw at the dig that I can't forget. The things that wake me from sleep in the darkest hours of the night," he added, pointing to his forehead.

"At Ras Shamra?"

The man nodded. "And other digs as well."

"Tell me."

The man stared at Benjamin for what seemed like several minutes, but was only a few seconds, then said, "In Tyre, Asherah was given the appellation *Qudshu*, or 'the holy one,' as if in some perverted moral sense she was a divine courtesan. She was quite the contrary. Her worshipers, led by male prostitutes called *qedishim*, 'sodomites,' glamorized lust and murder."

The man paused, and Benjamin had the feeling he was trying to gain courage to speak about something he found personally repugnant.

"At Ras Shamra we discovered a tablet, a fragment of what Dr. Schaeffer eventually named 'The Baal Epic,' in which a grotesque story is told. Anath/Asherah leads a fiendishly bloody orgy of destruction against mankind. Men, women, even children are butchered without remorse in the most horrible ways imaginable. All the while, this supposedly holy goddess wades ecstatically through human gore — up to her knees at first, and finally up to her throat. Throughout it all, she sadistically exults in her debauchery."

Benjamin grew pensive. He took several sips of his wine before he spoke, giving himself time to formulate a response. "I've heard rumors, of course, that there is a lot of that kind of thing being uncovered from digs of the era. But tell me, as an archaeologist surely you have seen this type of thing before. Why are you so upset? It's only myth."

The man stared at him with sad, unblinking eyes. "Are you absolutely *certain* of that?" was all he said.

Benjamin finished reading the account he'd written the day after his disconcerting dinner conversation with the French archaeologist and continued to slowly flip the pages of his journal. He wasn't really reading now. It was more like the past two years of his life were passing before him. The strange and disconcerting things that he'd discovered during the course of his excursions, especially those he'd made out from Damascus, now seemed to make sense. Oddly, he felt both relief and fear.

Regardless of how often his training told him the story contained within the bundle of linen was too fantastic to be real, something inside him knew otherwise. The parchments were a stunningly accurate historical record, written by a man who had lived at the time Pontius Pilate ruled Judea, the southernmost Roman division of Palestine. There was, however, an enigma that could not be ignored.

The story was so detailed, it had to have been penned by someone who had lived through the incredible occurrences. And yet, that was impossible, for the events chronicled covered a span of history spanning at least seventy-five hundred years. No man, not even Methuselah, had lived that long.

Benjamin sighed again and reached for the bottle of wine he kept for times such as these, when the magnitude of the revelation became a burden his spirit could no longer bear. He poured himself a glass, knowing it would relax him. After taking several sips, he turned to the first empty page and began writing.

October 31st.
Jerusalem.

This month started out dismally for me, in spite of it being *Rosh Hashanah*. I spent nearly ten weeks of sixteen-hour days battling the dust, the heat, and my own frustrations. There seemed to be no end in sight . . .

But, as usual, I'm getting ahead of myself.

Two months ago I received a telegram from George Amos, an antiquities dealer and a member of the Syrian Jacobite Church of St. Paul. He informed me that he had helped the Archbishop Metropolitan, Mar Athanasius Yeshue Samuel, obtain and authenticate five very old, very special scrolls.

Even though George's message was brief, there was something about his words that caused my heart to flutter and the blood to pump a little faster through my veins. More excited than I can remember being in a long time, I put everything else on hold and rushed back here from Damascus, all thoughts of finding material for the grist mill of my thesis temporarily displaced.

(There are times, and this is one of them, that I wonder about my choice of vocation. If my father Jacob were alive, he would most certainly disapprove of his youngest son obtaining a Ph.D. in ancient Semitic myths and legends. I can hear him now: "Why can't you be more like your brother Joseph? At least he is doing something practical. Something I can be proud of." As usual, Father, I don't have an answer for you.)

To continue . . .

It wasn't until after I talked with George face to face that I learned the true magnitude of the discovery. Over one hundred Biblical and intertestamental scrolls, dating from sometime between 50 B.C. and A.D. 70, were found in a cave not far from here, on the shores of the Dead Sea. Our ancestors referred to it as the Great Salt Sea, the Sea of the *Arabah*, or the Asphalt Sea. I swam in it only once. The water is extremely nauseous to the taste and oily to the touch. I neglected to wash with fresh water after my swim, and within a short time my skin was covered with a thick crust of salt.

(Forgive my digressions, but I am at heart a student of nature, and therefore I am compelled to elaborate on those wondrous aspects of God's creation which intrigue me.)

The most exciting discovery to date from Qumran is a parchment that has been given the name the "Isaiah Scroll."

Unearthing a complete document of a Biblical manuscript has created a storm of sensation; not only because it's the first major Biblical manuscript of antiquity ever to have been found, but also because it is more than a thousand years older than the oldest Hebrew texts preserved in the Massoretic tradition. Those texts, the basis for all recent Biblical translations, only go back as far as A.D. 900.

Needless to say, I was distraught at the possibility that I had missed the opportunity of a lifetime. Not since von Tischendorf discovered the *Codex Sinaiticus* in the monastery built by Justinian at the foot of Gebel Musa has there been such excitement in the archaeological community worldwide.

(I've been to the monastery, now dedicated to St. Catherine of Alexandria, and I've seen and read a few of the three thousand manuscripts in the library, some of which are older than the monastery itself. They're breathtaking!)

George put me in touch with a friend of his who is highly placed in the government, and I pleaded with him to help me get a permit to work the Qumran site. Unfortunately, my requests were categorically denied. And that is why I resolved to strike out on my own.

After six weeks of hard work, just five days after *Yom Kippur*, God rewarded my tenacity . . .

Benjamin reached for the wine bottle and grunted when he realized it was empty. He blinked and shook his head to clear away fatigue, then leaned back in the chair.

The sun had set, and darkness was poised to cover the city like a blanket. He knew that tonight the moon, having gloried in her fullness the past three nights, would hide like a demure maiden. Yet the stars seemed reluctant to perform their nightly promenade across the purple-black stage of the heavens. Suddenly a series of disconcerting images intruded upon his thoughts.

Deep within the slumbering city that lay spread out below the mount, an old man, his once abundant and jet black hair and beard now thinning and gray, began the task of preparing for the ensuing eight days of celebration and worship. It was just after midnight when he left his humble home and walked quietly through the dark-ened, deserted streets. His whole body tingled with expectancy as he inhaled the familiar musk odor of the city. He did not have to walk far, and upon reaching his destination he reached forth with a stubby, callused hand and unlatched the gate.

The old man, his senses attuned to the various rhythms in the sea of night surrounding him, moved among the animals with the practiced ease of one long accustomed to ritual. The collection of male lambs crowded in the pen — none younger than eight days nor older than one year — represented the finest sheep of twenty dif-ferent flocks. The initial selection had been accomplished in broad daylight and each had been chosen carefully to insure that none had blemishes or imperfections.

The old man, however, did not rely upon sight to tell him of imperfection. Instead, he depended upon his acute sense of smell for the final test. He was blind.

He smiled and sniffed the air. The odor was faint, but it was there. He'd been asked many times during his seventy years to describe the scent, and his reply had always been the same: "I'm not sure exactly. But I am sure of three things. I always smell the pecu-liar scent after only a short time among the lambs; I never smell it on more than one animal; and I know that the gift is from God."

Without further delay, he reached down swiftly and grabbed hold of a pure white lamb baying softly to his right. This is the one, he thought as he carried the animal inside the building adjacent to the pen, handing it over gently into the outstretched arms of the waiting priest.

The night gave way to morning, and the morning to afternoon. The old man had returned home, slept, and was now back at the Temple. It was time.

Although it was early afternoon, the room was dark except for the light provided by several tall candles. The color of the wax was almost as pure white as the coat of wool covering the lamb held in the arms of the priest.

The Levite, one of several present, carried the lamb to the altar, carefully stretched it out upon the deeply stained, grooved wood, and secured its four legs firmly with leather straps. Only then did he withdraw the razor-sharp sacrificial knife from his robe.

First the Levite, then other priests closed their eyes and began to sing in unison, filling the Temple with the sonorous sound of the Great Hallel. The old man added his own deep-throated voice to that of the others, singing with vigor. Outside, in the immediate vicinity of the Temple, the sounds of the city were swallowed up by the ritual chanting.

Gradually the singing stopped. The Levite opened his eyes and grasped the head of the lamb. He stretched the animal's neck backward, exposing the soft, vulnerable flesh to the light and the knife. His right hand was poised above his head.

Swiftly, with a precisely articulated motion, he brought his arm down, turning the blade ever so slightly as the knife dropped downward through its arc. In one deft stroke he drew the shining blade across the animal's neck, severing the jugular vein.

Several of the priests blew a threefold blast from their silver trumpets as bright red blood spurted from the wound. Special silver and gold ceremonial bowls caught the warm, sticky fluid, which was then splashed in one single jet at the base of the altar.

A small amount of blood escaped the confines of the altar and fell to the foot-packed ground. The desiccated, yellow-brown earth and the burgundy-red, liquid life blended together into a copper-colored mud.

The Levite grasped the dead animal by its hind legs, took a

length of rope, and secured the sacrifice from two hooks mounted in staves nailed together in the shape of a T. It was flayed, and the entrails were taken out and cleansed. Afterwards, the inside fat was separated, put in a dish and salted, then placed in the fire of the altar of burnt offering.

The ritual was repeated continually for several hours. There were many waiting, just like the old man, for their paschal sacrifice.

Once again twilight settled upon the city. The old man stood in the doorway of his small hovel and stared at the sky with sightless eyes. A penetrating shiver danced a promenade up and down his spine. For some strange reason he could almost feel the darkness seeping into his bones through the pores of his skin, and somehow he knew that even though there were no clouds in the ebony sky, there were also no stars.

Hastily he dipped the hyssop he held in his trembling right hand into the wooden bowl he cupped in his left and sprinkled the blood of the lamb upon his doorway, wondering why he felt so strange on this very special night.

The priest lit the incense. The room was smoky, the air thick with ketoret, the special blend of spices he'd prepared earlier. He took several deep breaths as he went about his tasks and smiled contentedly. His nose twitched as he savored the unique aromatic smell: frankincense, galbanum, stactate, onchya, and myrrh.

Finally, as the thick night began to seep into the cracks and crevices of the Temple, he trimmed the lamps in preparation for the evening prayer.

Startled by the unusual occurrence, Benjamin shook his head to clear it, not quite certain that the vivid images were merely a fragment of a long forgotten memory that had been dredged up from the recesses of his subconscious because of his exhaustion. He thought about lighting a candle, but decided against it. For some strange reason, the fading of the light was reassuring.

Bits and pieces of his Hebraic upbringing floated upon the choppy sea of his memory, like flotsam and jetsam bobbing up and down upon the ocean. Oddly, he felt like singing. He crossed his arms over his chest and rocked back and forth in the chair. The liturgy that rose up from inside him flowed from his lips unbidden. "In your streams all fish will leap. . . . In your rocks all plants will take root. . . . In your fiery vortex every man will be saved . . . from your peaks."

Benjamin was familiar with the words, a segment of an ancient Hebrew text, *Canticle of the Sea*, a kind of lyric sermon about everything that happened between the Red Sea and the peak of Gebel Musa, the mountain of Moses. But he had no idea where the melody came from.

He stopped singing and frowned with sudden insight. His ancestors saw the Sinai almost as a living entity, suffused with the life of God. Why then could he not bring himself to see and think that way? For him the desert was simply a vast museum of the past whose treasures were hidden beneath the arid landscape. And he was merely a modern-day detective engaged in the tedious task of discovering artifacts lost from antiquity.

Suddenly he was very tired. He felt old beyond his years. He pressed his thumbs against his eyelids, knowing he had to make a final entry in his journal before he could even attempt to sleep. He didn't want to forget, in later years, why he'd betrayed his Uncle Mattathias, his grandfather's dream, and Israel, his adopted home. Not to mention his God.

Bracing himself with the final gulp of wine that remained in his glass, he skipped down several lines so he could finish his earlier train of thought later.

Sleep has become my enemy.

In the hours between midnight and cockcrow, the nightmare that has been my companion now for nearly six months wakes me from fitful slumber, and I lay upon my cot sweating with the knowledge of my betrayal and the fear of what the increasingly vivid dream portends.

Perhaps it is a harbinger of the future, although I don't believe in that sort of thing. Nevertheless, I am compelled to cry out to the Almighty and ask His forgiveness.

I have decided not to reveal my discovery. I know that the parchments are a national treasure and that by keeping them for myself I am committing more than a mere theft. But I cannot give them up. They have become too important.

Benjamin closed the journal, stood up, and stretched. He walked to the balcony a second time and took a deep breath, filling his lungs with the musky odor of the city. It was a unique scent, peculiar to the Holy City. The cool, fragrant air helped to temporarily douse the fire smoldering within him. For a time his thoughts wandered to the Temple as it must have been at the time of Pontius Pilate. He wondered if what he was smelling was the accumulated residue of two thousand years of burning *ketoret*.

The blood of the lamb, he thought. *The paschal sacrifice. Is it possible there was truly only one? Are we that blind to the truth?* What was it Rabbi Markowitz, his mentor during the years leading to his *Bar Mitzvah*, had said: "When you wonder you wander . . ."

The wine had dutifully worked its magic, and Benjamin's mind began to calm. He watched the stars push through the curtain of night. For a moment he thought he saw several come together in the shape of a cross. Startled, he rubbed the tiredness from his eyes and muttered, "It must be an illusion." A scholarly voice within assured him the image had to be the result of his exhaustion — and the wine.

As the darkness deepened, he no longer felt the aches and pains of his body or the burden of his conscience. Finally he stepped back into the room and stretched out on his cot.

As he drifted into sleep, he thought it very fitting that he'd discovered the parchments on the fifteenth day of the seventh month — the Feast of Tabernacles, the most important of the three great annual feasts of his people. His Uncle Mattathias had told him that God had something special planned for him in Palestine, and he'd been right, perhaps even prophetic, in his utterance. Benjamin remembered the nearly three-year-old conversation as if it had been only yesterday.

"This is very special, Benji, just like you," Mattathias Kingman had said when he handed a well-worn, hand-sewn leather suitcase to Benjamin. "It's not every day that my favorite nephew turns twenty-one."

"Thank you, Uncle Matt. I'll take good care of it."

"I'm sure you will. You know, my father brought that suitcase with him to America from Russia," he added, a hint of sadness in his voice, "when he and your grandmother left Moscow in order to escape persecution by the Czar. He prayed that one day he would pack it for a trip to the home of his heart, *Erez* Israel."

Benjamin had looked into Mattathias' soft, hazel eyes, speckled with agate blue variegations, the captivating signature of the Kingman heritage, and was overcome with emotion. But, as usual, he was at a loss for words.

"Your grandfather never doubted, deep down inside, that he would live to see the establishment of the Jewish National State and the return of Jews to the Promised Land," continued Mattathias, his voice thick with emotion. "Unfortunately, his heart, like your father's, gave out before the dream became reality."

His uncle smiled with understanding, and his eyes sparkled with a gleam that someone who didn't know him well might have mistaken for mischief. "Now, however, not only do you have the opportunity to do what your father and mine could only dream about, but you will be a part of something we Jews have prayed about for more than two thousand years — the fulfillment of God's divine plan. An end to the *diaspora* — the return of Jews to the land God promised to Abraham. I've known since the day you were born, Benji, that God has something extraordinary planned for your life . . . and I believe you're going to find a portion of what it is He has in store for you while you are in Palestine."

When he'd pressed his uncle to elaborate, Mattathias smiled and told him an unsettling story.

"In the Scriptures there is a story about a man named Josiah. Three hundred years before he was born, a prophet foretold his birth and what it was he would accomplish."

"And what was that?"

"He became King over Israel at the age of eight when his father, Amon, was assassinated by his servants. It was a dark time in Israel's history — an age during which God's people had fallen into idolatry because their leaders had forsaken the God of their fathers and did not walk in the way of the Lord.

"When Josiah was twenty-six, the High Priest, Hilkiah, was laboring in the House of the Lord when he discovered something very valuable, something that had been lost to the children of Israel for many generations."

Benjamin was hooked. "Tell me — what was it?"

"The Book of the Law."

"The Pentateuch?"

Mattathias nodded. "He gave the Book to the King's scribe, Shaphan, and when the scribe read the contents to Josiah, the King tore his clothes and commanded the High Priest to go before the Lord and inquire for all the people, and for all Judah, concerning the words contained therein.

"Josiah eventually learned that in order for God to bless His people, they must turn from their idol worship and worship Him alone. As a sign of his desire to serve the one true God, Josiah reinstituted the Passover, which had not been observed since the time of the Judges. It is no surprise that Josiah's name means 'God healed.'"

Overwhelmed by his uncle's poignant words, though uncertain why, Benjamin broke down and cried, shedding tears he'd been unable to shed at his father's death. His uncle hadn't seemed surprised at the outburst, but simply hugged him and held him until his flow of tears had subsided.

Now, outside the hotel room, on the narrow street below, a wild dog howled. Several others answered, until it sounded like a pack.

Benjamin's eyelids fluttered like the wings of a butterfly

caught in a tempest, and in the moments before sleep he wondered if he were going to dream about giants again.

The bone-penetrating cold woke Benjamin from fitful sleep. For a moment he was disoriented. He blinked tired, red eyes several times. The gentle roll of the ship and the damp salt air reminded him where he was. *Thank God, I didn't dream*, he thought, shivering.

It was February 1949, and Benjamin was in his cabin, aboard the *Arabesque*, finally on his way home to America. His life in the desert was now a memory, his undiscovered crime merely an invisible mark etched upon his tortured soul. Like a scarlet letter. Or the mark of Cain.

He sat up and swung his long legs over the side of the narrow bunk. He reached for the coarse woolen sweater one of the crew had loaned him, conscious of the heavy fish smell that permeated it, as if it had been woven from strands of seaweed instead of sheep's wool. He quickly pulled it over the lightweight cotton shirt he wore, grateful for the itchy warmth against his goose-bumped skin.

He was not prepared for this kind of weather, or the suffocating smallness of his quarters. After four years of almost nomadic living in the openness of the desert, the small, stuffy cabin seemed like a coffin to him. He sighed heavily and dropped to the floor. "At least I haven't gotten seasick," he reminded himself as he pulled the thin chain above his head.

A dim yellow light revealed just how small the cabin was. He barely had room to turn around. Now that he could see, he reached for the gaberdine sweater George Amos had given him as a going-away present before he left Jerusalem.

Abruptly he stopped dressing and blinked. *That's strange*, he thought. He rubbed his eyes several times. A silken haze hung in the tiny quarters. And it seemed to be thickening right in front of him, just like his mother's thin soup thickened when she added cornstarch to it. He sniffed the air tentatively, and a rich, sweet smell filled his nose. "Frankincense!" he sputtered, stunned. "But that's impossible!"

He took another breath, deeper this time. All he smelled was the sweater. *I've been in this cabin too long*, he thought, remembering his hotel room in Jerusalem and the stars that had one evening seemed to form themselves into the shape of a cross. He shook his head and chuckled, amused at how easily his tired body played tricks on him. And this time he was sober too. It was time to get some fresh air.

He glanced somberly at the suitcase his uncle had given him and reassured himself that what was inside would be safe while he walked on deck. All the same, he locked the door behind him as he stepped out into the night.

The frigid salty air hit him in the face like a cold, wet compress, but he didn't mind. It refreshed him. He spread his legs, balancing against the steady roll of the ship, and grabbed the brass handrail with his left hand for additional support. He could feel the methodical hum of the Canadian tanker's huge Rolls Royce engines pulsing in the soles of his feet, and it reminded him of how his blood had pulsed in his veins the day he'd made the discovery that had irrevocably changed him.

Once he'd adjusted to the rhythm of the ship, he released the rail and looked up as he headed for the stern, finally realizing why it was so dark. There were no stars in the black, moonless night.

When he reached the rear of the tanker, he saw that he was not alone. An extremely tall man and a young boy stood side by side with their backs to him. He almost turned around — he didn't want company. But a solitary bulb on the bulkhead above them accented their two sepulchral silhouettes. They looked like they were perched on the edge of an abyss. His heart began to pound.

Unseen, Benjamin watched them. Then, without knowing why, he moved closer to them and blurted out the beginning of a Scripture that had begun to reverberate in his brain. "'Watchman, what of the night? Watchman, what of the night?'"

The boy turned first at the sound of his voice, and Benjamin felt an electrifying jolt course through his body. The lone light caught in the boy's ebony eyes, flecked with silver, held Benjamin captive. And what he saw there was colder and darker than the night. In fact, it was almost as if the boy's eyes *devoured* what little light there was.

Benjamin shivered and wondered why he'd ever left the security of his cabin.

"Hello. My name is Vaughn," said the boy politely, breaking the spell. "And this is my father. Who are you?"

Before Benjamin could reply, the man turned. He was lean, almost gaunt, with brown hair and dulled dark eyes. He looked withdrawn and defeated, almost ill.

Benjamin's attention was diverted only momentarily. His eyes seemed to have a will of their own, and they were drawn back to the boy. He would never have guessed the two were father and son. The boy's honey-colored skin, along with his jet black hair and vibrant eyes, stood in stark contrast to his father's sallow, tired demeanor.

"My name is Benjamin Kingman," he answered and tried hard not to stare at the unusual white scar at the top right of the boy's forehead. It was an incongruous physical blemish on the otherwise perfectly sculpted face.

The boy's father spoke in a monotone, as if he hadn't heard Benjamin's reply, and the words came out sounding like a memorized response to a secret password. "'The watchman said, The morning comes, and also the night: if you will inquire, inquire you: return, come.'"

The boy continued to stare with unblinking eyes. Benjamin felt flushed and chilled at the same time, caught off balance by the man's automatic response to his greeting and by his son's unsettling gaze. *What is going on here?* he wondered.

"You're Jewish," continued the man, abruptly changing his tone of voice. He spoke matter-of-factly, without any hint of displeasure.

Benjamin nodded. "And so were my mother and father," he

quipped, feeling light-headed and jocular in spite of the oddness of the whole situation. "And theirs before them . . . and theirs before that. I am truly the son of the son of the son."

The man laughed, and Benjamin had the feeling it was something he'd not done in a very long time. He joined in, suddenly relieved.

"Touché, Mr. Kingman," said the man. "And thank you for reminding me that a little levity goes a long way toward mending the broken heart."

"I assure you it was unintentional."

The man shrugged, then stuck out his hand. "Franklin Aurochs. And please forgive my son. He will soon be six-going-on-twenty." A strange look passed between father and son that made Benjamin wonder who was in control.

Benjamin shook the proffered hand. Franklin's palm felt dry and leathery, which once more made Benjamin think the man was in poor health.

"You caught me by surprise quoting from the Book of Isaiah. Are you a Rabbi?" Franklin asked.

"Hardly. I'm an archaeologist. I've been working in the Sinai for the past three and a half years." He glanced at Vaughn and wondered why his eyes kept returning to the sickle-shaped scar. "I'm a bit surprised myself. I don't know what came over me." He paused, sensing it was important that he and this man become friends, then added, "It would seem we have something in common."

"Oh?"

"Our knowledge of Scripture."

Franklin sobered suddenly. He turned his back on Benjamin and his son and leaned against the rail. "Perhaps," he said quietly as he fixed his gaze on the darkness that cocooned the tanker.

Benjamin moved to stand beside him and stared at the black water, watching the froth of foam trail behind the ship and disappear into the darkness.

"I was born in Germany," continued Franklin somberly, "but my father brought the family to America when I was seven. And for the past twenty years I've lived in China."

Benjamin suddenly felt nauseous. *German.* The war had been over for four years, but old hatreds die hard. Yet, he hadn't sensed any anti-Semitism in the man's demeanor — no anger or intolerance. "How is it that *you* are so familiar with the Scriptures?" he asked, swallowing away his queasiness.

"I was a missionary at one time."

"What happened?"

"I lost my faith."

"I'm not sure I understand," pressed Benjamin, amazed that he was being so persistent with someone he barely knew.

"When you mentioned the desert," explained Franklin, "my initial thought was of the first part of the Scripture you quoted. It's more appropriate. Do you know it?"

Benjamin nodded, amazed at the acuteness of his memory for a specific Scripture. "'The burden of the desert of the sea,'" he recited. "'As whirlwinds in the south pass through; so it comes from the desert . . . from a terrible land.'"

Franklin smiled a tired, thin smile and continued the verses by rote. "'A grievous vision is declared unto me; the treacherous dealer deals treacherously, and the spoiler spoils. . . . Therefore are my loins filled with pain: pangs have taken hold upon me, as the pangs of a woman that travails. . . . And the watchman said, Babylon is fallen, is fallen; and all the graven images of her gods he has broken unto the ground.'"

The night thickened about the two men as the haze in Benjamin's cabin had done earlier. Benjamin shivered and glanced at his watch. It was almost midnight. "Do you ever hear a voice inside your head?" he asked cryptically.

Franklin frowned and regarded his son. Benjamin followed his gaze and realized from the look in the boy's eyes that Vaughn had been listening intently to their conversation, as if he were a stenographer taking dictation. "Sometimes."

Benjamin nodded, making a decision. "Then we definitely have more in common than the desert," he said, wondering if the enigmatic child with the ebony eyes could somehow see the stain on his soul.

II

March 1986.

In the heavens above Washington, D.C., a fierce battle raged. Bolts of lighting arced through the atmosphere, searing the slate-gray sky with brilliant flashes, sending shock waves of thunder cascading to the earth below. Light from the sun fought to break through the maelstrom and reach the earth, but the clouds, heavy and black with water, formed a temporary impenetrable canopy over the nation's capital.

On the ground below, it seemed to Paul Michael Kingman that the rain, which had been pummeling the city nonstop for the past several hours, was going to go on forever. That thought, along with the miserable nature of the occasion, caused him to laugh. It was a cynical laugh. A laugh of defeat, not of hilarity.

The tall, sandy-haired man stood in the downpour without an umbrella and stared morosely at the plain pine coffin. "Death always wins," he'd remarked to his father just one week ago. "No matter how hard we fight, life always seems to be the last one to find out that it is not going to go on forever."

Of course his father had not heard him. His emaciated body languished in its five-week coma as Paul spoke, virtually all of its vital inner organs ravaged by the cancer still seeking some tender morsel of life upon which to feed. Thus the irony of the present moment was lost amid the clutter of the final eulogy in the rain.

The memory of Paul's last desperate attempt to communicate with his dying father heightened not only his pain at the loss of his only remaining parent, but his sense of utter personal failure as well. The resulting hollow ache within his belly gnawed at his soul like a starving rat.

Ignoring the familiar feeling, he pulled the collar of his slick, black Pierre Cardin raincoat tighter about his body and fixed his eyes on the coffin. Try as he might, he couldn't keep his mind from resurrecting the guilt that had lain dormant within him for longer than he cared to remember. It whipped at his sense of emotional equilibrium, even as the wind threw thumbnail-sized raindrops into his unprotected face.

In an effort to regain control, he called upon his last line of defense. He thought of the wind as a boxer and the hard drops of rain as the wind's fists. It was the fourteenth round. His opponent knew Paul's weak spots were exposed and was waiting for the moment when, from either exhaustion or bad judgment, he would let down his guard.

After several minutes, Paul chuckled cynically. Trapped in the abyss of misery, his imagination worked overtime to guide him out of the pit. He couldn't help it; it was the writer in him.

The rain fell harder, and he shivered, then remembered the last time he'd talked to his father — before the hospital, that is.

"Well, well, the prodigal son returns," said Benjamin when he opened the door. He scrutinized his estranged son with unforgiving eyes. They seemed to look right through Paul. "It would seem from the look of you that your latest sojourn in the wilderness has left you a bit worse for the wear. I suppose you've come home to repent," he added in a tone that kicked Paul in his gut.

"No, Father . . . I've come home to recover," he said, trying to postpone the arguing as long as possible.

Benjamin grunted and turned his back on his son, leaving the door open.

Paul stood motionless for a few seconds, as if he were a stranger, uncertain how to act. Finally he stepped inside and closed the door. It had been a long time since he'd been in his father's home.

The house was extremely well kept. Benjamin had always been a fanatic about cleanliness. Paul once heard his father tell his mother that it was because of the time he'd spent in Palestine, after the war. "The Sinai has a way of working itself into your bones, and you never forget its presence after that. Even if you want to forget, you can't," he'd said and smiled a cryptic smile.

The furniture was old, but in excellent shape, and because the house was old as well, the floors were hardwood. Each room had an oriental rug to soften the austerity of the meticulously buffed wood. Scattered throughout were the various antiquities his father had acquired in a lifetime of searching out the secrets of the ancient past.

After they'd eaten supper, Benjamin did the dishes, and Paul used the time to prepare emotionally for their evening together. He studied the artifacts in the den with the trained eye of journalistic appraisal. There was a Greek copy of *The Jewish War*, written by the great Jewish scholar from Jerusalem, Flavius Josephus, and a fifteenth-century copy of Seneca's *Epistles*, along with several German translations of Apocryphal and Pseudepigraphical works that had been written sometime between 120 B.C. and A.D. 200. How his father had acquired such valuable artifacts on a professor's budget was a mystery to him; but for some inexplicable reason, Paul had never pressed the issue.

There were two objects, however, that stood out among the others. Every time he'd been in his father's house, they caught his eye. He stared for several minutes at the glass case that housed a sword and a silver goblet, then walked over and placed his hands upon the glass, as if he might touch the encased objects his father had brought home with him from Palestine.

Benjamin had always been very secretive about those two particular artifacts. He refused to discuss them and yet, displaying them so visibly, seemed to use them as a taunt. Not for guests, but for himself.

There was something very special, and very strange, about his father's behavior toward the sword and goblet. There were times when Paul had almost believed Benjamin carried on a love-hate relationship with the ancient *objets d'art*.

Paul tapped the glass, bewildered, shook his head in amazement, and moved to the fireplace.

He paused for a moment in front of the photograph sitting on the mantel. It was a color portrait of his mother, taken just two weeks before she'd died, nearly fifteen years ago. He pulled it out of its frame and turned it over to read what he already knew by heart. On the back she'd inscribed her favorite Scripture: "For now we see through a glass, darkly; but then face to face: now I know in part, but then shall I know even as also I am known."

When he'd asked her why she liked that particular Scripture so much she'd said, "The Apostle Paul wrote that to the church at Corinth, over nineteen hundred years ago. He was writing about love. Without love we are nothing."

Paul wondered if that was what Orson Welles had been trying to say in one of the last interviews he gave before he died. When asked if there was any one thing in his life that he'd desired to achieve but had failed to accomplish, Welles had replied, "Learning how to belong. We are born alone . . . we live alone . . . we die alone. And it is only the illusion of love that keeps us from being truly alone."

Paul didn't know much about love, but he did know a great deal about his namesake. Ex-Jew. Ex-murderer. Formerly Saul of Tarsus, tentmaker. Devout Jew turned Christian.

Elizabeth Kingman had been a Christian. When her son was born she'd wanted to name him Paul Michael, after the most famous apostle and the most powerful archangel. Benjamin insisted that he be called Saul, which means "asked for" in Hebrew. Elizabeth prevailed, but the matter had always been a source of contention in their otherwise happy marriage.

Paul sighed. His name was a constant reminder of the battle that had been raging inside him since he was thirteen. Which was he to be? Jew? Christian? Both?

"Do you remember, when you were just a small boy, how I

used to read Scripture to you at night . . . before you went to sleep?" Benjamin asked, startling Paul from his reverie.

Paul replaced his mother's picture, then turned, wondering how long Benjamin had been standing behind him. He studied his father as if he were seeing the strangeness in a stranger dissolve into recognition — the stranger speaking words that bred familiarity, exorcising fear and doubt, bringing absolution for the unforgiven. The Hasidic absolution, not the Catholic.

"Yes, I do," he replied softly, wanting to add that he doubted he'd ever had the luxury of being a child.

"Do you remember the passage in Ezekiel . . . the one you always asked about?"

Paul nodded as his father quoted verbatim from the Old Testament. "'Behold, all souls are mine; as the soul of a father, so also the soul of the son is mine: the soul that sins, it shall die.'"

Hearing the words spoken again by his father after so many years had an unusual and unexpected effect on Paul: he became angry and lashed out at Benjamin. "You talk to me of sin? I learned at your knee that the *Talmud* speaks of three principles in life: Torah, service to God, and charity. It was you who told me that genuine charity flows only from the heart of one who truly understands that all we possess is God's and that we belong to Him. And you drilled into my head that the highest form of charity is helping man to help himself." He stared at his father, then added, "When have *you* ever lived up to those principles?"

Benjamin was caught off guard by his son's abrupt change of demeanor. "How dare you rebuke me. And why this sudden expression of concern for *my* faith? You always favored your mother's religion, God rest her soul. True, you went through with your *Bar Mitzvah,* but I knew your heart wasn't in it."

His father's accusation caused Paul to cringe inwardly. He knew better, however, than to let Benjamin see that his words had hit their mark. "You're right, Father, I've never cared much for the ritualism of orthodox Judaism."

"Why not?"

"Because it's a religion with a stony, unyielding heart. You, and others like you, survive by building a hedge around yourselves."

"What are you talking about?"

"You claim to be one of the chosen of God, and you wait for the day when the *mashiyach*, the Anointed One, will come and fulfill the promise of the prophets. Yet you seem to relish persecution and affliction." Paul sighed. "Almost as if you believe that the promise given to Abraham is fulfilled by acts of captivity, slaughter, and abandonment. And your spiritual circumcision only makes you suffer more."

"And what about you? Does *your* circumcision mean so little to you?"

Paul glanced at his mother's photograph. "Why do you insist that God requires the shedding of blood and the cutting of the prepuce in order for His covenant to have force and effect?" he asked, his voice trembling.

Benjamin followed his son's gaze and sighed, suddenly feeling broken. "Judaism is the *only* religion for *Jews*. However, we neither judge nor condemn the honest, devout worshiper of any faith. The *Talmud* tells us that 'The righteous of *all* nations are worthy of immortality.'" He paused, then added, "The Gentile who follows the *Torah* is as good as our High Priest."

Paul was thinking as his father talked. Being a child of the sixties, he disdained ritual and elitism. And because he'd decided in college that the pen was mightier than the sword, so long as that pen did not write with the taint of theological ink, he'd become a free-lance journalist. Ambivalence was the world's Achilles heel, and during the past decade he'd used his pen to strike at that weak spot as effectively as Hector had used bow and arrow. His college roommate, a political science major and an agnostic, found his choice of careers less than admirable. When Paul had asked him why, he'd replied, "The world deals harshly with prophets, honest politicians, and writers who make people think."

Benjamin grew pensive. He shuffled over to his favorite chair, opposite the fireplace. "Sit," he said sternly, motioning for Paul to take the chair across from him.

A guarded silence fell between the two men, an emotional chasm.

Paul was a writer. Words were his forte. Tonight, however, they seemed to be failing him. In spite of his earlier resolve, he and his father had fallen into a familiar rut. Nevertheless, as he scrutinized Benjamin, he sensed that there was something very different about him. His father seemed less agitated, more relaxed. As though a demon he'd been wrestling for many years had suddenly departed the arena.

Reflecting on the scene later, Paul was certain the demon had known his father was doomed and so had withdrawn from the unchallenging contest, seeking more succulent prey.

When Benjamin finally spoke, his voice was strong and clear, although he sounded weary. "Forty years I have sinned against God," he said undramatically.

"What?"

Benjamin leaned forward, straightening himself awkwardly, as though the rod of truth temporarily supported his failing structure, as though decaying bone was now replaced with the incorruptible gold of absolute certainty. He stared at his son with clouded eyes. "I found some ancient manuscripts in the desert, before I met your mother," he said heavily. "I was in Palestine . . . after the war."

Paul nodded. "I know. In '48, just after Israel was declared a state."

"I kept the documents, Paul. I'm a thief."

Paul was stunned. "But why?"

Benjamin shrugged. "I've asked myself that same question a thousand times. I suppose there really is no good reason. I just had to *own* them."

Paul stood up and ran his hand through his hair, overwhelmed at his father's confession. Benjamin's scruples concerning archaeology were unimpeachable. His impeccable credentials and his pride in scholastic excellence were exceeded only by the critical acclaim he received from his colleagues. Yet here he sat, admitting he had stolen a national treasure.

"Why are you telling me this now?"

Benjamin sighed and sat back. The chair seemed to swallow him. "I've violated my heritage . . . compromised the very things I've always told you were essential to our Faith." His head sagged forward, as if it had become a burden his shoulders could no longer bear. "I admit that I haven't led the life of balance the *Talmud* instructs us to attain. My love of learning has overshadowed all else. And because of that, I've sinned not only against God but against mankind as well. My prayers go unanswered because God will not intervene to redeem that for which I must atone."

"What are you going to do?"

When he finally replied, Benjamin's voice was full of agony. "I'm not sure yet. Somehow the documents must be made public —"

". . . for there lives no man on earth who is so righteous that he sins not." Paul was pulled from the memory of his last conversation with his father by the final words spoken by the Rabbi.

The rain continued to pummel his face. He tugged at the collar of his coat, refusing to give the storm an opportunity to best him. Part of him wished the weather would take on corporeal form so he could legitimately vent his anger and frustration.

Abruptly, in the midst of his imagined contest, a brilliant flash of lightning illuminated the afternoon sky. Paul's pupils constricted automatically to compensate for the searing light. "You've lost!" said a small voice in the back of his head.

Finally, unable to cope any longer, and not really caring that he couldn't, he broke down and did what he had been unable to do since his tenth birthday. He cried — unreservedly and unashamedly. "Good-bye, Father," he whispered as the rain diminished to a steady drizzle. Celestial and terrestrial tears mixed together on his cheeks, but no one paid any attention.

Afterward he thanked the Rabbi he'd met only an hour before the service, turned his back on his father's grave, and walked a short distance to the street to hail a cab. As he stood waiting at the curb, he wondered if the journal his father had bequeathed to him along with the key to a safe-deposit box would tell him what he had been unable to find out seven months ago.

III

On the other side of Washington, D.C., Yuri ben Raphah, as he called himself now, stared out the large east window that dominated the living room of his new residence. From fifteen stories up he watched the wind-whipped rain pummel the earth with pronounced fury.

He was tall, over six feet, with silver-gray hair. His shoulders were broad and well-muscled. To people who didn't know better, he appeared to be a man who had performed much physical labor in his life. However, his erect, unblemished posture, and the fact that there were no calluses on the palms of his strong, large hands, gave away his secret: he had never worked a day in his very long, very unusual life.

There was an air of solidarity about him that some might have thought arrogant. In truth, he was incapable of the emotion. In fact, emotion for him was a practiced exhibition, at least insofar as he actually expressed feeling, which was entirely on the physical level.

Had he been asked about the source of his youthful appearance, he would have replied cryptically, "Love is the source of all."

To those he met, having sought them out with purpose, he appeared to be clothed in something beyond material covering. People who talked with him could never seem to remember what he was wearing when they met or just exactly how and why he had come into their lives.

What they did remember, however, was the light. His whole being *glowed*. And his penetrating hazel-green eyes blazed with a luminescence that was bright and soft at the same time. They radiated power, yet they didn't intimidate. His face was a study in compassion, his overall demeanor thoughtful.

Unfortunately, death still stalks the unwary and ignorant, thought Yuri. He stood silent, not really seeing the rain that beat against the glass. How different the world was today. Many things had changed during the years he'd been away, and yet there was much that seemed familiar.

The room behind him was spacious. Although sparsely furnished, it radiated warmth. The floor was marble of a beautiful off-white color, with streaks of variegated soft pink and a gray mineral residue running through it. The natural discolorations softened the cold austerity of the rock, which came from the same quarry from which Michelangelo selected the stone used to carve his masterpiece *David*.

To offset the bare marble, several large, very old Persian rugs had been placed strategically throughout the living area. The weaver had made no attempt to draw attention to his craft with superfluities of design. Instead, the magnificence of his artistry revealed itself to the one who accepted, rather than anticipated, the handiwork.

Yuri turned from his musings and walked over to one of the few pieces of furniture, an exquisitely carved obsidian table inlaid with gold. The merchant from Damascus who'd sold it to the former owner of the penthouse where Yuri lived claimed Pontius Pilate sat behind it when he sentenced Jesus of Nazareth to be crucified. On top of it sat a first-edition Gutenberg Bible and a translation by Erasmus of the *Septuagint*. Above it on the wall hung a pen-and-ink Rembrandt drawing depicting Christ raising Lazarus from the dead.

After staring at the drawing for several minutes, Yuri picked up the newspaper lying next to the priceless sixteenth-century Bible. It had been folded to a particular page, and a certain part of the page had been circled in red ink.

He pondered the old photograph from the archives of UPI, captioned: NOTED ARCHAEOLOGIST AND PROFESSOR OF ANTIQUITIES BURIED TODAY.

The brief obituary described the man, the work that had brought him a measure of national attention, and the location of the funeral service. It also mentioned that he was survived by a son, living in the city.

Yuri set the paper down after a few moments of contemplation and gently lifted the Gutenberg out of its case. He handled it reverently, not so much because of its age, but because it was, for him, something he'd heard about but had never seen.

He turned the pages methodically and stopped in the Book of Joel. He scanned the page rapidly, not having to read the words; he knew them by heart. However, he'd never committed them to memory.

He began to read aloud from the second chapter. His voice filled the large room with a melodious sound, resembling that of a choir of angels singing softly, praising God.

"'Be glad then, ye children of Zion, and rejoice in the Lord your God: for He hath given you the former rain moderately, and He will cause to come down for you the rain, the former rain and the latter rain in the first month. . . .

"'And it shall come to pass afterward, that I will pour out My Spirit upon all flesh; and your sons and your daughters shall prophesy, your old men shall dream dreams, your young men shall see visions. . . .'"

He closed the book, held it to his chest with both hands, and pressed it into his body. Outside the highrise the rain slackened to a drizzle. Although the sun had not yet shown itself, Yuri knew it was there. He could feel its presence.

He picked up the newspaper and stared at the circled photograph. "I wonder if they realize how many millions of lives are at stake," he mused aloud. "I wonder if they really understand what's about to happen."

"Sarah," David McDaniel called to his secretary over his intercom, "do you have the phone number I requested?"

"Yes, Senator. Do you want me to dial it for you?"

"No. I'll make the call myself. Just bring it here," he growled, tapping his left hand impatiently on top of his desk. The white-gold ring produced a dull, resonant thumping sound as it struck the polished wooden surface, a huge piece of furniture that was handmade from the trunk of a single oak tree imported from the *Schwarzwald*, the famous Black Forest in southwest Germany.

He glanced at the framed family photograph on his desk and sighed, remembering happier days . . . When his son and daughter had not been strangers. Then, almost irresistibly, his eyes were drawn back to the top of his desk and the newspaper.

He grimaced as he studied the black-and-white photograph. The somewhat faded, grainy image brought back memories he'd buried in the recesses of his mind a long time ago. He picked up the newspaper, reading the obituary for the tenth time, his mind only half on what he read.

The fourth-term Senator from Colorado thought about the nature of power and his consummate ability to tame and wield the elusive elements which make for survival in the American version of the ancient Roman Senate. *Power.* He was sixty-six years old, and in his world knowledge was power. He'd come to the realization of that fact forty years ago when he was living in Palestine, writing articles for the *New York Times*. Money was also power, but without knowledge the possession of money was superfluous. He knew there were men who coveted gold and silver, but they were men who were easily manipulated. The metal of exchange in the world of the truly powerful — of which he considered himself to be one of the elite — was information.

"Are you sure you're OK?" asked Sarah when she came in from the front office.

"I'm fine, just a little tired." On McDaniel's wedding finger was a ram's-head ring, with two distinct, burgundy-red rubies where the eyes would normally be, and two small green emeralds that looked like horns. He caressed the unusual-looking piece of jewelry absently, ignoring the warmth that now radiated from it.

Sarah handed him the number, then shut the door on her way

out. She knew better than to disturb the Senator when he got like this.

Vaughn Aurochs scanned the vast Serengeti Plain with his binoculars and thought about how much Africa reminded him of his birthplace in northern China, at the edge of the Ordos Desert. The veldt stretched before him, seemingly endless. The magnified panorama viewed through the lenses was a shimmering ocean of heat and dust. The gently rolling landscape was pockmarked with clusters of wildebeests, elephants, giraffes, and an occasional lone rhinoceros.

Vaughn was unusually tall, considering his mother was Asian, and had broad shoulders and a lean, athletic build. His ebony eyes, striated with flecks of silver, sparkled with anticipation as he waged a silent battle with the implacable brightness of the early-morning sun. The harsh glare of the equatorial sunlight reflecting off the stark, rock-strewn plain burned his unprotected eyes. He ignored his discomfort and panned the horizon slowly, stopping briefly to stare at the twisted, thick trunk of a solitary baobab tree that appeared in his peripheral vision. After a few moments of contemplation, he continued looking for the prey he'd traveled halfway around the world to stalk and kill.

A slight breeze blew his unkempt jet hair off his forehead, exposing the unique birthmark that marred the skin above his right eyebrow, at the edge of his scalp.

Vaughn had expended a great deal of money seeking a way to erase his "scarlet letter." Finally, after a year of fruitless efforts, he decided that if he could not eliminate the aberration physically, he would eliminate it mentally. Now, whenever he looked at himself in the mirror, he never saw the sickle-shaped blemish. He also kept his hair combed in such a fashion that unless one knew the mark was there, it was rarely discernible.

He set down his binoculars and glanced at his watch, a Vacheron Constantin Geneve. He'd been staring at the plain for over an hour, and now he rubbed his dry eyes methodically, massaging away the circular imprint that had been pressed into the soft skin by the intensity of his grip. "I will not be denied this time," he swore.

Glancing briefly at the cloudless, cerulean sky, he grabbed his canteen and took several small gulps of the lukewarm water, allowing himself only just enough to alleviate the dusty dryness that clung to the inside of his mouth and throat. He noticed a flake of rust on the dash of the Land Rover and picked at it with his free hand until a chunk the size of a quarter came loose. He studied the oxidized piece of metal and remembered one of his last conversations with his father. He'd only been out of college a year, but already had plans to carve a niche for himself in his father's fledgling empire.

"The Greeks were right in calling the mother goddess Gaia and in creating gods that lived outside of time," Franklin had chortled one evening after dinner.

"What?"

His father laughed and opened a second bottle of Angelica, the almond-flavored liqueur upon which the Aurochs family's fortune was built. He poured himself a healthy snifter full — his fourth — and continued with his train of thought. "Time is the true oxidizing agent of mankind — it eats away at the fabric of men's souls, even as rust rots the products of the intellect's imagination and vision."

"You're only partially right, Father. The Greeks created the gods out of fear and ignorance. In time, either from rapture or deception, men's imaginations embellished and distorted them. Today men feel no need of them."

Franklin raised his snifter and saluted his son. "Well put," he said sarcastically. "I would expect nothing less from an atheist."

"I'm not an atheist, Father. My point is simply that I don't believe there are deities who intervene in human affairs."

"You and Epicurus."

"I wouldn't be quite so snide if I were you."

"Oh? And what, pray tell, are you suggesting?"

"Simply that you have become a man whose passion is pleasure, and that I find your attitude inconsistent with your former religion."

"How dare you!"

"Please, spare me the righteous indignation, Father. It was you who told me after we came to America that as far as you were concerned, God is just a myth and religion is simply a collection of myths rooted in unfulfilled human feelings, wants, and needs."

Vaughn pressed his fingertips together in the shape of a pyramid and continued, "I believe your exact words were, 'When a man's mind becomes idle he begins to wander through the labyrinths of uncertainty, searching for meaning and purpose to life, stalked by the Minotaur of doubt. We live, we die. There is no purpose save what occurs between those two breaks in eternity.'"

Franklin's face went livid. He slammed the snifter on the table, spilling what little Angelica remained. The thick amber liquid puddled on the polished wooden surface. "You're so proud of that photographic memory of yours —"

"Eidetic, Father . . . there *is* a difference."

Franklin's eyes were daggers. "I curse the day your mother sacrificed that Manchu breeding pig, but Chi Lin wanted a son so badly she would have done anything."

"I thought you told me she did it for you — because of Deborah . . . and Angelica."

"Enough!" ordered Franklin. He jumped to his feet and grabbed his head as it exploded in pain at the mention of the woman he'd married immediately upon graduating from high school and the name he'd posthumously given to their unborn daughter who'd died in a flash flood with her mother so long ago. "Get out now! I've heard enough!"

The fierce African heat sucked Vaughn into the present. He blinked twice and sighed, setting aside the canteen.

The thin piece of oxidized metal had turned to powder in his tightly clenched fist. He opened his hand and stared at the orange-red remnant for several seconds, then wiped his palm against his pants. The rust fell to the floor of the Land Rover, mixing with the dust of the veldt.

He reached across the seat and picked up the style section of one of the two newspapers that had been flown in especially for him. His wealth was such that those who worked for him did not think the practice unusual. No matter where he was in the world, he always read the *Washington Post* and the *Wall Street Journal*.

Surprisingly, what had caught his eye earlier as he leafed through the papers after reading the business sections was not something in the *Journal,* but something he stumbled upon in the *Post*. Benjamin Kingman was dead. And he was survived by a son. Vaughn had brought the notice along on the hunt because he couldn't stop thinking about the man he'd met as a small boy.

The day was getting hotter. He could feel the weight of it in his bones. Unconsciously he reached inside his khaki shirt and grasped the amulet he always wore around his neck. He pulled it out and stroked it, watching it gleam in the rearview mirror.

He'd received it in the mail on his forty-second birthday, seven months ago. When he first opened the package, postmarked from Damascus, he was amused that someone would send him such an oddity. He'd lifted the amulet out of the box by its silver chain and examined it.

The white gold trinket had the head of a goat, with two brilliant rubies as eyes, and the body of a fish. He'd examined the scaly body of the fish more closely and discovered it was actually a distorted phallus.

Later he'd learned that the amulet was an unusually sophisticated *fascinum* from Nimes, a town in the south of France named after Nemanseus, the genie of the sacred fountain. When the Romans conquered Gaul, they brought with them the ritual of goat worship. They built an elliptical amphitheater sixty-nine feet tall there in the first century A.D. for gladiatorial shows, chariot races, and naval spectacles. Sacrifices were also common.

When Juno's oracle had been consulted there about the prolonged barrenness of Roman women, the oracle reputedly responded with, "*Iliades matres caper hircus inition,*" meaning,

"Let the rough goat have intercourse with the Trojan women." The Romans toned down the oracle's dramatic command, incorporating a less bestial, though equivalently sacrificial, rite into the celebrated festival of Lupercalia, observed on February 15 each year. Although one of the significant tasks of this particular fertility festival was the caprifying of the fig, an emblem of the phallus, whereby the wild male fig tree was used to fertilize the cultivated female fig tree, there were those who argued that the ritual actually derived its name from the Latin *luere per carprum*, which means "to purify by means of the goat."

According to Cicero, Caesar was given the fatal diadem twined with laurel by a drunken and naked Mark Antony at the celebration of this festival in 44 B.C., and in the fifth century A.D. the Church, under Pope Gelasius I, appropriated a form of the rite as the Feast of Purification.

Some scholars believed that because the priests were called *Luperci*, the festival was associated with some form of wolf worship, the Latin word *lupus* meaning wolf.

The amulet felt hot in Vaughn's hand . . . Hotter than the heat of the veldt. He chuckled humorlessly, then muttered several unintelligible words. After a few moments he released the *fascinum* and stared out at the shimmering red-brown landscape. This was his last day on safari. He did not intend to go home empty-handed.

Once again he picked up the binoculars and scanned the plain, wondering when the lions would come to feed.

IV

Gabriella McDaniel was sure she was going to be late, and she wasn't happy about the prospect. She was giving a lecture at the university, and she'd agreed to a brief interview afterwards, against her better judgment. Being a Senator's daughter was not easy. Especially when that Senator was expected to become the next President of the United States and you were trying to step out from beneath his ubiquitous shadow.

Recently she had begun to cast a rather sizable shadow herself. She was twenty-eight, and she was finally being noticed — after a decade of hard work. People had been buying her works now for two years, but she consented to sell so few of them that she had only a small, very specialized following.

All that had changed in September when Antonio Raphaelo, the owner of one of the most prestigious galleries in the city, had asked her if she would consider participating in a special showing he was putting together. She'd jumped at the chance, and both of them were stunned when all fifteen paintings she displayed were sold within the first three hours.

Afterwards he pulled her aside and said, "Gabriella, my dear, it's obvious you have the gift . . ."

"Gift? What . . ."

Antonio smiled. "The gift of touching people's souls."

"I don't understand."

"You are familiar, of course, with Rembrandt's pen-and-ink drawing of Christ raising Lazarus from the dead?"

She nodded. "It is a classic example of chiaroscuro."

"Exactly. Rembrandt mastered the technique of distributing

light and shade throughout a picture so as to evoke the maximum emotional involvement." Antonio put his arm around Gabriella and counseled her with the expertise of a shrewd businessman who truly loves his work. "You, my dear, have a similar talent. Your work demands an investment from the viewer. And those who are willing to contribute a portion of themselves discover a kind of mirror into their own souls. Indeed, there was even one patron not present tonight who purchased your most expensive work simply upon my recommendation. And that, my dear Gabriella, is why I know you have the gift."

Her jade-green eyes grew big and round. "Who —?"

"Ah, now that is what I want to talk to you about. I've decided it's time you had your *own* show. Here in the gallery."

Her legs were weak, and she felt light-headed. "What!"

Antonio chuckled. "It's already arranged, so I certainly hope you are not going to say no."

She laughed then, realizing he was doing his best to put her at ease. "I could hardly say no to something I've dreamed about ever since I started painting. But what about a sponsor?"

Antonio's eyes gleamed.

She realized instantly that the person who had purchased her work sight unseen would be her sponsor as well. "Well, out with it — who is my benefactor?"

Antonio shook his head. "He conditioned his sponsorship on anonymity. You'll meet him in April."

"Oh, Antonio, you mustn't keep me in suspense. I don't know if I can wait that long to find out."

Antonio chuckled. "I'll tell you this much. He's a very power-ful man who likes beautiful things. However, even though his tastes are eclectic, he rarely purchases art. When he does, he only collects paintings which he deems to be of special interest. And don't ask me what qualifies because I've no idea. He's very secre-tive about such matters."

The shrill sound of a car horn wailing behind the cab she was riding in pulled Gabriella into the present. The cabby inched the car forward and glanced at her in the rearview window, then shrugged. There was nothing he could do.

Gabriella sighed and told herself it didn't matter if she was a few minutes late, then turned her thoughts to something more pleasant. In less than two weeks she was going to have her first one-woman show. For seven months she had worked feverishly. And for seven months she'd wondered who her mysterious bene-factor was. Despite repeated requests to Antonio, he would divulge nothing.

Today, however, she had to concentrate on her lecture and getting through her first interview. Stuck in traffic, she decided to make the best of the frustrating situation and mentally review her presentation.

Minutes later she saw the accident that had stalled the mass of cars. It was a bad one. A body, covered by a blood-soaked sheet, lay in the street next to a crushed car. As they drove by, Gabriella glanced at the body, her eyes inexplicably drawn to the scene of death.

A cold chill climbed from the base of her spine to the top of her neck and caused her to shudder involuntarily as she had a sudden premonition of her own death. Then, inexplicably, frag-ments of a conversation flooded her mind. ". . . so sorry, Gabriella . . . nothing I could do . . ." the man sobbed ". . . happened so fast . . . so much blood —"

The driver behind her beeped his horn again. The noise star-tled her, snapping her out of her macabre reverie. The cabby yelled a rebuke, which only Gabriella could hear because the win-dows were all up, then stepped on the gas.

The fractured memory floated at the edge of Gabriella's con-sciousness. Yet when she tried to put a time or place or face to the voice, she drew a blank. The brief but intense recollection left her feeling disoriented and queasy.

She turned around and looked back at the scene as they drove on, certain now that she could see strands of raven-black hair, so much like her own, sticking out from one corner of the sheet.

The day broke clear and crisp over the city, the rain that had continued nearly unabated for three days having finally stopped during the early hours of Saturday morning.

Paul awoke in the grips of a hangover. The front of his head throbbed like a construction worker's jackhammer pounding the asphalt. He didn't drink often, but when he did he preferred Angelica. Since he'd buried his father, he'd finished an entire bottle, and now his system was rebelling.

He lay in bed frowning, waiting for the pain behind his eyes to subside enough so he could get up and move about without feeling nauseous. Bits and pieces of the recurring dream that had plagued his sleep for three weeks now began to drift together into a fragmented picture.

After a time, eyes closed, he remembered it all. His drinking had loosed the full force and effect of the nightmare, pulling the heat of it from the recesses of his mind, kindling the firewood of fear.

The land was flat, the air hot and dry.

The two men working the field were forced to squint in order to block out the harsh glare reflecting off the dusty, rock-strewn landscape.

No rain had ever fallen upon the field they now tilled.

They had worked the fields every day for months now, from dawn until midday, when the heat became so intolerable that they were forced to rest until late afternoon. Only then could they return to the tilling and planting.

The younger of the two men — although both were youthful in appearance — sang quietly to himself as he worked, oblivious to the inhospitable environment. Small rivulets of sweat trickled down the crevices of his back as he stabbed the desiccated skin of the planet with his crude wooden hoe. His perspiration evaporated quickly upon contact with the air, leaving his body coated with a crystalline veneer of salt.

Although the two men were brothers, upon close scrutiny one might believe they had sprung from the loins of different fathers. Where his younger brother was tall, lean and fine-boned with narrow shoulders, the older was short and squat. His broad body sat atop stubby, thick legs, and his whole frame was covered with a thick carpet of jet black, coarse, curly hair.

It was apparent from the way the older one lashed out at the earth in feverish abandon that he was very angry. Every few minutes he looked up from where he labored, sweat pouring off his face, and shouted something unintelligible at the sky, carrying on a conversation with some unseen tormentor.

Finally, having given himself over to the voice inside his head, he threw down his tool and headed in the direction of the small hut he and his brother had constructed as shelter against the sweltering intensity of the day.

Abel looked up and wondered why Cain had left his work unfinished.

The relentless, uncompromising onslaught of the sun campaigned throughout the morning. After a time Abel finally headed for shelter, leaving the earth to battle the implacable heat in its own way.

He searched the small hut for Cain, but it was empty. Fatigued, he took several sips of water from the clay pot sitting near the entrance of the shelter, then sat down on the ground in the shadow of the hut.

He fell into a fitful sleep, and when he awoke, the sun was gradually slipping over the edge of creation. The dull orange-red glow of day's last light reflected off the opaque blue-purple canvas of the sky. The moon, hazy and lavender-white, hung low in the east, suspended like a giant pearl.

He attempted to sit up, but found he could not. His hands and feet were securely bound, stretching him upon the still-warm earth like a four-point star fallen from Heaven. He was firmly anchored to the ground by four small but strong wooden stakes.

A dull, throbbing ache pulsed painfully at the back of his eyes, making it difficult for him to focus. His mouth tasted like he had eaten sour fruit. He felt like vomiting.

Dazed and confused, he called out his brother's name, his voice barely above a whisper. Minutes passed without response.

Again he called out — more loudly this time. Again nothing.

Suddenly, a shadow fell across him, etched upon the twilight, silent and unmoving. Raising his head a few inches off the ground, he cried out, "What is happening, Cain? What is it you want? I am bound as one would bind an animal in preparation for sacrifice."

When his brother finally replied, a look of madness glazed his eyes. "You are most observant, brother . . . and it is to your credit that you remain so calm in the face of your fate." Cain looked down at the helpless figure before him. The intensity of his anger pierced the veil of composure on Abel's face. "Truly the sacrifice I offer up this night shall be worthy of the one who shall receive it," he added.

"You must not do this," pleaded Abel. Fear welled up inside him, threatening to overflow his normally tranquil state of mind. Oddly he was not afraid for himself, but for his brother. "You are deceived," he placated, regaining control. "Your lack of faith has opened the door, allowing the evil one to gain a further stronghold. He uses you to seal his covenant with death. Do not give place to him. Resist him . . . he is a lie."

For a moment it seemed as though the soft words of the younger would be able to turn the older from his chosen course of action. Yet before Abel could speak further, Cain withdrew his sacrificial knife, raised it high, and plunged it deep into the chest of his offering.

Blood flowed down Abel's stilled chest, mixing with the dusty, brown earth, blending into the blackness of night.

Again there was silence.

The sun disappeared over the rim of the world.

Darkness reigned.

Paul opened his eyes for the second time and shuddered with the memory. He felt strange. As if it was he who had been sacrificed. He'd had the dream every night since his father died.

And each night it became more vivid. It was almost as if his subconscious was trying to tell him something.

He lay in bed thinking, gradually becoming aware of the stillness in the room. He felt it, rather than heard it, as a man who has lost a limb "feels" the absent appendage even though it is no longer a part of his body.

Gradually the stillness intensified, almost taking on the physical characteristic of substance. The feeling was so tangible, Paul imagined he could *see* the quiet.

Time slowed.

He saw a haze in the room. He sniffed the air. There was no smell of smoke. He hadn't used the fireplace in days, yet the haze remained.

He watched, detached, as his right hand moved to his face and began rubbing his eyes. Illusion?

His body twitched involuntarily. It was not painful, just strange. Like the haze. He was fully awake. He was back in real time.

He looked at his alarm clock, wondering why he had not heard the snooze alarm. The large red digital numbers read 1:00 P.M. Over an hour had passed since he'd first awakened, yet it seemed like only minutes.

The telephone rang.

Paul threw back the covers, pulled himself out of his lethargy, and reached for the phone. Not only had the jackhammer-pounding behind his eyes departed, but his whole body was now tingling from the neck down.

"Hello," he said groggily.

"Mr. Paul Kingman?"

"Speaking."

For a few seconds there was silence on the line. Then a guttural voice said, "I am interested in the documents your father discovered in Palestine."

Paul sat up straight in the bed, his writer's antennae suddenly vibrating. "Who is this?"

"We've never met, Mr. Kingman, so at this point my name would mean nothing to you."

"How did you get my number? It's unlisted."

The sepulchral voice chuckled softly. "There is nothing unavailable to me. Please, indulge me for a few moments and I will put your mind at ease."

"I'm listening."

"I met your father in 1949. I was traveling with *my* father. The three of us were passengers together on a ship sailing from Alexandria to New York. The encounter was brief, but it left an indelible mark upon my mind."

"I don't understand why you're calling me."

"When I read of your father's death I learned that he was survived by a son."

"And?"

"The firstborn in an Israelite family enjoys special status. Since you are an only child, and your mother is dead, you inherit your father's entire estate. The parchments your father discovered on the shores of the Dead Sea forty years ago would be part of such an inheritance."

Paul's mind was spinning, and an eerie sensation crept up his spine. He was trying to remember the conversation he'd had with his father in September. He was certain his father had told him no one knew of the existence of the parchments. And how did the voice know about his mother?

The hypnotic voice on the phone beckoned. ". . . your father discussed his discovery with my father —"

Paul needed time to think. He had not even read the journal his father had left him yet. "Look," he interrupted, "I don't know what this is all about, but I have no intention of discussing the private affairs of my family with a voice on the phone."

The silence on the line seemed to reach through the receiver and wrap itself around Paul.

"Fair enough, Mr. Kingman. You'll be hearing from me."

The line went dead. Paul hung up the phone and stared at it, perplexed. "This has to be the strangest Saturday I've ever had," he muttered as he headed for the shower.

He glanced at his clock again, shaking his head. He couldn't believe how the time had gotten away from him. He was going to have to hurry to keep from being late for his interview session.

He turned the water on full-blast in the shower, making it hotter than usual. As the steam began to fill the bathroom with a warm mist, he wondered not only about the strange phone call, but about just exactly what it was he had seen in his room. As he stepped into the skin-tingling spray, he doubted he'd be able to wash the memory of the nightmare from his thoughts as easily as he rinsed the sweat from his body.

V

Gabriella arrived at the university campus for her lecture and the interview to follow. She paid the fare, then stepped out of the cab and into the wind, hugging her materials to her chest as she ran toward the red-brick building known as Thompson Hall. The strong gusts blew long strands of her hair behind her and exposed the soft angles of her cheeks. There was a determined look on her face that belied the butterflies in her stomach.

"My first big interview and I'm late," she muttered as she ran. She'd gotten up extra early this morning just so this wouldn't happen, but she hadn't counted on the accident. She wanted to impress the man whose credentials seemed quite impressive over the phone. "I've been published in *Time*, *Newsweek*, and *Rolling Stone*, Miss McDaniel," he had said when he called.

"*Rolling Stone*?"

"Yeah. I did an interview with Harry Chapin just before he was killed in a car accident."

That bit of information was what had made up her mind. Being published in *Time* and *Newsweek* gave the man credibility, but the fact that he'd interviewed the musician who was arguably one of the twentieth century's premier balladeers told her he would understand what it was that drove her to paint. And that was something she'd wanted to share with someone for a long time, but until now had been reluctant to.

She glanced at the lone dogwood tree standing before the hall as she ran past it. Although spring was still several weeks away, there were a few buds on the tree's barren branches. *Signs of new life everywhere*, she thought.

She entered the lecture auditorium trying to remember a story her grandmother had told her about dogwood trees. But at the sight of twelve pairs of eyes staring at her expectantly, she forgot about everything except that she was late. The butterflies began to flutter with greater intensity.

"Ladies and gentlemen, I apologize for being late," she said out of breath, trying to quickly assess the looks on the faces before her as she arranged her materials on the podium. "I've chosen to talk to you today," she continued, "about my very favorite subject — light. I hope that when our time together is over you will have come to the point of sharing a small portion of the enthusiasm I hold for what Emerson called 'the first of painters.'"

A sandy-haired man in the center of the room interrupted. "'There is no object so foul that intense light will not make it beautiful.'"

Gabriella glanced at the man, surprised at his utterance of the quote. It was one of her favorites. Their eyes locked for a moment. The contact jolted her. Flustered, she looked away and scanned the other faces in the room and wondered where she should begin her discussion. Her mind drew a blank.

Surprisingly, her eyes were drawn back to the man. As she met his gaze, she noticed he had deep blue eyes that sparkled with specks of hazel. He was staring at her — or rather he seemed to be looking *inside* her, as if he saw something there that jolted him.

The momentary distraction caused her heart to flutter. She shuffled her notes in front of her, organizing them along with her thoughts. Before speaking, she regained control, telling herself that the encounter had been nothing.

"Whenever we turn on a light in a room, we are not, in the purest sense, actually seeing the light itself," she began hesitantly. "Rather, the eye constantly 'photographs' the images produced by the reflection and refraction of light off the physical objects in the room, including the light bulb. What the eye sees is actually the result of the slowing down and dispersion of light into a very narrow band of the electromagnetic spectrum. In the same way that sound is the result of vibrations in the air, color is the result of vibrations of light.

A hand popped up in the middle of the class, and when Gabriella recognized the student, the woman said, "I'm a little confused. Could you clarify what you're talking about?"

Gabriella smiled and said, "Certainly." Leaving her notes behind, she turned and walked over to the portable blackboard standing in the corner of the room and wheeled it over behind the podium, then picked up a piece of chalk and began to diagram a musical scale, from low C to high C, as she talked.

"Let's look at something I'm sure you're all familiar with, the musical scale, and then we can use it to make an analogy to light. In music there are seven notes of the scale, the eighth being a repetition of the first. Each musical note has a precise vibration, its signature if you will." Beside the scale, Gabriella drew a large ear. "The human ear is capable of detecting and conveying to the brain sounds comprised of these notes only within a narrow band," she continued.

"Sound enters the ear and impacts upon a tiny organ, similar to a miniture harp with over ten thousand strings, called the organs of Corti, so named for the Italian who discovered them. Because of the complexity of these two 'miniture harps,' the ear can convey to the brain virtually every conceivable sound, but only within certain limits."

Now she drew a large human eye, along with several horizontal lines to indicate rays of light impacting the iris and cornea, then said, "According to physicists, light is electromagnetic radiation to which the organs of sight react. We know that light travels at 186,000 miles per second and ranges in wave length from 4,000 to 7,700 angstrom units."

Gabriella turned and glanced briefly at her audience. She noted that there were still confused looks on several faces.

"Stay with me on this," she said hastily. "It's really not all that complecated. The angstrom is simply a unit of length, equal to one ten-millionth of a millimeter, that scientists use to measure electromagnetic radiation."

She finished her diagram and put the chalk down, then wiped her hands and stepped back up to the podium. "Now let's tie this all together. As there are seven basic notes in music, there are also seven basic colors—three primary and four secondary—from which all other colors are derived. Even as the human ear has a limited range in which it can detect and convey sound vibrations, using the organs of Corti, so too the eye has a limited range in which it can see the vibrations of light using the retina.

"This information is very important to the artist, because it is the manipulation of color, or more precisely, the harnessing of light throught the ordering of color that makes painting possible."

Gabriella paused, unsure of how deep she wanted the discussion to get. She decided to stay with the basics for the time being and see where that took her.

"Leonardo da Vinci was the first individual to make a significant contribution to the understanding of the uses of light in artistic works," she said, all professionalism now. "He developed the idea of light traveling in a straight line and utilized practical applications of his theory in his drawings and paintings. It wasn't until 1604, however, that a complete description of diffraction, the spreading of light into shadows, was given by the Danish astronomer Johannes Kepler."

Gabriella, all thoughts of confusion and trepidation banished from her mind, began to enjoy herself. Her eyes glistened with excitement as she warmed to the topic. Her enthusiasm was contagious and quickly spread to her audience. She continued her story. "As the nineteenth century drew to a close, the wave theory of light was generally accepted and seemed capable of explaining all known optical phenomena. Unfortunately, as in the case of most scientific disciplines, the absolute resolution of the question, What is light? was not to be.

"The problem that late nineteenth-century and early twentieth-century scientists such as Einstein faced was that there are some situations where light behaves like waves and others where it behaves like particles. It became apparent to researchers that it would be necessary to have a theory that predicts when and to what extent each kind of behavior manifests. That theory is known as Quantum Mechanics and, fortunately for us, falls outside the scope of our inquiry."

The audience chuckled.

"Are there any questions at this point?"

A hand popped up in the back of the room. "Why so much detail about the history of light?" asked a young man.

"Because the study of art *is* the study of light. Without light there would be no art. And without art man would be destitute of some of the most reliable mirrors of his soul: color, perception, depth of field, tinting, shading — all the objective, physical elements of art that, through various choices of medium, give physical reality to the subjective, ethereal substance of thoughts, ideas, feelings."

Paul had been listening intently to everything the beautiful raven-haired woman had been saying. He couldn't help himself.

When she'd first walked into the auditorium, he again felt the tingling sensation he'd experienced in his room upon waking. And, although he couldn't explain it, he'd also seen that same haziness. Only this time it seemed to be hovering just above the woman's head.

And when she'd looked into his eyes, just before starting her talk, he'd felt as if he'd grabbed hold of a high-tension power line. The galvanizing effect of her questioning gaze catalyzed a reaction that had been building inside him from the moment he'd seen her.

Thinking to himself that this was turning out to be a very strange Saturday indeed, he raised his hand.

"What you're telling us," said Paul when Gabriella acknowledged him, "is that the mind, though not necessarily the source of creativity, is the medium of expression for creative thought. Art, then, is merely the means by which the individual — the artist — communicates a specific concept or idea. In essence the physical act of rendering thought into art — be it poetry, music, painting or writing — is the act of translation."

All eyes were looking at Paul. Conscious of the effect his words were having, he made his point without flair. "Light, then, is an impartial participant. It simply illuminates what already exists, leaving *interpretation* to the recipient."

The room remained quiet for several moments. Gabriella stepped into the silence, making sound her servant. "That was very well put, Mr. —"

"Kingman," supplied Paul and smiled nonchalantly. He realized from the intensity of her gaze that he had accomplished what he hoped would be the means of obtaining a formal introduction.

Gabriella willed her eyes to move from Paul's the same way she would forcefully will her feet to move from a small pool of quicksand threatening to draw her into its depths. Her heart was beating rapidly, and she wondered idly if Mr. Kingman had any idea of the effect he was having on her, certain he would notice that the arteries in her neck were pulsing madly.

"Mr. Kingman has just provided us with the material we need to construct our bridge over the abyss of subjective interpretation . . ." was all she managed before she was interrupted by a scratchy, irritating voice from the rear of the room.

"The term 'subjective interpretation' is redundant."

All eyes shifted to the speaker. He was very tall and very thin. His clean-shaven face looked almost porcelain-white against the bright red shirt that lay open at his neck, exposing a hairless chest. His long, dirty-brown hair was tied back in a ponytail, and he was wearing jeans tucked into a pair of worn, snakeskin cowboy boots. Except for his pasty-white complexion, he looked very bohemian.

"Interpretation is, by definition, the act of explaining," he continued arrogantly. "Insofar as the content of art is concerned, interpretation is, of necessity, subjective. Thus, tainted as it is with experience, interpretation must be excluded from the realm of objectivity."

Something about the man jarred Gabriella, but it took her a few moments to decide what it was. Finally she realized that the silver goat's-head amulet hanging from his neck seemed to be out of place with the way he was dressed. Although she had no good reason, she found the piece of jewelry disconcerting. She was curious, but at the same time oddly repulsed.

"Well, it seems we have at least two philosophers in our midst," she said, not wanting to lose control of the lecture. She put the strange thoughts out of her mind. *This is no time to get distracted*, she told herself.

The audience began to fidget, and she could tell by the looks on their faces that the discussion was confusing them. All except the sandy-haired man. She noticed that the enigmatic Mr. Kingman was not confused at all. His demeanor was merely one of perplexed curiosity, as if he were looking beyond the visible into the invisible, seeing something in her that he could not quite put a label on, but at the same time recognizing its presence because what he saw was familiar to him.

The look in his eyes reminded her of the look she'd seen on a young boy's face in the Louvre Museum nine years ago. He could not have been more than twelve or thirteen years old. He stood rapt before Michelangelo's *David*, and the radiant look of unabashed desire on his face gave away the secret of his heart: he sheltered a passion for the artistic expression of love.

However, it wasn't a look that betrayed a yearning for sexual release. It wasn't anything as coarse as that. Rather it was one which spoke of his recognition of the artist's expression of a far more sublime and infinitely longer lasting concept of love. She was drawn to the boy because of the intensity of his absorption. She moved close to him and stood beside him silently, sharing but not intruding upon the moment. The minutes passed like seconds.

Finally, as if he'd been aware of her presence all along, he spoke. His words were so intimate she thought for a moment he was speaking to someone else. "This is my third time to see him. Sometimes he seems to come alive, and I imagine he steps down off his pedestal and runs through the meadows with me, laughing and singing. We run together across the fields, playing among the flowers, dancing beneath the clouds. Then he scoops me up into his strong arms and hugs me to him as if I am a brother he hasn't seen in a long time."

Gabriella had been stunned by the depth of the boy's vision. Not to mention that he was extremely articulate for one so young. He had eloquently vocalized a concept apologists had been trying to establish as an absolute for centuries.

"Did you know that the *David* was cut from an imperfect piece of marble?" she asked hesitantly, hoping to engage the lad in further conversation.

"Of course . . . That's why the work is perfect," he replied, looking her straight in the eyes before walking away and leaving her standing open-mouthed.

Gabriella pushed the memory from her mind and continued her discussion without further interruptions. The time passed rapidly, and before long a bell rang loudly. She concluded her talk, surprised at how the hour had flown by; it was almost as if her lecture had occurred in the blink of an eye.

She began to collect her material as her audience filed out of the room. When she looked up from the podium, the sandy-haired Mr. Kingman was watching her intently. "You've been staring at me that way for almost thirty minutes, Mr. Kingman," she said, trying to sound annoyed, "and I don't believe you've found a moment to blink."

Paul smiled and stood up. He pretended to rub his eyes in mock unbelief, as a cartoon character will do when he encounters something fantastic.

Gabriella laughed at the impersonation in spite of herself. She couldn't resist the comical look on his face. She shook her head in admiration for his ploy, and her long black hair glistened with just a hint of burgundy. The effect produced by the diffusion of the sun's last rays through the windows of the room was dramatic.

"If I didn't know better, I'd swear you are . . ." Paul hesitated, seeking a word to express what he saw. ". . . *glowing!*" He wasn't sure whether it was a trick of the lighting or something far more subtle and intrinsic. Whatever it was, he was definitely intrigued.

Gabriella felt color suffuse her cheeks. "Well, that's a first," she said dismissively and walked briskly past where he stood with his hands awkwardly thrust deep into his pockets.

Before she could leave the room, however, he stopped her with his words. "I'm much better at *penning* words than I am at speaking them" — he held up his right hand, palm outward — "and I have the calluses to prove it."

Gabriella stopped and turned. She eyed him cannily. "No doubt you're a blossoming writer whose acerbic wit is surpassed only by his supposed naiveté where women are concerned," she countered in a cracked, deep-throated imitation of Katherine Hepburn.

Paul laughed. "Very good. We make a great pair — just like Tracy and Hepburn."

"Not quite," she retorted, hoping to put him off, not sure why she should. She stepped into the hallway, leaving Paul in her wake.

The sun had slipped below the windowsill. The cold, riding piggyback on the deepening shadows, reminded Paul that March had not relinquished its authority to spring. The Vernal Equinox was upon them — day and night shared equally, pitting time against itself. The rare event occurred only twice each year. Both times the event mirrored change.

Paul rushed out of the room, anxious to catch Gabriella before she could disappear. He wanted to find out more about her. He caught up with her and stopped her again, this time physically. He grabbed her by the arm just as she was passing the crooked, solitary dogwood. "How about I interview you over dinner, Miss McDaniel?" he asked suddenly.

"You . . . ?" was all she could say.

Paul nodded and grinned from ear to ear. He enjoyed seeing the surprised look in her eyes. It gave her face an air of vulnerability he hadn't noticed while she'd been speaking.

"But I thought —"

"I know," he interrupted, chuckling. "It's a bad habit I have. I like the element of surprise. Not to mention that traveling *incognito* has certain advantages for someone in my profession."

Gabriella looked at him with renewed interest. "Are you always so abrupt? And so forward, Mr. Kingman?"

"Paul, please. And no, I'm *never* abrupt."

Gabriella smiled without thinking. "Never?"

"OK, how about *almost* never?" Paul let out a sigh, sending a puff of frosted air sailing on the breeze that rustled the long, thin branches of the dogwood.

They both laughed.

It was time to call a draw.

Gabriella brushed her hair out of her face and simultaneously tightened the thin jacket she wore, conscious that the temperature was dropping fast now that the sun had set. Although it was not yet dark, what light there was seemed to have melted into the air, thickening it as cornstarch thickens gravy, giving their surroundings a blue-gray coloration.

"March is unpredictable," she said and shivered. "I never know whether to wear a heavy coat or shorts."

Paul offered her his jacket, which she declined. "The wind shows up when you least expect it and ruffles everyone's feathers," he said and winked.

Gabriella arched her eyebrows. "You *are* a poet, aren't you, Paul?"

Paul shrugged. "What can I say?" He looked at her mischievously and added, "I'm a writer with an acerbic wit and tons of naiveté."

"Touché," said Gabriella.

"Great. Now that we've been properly introduced, how about Kingman's Wharf for dinner? My place is very private —"

"I'll bet."

"I promise it will be strictly business. If we go to a restaurant, someone is bound to recognize you. And then I'd never have a chance to find out what makes you tick. Besides, I'm a great cook."

"I thought it was my *art* you were interested in."

"That was before I met the artist."

"Just what kinds of things *do* you write about?"

Paul smiled. "You mean you've never read anything I've written and you granted me an interview?" He was grateful that his call a week ago had convinced her to talk to him.

"You caught me at an opportune moment."

"Oh?"

"We'll discuss that during the interview."

"Then you'll come?"

Gabriella studied him, surprised she was so suddenly and unequivocally attracted to him. She smiled and nodded.

"That's great," said Paul, suddenly feeling like a schoolboy who's just landed a date with the prettiest girl on campus. "I promise you won't be disappointed."

"With the interview or the dinner?"

"Both. Just think of me as an emancipated writer who in spite of his awkward attempt at getting the astonishingly beautiful —"

"Don't forget glowing."

". . . and *glowing* Gabriella McDaniel to have dinner with him is a magnificent storyteller who happens to cook a mean blackened redfish, New Orleans style."

"Well, I must say I can't remember ever having blackened fish before."

"You'll love it. How would Tuesday at 8 o'clock be?"

"Shall I dress formal?"

"Hardly. The Wharf is definitely casual. Jeans and a warm sweater will be fine. Unless of course the weather changes."

"And then?"

"Wear shorts," Paul said judiciously and winked again.

"There *is* one condition."

"Name it."

"You said you were a storyteller. So you must tell me a story

. . . one you've never told anyone else." Gabriella stuck her hand out. "Deal?"

Paul looked at her for a moment, as he'd looked at her in the auditorium, then grasped her hand in his. "We most certainly have a deal."

What an extraordinary day, he thought as they headed for the street.

This is crazy, she thought as Paul hailed a cab.

VI

A variety of pungent aromas greeted Gabriella as she entered Paul's home. She was immediately reminded of the musky odor that suffused the city of Jerusalem. She'd once spent five days in the Holy Land, and what she'd seen and felt during that experience indelibly impressed itself into her consciousness.

Paul smiled and ushered her into the living room. "I hope you're hungry," he said, taking her coat. "I got carried away with the fish. There's enough here to feed four."

"As a matter of fact I'm famished," she replied, surprised at how relaxed she felt. When Paul had first asked her to have dinner with him, she'd been a bit nervous. It had been a long time since she'd had dinner with a man other than her father or her brother. But she'd soon found herself looking forward to the experience.

"Great. Make yourself comfortable." He headed for the kitchen. "I have to check on dinner."

Gabriella surveyed the room. Paul's house was constructed from a combination of wood and stone, and the subtle combination, along with the casual style of the furniture, gave it a warm, cozy feeling.

Not all of the scents she'd noticed when she stepped through the front door were from the kitchen. She now discerned the smell of cedar. The thick, heady aroma of the rough-grained wood made her head tingle. It also resurrected the memory of an incident that had occurred during her trip to Israel.

"I love the smell of your house, Paul." *And I feel safe here for some strange reason*, she thought.

He stuck his head around the wall separating the kitchen from the living room and asked, "Fish?"

The look on his face made her laugh. "No, silly. Cedar."

Paul smiled. "I'm glad you approve."

Gabriella joined him in the kitchen. She leaned against the refrigerator and watched as he worked quickly and efficiently, juggling several tasks at once. Although he wasn't muscular, he had a rugged sort of magnetism about him. Like Harrison Ford in the *Indiana Jones* films. And from the way he moved in the kitchen, she was sure whatever Paul did, he worked hard to do it well. She liked that quality in a man. It meant he didn't take himself for granted.

"Can I help with anything?" she asked leaning forward.

"No thanks. Just stand back and watch the chef do his thing. I've spent a lot of years perfecting my technique."

"OK, but if that's how it's going to be, you're going to have to put up with my inquisitive nature."

Paul glanced over his shoulder. "Sounds like I better put you to work . . . fast."

"Too late. I already have a question. Do you play the piano?"

"What?"

"You have perfect hands for playing the piano."

"Funny you should mention that. My mother always told me I had 'piano hands,' and I love to listen to other people play. But I never had the patience to sit down and practice. I keep telling myself that one of these days I'll take it up."

"What did you do when you were a boy?"

"The same things I do now. I read a lot, and I'm a movie fanatic."

"Who's your favorite author?"

"Now that's a tough one. I guess if I had to pick my all-time favorite it would be a toss-up between John D. McDonald and Phillip K. Dick."

"McDonald I've heard of, but who's Phillip K. Dick?"

"He was a prominent science fiction writer who died a couple of years ago. One of his novels was even made into a movie."

"Which one?"

"*Do Androids Dream of Electric Sheep?*"

"I beg your pardon?"

Paul chuckled. "That's the name of the book. The movie was called *Blade Runner*. Harrison Ford played the lead."

"I thought I'd seen everything he'd done."

"You're a fan then?"

Gabriella nodded and chewed her lip, wondering about the coincidence between her thoughts and the conversation.

"It's a pretty unique love story, with an unusual plot twist. Ford falls in love with a woman who is not at all what she appears to be. His character hunts down rogue androids for a living, kind of like a futuristic bounty hunter. The bounty hunter falls in love with a woman he meets at the corporate headquarters of the company which developed the amazingly human replicas.

"During the course of his investigation, the bounty hunter discovers the woman is an android. Initially she is unaware she's not human, and it's Ford who uncovers the truth and reveals it to her. It makes a very interesting tale."

Paul reached for the special seasoning he'd prepared earlier, then picked up the redfish and pressed it into the blend of spices, making sure both pieces were totally covered. When he finished, he expertly seared both sides of both pieces, then gently laid the two pieces in the skillet on the front burner and turned down the heat so the inside of the fish wouldn't cook too fast.

"You know, the smell of cedar in your house reminds me of something unusual that happened to me when I was nineteen," Gabriella said, changing the subject. Paul's words made her uncomfortable, and she wasn't sure why.

"Shall I get my tape recorder?"

She eyed him speculatively, noting the glint of amusement in his eyes. After a moment's hesitation she replied, "Not if you want this evening to go any further."

He laughed easily and said, "Just kidding. It would be a crime to let all this delicious fish go to waste."

"Are you familiar with the cedars of Lebanon?"

Paul nodded.

"Well, I was traveling through Europe nine years ago, and on impulse I decided to go to Israel. I rented a car in Tel Aviv and spent five days touring the country. On the third day there I went to Jerusalem, where I chanced upon a solitary cedar on the outskirts of the city. I got out of the car and stood before the magnificent tree with my eyes closed, imagining what a stand of them would look like. The day was especially hot and dry. Suddenly a breeze began to blow. It felt cool and refreshing, and I felt as if I were floating on the backs of the clouds."

Paul stopped stirring the vegetables and listened intently. He sensed that Gabriella was sharing a very private moment with him, perhaps even something she'd never talked about with anyone else.

"A soft, almost melodious voice spoke in my ear. At first I was startled. But as the man spoke, his words were like the soothing balm —"

"Of Gilead," completed Paul, whispering. Oddly, he felt as if he knew exactly where the story was headed.

Gabriella nodded and continued. "'Keep your eyes closed and listen with your heart,' the voice told me. It was so close that I imagined the breeze was actually speaking. 'Take a deep breath,' commanded the voice, 'and fill your lungs with the scent.'

"I breathed in. 'Now rest your mind and use your spiritual eyes instead of your physical ones. Imagine a stand of tall trees with fair branches and shadowing shrouds; trees that are noble enough to be used for the masts of ships . . . for carved work of the most sacred kind. See their reddish-brown bark and sturdy trunks. Imagine that you are standing in the shade of their branches, looking up through bright green needles, gazing at the dark brown cones growing among the branches.'

"The soft, firm voice paused, and suddenly I realized that I was actually seeing the stand of trees . . . just as the voice had described it. Incredibly I was viewing the large clump of cedars from a distance and standing in the midst of them *at the same time*. It was like nothing I had ever experienced before. I felt as if I'd acquired a new sense of perspective. A phrase my father liked to quote when I was growing up ran through my head: *The viewpoint depends on the point of view.*"

Gabriella looked at Paul with emerald-green eyes that glistened with emotion. She felt a strange tingling course through her body, just as she had felt when she was in Jerusalem. Her heart began to beat faster. She wasn't sure why she was telling him this, but felt compelled to finish the story.

"As I looked up through the needles, I could see the sunlight sparkling through the green color. A sense of peace descended on me. I almost felt drugged, although I've never used anything stronger than aspirin.

"Then, all at once the breeze stopped. The voice was gone. The ensuing silence wrapped me in its embrace. I felt momentarily dislocated, as if for an instant I'd stepped out of time and into eternity.

"I opened my eyes slowly, expecting to see the man who had spoken to me, but there was no one around. I glanced at my watch and was stunned to discover that an hour had passed since I'd first closed my eyes."

"Did you see a haze?" interrupted Paul, his eyes narrow and penetrating. Gabriella's account sounded disconcertingly similar to what had happened to him the morning they'd met.

"No, not that I remember. Why?"

"Just curious. What happened next?"

Gabriella sniffed the air. "I think your fish is burning."

"Never!" said Paul. He grabbed the skillet and quickly slid it off the burner. "It's only the zucchini, and there's plenty more where that came from." He replaced the skillet with a pan filled with water and a combination of brown and wild rice, then turned to open the refrigerator. "Uncle Ben's Instant, but you can't tell the difference," he explained. "How about a glass of wine?"

"No thanks — I don't drink."

"OK. What *can* I get you?"

"Coffee. I'm a fanatic."

"Coming right up. Meanwhile, finish your story. I can't bear the suspense."

"I thought you were the one who was going to tell *me* a story."

Paul smiled. "We have plenty of time."

Gabriella arched her brow, then said, "I recounted my experience to the young man from Beirut who ran the desk at the hotel later that same afternoon. 'So you have been to Besherreh, north of Beirut,' he said.

"I told him I'd never been to Lebanon.

"'Perhaps you have seen such trees elsewhere,' he offered. 'There is no such stand of trees located anywhere in Palestine. The cedars range from the Himalayas to the Atlas, and from central Asia Minor to Lebanon.'"

"Obviously you hadn't," interjected Paul.

Gabriella nodded. "Later that night I asked an old Jew I met in the lobby about the cedars."

"Aha. And no doubt he told you that the tree was sacred — that it was considered by the Hebrews to be the 'king of trees' when compared with the other types of trees found in the Holy Land."

Gabriella's mouth dropped open. "You read minds too?"

Paul chuckled. "Much of Solomon's Temple was built with cedar wood," he continued, "as well as his house and other important public buildings in ancient Jerusalem. The sacred grove at Besherreh, in Lebanon, still bears the ancient name 'the cedars of the Lord.' Even the heathen used cedar for roofing on the temple of Diana at Ephesus and for that of Apollo at Utica."

"You're Jewish!" exclaimed Gabriella, wondering why that fact pleased her so much.

"Only half."

"What?"

"My mother was a Gentile."

"Oh. Was she a Christian?"

Paul looked at her strangely and nodded.

"So am I," she said, then added, "I thought there were strict rules in Judaism against intermarriage."

"There are," he replied in a tone that told Gabriella now was not a good time to pursue the issue.

"Coffee's ready," she said, once again changing the subject.

"And so is dinner," added Paul, taking her cue.

They talked as they ate, getting to know one another, and discovered they had a variety of interests in common. Paul shared a bit about his work and travels, and Gabriella talked about her struggles as an artist. Listening to her talk, Paul had the feeling he wanted something more from this woman than an interview. He wanted her friendship, and possibly her love. The abrupt thought startled him.

"That was excellent," said Gabriella as she finished the last bite of spicy redfish.

"A Paul Proudhomme specialty," he replied, speaking in an exaggerated French accent, deliberately mispronouncing the famous chef's last name.

They laughed together, and Gabriella said, "I can't remember when I've enjoyed myself so much. And I haven't laughed as much in the last few years as I have tonight."

"That goes for me too," added Paul, thinking that he'd met a very special woman, a woman who, for the first time in many years, made him think about something other than his next story.

As they were clearing the dishes Gabriella said, "Now, you did promise to tell me a story."

Paul looked at her with a gleam in his eyes. "One I've never told anyone else."

Gabriella nodded, uncertain why she felt excited by the prospect.

He led her back to the living room and motioned for her to sit on the floor. He threw her a small pillow from the couch, then gathered up kindling for a fire.

The fireplace was large, and the river-stone that comprised the chimney was speckled with flecks of silver and quartz. When Paul finally had the fire going strong, the soft yellow light from the flames danced across the face of the glistening granite. The freezing March wind had made its nightly debut while they ate, causing the temperature to drop steadily outside the house. The two windows on either side of the fireplace were coated on the outside with a translucent veneer of ice.

Gabriella could see Paul's face reflected in the right window as he knelt and methodically stoked the fire. His jaw was set, as if he were devoting all his attention to the task before him, even though it was routine. His eyes seemed to dance with the firelight, jubilant with the warmth and agility of an inexhaustible dancing partner.

Gabriella noted, with the artist's eye for texture and tint, that the yellow coloring of the flames toned down the intense blueness of his eyes, softening them to a pastel shade of green. But it was not the subtle change in the intensity of the coloring in his eyes nor the determined set of Paul's jawline that intrigued Gabriella.

She sensed anguish lurking beneath his seemingly serene expression. True, she saw a great deal of strength in his reflection. But she also saw pain. She wasn't quite sure, but she believed Paul was wrestling with something he didn't want to reveal. She wondered what it was.

Paul turned from the fire and caught Gabriella staring at him. "Well, now that we have the basics taken care of — food, shelter, and a brightly burning fire to keep away wolves and demons — let's talk turkey."

Gabriella frowned and started to say something, but Paul interrupted her. "Sorry. I inherited my father's love of colloquial aphorisms. They're so much a part of my vocabulary, sometimes I forget."

Gabriella was still frowning. "Why did you say what you just did?" she asked.

"About aphorisms?"

"No, before that. About wolves and demons."

Paul shrugged. "I don't know. It's a phrase I picked up from my research, I guess. I did an article on Eskimos a couple of years back after traveling to Alaska and Siberia. We talked about wolves and spirits, among other things."

"How did the subject come up?" asked Gabriella, intrigued at the twist their conversation was taking.

"The American Eskimos believe evil spirits can possess a man; that they are nomadic, traveling wherever they wish the man's body to take them, bringing ruin and chaos to all who come into contact with the unfortunate individual. They feed off his life until they consume his soul."

"And you got this information firsthand?"

Paul nodded. "One night I was with a group of Nunamiut in the central Brooks Range," he said, "about one hundred miles north of the Arctic Circle. We'd built a fire on the tundra and were cooking some caribou meat one of the Eskimos had killed when a huge she-wolf appeared out of the darkness and watched us. I can still see her shining yellow eyes staring at us from the edge of the firelight. Normally a female wolf weighs about eighty to eighty-five pounds. This one had to have been over a hundred."

"That's a big wolf," agreed Gabriella, getting caught up in the story.

"No kidding. I estimate she was over six feet from the tip of her nose to the end of her tail. Even though it was hard to see in the light, I'd be willing to bet she was close to three feet high at the shoulders."

Paul paused, then said, "But it was the coloring of her fur that really snagged me." He used his hands to describe what he'd seen as he talked. "The guard hairs that saddled her shoulders, all the way up her neck and down her spine, were slate blue. The underside of her tail, the insides of her legs, her belly, and the underside of her muzzle were pure white, with ocher striations. The area around her eyes and ears was also white, with reddish overtones. I tell you, her blue pelage blended with the night in a way that made those tawny eyes glow, giving her a surreal quality."

Gabriella listened intently to Paul's story, and her eyes watched the subtle, artful changes his face made as he talked. Even though she had known him only a short time, she had already started to realize that he used language the way she used paint, only his canvas was his audience's imagination. He was very adept at creating vivid images with his words.

"Not only was I struck by her size and coloring, but by her apparent lack of fear," he continued enthusiastically. "Eskimos hunt the wolf regularly, and any one of them could have shot her on the spot."

"Why didn't they?"

"That's the strange part. One of them spoke loudly — it seemed to me, almost deferentially — in Inupiatun to the wolf. He spoke for several minutes, and oddly I had the sense he was having a dialogue with the wolf. I fumbled inside my pack, trying to find my camera, and when I finally grabbed it and looked up, the wolf was gone."

"What was the Eskimo saying?"

Paul shrugged. "When I asked my guide, he told me the man had recognized the spirit of a demon in the wolf. He acknowledged the demon's presence, then told it where the remnant of the caribou carcass was so it could feast on the flesh and blood. The guide said that was the only way we could be sure the demon wouldn't bother our hunting party."

"Did you believe him?" asked Gabriella, toying with the sofa pillow.

Paul shrugged. "Not at first. I thought he'd exaggerated the translation for my benefit, because I was doing a story."

"What changed your mind?"

Paul shifted his position and turned to face the fire. He was sitting very close, and Gabriella could feel heat radiating from his body. She forced herself to concentrate on what he was saying.

"When I went to Siberia, to interview the Russian Eskimos, I had a similar experience. Only this time it was more dramatic. Once again we were huddled around a fire in the middle of nowhere, trying to keep warm. Suddenly one of the Russians started jabbering away and pointing toward the edge of the firelight."

"And?"

Paul stared at the fire. He watched the orange-yellow flames consume the pine logs and with astounding clarity remembered the night on the tundra in Russia, thousands of miles from America and sanity. The memory was so vivid, it seemed like only yesterday.

"I looked where he was pointing and saw nothing but darkness. I stood up, intending to walk over to where the man was pointing. But for some reason I still can't explain, I only took a few steps, then decided against leaving the security of the fire and returned to the circle of men.

"The Siberian became increasingly agitated. His voice got louder. Finally he began to chant. I looked at my guide. His eyes were riveted on the dark as well. Then, as suddenly as he'd started, the Russian stopped his litany. The silence was unnerving. It seemed to cloak our small group like a cocoon. I had the distinct feeling that I'd witnessed something very unusual — something no other white man has ever observed."

Paul paused as the heat from the fire caused a pocket of dried sap to explode, sending a white-hot stream of vaporized liquid up the chimney. The loud *crack!* split the air.

Gabriella didn't seem to notice. She was listening intently to what Paul had to say.

"What exactly the Siberian saw, and to what he'd been speaking, I don't know. But the look in his eyes —" Paul stared into the depths of the fire as he talked. "— made me cold inside. I tried to get rid of the chill by sitting very close to the fire . . . but it didn't work."

"What happened after that?"

Paul turned to face Gabriella. "I didn't sleep at all that night, and I made sure the fire never went out," he said, then stretched his arms over his head. "In the morning I asked my guide to tell me what had happened. All he would say was, 'No talk about demons. Talk about walrus, whale, and caribou — but no talk about the dead living.'"

"The dead living?"

"Yes, that's what he said. I thought at first I'd misunderstood his English. Later I remembered that both he and my American guide said the Eskimos built fires to keep away wolves and demons."

"Did you put those two experiences in your story?"

Paul looked at her and laughed, deliberately punctuating his tale with mirth. "How do you think I sell so many stories? I have a flair for the dramatic."

Gabriella smiled, but the frown didn't leave her brow. ". . . *um elfe kommen die wolfe, um zwolfe bricht das gewolbe,*" she whispered and wrapped her arms about her. Paul's story had touched something within her, but she wasn't quite sure how to express what she felt.

"What?"

"It's from a German folk rhyme that helps children learn the hours of the day. The ending says: 'at 11 come the wolves, at 12 the tombs of the dead open.'"

Paul stared at Gabriella with fascination. "Go on," he said, wanting to hear more.

"Humans have wrestled psychologically with the wolf from the time of Aesop and before," Gabriella explained as she tried to put into words what she was feeling. "But it was during the late Middle Ages, at the start of the Renaissance, that the link between the wolf and a period of half-light came together. The Latin idiom for dawn is *inter lupum et canem* — 'between the wolf and the dog.'"

"Meaning?"

"Darkness and savagery are symbolized by the wolf, enlightenment and civilization by a tamed wolf — the dog."

"Hmmm," said Paul, thinking out loud. "That's very interesting."

"There's more." She hugged the pillow to herself as if to ward off the darkness.

"Oh?"

"From classical times the wolf has been a symbol of things in transit. He's a twilight hunter, seen by man at dawn and dusk. During the Middle Ages it was thought that his howl, like the crow of the cock, heralded dawn — the end of night, the hours of the wolf."

"Hours of the wolf?"

"Famine, witchcraft — and carnage."

Paul's writer's antennae were vibrating. "During my research for the article on Eskimos," he interjected, "I discovered an interesting fact. The Bella Coola Indians believe that someone once tried to change all the animals into men, but succeeded in making human only the eyes of the wolf."

Gabriella's frown was finally gone. "Well, my point is, the Roman Church, which dominated medieval life in Europe for hundreds of years, exploited the sinister image of the wolf by associating it with devils."

"Why?"

"Because the clergy wanted to firmly fix in the minds of men the fact that the Devil was real."

"That's not surprising. We Jews have similar myths. My ancient ancestors were not interested and did not believe in impersonal forces."

"That's not what I meant." Gabriella fixed Paul with a penetrating gaze. "Even though the clergy's intent was Scripturally based, the methods they used were designed more to smother social and political unrest — and to maintain secular as well as religious control by flushing out 'werewolves' and putting them to death — than to educate believers about incarnate evil."

"Why are you telling me all this?" Paul asked.

"Because what's even more interesting is that in both Greek and Latin, the words for wolf and light are so similar that one was sometimes mistaken for the other in translation. The association with the Devil resulted from the fact that in Latin the word for wolf is *lupus*, while the word for light is *lucis*. The name Lucifer, given to God's fallen angel, is a contraction of *lucem ferre*."

"To bear light," said Paul, a glimmer of understanding coming into his eyes.

Gabriella nodded. "Exactly. The greatest prophet of the Old Testament, Isaiah, referred to Lucifer as 'son of the morning.' It should be obvious why the wolf of the Middle Ages was referred to as 'the devil, devourer of man's soul.'"

Paul grabbed hold of the metal tongs next to the fireplace and poked the burning logs, sending a torrent of flaming sparks and ash up the chimney. He added two more logs to the fire, set the iron tongs on the floor next to the dwindling pile of wood, then said, "If you're leading me where I think you're leading me, this could get pretty far out."

Gabriella arched a brow. "Oh?"

"Yeah. Someone else may have had a pretty good idea of what you're suggesting . . . Although I'm not sure I agree."

"Tell me."

> "'O, be thou damn'd, inexorable dog!
>   And for thy life let justice be accus'd.
> Thou almost makest me waver in my faith,
>   To hold opinion with Pythagoras,
> That souls of animals infuse themselves
>   Into the trunks of men: thy currish spirit
> Govern'd a wolf, who, hang'd for human slaughter,
>   Even from the gallows did his fell soul fleet,
> And, whilst thou lay'st in thy unhallow'd dam,
>   Infus'd itself in thee; for thy desires
>   Are wolfish, bloody, starv'd and ravenous.'"

Gabriella gave Paul a questioning, furtive glance.

"Shakespeare," he supplied, "*The Merchant of Venice*."

"Well, I guess that makes us even — me with my German fairy tale and you with your Shakespeare."

"Aha . . . I knew it," said Paul mischievously, "there's definitely hope for us yet."

"You think so?"

"I know so."

Time to change the subject, thought Gabriella. "Is your encounter with the wolf the story you'd planned on telling me?" she asked.

"Actually it's not," answered Paul. A distant look filled his eyes. "I don't know why I told you about it . . . I haven't thought about that experience in years."

"Good. I want something original, something you've never published. Something . . . *special*."

Paul grimaced good-naturedly. "Why do I have the feeling there's more to this request of yours than meets the ear?"

"Because you've proven to be a man who knows a great deal about the vagaries of a woman's inquisitive nature."

"Aha — the truth will out. I've got you now, Moriarty."

Gabriella laughed musically.

Paul reached out to hold her hand and was surprised to find it was cool to the touch despite the heat from the fire. "Actually I've given the matter a great deal of thought," he said, enjoying the moment of physical contact. "I'd like to share something personal."

Gabriella realized Paul was about to share with her whatever it was he'd been agonizing over. And somehow she knew she would be able to help. She drew back her hand and said, "Well, in that case, out with your deep, dark secret."

Paul sighed and stood up. "Not tonight."

Gabriella was taken back by his sudden brusqueness. "I'm sorry . . . Did I say something wrong?"

Paul grimaced. "No, it's not that. It's just that now isn't a good time. But I would like to see you again."

Gabriella let him pull her up beside him. "Are you sure?"

"Beyond a shadow of a doubt." Paul went to the phone and called for a cab. "They'll be right over," he said as he hung up.

"You never did ask me any questions about my art work, you know."

"Perfect. How about we get together Friday and I'll ply you with a thousand questions?" He walked her to the door.

"You know what they say. A picture —"

Paul chuckled and completed the phrase. "—is worth a thousand words."

"Friday sounds wonderful," Gabriella said as she put on her coat. "Where?"

"How about my office?"

"You're on. We'll have lunch. My treat."

Paul nodded and opened the door. A strong, cold gust of wind whipped at Gabriella's hair, blowing long strands of it into Paul's face. He breathed in the fragrance and was startled. He smelled *frankincense*.

There were no leaves on the maple trees outside Paul's house, and the wind whistled through their branches. The result was a soft, scraping noise that sounded vaguely like a song without harmony or rhythm.

Suddenly Gabriella turned to Paul. "The day we met I was trying to remember a story my grandmother told me about the tree standing outside Thompson Hall."

"The dogwood?"

"Yes. Legend has it that at the time of the Crucifixion the dogwood was comparable in size to the oak tree and other monarchs of the forest. Because of its firmness and strength it was selected as the timber for the cross; but to be put to such a cruel use distressed the great tree.

"Sensing this, the crucified Jesus told it, 'Because of your sorrow and pity for My sufferings, never again will the dogwood grow large enough to be used as a gibbet. Henceforth, it will be slender, bent and twisted, and its blossoms will be in the form of a cross — two long and two short petals. In the center of the outer edge of each petal there will be nail prints — brown with rust and stained with red — and in the center of the flower will be a crown of thorns. And all who see it will remember.'"

Paul stood speechless. He wondered why Gabriella's words moved him so. He wasn't a religious person at all; yet something in her words tugged at his soul.

The cab pulled up to the curb, and Gabriella turned and walked briskly down the steps. She pulled her coat tightly about her to ward off the penetrating cold. Paul followed hastily and caught up with her just as she reached the cab. He opened the door for her and asked, "What kind of perfume are you wearing?"

Gabriella smiled knowingly as she slid into the backseat of the cab and replied, "I'm not."

Thirty-five thousand feet above the North Atlantic the air was thin, ice-cold, and unbreathable. Sitting in the first-class section of a 747, Nathan McDaniel wondered what the air would be like in Heaven. He chuckled at the thought and stared at the face he saw reflected in the small window of the jet as he gazed at the abundance of stars adorning the dark canvas of night. Assuming he made it, of course.

The time away from Washington had rejuvenated him in more ways than one. Even though he was returning to a city that held a number of unpleasant memories, he felt more alive than he had in several years.

His hair was still thick and black, unlike his father's, which was thinning and had started to turn gray. There were fewer lines around his blue-gray eyes than when he'd left, and he'd lost about ten pounds, diminishing the small paunch he'd developed as he approached middle-age. He was happy about the weight loss; not being quite six feet tall he'd always felt better at 165 than 175.

He was on his way home to America — less than two months before his thirty-eighth birthday. Two years ago he'd left for Europe, frustrated and burnt out, intending to loaf for a while. Originally he'd planned to travel for a time, then settle on a Grecian island, perhaps Mykonos or Corfu, and indulge himself by doing nothing.

However, what he'd accidentally stumbled upon during the first few months of his self-imposed sabbatical had changed all that. There had been little time to relax after that.

He sighed and rubbed his eyes, then sat back in the seat and let the droning of the plane's engines lull him into relaxation. He reflected on the last speech he'd given — just before he'd left

America, and just after he'd quit as his father's campaign manager and political adviser.

He had been talking to a group of Kiwanians — who some said derived their name from the ancient Babylonian god the Greeks knew as Saturn — concerned about certain disturbing economic and political trends developing in the world. As he looked out over the small sea of faces, the sense of frustration and disillusionment that had been building up inside him for months threatened to overwhelm him.

"The enemy we face today," he'd said without preamble, "is not a man, a country, or even a particular type of government." The blank looks he saw only increased his sense of desperation. "It is the belief that man's intellect can and will provide solutions for society's problems."

He ignored the soft murmuring.

"My father, the esteemed Senator David McDaniel, has over the past fifteen years developed and refined that concept into a political dynamo that will very likely propel him into the White House. He is a man with a vision. A vision so comprehensive, it includes each and every one of you.

"His speeches are filled with passion and fueled with the rectitude of a man who believes in destiny and the fulfillment of dreams. A man who is certain there is nothing mankind cannot accomplish if we simply put our minds to it. At first blush, it would seem almost criminal to contest the veracity of his vision."

He paused to let his words sink in. People turned to look at one another, and the first signs of fearful uncertainty showed in their eyes. He'd known then that he had their attention. He prayed they would believe him.

"But you, ladies and gentlemen, must ask yourselves a very important question: Whose dreams and whose destiny is he talking about? Who is it that stands to benefit most from the dream he speaks about with such eloquence?"

Several people coughed and cleared their throats. The bluntness of his statements had caught his audience completely off guard. They were clearly getting more than what they had bargained for.

"If you drink from the cup of communion he and his cronies offer up as a means of absolution from the sins and ills of the world," he continued, "beware of those with whom you break bread."

A low murmur had begun to spread through the audience, but he was now committed beyond the point of no return.

"The man whom you invite into your homes via television, the Senator who speaks so eloquently about the necessity for world peace and global harmony, is not what he appears to be."

The murmuring grew louder.

"His face is not the face of the god of your salvation." His head had begun to throb, but he couldn't stop. "I warn you: if you partake of the silver cup of his truth, you will inevitably taste lead, even as the invincible Roman Empire did. The wine of his promises will sour inside you once you realize the price you'll have to pay."

The room had grown suddenly quiet, and the ache inside his head moved to his stomach.

"In closing, let me share with you a quotation from the nineteenth-century German philosopher Friedrich Nietzsche:

"'Oh man! take heed
Of what the dark midnight says:
'I slept, I slept — from deep dreams I awoke:
'The world is deep — and more profound than day would
have thought.
'Profound in her pain —
Pleasure — more profound than pain of heart,
Woe speaks; pass on.
'But all pleasure seeks eternity —
A deep and profound eternity.'"

The audience had remained silent, stunned. He wanted to smile as he left the podium, but he couldn't. They had heard him, but it didn't matter. He couldn't stay any longer. Especially since he'd have to face his father.

". . . get you anything?"

Nathan's eyes snapped open, and he looked into the soft, round face of the flight attendant. "I'm sorry . . . I was day-dreaming."

She smiled and said, "A bit late for that. It's almost 3 A.M. Washington time."

"How long before we arrive?"

She glanced at her watch and replied, "A good three hours, if the weather holds."

"In that case, the answer is no. I could use some sleep."

The stewardess reached above his head and turned off the light. "I'll wake you just before we land."

As Nathan drifted into sleep, a wisp of a smile crossed his lips. He was thinking of how nice it was going to be to surprise his sister.

VII

The frozen ground was beginning to thaw. After six months of cold, windy mornings, rainy afternoons, and occasional snowy nights, the earth was giving notice that the new life she harbored within the warmth of her womb was ready to burst forth into the light of spring.

April was insistent and precocious . . . March reluctant and fading.

Gabriella liked to work early in the morning and late in the afternoon because that was when the light shining through her studio windows was the most dramatic. On this particular morning she'd been sitting in front of an easel for over an hour, thinking.

A paintbrush was absently stuck in her mouth. Her once-white painter's smock was splattered with a variety of colors. The canvas she was working on was not. It gaped at her relentlessly. If she'd allowed her imagination to get the better of her, she could easily believe the blank canvas was rebuking her for her lack of creative expression.

Only one week remained until her show and she was having trouble finishing her work, but she couldn't get Paul Michael Kingman off her mind. She'd never met a man like him. She wasn't quite sure why he was so different from other men she'd met, but whatever it was, she knew it was something special. Unfortunately, she didn't have time for a relationship. Other than God, right now her work was the most important thing in her life. And besides, the last time she'd let her emotions get the better of her, she'd come very close to giving away a part of herself that was very special. She was determined not to repeat *that* mistake, no matter what. Nevertheless, she found herself thinking about Paul Kingman more than she liked to admit. Aside from her emotions, there was something else holding her back — a problem she couldn't ignore. When she'd first started to study the Word in earnest, someone had told her that the Bible had an answer for every question, a solution for every dilemma, but that people often ignored those answers which didn't fit with what they wanted to hear. So far she'd found that to be the case. Now she had to deal with the issue on a personal level.

Last night she'd been doing her daily Bible reading and had reread a Scripture she'd forgotten about. The Apostle Paul had written to the church at Corinth and admonished them not to be "unequally yoked together with unbelievers: for what fellowship has righteousness with unrighteousness? And what communion has light with darkness?" It was clearly a word for her from the Lord, but what was she to do about it? Even though she had only known Paul a short time, she believed that the Holy Spirit was at work in his life and that ultimately he would come to accept Christ as his personal Savior. However, she had no idea how long it would take. And where did that leave her in the meantime?

Ironically, as she wrestled with her emotions and her Biblical beliefs, the words from one of her favorite tunes kept running through her mind. It was a song by Billy Joel called *Vienna*:

Slow down you crazy child,
*   You're so ambitious for a juvenile,*
But then if you're so smart, tell me . . .
*   why are you still so afraid? . . .*

Slow down,
*   you're doin' fine,*
You can't be everything you want to be,
*   before your time . . .*

You got your passion,
       you got your pride,
But don't you know
       only fools are satisfied?

The doorbell rang, startling her out of her reverie. She stuck the paintbrush behind her ear and headed downstairs. When she opened the door, her mouth dropped open with surprise.

"Hi, sis, long time no see."

"Nathan!" she squealed.

Nathan smiled and grabbed his sister in a bear hug, lifting her off the floor. "It's good to see you. I've been thinking about this moment for two days."

"Put me down, you brute. I may be your little sister, but I'm not *that* little any more."

Nathan laughed and complied.

Gabriella shut the door and stepped back so she could look at her brother. He was dressed casually — black Reeboks, a pair of faded blue jeans, and a maroon sweater. And he'd lost weight. "You look great. Quite a change from Armani suits and silk ties."

"Let's not talk about that — it's still a sore spot."

"Come on, it's been almost two years."

Nathan did not respond.

"OK. When did you get back?"

He looked at his watch. "About two hours ago."

"Got tired of the life of leisure, eh?"

"Not exactly. You have any of that famous Java brew of yours ready?"

"Right this way."

It was like he'd never left. She led him to the kitchen and poured them both a cup of steaming *cafe au lait*, fixing it just as she'd been taught by a woman who owned a *patisserie* on the *Champs Elysees*. She also fixed them each a croissant and put some yogurt and her brother's favorite fruit on the table.

"So tell me about Europe."

Nathan dunked one of the plump, fresh strawberries in his

coffee and popped the whole thing in his mouth. He stared at his sister while he chewed. "Well, it wasn't quite what I expected."

"How so?"

"I'm not sure you really want to know."

Gabriella frowned. "Uh oh, sounds serious. I thought we'd agreed you were going to relax, have a good time, rediscover your lost childhood."

Nathan chuckled. "Those were *your* words, not mine."

"You sound like the big bad wolf tried to eat you."

Nathan's eyes suddenly clouded. "Why did you say that?"

Gabriella shrugged. "I don't know. I had an unusual conversation about wolves and demons the other night. Guess it's still on my mind."

"Demons?"

"Yeah. You always said I was a little crazy."

Nathan glanced at his sister speculatively and replied, "I've been wrong about a lot of things, sis. In fact, something happened to me a week ago that I still haven't figured out."

"Tell me."

"I was in Paris tracking down some information on the Kronos Corporation's business activities in —"

"Europe!" interrupted Gabriella. "Father's company doesn't do business in Europe."

"It does now. I'll tell you about that later also."

"OK. Sorry I interrupted."

"Anyway, I took a drive and ended up at Chartres Cathedral."

"That's quite a drive."

Nathan shrugged. "After spending a couple of hours walking around, I had a sudden urge to go to confession. I hadn't been in quite some time."

"Neither have I."

Nathan stared at his sister, wondering if she had any idea of what he was about to tell her. "I found a young priest and asked him to hear my confession. Afterwards he invited me to his home for coffee. We talked for hours about a variety of things. Near the end of the conversation he said something that caught me off guard."

"Oh?"

"He said, 'You know, Mr. McDaniel, one of the things Jesus accomplished with His death was to bring forth the ministry of the Holy Spirit. The Bible tells us we who believe are temples of the living God and that His Spirit dwells in us to guide us and teach us in all things. Jesus said, "He that has My commandments and keeps them, he it is that loves Me: and he that loves Me shall be loved of My Father, and I will love him and will manifest Myself to him."'"

Gabriella's eyes were glistening with emotion. She had sensed from the moment she laid eyes on her brother there was something different about him, but she hadn't been sure what it was. Now a glimmer of hope burned within her heart.

"On the drive back to Paris I couldn't get the priest's words out of my mind. I kept repeating them to myself over and over, so I wouldn't forget them. The more I thought about what he'd said, the more intrigued I became." He stopped talking long enough to take a quick sip of coffee, then resumed his story.

"By the time I got back to Paris, it was late. But I managed to find an open bookstore and bought a Bible so I could look up the Scripture myself. Had a heck of a time finding it."

Gabriella smiled.

"I read the whole Gospel of John that night. Couldn't sleep at all. I felt like I'd been hooked up to a high-tension wire for a week. Just before the sun came up the weirdest thing happened." He paused, then asked, "Do you believe in angels, sis?"

She nodded, and her heart began to beat faster.

Nathan sighed, relieved. This was going to be easier than he'd thought. "I'd turned off the light and was lying in bed staring at the ceiling, thinking. All of a sudden the room was filled with light. I knew immediately something strange was going on. One minute the room was pitch-black, the next it was like the sun had fallen into the room."

Gabriella was suddenly excited. "Exactly *when* did all this happen?"

"Last Wednesday."

Gabriella gasped. "Go on."

"At first I thought I was dreaming. But I wasn't. It was all real." He hesitated, then added, "I know this is going to sound crazy, but there was a man standing at the foot of the bed. He was huge, maybe over seven feet tall. It was hard to tell. Oddly, other than that I don't have any specific recollection of what he looked like. All I can remember when I think about him is his height . . . And the light.

"Then he spoke to me, and I could swear that his voice sounded like choir music. But his words sent a chill up and down my spine. 'Be sober, be vigilant: because your adversary the devil, as a roaring lion, walks about, seeking whom he may devour.'"

Nathan eyed his sister sheepishly. "You probably think I've gone over the edge. But I swear to you that's exactly what happened. Ever since then I've been reading the Bible. The words are right out of —"

"The First Book of Peter."

"You know it?"

Gabriella told him about the voice she'd heard in Israel, and about her own encounter with one of God's mighty messengers, and finally about her conversion experience.

"Whew," said Nathan when she was finished. He sat back and stared out the window, a somber look on his face. He noticed that even though Gabriella lived in the city, she'd found a place surrounded by trees. His sister loved trees, especially cherry trees.

He remembered that the man who owned the property before her was Japanese, and he'd planted a variety of the colorful trees: The *Amanogawa*, which was narrow like a Lombardy poplar with pale pink flowers. The *Kanzan*, with its dense masses of deep-pink, double flowers. The *Shirofugen*, which had large, double white flowers and purple leaves. And the largest flowered cherry, the *Tai-Haku*, with blossoms three inches wide.

The blossoms on all of them were in full bloom, and the effect produced by the sunlight streaming through the profusion of color was breathtaking. Still, his mind would not calm.

Every time he thought about the incredible occurrence, he felt overwhelmed. In all of his life he'd never experienced something so alien to his worldview. He found it almost unbelievable that a solitary event had so irrevocably affected his outlook on life.

Gabriella was startled by her brother's sudden change of demeanor. "Talk to me, Nathan. What are you thinking about? Something else is on your mind, isn't it?"

"The Kronos Corporation," he replied as he pushed all other thoughts aside.

Gabriella stood up and added fresh coffee to her cup. "This is about Father, isn't it?" she asked, trying to keep the frustration out of her voice.

Nathan nodded and finished his croissant.

Gabriella sat back down and handed her brother a fresh cup of coffee. "Well, are you two going to be reconciled?"

"Not if what I think is happening is true."

"Oh, Nathan, what is it now? Why can't you and Father simply agree to disagree? You're different people with different values and dreams, and that's OK."

Nathan sighed. "You don't know him the way I do, Gabriella. There's a side to him few people have ever seen. He hasn't been the same since —"

"Since the first campaign," interrupted Gabriella, a harshness creeping into her voice she wished wasn't there. She hated to argue with Nathan, but she knew there were times when her brother couldn't see the forest for the trees. And this was one of them. "We've been over this a hundred times. You did the right thing by quitting. It was time for you to do something for yourself. And besides that, you needed the break. It seemed like all you did was work. You never had any fun . . ."

". . . since Mother died," finished Nathan, watching his sister intently. He knew he was opening a can of worms. He also knew it had to be done. There was too much at stake for him to continue deceiving his sister.

Although Gabriella's outward demeanor didn't change, inside she was a jumble of emotions. She had so few memories. One thing she did remember was that her mother laughed and smiled a lot. And she'd been extremely beautiful.

How she hated having been robbed of her childhood. Her mother had felt the sting of death, but did the grave have the victory? She hoped the answer was no.

"That was over twenty-five years ago," she said, willing the past to stay out of the present. "You can't blame your problems on Mother's death."

The anger in her voice slapped Nathan in the face like a cold wind. He felt her pain, but he'd already made his decision. He prayed it was the right one. "I'm not *blaming* anyone. I'm simply trying to tell you that sometimes all is not what it seems to be. There are things you just don't understand."

"What kind of things?"

"You don't know what happened."

"What are you talking about? We've discussed it before. Mother was killed by a drunk driver."

"That much is true . . . But there's more."

Gabriella suddenly felt uneasy. She wasn't sure she wanted to hear what her brother was about to say. She loved her father deeply, even though during the last five years they had not had much contact. He was busy with all of his committees, and she had been busy trying to figure out what she wanted to do with her life. She was dedicated to being an artist, but that was only one part of who she was. There was something else inside her waiting to be born. It was that "something" that made her art so special. Ever since she was a little girl, a voice inside her had guided and protected her.

Two years ago, just after Nathan left for Europe, she'd discovered that the voice she'd come to depend upon was God's voice. That revelation had changed her life. And now that voice was telling her to be patient and listen. She believed in her spirit, but her mind and body were rebelling.

"Go on," she prodded. "What about Mother's accident?"

"The driver was Father."

"I don't believe you!" But even as she voiced her denial, she knew by the sick feeling in the pit of her stomach that her brother wasn't lying. Suddenly she realized where the fractured memory had come from the other day when she'd seen the accident on her way to the university. The voice had been that of her father, waking his nearly five-year-old daughter and asking her for forgiveness in the middle of the night.

Nathan reached across the table and grasped hold of his sister's hands. She was trembling. "I know this is difficult for you, sis, but believe me, it's twice as difficult for me. I've wanted to tell you the whole story a hundred times, but I couldn't."

"Why not?"

"Because Father made me promise never to tell you. He didn't want you scarred."

"I'm tough," she countered, feeling just the opposite. "And I'm tired of the men in this family treating me as if I were a fragile butterfly. I've fought hard to keep from being swallowed up by Father's ubiquitous shadow. If anybody should understand that, you should."

Nathan looked deep into his sister's eyes and saw a strength there he'd never seen before. There were rough seas ahead, but he needed Gabriella as an ally. Somehow he was going to have to convince her of the truth about their father. The problem was, he wasn't sure he'd convinced himself.

"It was two weeks before the assassination," he continued thickly as the memory flooded his mind.

"Kennedy's?"

Nathan nodded. "Dad had been asked to accompany the President to Dallas. He'd gotten a lot of publicity as a result of the *Torcaso* case, and the spotlight was on him."

"That was his last case, wasn't it? The one he argued before the Supreme Court. They ruled that the First Amendment upheld a person's right not to believe in God."

"Right on all three points. The President wanted to meet Dad. There were rumors of a possible position high up in the administration. Dad was very excited. Mother wasn't."

"Why not?"

"Mother was Jewish. She was born in Palestine, and her parents were very religious. Her heritage was important to her."

Gabriella gasped. "But Father told me she was an orphan."

"Will you let me finish?" said Nathan, exasperated. "Mother *was* an orphan. Her parents were killed shortly after she was born. She was raised by monks from a monastery dedicated to St. Catherine of . . ."

Gabriella barely heard her brother. She couldn't believe what she'd just been told. What an incredible twist of fate. Paul's father was Jewish, and his mother was a Gentile. Her father was Catholic, and her mother was Jewish. She wondered what he'd say when she told him.

". . . they named her Vashti, after the first wife of King Ahasuerus."

"How do you know all this?" asked Gabriella, perplexed at the depth of her brother's knowledge and wondering why he was going into such detail.

"I've been doing a lot of research the last two years."

"Research?"

"I'll tell you about it later. Anyway, it was the night before Dad was supposed to leave for Dallas. They'd gone to dinner and left you with me. It was rainy and cold. The weatherman predicted a freeze.

"On the way home they were arguing. Mother asked Dad if he was going to tell the President the truth about her ancestry. He told her the time wasn't right. She accused him of being ashamed of her and told him that if anybody would understand, Kennedy would.

"Dad wasn't paying attention to his driving, and the car hit a patch of ice. He'd been drinking, and his reactions were off. They

crashed into the embankment doing sixty. Dad was barely hurt."
He paused, then added, "Now you know the real reason Senator
McDaniel hasn't had a drop of liquor in twenty-five years."

"You mean the two of you have lied to me all these years?
You've conspired to keep me ignorant?"

"It wasn't like that, sis."

"Oh no? Death cheated me of a very special relationship. But
you and Father robbed me of something more. By avoiding talking about her, you hid memories that could have helped. Why?"

Nathan sighed heavily. "I always knew it was wrong, but I
kept telling myself the time wasn't right. Remember the summer
we went to Grand Lake — when you were twelve?"

Gabriella nodded, praying silently that God would take the
pain away. "Raindrops keep falling on my head . . ." she whispered.

Nathan smiled. *"Butch Cassidy and the Sundance Kid.* We
acted out the scene where Robert Redford took Katherine Ross
for a ride on the bike." He paused, remembering happier times.
"I wanted to tell you then . . . But I didn't. I decided you weren't
old enough. You were *never* old enough. That's how I rationalized
it."

"Why tell me now . . . after all these years?"

"Because of what I discovered in Europe."

"And it concerns Father?"

Nathan nodded.

Gabriella studied her brother intently. She could tell by the
look on his face that whatever he was about to tell her wasn't
good. Oddly, the thought crossed her mind that she wished Paul
was here so she could ask his counsel. *Now where did that come
from?* she wondered.

"I believe Father is involved in something horrendous . . .
something so diabolical that even though it appears to be good
it will ultimately enslave every person who believes in and supports him," said Nathan. "And I need your help to prove it," he
added, watching surprise and anger battle for supremacy in his
sister's sparkling green eyes.

VIII

Paul's soul ached.

It felt like the fabric that bound together his mind, will and emotions was under relentless attack from ethereal, celestial forces whose existence he could sense but not grasp. Doubt stalked him in the labyrinths of his imagination. And as usual he wasn't dealing with it very well.

He was sitting at his antique rolltop desk in the small office he maintained inside the Kronos Building. Outside, the symphony of alto and tenor wind and soprano rain drummed musically against the window, intermittently punctuated with the bass and baritone thunder.

He looked up from his musings in time to see the sun swallowed up by a large black rain cloud in the shape of a blacksmith's anvil. It made him think about Hephaestus, the ancient Greek god of fire and metalworking. Perhaps he was hard at work in the heavens. Known as Vulcan by the Romans, he was said to be the only flawed immortal who worked, having been born lame.

Paul sighed heavily, wondering if the sinews of truth holding together his sanity had been weakened by his unbelief. The only unguent that soothed his uncertainty was the faith in his heart spread repeatedly upon his doubt like the once-famous salve, the balm of Gilead.

In moments like these he was almost certain he could see into the unseen realm of the spirit. And he was frightened of what he might find. The battle that had smoldered inside him for years had been rekindled by his father's death. Also, he was fighting off guilt for not having seen that his father was ill last fall. He knew it was foolish to feel that way, but he couldn't help himself. The old familiar ache had settled in, and that frightened him. He thought he'd finally banished that particular emotional parasite.

Seven years ago, just after he'd graduated from college and before he'd become a well-known writer, he'd gone through a time when he felt empty and alone. Even though it appeared to those around him that he was on his way up in the world, inside he hurt. He'd tried to describe the feeling by writing about it, but the words never came out right.

Eventually he decided he had a spiritual cancer.

Like Prometheus, the Titan who stole fire from Olympus and gave it to mankind in defiance of Zeus, he was bound to the rock of penitence. His eagle, favorite bird of Zeus, was a cancer, his soul the liver upon which the eagle feasted. The torn and bloodied vessel storing his identity was regenerated nightly as he slept. In those days there were many mornings when he longed for a Hercules to come and set him free.

He stood up and stretched, hoping to ease some of the tension. It was time to take a break from reading his father's journal. He stared at the overworked computer he'd nicknamed "Sam" in honor of two of his favorite figures from history — the Biblical Samuel and Samuel Langhorne Clemens, the real name of Mark Twain.

A knock at the door pulled him from his musings. He opened it, only to stare into a disconcerting pair of ebony eyes. It was like looking into a deep cave. Were it not for the fact that there were shining specks of silver in them, he would have sworn that the man's eyes devoured light.

He also felt a sudden chill — as if the heat in the room had been abruptly sucked out of it.

"Mr. Kingman, I am Vaughn Aurochs. We spoke briefly on the phone."

"Come in," Paul said, not sure why he felt so strange. "Please, sit down," he added, indicating the large wingback chair next to the couch under the window.

"No thank you, I prefer to stand."

Paul didn't know what to say. The situation seemed very awkward. Vaughn was over six feet tall, and Paul realized that if he sat down while the imposing man across from him stood, it would be like talking to a giant. He decided that he too would remain standing.

Vaughn was dressed impeccably in a charcoal-gray silk suit, starched white shirt, and burgundy tie. Paul, on the other hand, was wearing a lightweight blue and red flannel shirt tucked into a pair of khaki-colored corduroy pants. Vaughn's expensive shoes were made of leather. Paul had on a worn pair of Nike running shoes.

"Let me get to the point, Mr. Kingman. I came here because I wanted to apologize for being so abrupt the other day . . . And to make you an offer."

"Oh?"

"I collect antiquities. The parchments your father discovered in the desert nearly forty years ago hold a special interest for me."

"That's odd. My father told me no one knew about the documents. How is it that you're aware of them?"

"I told you that on the phone," replied Vaughn, his voice taking on an edge that pricked at Paul like a barely audible high-pitched sound will do.

"That's true, you did. But I'm not exactly clear on how you came to meet my father."

Vaughn turned and walked to the window. He looked down at the city's largest park, ten stories below. Paul sat down at his desk and casually put his father's journal in the top drawer.

"I read your article on the Eskimos," Vaughn said, his voice sounding distant. "I especially liked the section on the wolves. Fascinating animals, aren't they?"

Paul stared at Vaughn's rigid back. "Yes, they are. There aren't many left, however. They've been hunted down and killed, almost to extinction."

Vaughn nodded as Paul spoke, then turned to face him. "My father was a missionary to China . . . under the auspices of the Jesuits. That's where he met my mother. She died shortly after my sixth birthday. Franklin Aurochs — my father — and I were on our way back to America when we met your father on board ship."

"In 1949?"

Vaughn nodded. "I overheard your father tell mine that he'd discovered some rare documents in the desert. I'd forgotten about the conversation until I saw your father's obituary in the paper. So you see, the documents have dual significance for me."

Something about this conversation isn't quite right, thought Paul. His writer's antennae began vibrating again. How was it that Vaughn could remember a specific conversation that was nearly forty years old — one that had taken place when he was only six? Paul felt Vaughn was lying, but there was more — a hint of an evil presence in the man.

"I'm prepared to offer you a substantial sum of money for those parchments, Mr. Kingman."

"Sight unseen? They might be worthless."

Vaughn shook his head. "Not to me."

"Well, I'm sorry to disappoint you, Mr. Aurochs, but the parchments aren't for sale."

A cold, calculating look seeped into Vaughn's eyes. The light in the room seemed to grow dim. "You're aware, of course, that by withholding the documents your father committed a criminal act. I'm sure there are individuals — both here and in Israel — who would be very interested to learn about the existence of those documents . . . Not to mention their theft."

Paul stood up. "I think it's time for you to go. We don't have anything further to discuss." Paul was angry but not fearful. Even if what Vaughn said was true, and he didn't believe it was, he had the feeling that Vaughn would not complain to the authorities.

"What did your father die from?" asked Vaughn abruptly.

Paul frowned. What was going on here? "Chronic lymphocytic leukemia."

"That's cancer of the blood, isn't it?"

"In a manner of speaking."

"Please excuse my morbid curiosity. Both of my parents are dead as well."

"Oh, I see."

"No, I'm not sure you do. Have you ever heard of lupus, Mr. Kingman?"

Paul nodded, thinking about the fact that in Latin *lupus* meant wolf. "It's a non-fatal skin disease, isn't it?"

"One form is. The other, systemic lupus erythematosus, is a chronic disorder which, if it remains undiagnosed, is fatal. Both my mother and father died from it. And that's extremely rare, considering that only about 15 percent of those diagnosed with the disease are men, and only 1 percent die."

"I thought the disease wasn't contagious."

"It's not."

The silence in the room was deafening. Outside the rain had slackened to a drizzle, but the sky had grown darker. Oddly, Paul was reminded of the opening lines of T. S. Eliot's famous poem *The Wasteland*:

> *April is the cruellest month, breeding*
> > *Lilacs out of the dead land, mixing*
> *Memory and desire, stirring*
> > *Dull roots with spring rain.*

As Vaughn walked out the door, he stared at Paul with hooded eyes and said, "Think about my offer, Mr. Kingman. I'm a very persistent man when I really want something."

After Vaughn left, Paul drummed his fingers on the desk, chasing his thoughts. It started to rain again — first lightly, then harder. Large, silver drops fell from the thick, black clouds in great sheets, like sparks flying from molten metal being hammered upon a smith's iron block.

Paul opened the drawer, pulled out Benjamin's journal, and began reading.

April 14th, 1948.
Damascus.

The exact origin of the city's name is unknown. Some call

it *City of the Sun*; others believe it means *The Righteous Blood*, because Cain slew Abel here. For me the city, like all great cities, paints a picture in my mind. Cairo a pyramid, Shiraz a rose. When I think of Damascus I see running water . . . a river of it flowing out of Lebanon, smearing soil over the desert for a hundred and seventy square miles, giving birth to the miracle of trees.

If I close my eyes tight enough I can see, not just a single river of flowing water, but three rivers. I'm on the site of the original Garden of Eden. I'm standing beside Adam and Eve, watching the sun set on creation. Before the serpent beguiled and deceived them. Before there were . . . *distractions*.

I want to ask them a thousand questions, but I can never bring myself to speak. I stand mute before the first-created of God, struck dumb by the purity and unfettered magnificence of their splendor.

But enough of my personal fantasies. I need to write about what happened today.

I followed the Barada River to the ancient Grecian city of Abila. Today the river is little more than the size of an English woodland stream, but still the inhabitants along its banks refer to it as the *River of Gold*.

On the outskirts of the city I began climbing toward the crest of a hill. The ground was littered with chunks of limestone, and the earth was parched, the thin topsoil easily disturbed by the slightest breeze. Scrub brush grudgingly shared the hillside with dwarf oaks. And of course there were the flowers; purple and yellow flowers, most of which had dried up in the heat. However, some were still living, and they provided a refreshing distraction from the barrenness of the surrounding landscape.

But it is not the image of the land that is fixed so commandingly in my memory. It is the tombs. They speckled the mountainside like dozens of gaping, sunken eyes, staring out at the day with blackened pupils.

I finally reached the crest, only to find that I still had an almost precipitous climb before me, up the vertical face of rock forming the base of the plateau that was my destination.

By the time I reached the summit it was mid-afternoon. The pastel blue sky had adopted a silky-white haze, almost as if in afterthought to the sun's original plan for the day.

At last I stood before the tomb on the Mountain of Abel.

I shuddered, as though a stifling summer *sirocco* had blown in off the desert unexpectedly. Suddenly I was very tired. I sat down and rested against a small fir tree — sacred to Pan, the ancient Greek god of the forests, flocks, and shepherds. I ate some pomegranates and remembered other tombs I'd visited.

In Betima, near Hermon, I saw a sepulchre thirty feet long. Legend says it was the burial place of Nimrod. The local people are convinced that because of his sins, the dew never falls on his grave.

Then there was the Mountain of Shiit, in Lebanon; a long, slender tomb inhabitants say is that of Seth, the third son of Adam. There were many others, a surprising number of them twenty feet long or better.

As I sat atop that hill, eating my pomegranates, looking out over the plain below, I thought about giants mentioned in Scripture:

In Deuteronomy, Og, King of Bashan, whose grave was thirteen feet long and six wide. In Chronicles, the last days of the ogre-kings, the Titans of Gath and Gezer, whose spear shafts were like weaver's beams and where it is written that the sons of Anak made the spies of Moses look like grasshoppers. The Rephaim, lurking under the waters, the Emmin and Zazummin, bellowing among the rocks of Moab and the land of Lot. Amos declaring that the Amorites were like the height of cedars and strong as the oaks.

I remembered the account in Genesis that has plagued my dreams now for nearly two years:

There were giants in the earth in those days; and also after that, when the sons of God came to the daughters of men, and they bare children of them, the same became mighty men which were of old, men of renown.

Paul paused, a glimmer of an idea forming in his mind. He flipped the pages backward rapidly, looking for an earlier reference to the Rephaim. He was sure the word meant "spirits of the deceased."

When he got to the entry for August 10th, 1947 a name on the page caught his eye. At the sight of it he completely forgot about what he was looking for.

Met an interesting man last evening while attending a party at the home of my friend George Amos. David McDaniel is a journalist who has been covering the War for the *New York Times*.

He's gregarious and not a little bit irreverent. However, he intrigues me. We talked of many things.

When I asked him whether or not it was politically expedient for the world to allow us Jews to have a homeland he replied, "Politics, Mr. Kingman, is for those who don't share God's sense of timing. We are not involved in politics here in Jerusalem. We are involved in the fulfillment of God's covenant . . . and not just with the Jews."

I pressed him to explain and he said, "The establishment of a Jewish National State may seem to the uninformed to be simply a political decision. I assure you, it is much more than that. A new age is unfolding. Not only have we been chosen to witness the global drama that's beginning, but we will participate in it as well."

What sticks in my mind even more than his words is my impression that he is a man who idolizes truth. He courts the *absolute* like most men court women. His passion is not perfection. It is power. Absolute power. And he has an almost hypnotic way of getting one to agree with his viewpoint.

Even if it is flawed.

Paul sat back in his chair. Incredible as it was, Gabriella's father and his father had known one another. Apparently they'd met before Benjamin Kingman discovered the parchments. He wondered if there were more references to the Senator in the journal. He flipped through page after page, scanning them for information on David McDaniel.

When he began reading again, part of his mind was thinking about how intertwined his and Gabriella's lives had become.

IX

"What do you mean *we* might have a problem? You're the one who said it was imperative that *you* get your hands on the parchments," David McDaniel snapped.

Vaughn listened impassively, a glazed look clouding his eyes. He was thinking of the night on the *Arabesque* forty years ago when he'd met Benjamin Kingman . . . And of his more recent conversation with Kingman's only son.

David McDaniel couldn't help but think that the look reminded him of snakes he'd seen at the zoo when he was a boy. They had that same milky glaze on their eyes when they were feeding. "I can't believe you came *here*," he added angrily, working hard at not yelling. "We agreed that any time we met, it would be in *your* office."

"It's almost midnight, Senator. I doubt if anyone but you or I is in the building."

"You found *me* here, didn't you?"

"All right, Senator, leave the matter to me. I'll take care of everything. You needn't concern yourself further."

Vaughn stood up abruptly and went to the window of the spacious office, pushing thoughts of the past out of his mind. He was pleased with David McDaniel's anger. It would be easy to manipulate. He also knew that he'd made the right choice. If nothing else, this room told him that.

The Senator's office had been decorated with one subtle purpose in mind. Whoever sat in front of the magnificent desk from the *Schwarzwald* sensed — even if they didn't immediately believe — that whatever power they wielded *outside* the office became irrelevant within it.

Inside the Citadel, as it was referred to privately, David McDaniel was King. And few people knew how large his kingdom really was. The poor souls who had discovered just how far his long arm could reach were no longer around to talk about it.

Vaughn chuckled, remembering. He'd first heard about the Citadel last summer when he began to focus his attention on finding the perfect man for his needs. He was at a cocktail party and overheard the tail end of a conversation.

". . . and I tell you, Malcolm, his office was more like the den of a lion than a room where political negotiations are conducted."

The man named Malcolm had chuckled and replied, "I know what you mean. But count your blessings, old chap. There are those who, being far less fortunate than you and the Biblical Daniel, have come out of that office so severely mauled they have disappeared into the dust of political anonymity."

"No doubt you're referring to former Senator What's-his-name from Arizona."

Malcolm had laughed loudly. "See, I've already cheered you up. All the poor sod said was, 'The engravers who etched McDaniel's name on the door to the Citadel neglected to complete their work. They should have added Dante's warning in small print: *'All hope, abandon, ye who enter here.'*'"

"I don't find this conversation amusing," said Senator McDaniel, becoming increasingly agitated. The rebuke snapped Vaughn back into the present. "And I don't like you standing behind me when I'm talking."

Vaughn turned from his perusal of the city and went over to stand with his back against the bookshelves that stretched from floor to ceiling. The pose was so casual, it unnerved McDaniel.

Actually he was more angry with himself than with Vaughn. Whenever he looked into those emotionless, ebony eyes, he felt as if he'd plunged headfirst into a black sea of coldness from which there was no escape. This was *his* office, yet for the last half hour he'd been suppressing an almost overwhelming urge to flee the scene. No other human being he'd ever met had had that effect upon him. That fact both disturbed and intrigued him.

"Are you finished?" asked Vaughn laconically.

"Hardly. I'm waiting for you to tell me why you came here tonight."

Vaughn snared the Senator with his eyes. "Because of a man named Nimrod."

Nathan had been walking around in the cold April air for two hours, wrestling with his thoughts. Remembering the unpredictability of Washington weather, he'd dressed in lightweight wool pants, a long-sleeved shirt with a blue tweed sweater, and a gun-metal gray London Fog trench coat, just in case it rained.

He and Gabriella had spent the day filling one another in on the past two years. She'd insisted that he stay with her until he decided what he wanted to do. And that was the problem. He wasn't sure what he wanted to do.

He'd realized after talking with his sister that his father had become even more powerful than when he'd left for Europe. "He may even be more popular than Kennedy," were Gabriella's exact words. That observation sent a shiver down his spine.

Nathan stopped his seemingly aimless circumnavigation, realizing that his feet had finally made the decision for him. He looked at the steps in front of him and reached into his pocket. This would be the perfect time. It was late, and he doubted that anyone but Security would be in the building. He pulled out the keys to his father's office and wondered if the Senatorial pass he carried in his wallet was still good.

"Who?"

"I'm surprised, Senator. I would have thought that you, of all people, would know about the first great personality in human history in whom earthly imperial power was vested."

The Senator grunted. "Your sense of humor escapes me." For

a moment McDaniel thought he was actually going to see some emotion from this man who never seemed to show any.

A flicker of something sinister flashed in Vaughn's eyes, eyes that at times looked like those of a dead man. It was gone in an instant.

"Nimrod understood the power of consolidation," continued Vaughn in the scratchy, guttural voice McDaniel had become accustomed but not adjusted to. "He was the first man to recognize that in order to unify a large number of diverse people there must be sacrifices. And in order to get the populace to sacrifice, one must have a purpose worthy of their self-denial."

"I'm listening."

Vaughn reached up and pulled a book from the shelf, running his hands over the leather binding as he talked. The title did not escape the Senator's attention. It was Sun Tsu's *The Art of War*.

"*You* are the key, Senator."

McDaniel blinked, uncharacteristically caught off guard. "I beg your pardon?"

Vaughn smiled, knowing the Senator's weakness. "You were a journalist during the War. No doubt you're familiar with the Hundred Days of Reform."

McDaniel frowned. "China. 1912. The People's Revolution."

Vaughn nodded. "One individual who played a commanding part in that momentous occurrence was a famed political propagandist named K'ang Yu-wei. Disturbed by China's growing weaknesses, evidenced by her defeat at the hands of the Japanese in 1894 and 1895, he designed a dramatic reform program. A systematic revision of Chinese life that would marry the military and industrial techniques of the West with a revitalized form of China's ancient spiritual heritage."

"The Empress Dowager crushed that movement and imprisoned the Emperor," interjected McDaniel dryly. He'd kept his eyes on the book, wondering if Vaughn had picked the title at random.

"Patience," replied the enigmatic man as he replaced the rare edition on the shelf without opening it. "K'ang studied Confucius . . . especially his teachings which were collectively called 'the

Great Way.' He was convinced that humanity steadily progresses, according to a *fixed* sequence, toward the 'Age of Universal Peace and Great Unity.'

"First there is a clan, then a tribe, then a nation. And from the nation the Great Unification is formulated. That is the way of the political realm. The concept is applicable in the social sphere as well. Political progression defines the ruler/subject relationship; social progression defines the relationship between husband and wife, father and son.

"Eventually the concept embraces the entire human race, leading to the Great Unity. The cycle is complete when man returns to individuality. Evolution progresses from Disorder to Approaching Peace, and from Approaching Peace to Universal Peace."

"You've lost me."

Vaughn ignored the comment and continued as if he were instructing a brilliant pupil who was so smart he was having a hard time with basics. "Confucius was born in the Age of Disorder. K'ang lived in the Age of Approaching Peace. You and I, however, sit poised upon the edge of a time during which there will no longer be nations or racial distinctions. Customs everywhere will be the same. Uniformity will usher in the Age of Universal Peace."

"Sounds like you're trying to pour new wine into old bottles."

Vaughn stared at him intently, but said nothing.

McDaniel sighed, realizing he'd been snared. The conversation had opened his eyes to a vision much grander than his own. Yet it was a logical extension of what he'd been called to do in the desert so long ago. He just hadn't allowed himself to believe that he would be the one to undertake the task. He needed time to explore the possibilities. "There have been numerous individuals who have had similar aspirations and —"

"An individual from one Age cannot operate successfully in the institutions of the Age before him or after him," interrupted Vaughn. "To do so would result in significant discord. The regulations of Confucius demand that they be employed according to the proper time frame. The theory of the Three Ages is following an inevitable course which cannot be diverted.

"The problems faced by government arise not because of shortsightedness or long-term implications, as is often argued, but because it is *unacceptable* to operate in institutions that are of a past Age."

"What did Confucius have to say about the time of Universal Peace and the Great Unity?"

"Very little."

"Oh?"

"The emergent process is complex, Senator, and it must unfold in accordance with the times. The world in the age of Confucius was still young and immature, like a child which in the course of its upbringing cannot be abruptly made into an adult simply by suddenly stripping it of swaddling clothes."

"And what about K'ang?"

"At the turn of the century, governments the world over were undergoing major transitions. K'ang realized intuitively that he could only develop institutions that were appropriate for the Age of Approaching Peace." Vaughn spread his hands expansively and added, "No matter what one attempts to do, if the institutions are inappropriate for the Age, the ultimate result can only be one thing — disharmony."

"What you're saying, then, is that when the time is right the changes appropriate for the Age unfold themselves."

Vaughn nodded appreciatively. "Exactly."

The security guard had scrutinized Nathan's identification for several minutes, then waved him on. The Senator's son held his breath as he placed the key in the door and turned it. It worked! Now all he had to do was remember which file cabinet held the information on the Kronos Corporation.

And pray his father hadn't changed the locks.

As he let himself into the darkened outer office he heard voices. He noted the pencil-thin shaft of light at the base of the door leading into his father's inner sanctum. What was he doing here at this hour?

Nathan walked over to the door, straining to see in the dark. He prayed that Sarah hadn't rearranged the furniture. His heart was beating rapidly. When he reached the oak door he took several deep breaths. *Incredible,* he thought as he placed his ear against it, *I'm about to spy on one of the most powerful men in the country — my own father.*

". . . Rainbow International now controls, both directly and indirectly, 75 percent of the world's food production and distribution, 42 percent of the world's major manufacturing industries, and 80 percent of the world's telecommunications industry. For the first time in the history of mankind, the means to bring about global harmony is in the hands of one multinational corporation."

Vaughn was standing in front of the Senator, who was seated. The billionaire reached down and picked up the Senator's pen off his desk along with a piece of stationery and began scribbling something on the paper as he talked. McDaniel leaned forward to get a better look.

Vaughn had drawn three parallel lines, with a horizontal line on top, so that it looked like a genealogy tree. Above the line he'd written in bold caps: NEW WORLD ORDER.

"What I'm talking about, Senator, is sociopolitical interdependence. And in order for this interdependence to work on a global scale, three things must be present. First, international trade. Without it, there can be no interdependence. Second, an international system of payment. This is absolutely essential to keep the first root from shriveling up and dying. And finally, the cement that binds the other two together — physical security. Without this third aspect, neither trade nor payment can be accomplished safely."

"This is beginning to sound like a history lesson," complained McDaniel.

Vaughn chuckled. "It's much more than that, Senator. Much more. Now pay attention."

McDaniel bristled at Vaughn's air of superiority, but said nothing. He was intrigued by what he was hearing, and he'd learned a long time ago that if one wanted to understand the mind of an adversary, it was best to speak little and listen much. What was it Sun Tsu had written? "Subtle and insubstantial, the expert leaves no trace; divinely mysterious, he is inaudible. Thus he is the master of his enemy's fate."

"From the middle of the nineteenth century until the end of the Second World War," lectured Vaughn, "nations utilized networks of bilateral agreements along with treaties of friendship, navigation, and commerce to conduct trade. However, in order for these types of trade arrangements to prosper and continue, there had to be one prominent power which served as the final arbiter in the marketplace. It had to have substantial military and naval strength — along with significant political clout — in order to provide stability and economic stimulus on a global scale. And, most importantly, that nation had to have a strong sense of mission."

"You're speaking about Great Britain, of course," interjected McDaniel.

"Precisely. But World War II changed all that. Hegemony passed to the United States. Simultaneously, because so many nations had to rebuild their devastated economies all at once, multilateral trade became the most desirable option over the old system of bilateral networks. The first root of our tree was now in place.

"The second root, the problem of multilateral payment for this expanded trade concept, was solved by the passage of two far-reaching pieces of legislation." Vaughn scribbled as he spoke. "The first was negotiated in Switzerland in 1947 — the General Agreement on Tariffs and Trade. Proponents of the GATT, as it is often referred to, hammered home the idea that isolationism produces chaos in the marketplace. That same year, following the

GATT like a paternal twin out of its mother's womb, came a series of agreements signed in Bretton Woods, New Hampshire."

"Creating the International Monetary Fund," finished McDaniel dryly. "You're not telling me anything I don't already know. What's your point?"

"My point, Senator, is that it is time for the next sociopolitical evolutionary jump."

Senator McDaniel stood up and went to the window. He stared out into the night. The Washington Monument was lit up like a rocket poised on the pad for lift-off. The building had been a symbol of power in the nation's capital for almost a century and a half.

Something tugged at his memory from the recesses of his mind. Something he'd heard or read.

"What about government? And physical security? The third root of your imaginary genealogical tree?" he asked distractedly.

"A Ten Nation Coalition headquartered in Europe. The Kronos Corporation's business dealings there will provide the necessary foundation."

McDaniel turned to face Vaughn. "Why Europe? Why not the United States?"

"Because, Senator, the times have changed. The infrastructure of effective economic and political leadership for the once flourishing British Empire and the now floundering United States was supported in both instances by two traits which no longer exist in either nation: an obvious and well-fed patriotic attitude and a moral consensus rooted in common religious beliefs. Not to mention the fact that the United States no longer has the essential requirement of financial hegemonic leadership. That has passed to Japan and others."

Vaughn joined McDaniel by the window. "The plain truth, Senator, is that America can no longer provide the economic drive and financial stability that are necessary for an increasingly complex and rapidly changing multilateral system of trade."

McDaniel wasn't convinced yet. "Why not?"

Vaughn shrugged. "Partially because there has been a resurgence of bilateral and regional trade agreements that make GATT a dinosaur. Almost everyone recognizes that regional initiatives are playing an increasingly important role in promoting free trade, closer economic cooperation, and stronger growth among nations. And partially because we can no longer talk about world trade in terms of individual nations. It's time to start thinking in terms of blocs."

"Such as?"

"North America, Europe, and the Asian Pacific."

"You're referring to the Free Trade Agreement between the United States and Canada, the European Economic Community, and the Pacific Basin Forum."

Vaughn nodded.

"And how will we stabilize the money supply?" asked McDaniel as he remembered the insightful words uttered by Meyer Rothschild in 1756: "Give me the power to control a nation's money, and I care not who writes its laws."

Vaughn smiled inwardly at the "we." "A World Economic Council that operates under the authority of the World Government. When we complete the link-up between Rainbow International's Cray computers and similar systems in Japan and West Germany, we will be able to monitor every business transaction on the planet. Then we shall bring to pass the vision of men such as Montagu Norman."

"Who?"

"The former Governor of the Bank of England. He served for four years in the early twenties and believed that the hegemony of world finance should reign supreme over everyone everywhere, as one supernational mechanism."

McDaniel was jolted by Vaughn's words. His own dream had merely been to achieve the Presidency of the United States. What Vaughn was talking about went far beyond the Senator's own limited vision. The Chinese-born billionaire with a German surname and American citizenship was talking about leadership on a scale that few men since Alexander the Great had envisioned as being possible.

The Senator became excited as he thought about the possibilities. What a magnificent obsession! And it could be accomplished without much difficulty; the technology was available. More importantly, the time was ripe. People the world over were clamoring for someone to stand up and grab the bulls of terrorism, poverty, hunger, pollution, racism, and political insecurity by the horns and subdue them. With the backing of Rainbow International, he could be that individual!

At the edges of his consciousness a nagging irritant prodded him, just as a cowboy prods cattle, herding them to market for slaughter. *What was it?* McDaniel knew it was in there somewhere. He could feel it swirling at the periphery of his memory. He struggled to bring the elusive recollection into focus, desperate to know what it was. Abruptly he had it!

A blinding flash of light exploded behind his eyes. He could feel the fire of it like dragon's breath upon his conscious mind. His body flushed with the heat of understanding.

It was the mention of Nimrod that lit the fuse. And it was the doubt and fear he'd buried deep within himself so long ago that finally kindled within him as he considered Vaughn's idea.

He knew Nimrod founded Nineveh, the ancient capital of Assyria, where the code of laws promulgated by Hammurabi was written. He was also the founder of Babylon. Both city-states were located in Sumer, the region comprising the eastern end of the Fertile Crescent, known as Shinar to the ancient Hebrews. The great prophet Isaiah named Shinar as one of the places from which the Jews would be regathered at the end of time.

Forty years ago he'd had an experience that he'd never shared with anyone before. And it had changed his life. Shortly thereafter he began studying everything he could find about Mesopotamia. That was when he'd stumbled upon a translation about the legendary Sumerian king — *The Epic of Gilgamesh*.

When George Amos introduced him to Benjamin Kingman, he'd asked the lanky Jew who Gilgamesh was. "You ever read the Book of Genesis?" Kingman had replied. When he admitted he hadn't, Benjamin said, "Many archaeologists believe he was the Biblical Nimrod."

"Why is that?"

"Gilgamesh lived in Erech, the city of Nimrod, located on the left bank of the Euphrates, about one hundred miles southeast of Babylon."

"And what about you?"

The archaeologist shrugged. "Who knows? It's possible. The oldest ziggurat — a kind of sacred temple tower — was discovered there. Along with Ur, the birthplace of Abraham, it is one of the oldest cities of southern Babylonia."

The forty-year-old memories flooded McDaniel's mind, and he was unable to staunch the overwhelming flow.

Now, instead of merely remembering the words he'd read with fascination, he was actually *living them* inside his head. He had no idea how or why, but he did know he was seeing the same vision the ancient author of the epic poem had seen.

Time ceased to exist. The author's vision, the reality of the event, and his own vision of the event were suddenly one. The three distinct perspectives of past, present, and future became fused into a unity. Although each perspective remained separate and distinct, maintaining its individual character, each was now part of something greater, something more complete.

Each existed as an actuality to be, outside time but within eternity. It remained only for the moment to be born, out of eternity and into time, and the vision would become reality. The memory that was no longer simply remembrance burst through his consciousness, dazzling him with its power. The vision raced through his mind like a virus replicating itself as he witnessed the future event as it unfolded:

> *Thunder was roaring in heaven*
> *which earth with her echo resounded,*
> *Sombre the day in its travail,*
> *bringing forth darkness widespreading,*

Blazed forth the lightnings —
  from heaven were kindled the fires celestial,
  Pestilence sated its maw,
  yea Death was filled to o'erflowing.
Sank then to darkness the glare of the sky
  sank also the fires,
  Crashing to earth, the great molten masses
  turned into cinders.

The Senator's mouth was suddenly dry. He tasted salt. With a start he realized he was sweating profusely, even in the chill of the room. He reached into his coat pocket, pulled out his handkerchief, and wiped his face.

The whole vision had taken only seconds to unfold. It seemed like an hour.

Vaughn's words pricked his ears and pulled him into the present. ". . . and when you speak, people hear what they have wanted to hear for a very long time."

"So you want me to be your Caesar," he said, struggling to regain his composure.

Vaughn captured McDaniel's eyes with his own, ignoring the sarcasm. "Your words have power, Senator. I've seen the reactions when you speak. Something from deep inside you reaches deep down into the people, to the very depths of their souls. And . . . they . . . *listen*."

Nathan had difficulty hearing what was being said through the thick oak door, so he very quietly opened it just a crack.

Now he couldn't see very well, but he could hear clearly. And what he heard made him gasp.

He recognized his father's voice, but who was the man doing most of the talking? He had to find out. Gently he opened the door further, praying the two men would be so engrossed in their conversation they wouldn't notice.

He didn't know what he'd say if he were caught.

Abruptly the voice he didn't recognize stopped speaking. Nathan realized he was sweating, in spite of the fact that the heat in the office had been reduced to a night-time setting hours earlier.

Had they seen him?

Seconds passed like minutes.

He'd heard enough. It was time to leave. Tomorrow he'd come back and confront his father. He closed the door gently, wondering if anyone on the other side was paying attention.

He didn't notice that he hadn't quite closed it all the way. As he left the building, he also failed to notice the tall, pale man in the snakeskin boots watching him from the shadows.

X

Yuri ben Raphah had also followed Nathan all evening.
When he saw him enter the Senate building he hung back,
deciding it was better if he waited outside. He was not supposed
to interfere with events. He was present only to assist if things
got out of hand. To some he was known as a Watcher.

He'd been waiting a little over an hour, as man reckoned
time, when Nathan suddenly reappeared. Yuri drew a deep
breath, a parody of a human gasp, at what he saw in the shadows, just behind Nathan. He wasn't shocked, just surprised.

Events were accelerating.

"Rephaim!" he muttered, moving closer. He looked around,
making sure there was only the one. As he got closer, he recognized the particular demon that had attached itself to the pale
man in the snakeskin boots.

The demon was old and powerful. They had fought one
another at the Vale of Siddim, the area now submerged by the
waters of *Bahr Lût*, when King Chedorlaomer invaded the Jordan
Valley at the time of Abraham. Before the great battle, and before
the destruction of Sodom and Gomorrah, the plain had been
called the Valley of the Fields. Afterwards it was known as the
Valley of the Demons. The region was still full of slime pits; it was
there the Egyptians got the bitumen they used to embalm their
dead.

The demon's host was so absorbed in watching Nathan, he
was unaware of Yuri's presence.

Yuri watched as Nathan left the area. He was surprised the

demon didn't follow. Instead, the host kept looking up the steps toward the building.

Although it would be easy for Yuri to enter the building unnoticed and find out what was holding the demon in check, he decided he'd better get over to Paul's house.

Rephaim were rarely alone.

The wolf stared at Paul with tawny eyes. Her lips were pulled back in a snarl. A low growl came from her throat.

She attacked without warning. Paul screamed.

In the blink of an eye the scene changed.

The wolf was now a lion. He was huge. His golden yellow mane was imposing. The muscles on his legs rippled, even though the huge cat was reclining under a baobab tree. The king of beasts licked its chops with a pinkish-red tongue. Paul felt like running, but he couldn't. He fought hard to control the fear rising up within him, threatening to overwhelm him.

The scene changed again.

It was hot. And dry. His mouth tasted like dust. He felt nauseous, as if he'd been drugged. He was staring at the twilight sky. The moon looked like a giant pearl suspended in the orange-purple heavens. His whole body ached, especially his arms and legs. His back felt as if it were supporting the parched earth rather than vice versa. He tried to get up and discovered he was bound hand and foot to four stakes.

"Oh, God, no!" he mumbled as harsh laughter came from the lips of the man covered with coarse, curly black hair standing over him. He saw the man raise the knife above his head.

That was when Paul began to scream in earnest.

The screams woke Paul from his nightmare. He sat up gasping for air. He felt as if something had been choking him. His throat was raw, and he was having trouble making saliva.

The dream had been so real this time that it took several minutes for him to realize he was not the one who'd been sacrificed. He was home . . . In bed . . . Safe.

He looked at the clock. Two A.M. He needed a glass of water. He went to the bathroom and drank the cool liquid. It tasted wonderful and soothed his aching throat.

"Must be coming down with something," he said to himself as he headed back to bed.

He lay down and pulled the covers up, wondering why the house was so cold. He was sure he'd set the thermostat before he went to sleep. He was too tired, however, to get up and check.

In spite of his exhaustion, or perhaps because of it, he didn't immediately go back to sleep. He wrestled with his fear and lay thinking about what he'd read tonight in the parchments. It was almost too fantastic to be believable.

Paul frowned. *That's strange,* he thought. The room seemed to be getting *darker*. At the same time there seemed to be a red haze forming. He glanced at the red digital numbers on the clock, then back at the foot of his bed. It wasn't possible for the weak light to be producing the strange fog.

The haze at the foot of the bed was getting brighter. It almost seemed to be pulsing. Fear washed over him in waves. Suddenly his throat constricted. He couldn't catch his breath. His chest felt as if someone were standing on it. "What's going on?" he moaned.

Outside the bedroom window a dog howled.

Gabriella was suddenly wide-awake.

She'd been in the midst of a very strange dream. A silver-haired man had been talking to her, telling her about blood.

"The life of the flesh is in the blood, and I have given it to you upon the altar to make atonement for your souls; for it is the blood that makes atonement for the soul," he'd said in a musical voice. She thought it sounded like a choir of angels singing and remembered what Nathan had said about what he'd seen in Paris. "The blood is the key," the glowing man repeated almost emphatically, as if he were trying to impress her with something beyond his words. She knew the quote was from the Book of Leviticus, the Old Testament book of the blood. But what did the stranger's cryptic admonishment mean?

Her nose twitched. She sat up, and as she did, the smell of frankincense overwhelmed her. Abruptly she had an overwhelming urge to pray. No, it was more like a command. She got out of bed and down on her knees and began to pray in the manner she'd been taught.

Oddly, although she was wearing only a sheer nightgown, she wasn't cold. In fact, her whole body felt warm, as if she'd just been immersed in a pool of warm, scented oil.

As she began to pray in the Spirit, she glanced at her clock. It was just before 2 A.M.

Nathan tossed and turned. He was asleep on the divan in his sister's studio. He kept seeing his father on the night his mother had died. He'd fallen asleep on the couch waiting for the two of them to come home. In the early-morning hours his father's voice had awakened him.

"Papa?" he'd said.

His father hadn't heard him. He was standing in front of the new color TV he'd bought for his wife as a Christmas gift, two months early.

He was talking to the blank set as if it were alive and could hear him. The set was unplugged, the cord lying on the floor curled like a slumbering snake. "Why have You abandoned me, God? Why have You shown me the lightning of your terrible swift sword? Where are You now?"

"Papa, what's wrong?"

His father turned, and Nathan saw tears streaming down his face. He looked beat-up. His nose was bandaged, and there were dark circles under his eyes. "Forgive me, son — I've killed your mother."

Nathan woke with a start, gasping. He was having trouble

breathing. Where was he? He remembered he was at his sister's and relaxed. Then he thought he heard chanting. He sat up and listened. It was coming from downstairs. And it sounded like Gabriella's voice.

"What in the name of . . ." he muttered as he got out of bed and glanced at his watch. "It's after 2 o'clock in the morning."

Paul wrestled with the night.

He didn't know what was going on, but whatever it was, he'd never experienced anything like it before. The darkness seemed to take on corporeal form. The air was so thick it was almost tangible, and the stench in the room nearly made him gag. It smelled like a thousand matches had been lit and extinguished simultaneously.

Suddenly he was chilled to the bone. It wasn't just that the room was chilled, but more like a pocket of brutally cold air had settled in around him and enveloped him. He started shivering and couldn't stop. "I know I turned on that blasted furnace," he muttered.

The howling outside his window had gotten louder, and his imagination was working overtime, telling him it wasn't the kind of noise an earthly animal makes.

The thought was pushed from his mind by the sound of the telephone ringing. As he fumbled for the receiver, the reddish haze vanished as suddenly as it had appeared.

"Hello."

"Paul, it's Gabriella. Are you OK?"

Paul's spine was tingling. "Gabriella?"

"Are . . . you . . . OK?" Her voice was insistent.

"Of course," he lied. "What makes you think I'm not?"

There was a pause, and Paul thought he heard another voice in the background. It sounded like Gabriella was having a conversation with someone else.

"Gabriella, what's going on? Is someone there with you?"

"My brother. He just got in from Europe yesterday morning. Both of us were having trouble sleeping."

"Is that why you're calling?" He tried to inject humor into the question. "To make introductions?"

Gabriella ignored his attempt at levity. "I've been up praying for the last half hour, and I couldn't get you off my mind. I was certain something was very wrong."

"Women's intuition?"

"There *is* something wrong, isn't there? I can hear it in your voice."

Paul was silent for several minutes. He flipped on his bedside lamp and gasped, then blinked several times. He sat staring at his bedroom doorway.

"Paul . . . what is it? Talk to me!"

"Nothing. I just had a bad dream." He shook his head to clear it.

"What kind of a dream?"

"I'll tell you about it on Friday."

"We're still on then?"

"Why wouldn't we be?"

"No reason. I just wanted to make sure. Sorry I woke you. I just felt so strange."

"You didn't wake me, Gabriella. Hey, when *do* I get to meet your brother?"

"Hold on . . . How about Saturday?"

"Sounds great. Where?"

"I'll tell you Friday."

When Paul hung up the receiver, he got out of bed and walked over to the door. The hair on the back of his neck was still standing on end. He opened it cautiously, then walked through the house turning on lights as he went.

Nothing. He laughed at himself and shook his head. He hadn't been scared of the dark since he was a kid.

On his way back, he checked the thermostat. It was on, and the temperature was set at 76. He stared at the small silver box, lost in thought. Ten minutes later he was back in bed, still muttering. "What a night!"

He was having trouble convincing himself he'd felt a cold blast of air in his room . . . that there had been two orange-colored eyes peering malevolently at him from the darkness . . . and that the silver-haired man he'd seen standing at the foot of his bed when he had turned on the lamp was just a figment of his imagination.

XI

Gabriella stared out the window and smiled. The April sun seemed to have found a heretofore untapped source of summer strength. Often in winter, in the heart of a city, the brilliant, crystalline character of the morning sunlight — so noticeable in summer — is diminished into a subdued shadow of its natural splendor by the gray-whites and silver blue-blacks of concrete and steel. Not so on this very special spring day.

It was Friday, and Antonio's was alive with the color of light.

Antonio had closed the gallery temporarily so he could prepare for the opening of Gabriella's show at twilight. She turned from the window and continued supervising the placement of the forty-five paintings, making suggestions as Antonio's helpers scattered them throughout the room.

As her eyes darted from one painting to another, her heart began to pound. The colors she'd chosen to chronicle her tryst with time were as effervescent and alive as the warm sunlight shining through the glass façade behind her. Each seemed to have more than one life; the exact number depended upon how much or how little of the natural catalyst was present.

She looked at her watch. It was after 11. She was going to have to hurry. "Antonio, I'll be back before the sun sets," she yelled as she turned and raced out the door.

Antonio shook his head and muttered, "Artists . . . they're a breed apart."

David McDaniel looked up from the report he was reading, irritated by the buzzing of the intercom. He punched the button. "Sarah, I thought I told you not to bother me."

"It's your son, Senator. He's here and would like to see you."

McDaniel was shocked. "Send him in," he said gruffly. Gathering together the papers on his desk, he put them in a manila folder, then stuck them in the top drawer.

In the outer office Sarah looked at Nathan and winked. "You're in luck," she said, smiling sarcastically. "He's in a good mood."

Nathan chuckled. "Some things never change, do they?"

Nathan stepped into his father's office and closed the door behind him.

"So, did you find your answers?"

"Hello to you too, Father. It seems like only yesterday we were having a similar conversation."

McDaniel glared at his son. "I guess not." He answered his own question, leaning back in the huge leather chair. "Are you going to stand while we talk?"

Nathan sat down and studied his father. He looked tired. No, it was more like he was drained. And yet his eyes glistened with energy — as if they held a secret they were anxious to share.

"Does Gabriella know you're back?"

Nathan nodded. "I'm staying with her temporarily."

"I see. And what are your plans?"

Nathan shrugged. "That depends."

"Oh?"

"On what you have to say."

His father frowned. "I don't understand."

"She knows about Mother. I told her the truth."

The Senator sighed. "And?"

Nathan was suddenly indignant. "You really are something else," he said, shaking his head. "You act as if lying is no big deal. I guess that's to be expected, however. You've had a lot of practice over the years."

"Why this sudden remorse over what we both agreed was

best for Gabriella? And who do you think you're talking to, anyway? Some naive freshman Senator who doesn't know what it takes to stay on top?"

"That's what it's all about, isn't it, Father? Winning. Who cares about truth? Or right and wrong." Nathan was trembling. "Some people are addicted to alcohol, others to drugs. The high you crave comes from manipulating people. The more control you exercise over others' lives, the more you want. You'll never get enough, will you?"

"Get off that high horse of yours, Nathan," said his father, standing abruptly. "We've been over this ground before. You made a choice two years ago." He glanced out the window. "I don't agree with it, but I respect your right to make it. I don't understand why you can't get it through that thick head of yours. That's what life is all about. Choices."

"Will you just *once* stop being the politician and talk to me man to man?"

His father turned and eyed him speculatively. "I thought that's what I was doing."

Nathan stood up, frustrated. This wasn't going well at all. Why did he always feel like he was playing catch-up when he talked with his father? He decided to make an end run.

"You told me a few years ago that you divested control of the Kronos Corporation after you realized there were going to be possible conflicts of interest in the future."

"What does that have to do with what we're talking about?"

"Everything. You asked me earlier if I'd found my answers in Europe." He stared at his father intently, wondering just how much of what he'd learned he should disclose. "In a way I did."

"Well, I'm waiting."

"*Your* company now has offices in nine major cities in Europe and the Middle East. Each of those cities is located in countries that were once part of the Holy Roman Empire."

"So?"

"You admit it?"

The Senator shook his head. "I haven't the faintest idea what you're talking about. I've told you, it's no longer my company. And even if it was, what is all this foolishness about the Holy Roman Empire? You make me sound like some sort of Caligula."

Nathan wasn't about to give up. "Have you ever read the Book of Revelation?"

The question hit the Senator like a ton of bricks. He had to work hard at keeping his face a mask. Another dead memory from his long forgotten past had just been resurrected. Benjamin Kingman had asked him a similar question about the Book of Genesis forty years ago. Beginning and ending. Coincidence?

"I've had enough of this nonsense."

"Have you?"

"No. But I'm sure you'll tell me why I should."

Nathan's anger was suddenly gone. As quickly as it had flared up it disappeared. He was so surprised, he didn't know what to say next. "Never mind. You wouldn't believe me if I told you."

His father shook his head in amazement. "I can't figure you out, son. One minute you accuse me of being a self-serving liar, and the next you're mumbling religious mumbo jumbo. What's gotten into you?"

Nathan sat forward and balled his fists. "Tell me why the Kronos Corporation has been buying substantial amounts of stock in virtually every major financial institution in Europe and the Middle East. It's become like an octopus, with tentacles reaching into the world's most important centers of global finance."

"It's no longer my concern."

"What about Rainbow International?" he countered. "Is that your concern?"

His father looked at him quizzically, giving away nothing. "I beg your pardon?"

"Come off it, Father. I know you've always had big plans for the Kronos Corporation. Are you planning a merger?"

The intercom buzzed insistently. His father reached over and pushed the button. "What is it?"

"You asked me to remind you about your luncheon meeting."

He looked at his watch. "Thank you, Sarah. I didn't realize it was that late." He stared at Nathan with hooded eyes. "I really don't know what you're talking about, son, and I'm afraid I don't have time now to discuss the matter."

"I'll find out, you know . . . Just like I found out about the slush fund you used to ruin your opponents in the last election."

His father chuckled. "There's nothing to find out, Nathan. And as for the alleged 'slush fund' . . ." he shrugged noncommittally ". . . there was never any proof."

"*You* know it existed, and *I* know it existed. That's proof enough."

His father paused at the door and said, "You made a mistake telling Gabriella about your mother, and you're making an even bigger mistake now. I don't know what you want, but it's obvious that in your time away you've forgotten that it's best to let sleeping dogs lie." He opened the door. "Now I really must be on my way. Give my love to your sister."

The steel-and-stone monolith that was the Kronos Building rose above Washington like a modern-day Tower of Babel. Twenty stories tall, it dominated the surrounding environs and offered its tenants an unobstructed view of the city for several miles in any direction.

At the entrance of the building were two mammoth lions. The bronze skin of each "king of the beasts" had been polished to the point that even on cloudy days the copper-yellow metal seemed to shine with a light all its own.

The male sported a huge mane, accentuating his proud, square-shouldered posture. He stood erect, his demeanor menacing, while the female was supine, resting languidly at his feet, an air of quiet contentment on her face. Both were positioned upon a rock façade carved to resemble the African veldt.

As Gabriella entered the building on her way to Paul's office, she was reminded of the Scripture Nathan had mentioned to her.

The sight of the two gigantic African cats combined with the memory of her brother's story caused her to shudder.

As she stepped through the doors, she had the feeling something extraordinary was going to happen to her very soon. When she stepped into the elevator and punched the button for the tenth floor, she began praying silently.

Paul was standing on the balcony, staring down at the large park bordering the building, when Gabriella arrived. She was carrying a small wicker picnic basket.

The sky was a soft, pastel-blue canvas in the aftermath of a short-lived spring thunderstorm, and the clouds were great puffs of white fading to gun-metal gray. The sun, reflecting off the giant celestial cotton balls, carved coral-pink pictures on their backs.

"Penny for your thoughts," she said, startling him.

He turned and smiled. "I was thinking about you."

Gabriella was caught off guard by his direct response. "Well then, that's worth a lot more."

Paul laughed. "I like a woman with a quick mind. You didn't even blush."

"Was I supposed to?" she asked coyly, glad once again for her honey-colored skin.

"Only if you think I'm worthy."

"Well, that remains to be seen."

What's in the basket?" he asked, changing the subject.

"Lunch. Courtesy of The Bagel Knosh."

Paul arched his brow.

"I did their logo when I was a starving artist," she continued. "The owner agreed to feed me pastrami, and in return I made sure he has the most unique logo of any deli in town."

"Somehow I don't picture a Senator's daughter as a starving artist."

"Oh?"

Paul shrugged. "I guess I'm an incurable romantic."

Gabriella was enjoying the playful bantering. "Great. Then you'll love Saul's pastrami on rye," she said, handing him one of two huge sandwiches. "I hope you like kosher dills. I brought two apiece."

"Saul?"

"He owns the deli." She handed him a checkered tablecloth and scanned the office quickly. "I vote for the balcony. What about you?"

"It's unanimous."

Gabriella pulled more food out of the basket as she talked. Paul watched her, amazed that she had packed so much into such a small space. The last thing she took out was a small bouquet of flowers. When she was done he said, "You forgot the ants."

Gabriella laughed. "Well, I can't think of *everything*."

About halfway through his huge sandwich Paul said, "I have to tell you that this is the most fun I've had eating lunch in a long time."

"Thanks. I'll tell Saul."

Paul chuckled. "But there *is* just one small thing . . ."

Gabriella took an especially crunchy bite out of her pickle, then giggled as Paul wiped the juice from her chin. "What's that?" she asked when he was through.

"Why do I have the feeling you're not taking me very seriously?"

"I don't know . . . You tell me."

"Pastrami on rye. *Kosher* pickles. The Bagel Knosh!"

Gabriella's laughter was like music. "OK, OK, I guess this is a bit overdone. But I had to make up for the other day."

Paul frowned.

"At the university."

"You know, Miss McDaniel," he groaned in mock agony, "if you continue to behave this way I may never finish my interview."

"What you didn't finish," she said, shaking long strands of her hair off her face, "was the story you promised to tell me the other night."

Paul smiled. "You're relentless."

"Only with people I like."

"I pity those you love."

The sudden silence was punctuated by the sound of distant thunder. The rain clouds were starting to move in again.

"Well?"

Paul sighed and set down his sandwich. "My father died a week ago Wednesday."

"Oh, Paul . . . I'm sorry. I had no idea . . ."

He could tell by the look on Gabriella's face that she was genuinely concerned and not just being polite. "That's OK," he interrupted. "There was no way you could know. Anyway, he and I weren't real close. Mother died when I was fifteen, two years after my *Bar Mitzvah*. Not long after that I left for college."

Paul watched as a pair of birds floated on currents of air high above the building. *Maybe they're eagles*, he thought, remembering he'd read somewhere that the majestic birds' wings were so strong all they had to do was extend them and let the wind do all the work.

"Benjamin — my father — and I kept growing farther and farther apart. Time and circumstances corroded the bond we once had. He told me once that even though he knew a father determines the blood type of his progeny, he was sure it was my mother's blood flowing in my veins and not his."

"That seems like an odd thing to say."

Paul closed his eyes and shook his head. "Not if you're a Jew married to a *goy*."

"What about if you're a *goy* married to a Jew?"

Paul was startled by Gabriella's question. His eyes snapped open. "What do you mean?"

Gabriella stared at him thoughtfully. "Would it be different if the man was a Gentile and the woman was Jewish?"

Paul considered the question, not quite sure how to answer it. Finally he replied, "The Jewish wife traditionally assumes full responsibility for establishing an atmosphere of piety and reverence in the home and for insuring that Jewish ideals are instilled into the children. As a mother, she sets the spiritual tone by taking responsibility for the character development of her children. She holds the family together in the face of adversity.

"The wife's most important role, however, is that of counselor to the entire family. The *Talmud* says: 'No matter how short your wife is, lean down and take her advice.'"

"Whoever wrote that must have really understood women."

"You shouldn't be so quick with your compliments."

"Oh?"

"Although the sages of Judaism advised husbands that the best way to have a blessed home was to respect their wives, to this day Orthodox Jews do not permit women to institute divorce proceedings, nor are they allowed to make up a part of the *minyan*."

"What's that?"

"The quorum of ten Jews required for all religious ritual."

"Hmmm. And who names the baby in Jewish families?"

"Why are you so interested?"

"Woman's curiosity."

Paul shrugged. "Theoretically the father. Boys are named on the eighth day, at the time of circumcision, and girls are named in the synagogue on the Sabbath following the birth. Both receive a threefold blessing at the time of birth: May this child grow in vigor of mind and body for the *Torah*, to be an intelligent and informed human being — for *chupah*, to reach the marriage canopy — and for a life of good deeds."

Gabriella was thoughtful. "OK, I've distracted you enough. Out with your deep dark secret."

Paul eyed her appreciatively. He wondered if he was that transparent or if she was merely that intuitive. Whatever the answer, she had a way of getting him to open up and talk about himself. Surprisingly, he didn't mind. He found her persistence refreshing.

"I've been having this dream about Cain and Abel . . ."

Nathan sat on the divan in Gabriella's studio, staring at the newspaper clipping he'd brought with him from Paris. It was from the January 6 European edition of *USA Today*.

He knew now that he was on to something incredible. Something so unbelievably real that even after eighteen months of nonstop investigating he'd had a hard time believing the truth of it . . . Until today. The conversation he'd overheard the other night in his father's office and his father's subsequent denial of any connection to Rainbow International convinced him that what he'd stumbled upon was not a figment of his imagination.

He read the advertisement for the hundredth time, putting the pieces of the puzzle together in his head.

OPEN LETTER TO 144,000 RAINBOW PEOPLE

Beginning at dawn everywhere on the earth August 16th, 144,000 humans are being called upon to create a complete field of trust, surrendering themselves to the planet and the higher galactic intelligences which guide and monitor the planet. At that time, and continuing through Monday, August 17th, the higher galactic intelligences will be transmitting a collective planetary vision, as well as messages of personal destiny, to and through these people. These dates represent a window of galactic synchronization; the first to occur since humans began testing atomic weapons, July 16th, 1945.

The testing and release of radiation into the atmosphere of the earth set up a signal which drew the attention of the higher galactic intelligences. The manifestation since that time which humans refer to as UFO's or Flying Saucers has never been officially acknowledged in a public manner by the earth.

The message of the higher galactic intelligences has been benign and compassionate, yet the dominant governments have chosen to use this information as a further instrument of fear. And all that the higher galactic intelligences have wished for humans to learn on a planetary scale is this: the only way to break the cycle of fear to which they have made themselves hostage is by creating a complete planetary field of trust.

The only acknowledgment the higher galactic intelligences

wish from humans is the creation of a complete field of trust. The optimum times for the creation of this planetary field of trust is August 16th and 17th of this year. The minimum number of humans required to complete this field of trust and be with each other in conscious acknowledgment of their common act of surrender to the earth is 144,000.

By their coming together wherever they may be beginning at dawn August 16th and 17th, these 144,000 will establish a receptacle of galactic transmission. This will create a signal more powerful than the atomic signal in Los Alamos in 1945. In response, the higher galactic intelligences will stream communications in high-frequency beams to and through these 144,000 Rainbow Humans, catalyzing the mental field of the planet. The integrity maintained by these 144,000 humans over the two-day period will be felt by virtually every other human on the planet, one way or another. Everyone will know and, depending upon their mental and spiritual development, will respond accordingly.

The opportunity presented by these dates is unprecedented. The vision of the earth will be collective and common once again.

Peace will come!

There were still several pieces he hadn't put together. Like the number 144,000. He knew the number was significant. He'd heard it mentioned before in context with the Antichrist, but he couldn't remember where. There was just too much he *didn't* know. He set the paper down and laid back on the divan, suddenly exhausted.

He knew he was going to have to tell Gabriella everything. He couldn't do what needed to be done without her help. And there wasn't much time.

"So now you know what I've been wrestling with for three weeks. What do you think? Am I going nuts?"

"No, you're not crazy, Paul, but you might just think *I* am if I tell you what I'm thinking."

"Try me."

"First I need to tell you about something extraordinary that happened to me three days before I met you. I think it will make what I have to say about your dream easier to swallow . . . and more believable."

"Sounds pretty serious."

"It is."

"I'm all ears."

It started to rain lightly. The sky was rapidly turning black. They gathered up the remnants of their picnic and ducked inside.

Paul's office was decorated sparsely. Besides his antique rolltop desk, there were a couch and two wingback chairs. Paul liked to refer to it as his "hobbit hole." He was an avid fan of J. R. R. Tolkien's rendition of Wagner's Ring Cycle fantasy. Many writers had made use of the German composer's version of the interrelation of myth and reality chronicling the battle between good and evil. But as far as Paul was concerned, Tolkien was the best.

"I'd been fasting and praying, seeking revelation from God about what He wanted me to do," continued Gabriella once they were settled on the couch. "On the evening of the third day I was overcome with the presence of the Holy Spirit. My whole body seemed to be on fire; it tingled with the anointing power of God."

Paul had a skeptical look on his face, but said nothing.

"Suddenly the air around me began to *rustle*. Slowly I opened my eyes. In the corner of my room, in front of the brass reading lamp my father gave to me on my seventeenth birthday, the air was shimmering and glowing with a pure white light that was brighter yet softer than the light coming from the lamp."

She closed her eyes, remembering. "The light from the lamp was diffuse, formless, subtle. But the light in front of the lamp was distinct . . . penetrating without being harsh. The form in the light was very large and spoke to me.

"He said, 'My name is Gabriel. I am sent to you from the Lord

God Almighty as a messenger. The Lord your God would say to you, Gabriella: Without a vision, without revelation, the people perish. Go forth and speak My Word and you shall not be ashamed. Write this vision upon the tablet of your heart so that you shall not forget. The vision is yet for an appointed time, but at the end it shall speak and not lie: though it tarry, wait for it; because it will surely come, it will not tarry.'

"Then the light was gone, except for the light from the brass lamp. I had goose bumps all over my body, and I felt as if I'd been immersed in warm, scented oil." She looked at Paul sheepishly, then added, "That was the first time I smelled frankincense."

Paul's eyes were the size of silver dollars. Normally he'd have been a doubting Thomas. But he remembered the night she'd come for dinner . . . when he'd smelled frankincense on her as the gust of wind had blown her hair into his face. He was familiar with the unique scent because he'd smelled it in Jerusalem when his father took him to Israel as a high school graduation present. "Tell me about my dream," he said emphatically.

Gabriella smiled at the small victory. She knew he'd made the connection, and she was pleased that he believed her, that he didn't think she was crazy. It was a start. "The most common translations of the Bible recount that Cain slew Abel, right?"

Paul nodded.

Gabriella rubbed the back of her neck, then crossed her arms, suddenly feeling chilled. "What if Cain didn't merely kill his younger brother? What if he actually *sacrificed* him?"

"So . . . why would that be significant, assuming of course that's what the Hebrew actually says?"

"Type and shadow."

Paul frowned. "You've lost me."

"Much of the Bible is a type and shadow of something else. The two most obvious types are Christ and Antichrist."

"Go on."

"Satan is Antichrist . . . the great counterfeiter. When he was known as Lucifer, the anointed cherub, he was cast from Heaven because he lusted to be like the Most High God. Later when God created man and placed him in the Garden of Eden and gave him authority over all the earth, Satan felt cheated. He believed he, not Adam, should have that authority."

"Well, he got that by deceiving Eve, didn't he?"

"Exactly. But he needed to seal his theft. He was sure he knew what God would do as a seal of His covenant."

A light went on in Paul's head. He was astounded by the obviousness of it, yet was reluctant to believe it possible. "A *blood* covenant," he whispered, shaken by the revelation. "Rephaim. Giants. It's starting to make sense!"

Gabriella looked perplexed as Paul sat down on the couch, overwhelmed. She joined him. "What are you mumbling about?"

Paul stared at her, not sure where to begin. "Your father and mine met nearly forty years ago in Jerusalem," he said solemnly, confusing her even more. "Let me tell you about it."

XII

In spite of the fact that Paul had agreed to come to the opening of her show, Gabriella was upset when she left his office. She'd been shocked at Paul's revelation about their fathers. "Are you absolutely certain?" she'd asked, stunned that such an incredible coincidence could have woven her and Paul's lives together before they were born . . . before either of their respective fathers had even thought about marriage.

Maybe it wasn't coincidence, she thought as she hailed a cab. At any rate, the more Paul had talked, the more she knew she had to speak with her father about that and other matters . . . immediately. If she hurried, she'd have just enough time to pay the Senator a visit before the opening at the gallery.

"Did you get the invitation I sent?" she asked as she breezed into his office and hugged him. Sarah had managed to reschedule a visit from representatives of the Colorado League of Women Voters to make room for Gabriella.

"Invitation?" he echoed, stepping back and gesturing for her to sit down across from him.

Gabriella moaned and slumped down into the same chair Nathan had occupied earlier in the day.

"I'm sorry, muffin," added her father hastily, using the affectionate term he always used when he was apologizing to her for his failings as a father. "I didn't realize it was today."

"Not past tense *yet*. My show opens at twilight. Will you come?"

The pained expression on her father's face gave her the answer before he spoke the words. "I can't, sweetheart. I'm hav-

155

ing dinner with the Secretary of State." He shrugged. "Politics . . . You know how it is."

Gabriella sighed. "Yes, unfortunately I do. No doubt you're going to solve all the world's problems while eating roast lamb and drinking California wine."

It was their private game. They'd played it since her father had become a Senator. Every time he had an excuse for not being able to do something she wanted, it was because he was having lunch or dinner with somebody *important*. He always made it sound as if he *had* to go. The truth was, he enjoyed all the fringe benefits of being an extremely powerful and influential Senator.

In retaliation, she always accused him of attending the seemingly never-ending social invitations simply so he could drink whatever wine was in vogue. It was their private way of dealing with the negative side of holding public office. Her father's time was never his own.

"Argentinean."

"What?"

"California wines are out — Argentinean wines are in. And you know what I think of South American wines."

Normally she would have replied along the lines of, "Well then, you'd better watch out for the women. I hear South American women will trip you and beat you to the floor." It didn't matter what type of wine or woman was represented, the dialogue remained more or less the same.

Today, however, there was no repartee. She was aching inside, and she needed her father to recognize her pain and comfort her. She needed him to be a father, not a politician.

The Senator studied his daughter. "There's something else bothering you, isn't there?" he said, knowing exactly what was wrong, but unwilling, as usual, to give up his edge.

Gabriella stared at her father with penetrating eyes. "Tell me about Mother," she blurted out. "Something . . . Anything . . . I'm tired of being lied to." The words kept rushing out, and she seemed unable to keep from saying them. "I need an anchor for my soul. Too many things are happening too fast, and I'm not sure what's going on. I'm not even sure I know my brother and father any more."

Her father stared at her for several minutes before he spoke. "I'm going to tell you something I've never told anyone," he said solemnly, knowing he had to do something dramatic to counter-act the effect of what Nathan had told her. "Not even your brother knows about this . . . and he knows more than he should about a lot of things."

Gabriella sat up straight in the chair. Her father had just done something totally out of character — he'd actually paid her brother a compliment. That was a substantial pat on the back, coming from a man who passed out accolades like the Pentagon passed out top-secret security clearances — sparingly and only after thorough investigation.

But there was something more. Something so subtle, so pointed, that only someone who knew how close she and Nathan really were would ever pick it up. Her father was telling her, in no uncertain terms, that Nathan was to back off. Whatever it was he'd uncovered, the Senator knew about it. And he was letting her know he didn't want Nathan pursuing it.

"I am what I am today, and you are who you are, because of what happened in the Negeb forty years ago," her father contin-ued, a distant look seeping into his eyes.

"That's part of the Israeli state today, isn't it?"

Her father nodded. "Thirty-six hundred square miles of dry desolation south of Biblical Judea. I traveled there once, between writing assignments for the *Times*. To Beersheba and Kadesh-Barnea."

Gabriella knew that Beersheba was almost midway between the southern end of the Dead Sea and the Mediterranean Sea. It was the site where Isaac's father, Abraham, entered into a covenant with Abimelech, the Philistine King of Gerar, regarding the use of a well. Wells were the key to tapping the hidden lifeblood of the desert; the water that flowed from underground springs brought life where there would otherwise only be death.

"I left Jerusalem early one afternoon in a borrowed army jeep and drove south on impulse. I passed through Hebron, where it was said the race of giants known as the Anakim once lived and where, later, King David built his royal residence. Late in the day I arrived at the site of the 'well of the oath,' also known as the 'well of seven.'

"As the sun was going down I walked among the ancient ruins, scattered over a three-mile circumference on the hills to the north of the city." The Senator paused, and his eyes glazed over. When he resumed talking, his voice was full of emotion. "The sky was the color of amethyst as the orange-red ball of fire sank below the horizon. The somber reddish-purple twilight washed over me like a cleansing rain. As a way of forgetting about the war, I played a game and looked for and found five of the seven wells before dark.

"Later I tried to sleep in the jeep, but couldn't. So I headed to Kadesh-Barnea. It's ninety miles south of Jerusalem, so it took all night.

"Just before dawn the car was suddenly engulfed in a bright light." His voice conveyed the fact that he was doing more than simply remembering the experience — he was reliving it. "I saw the light gather together around the jeep with the edges of my peripheral vision before it fully registered that the entire vehicle was swathed in a shimmering white luminescence." He closed his eyes.

Gabriella was mesmerized by his story. At the same time she realized something important, and it shocked her. When her father first began speaking, she was sure he was finally opening himself up to her in a way that he'd never done. But now it occurred to her that in his own very special way he was actually bribing her.

She remembered something he'd told her during the last campaign — after she'd seen him open himself up to a crowd in a moment of unusual vulnerability, bending the antagonistic people to his will. "When the stakes are high enough, and you're absolutely *certain* you're in control, let the people see you naked for a brief moment. Then they'll give you whatever you ask for."

When she asked why, he replied, "Because in spite of their vanity they think of you as being better than they are. Giving them a glimpse of your humanity reassures them that *you* don't think you are. It's the perfect bribe."

She was so absorbed in his story at the moment that she didn't have time to be hurt. "Go on," she urged.

Her father opened his eyes. "I stepped on the brakes abruptly, and the jeep screeched to a halt. I remember being surprised by the light because I was driving northwest. 'It can't be the sun,' I told myself. I looked first at my watch — which showed that it was only 4:30 A.M. — and then at my rearview mirror."

"What happened?"

"The Light spoke! The voice was warm and melodious. It said, 'I Am That I Am. Do not fear. Go forth and proclaim My Kingdom. Tell the people that the Great I Am is coming.'"

"That's all?"

Her father nodded.

"What did you do?"

"I turned off the engine and sat very still — for a long time. I was trembling. Part of me kept saying, 'You've finally lost it, McDaniel. Just like they said you would. The desert finally did a number on you.'"

"And the other part?"

Her father shrugged. "I'm *still* not sure about that."

Gabriella sighed, wondering why he fought God so hard. *Because he thinks of himself as a "good man,"* came the sudden revelation. *He doesn't drink, smoke, or chase women. He works hard at his job. And for him, that's enough. He's certain he'll go to Heaven and not Hell, if such places really exist. And he's* not *certain about that.*

Shaken by the sudden insight, Gabriella pushed the disturbing thoughts out of her mind and forced herself to concentrate on what her father was saying.

"Gradually dawn came, and I started the jeep and resumed my journey. Before the sun had time to scorch the already parched earth, I arrived at Kadesh-Barnea."

Gabriella knew from her time in Israel that what was originally called Rithmah was renamed "consecrated sanctuary" (Kadesh-Barnea in Hebrew) during the first time the descendants of Abraham set up camp while journeying from Egypt to Palestine — when the Tabernacle rested there. Later, at the same site, the Israelites were sentenced by God to wander in the desert for forty years because they had rebelled against Him, even going so far as to choose a captain to lead them back to Egypt, back into captivity. That's when the name was changed again, to *En-Mishpat*, "fountain of judgment."

"I walked those dusty streets, oblivious to the people, not understanding why I felt compelled to wander around the city. My mind was on the light. I was convinced I'd dreamed the whole thing."

"Why?"

"Because it was all too incredible. I knew no one would believe me. That is, until I met your mother."

Gabriella's breath caught in her throat. She knew that what her father had just told her and what he was about to tell her were connected.

"Just before noon I decided it was time to return to Jerusalem. As I reached the jeep, my eyes were drawn to the well in the center of the market where I'd parked."

"And?" she blurted out.

Her father smiled. "I saw the most beautiful woman I'd ever seen in my life. She was bent over the lip of the well, straining to raise a bucketful of water from the depths of the spring. I couldn't take my eyes off her."

"Tell me *everything*!"

"She was tiny, just over five feet tall, with thick black hair tied back off her face. Her skin was the color of a radiantly brown autumn leaf. She was dressed simply, wearing only a caftan, tied at the waist by a faded red-and-gold sash, and sandals.

"I found myself moving toward her, mesmerized by her beauty. When I reached her side I grabbed the rope and pulled the bucket of water up to the edge of the well. She looked at me and smiled." McDaniel paused, then added, "When I gazed into her eyes, I almost dropped the bucket. They were the purest color of jade I'd ever seen."

Gabriella closed her own eyes, suddenly seeing the image reflected on the backs of her eyelids, as if it had been etched there by the intensity of her father's words. She could almost feel the desert sand beneath her feet and the hot, dry air on her face.

"I asked her what her name was, stammering in my broken Hebrew. She smiled and replied in English, 'Vashti.'"

Gabriella opened her eyes, and there were tears in them. "Why didn't you tell me any of this before?"

He shrugged. "The memory was too painful. Every time I look at you, I see your mother. You could be her twin when she was your age."

Gabriella knew he was talking about her eyes and skin. Wherever she went, people stopped and stared. Especially men. At first, when she was younger, she'd been offended. She thought it quite rude that people looked upon her as some kind of unique doll. Later, in her late teens and early twenties, she'd been flattered. Now she ignored the attention and was careful how she dressed. But the color of her eyes still made people look twice.

"I wish you'd told me about her sooner. It's like she never existed. And it's obvious you loved her deeply."

Her father said nothing, and Gabriella realized he hadn't heard her. She felt awkward. She looked out the window and realized with a start that the afternoon had slipped past while they'd talked. She glanced at her watch and jumped up. "I have to run, Father," she said, throwing her purse over her shoulder. "You're sure you can't cancel your Argentinean wine tasting party and come see your only daughter's coming-out show?"

Her father chuckled, snapping out of his reverie. Realizing he'd accomplished his purpose, he stood up and spread his hands. "Settle for a hug and a promise I'll probably break?"

"I'll take the hug. Save the rhetoric for the Secretary of State. He appreciates it. I don't."

After his daughter left, the Senator sat at his desk for a long time, thinking. Vaughn had told him about Gabriella's involvement with Benjamin Kingman's son. Strange how fate worked. He wondered if Gabriella knew he'd known Paul's father.

When Vaughn had told McDaniel about the parchments, and that it was imperative that he own them, the Senator had suggested that the billionaire offer to purchase them. "Tell Kingman they have sentimental value to you. After all, your father was a missionary, wasn't he?"

"Not exactly. But you have given me an idea."

Unfortunately, money hadn't motivated the young Mr. Kingman to part with the documents. Why was Vaughn so interested in them anyway? That question bothered Senator McDaniel for more reasons than one.

He'd known the enigmatic Vaughn only nine months. And in that short period of time he'd been unable to find out more than a bare minimum of information on his new partner. Interestingly, one of the few things he'd learned was that Vaughn's last name was the word for a European wild ox that existed in Germany at the time of Caesar but became extinct during the Middle Ages. When he'd questioned Vaughn about it he'd replied, "The animal you speak about was hunted as game by one of the greatest conquerors of Assyria, seven hundred and fifty years before the birth of Christ. It stood over six feet high at the shoulders and was tremendously ferocious and absolutely untamable."

The Senator shuddered. The description was appropriate.

When Vaughn first told him he'd handle the situation regarding the parchments, McDaniel thought nothing of it. His mind was on the other ideas the savvy businessman had shared with him. Now he wasn't so sure. Particularly since Gabriella was becoming involved with Paul Kingman.

And of course there was Nathan to think about. If nothing else, his only son was persistent. Especially when he smelled a scandal.

It's time I pay a visit to Mr. Paul Michael Kingman, the Senator

thought as he took the file marked Solomon Bull-Ox Enterprises
out of the top drawer of his desk and began reading where he'd
left off.

XIII

The day had passed quickly for Gabriella. The transparent yellow-gold character of morning had given way to the hazy, almost translucent oyster-white of afternoon, followed by the opaque gray-blue of early evening.

Antonio had halfheartedly berated her for waiting until the last minute to return. She'd kissed him on the cheek and replied, "You know us artists, Antonio. We're a breed apart."

As the character of the light changed in relationship to the sun's arc through the sky, so too the character of Gabriella's paintings changed in relationship to the amount of light present in the gallery. Little by little, as the long shadows of late afternoon sucked the yellow-gold tendrils of warmth from the room, Gabriella's paintings began to give off a resonant inner light of their own. It was as if having stored the sun's energy during the day, the paintings now drew upon the captured light, coming alive with a striking radiance.

Finding a moment for herself, she stood in front of her favorite piece and admired it. After several minutes she glanced at the door, then at her watch for the tenth time, and wondered where Paul was. He'd promised to be at Antonio's by 7 and it was already after 8. She was just starting to get really angry when a warm, deep-throated voice behind her said, "Wasn't it Horace who said, *'Ut pictura poesis'*?"

Startled, Gabriella turned. She stood face to face with a very tall, deeply tanned, extremely handsome man. He was smiling appreciatively at her. She stared into his ebony eyes, speckled with silver, and had the feeling he was enjoying the fact that he'd surprised her.

Oddly, although the man's eyes sparkled, and despite the fact that he was smiling warmly, Gabriella had the distinct impression that the life she saw there was artificial and the warmth behind the smile contrived and calculating.

Her spine tingled. She knew immediately that she must not give any ground to the stranger standing before her. "I assume you're referring to the painting," she replied, her voice steady and authoritative, even though her heart was pounding. "And if you are, then, like most people, you've missed the point Horace was making."

The dark-haired stranger continued to smile effusively, unruffled. "Perhaps." His eyes were like cameras, recording everything. "Then again . . . perhaps not," he added softly. A hint of amusement rode the counterfeit light in his eyes, as a wisp of paper rides the wind. "Some paintings, like some poems, should be viewed close up, whereas others are but appreciated from afar. Some court the shade . . . and others endure scrutiny in full light, unfearful of the demands of the most penetrating criticism. Horace preferred the latter."

"And you?"

The man's smile slowly dissolved, and Gabriella noted a hardness in his face.

"That depends upon the subject."

She turned her back on him abruptly. It was an act of defiance, not rudeness. She had the distinct impression that the man was accustomed to hypnotizing people with his words and his contrived impromptu familiarity. She had no intention of letting him beguile her with his casual eloquence.

"What do you think of the subjects of this particular painting?" she asked, miffed.

"They both have a kind of liquid fire in them," he replied, keeping his eyes on the raven-haired woman he'd come to meet. "In fact, the one seems to be an obvious extension of the other. And *both* are exquisite."

In spite of her earlier resolve, Gabriella found herself becoming flushed. The stranger moved closer, stood beside her, and scrutinized her work. His right shoulder casually brushed her bare, left upper arm. She was sure she felt a brief, soft crackle of electricity arc between them, and she resisted the impulse to move away.

He was so close she could smell the faint odor of his cologne. It smelled like almonds.

He said, "To quote the great English bishop and poet John Donne:

"'Her pure and eloquent blood
  Spoke in her cheeks, and so distinctly wrought
  That one might almost say her body thought.'"

"I'm impressed, Mr. —?"

"Aurochs. And my intention was not to impress . . . merely to compliment."

"Indeed . . ." she replied, then turned and appraised *him*. "It seems you are a man who appreciates the poetics of art."

He chuckled, enjoying her feistiness. "Do I detect a note of disdain in your voice for the proverbial Renaissance man?"

"Not at all. In fact da Vinci and Michelangelo are two of my favorites. It's just that there are many in my profession who embrace the concept of humanism with far more zeal than I."

"Then you would disagree with the idea that present-day humanism builds upon and reveals a continuity with the vital humanist tradition of the Renaissance by carrying on the spirit of its great authors and artists in a contemporary form."

Gabriella was indignant. "You mean the idea of the 'universal man,' the many-sided personality, delighting in every kind of earthly achievement?"

"Exactly. I believe it was Protagoras who said: 'Man is the measure of all things. . . . As to the gods, I have no means of knowing either that they exist or do not exist. For many are the

166

obstacles that impede knowledge, both the obscurity of the question, and the shortness of human life.'"

"I hate to burst your bubble, Mr. Aurochs, but I disagree with the basic premise of humanism. An attitude toward the universe that considers all forms of the supernatural to be myth is inconsistent with my experience."

Vaughn remained silent. Both he and Gabriella seemed oblivious to all the activity going on around them.

"Humanists place ultimate faith in man," continued Gabriella emphatically, a little surprised at the direction of their conversation. "They believe — erroneously — that human beings possess the potential to solve their own problems. They place their faith in reason and the scientific method, adding a dash of courage and vision to the murky soup of their man-centered philosophical brew."

"And what's wrong with that?"

"Nature, for the humanist, is simply a constantly changing system of matter and energy existing independently of any mind or consciousness. Believing in humanism means believing that man is the master of his destiny. The humanist fails to recognize that all of creation, including man, is far too complex and far too beautiful to have simply evolved."

Vaughn was suddenly distant. When he spoke, the chill in his voice seemed to fill the room. "The Christian West has been confused and corrupted for almost two thousand years by St. Augustine's idea that everyone is cursed who places his hope in man. Man's failure — indeed, his refusal — to recognize that the reasoning capability of intellect is the only tool with which he can free himself from the disintegration of society will be his downfall — especially if he continues in the delusion that some celestial arbitrator will end his misery."

"And what do you believe, Mr. Aurochs?"

"We must recognize that our only home is this mundane world. Man's destiny and his promised land are to be found in the here and now or not at all. Even the Old Testament Hebrews, despite their fervent and robust mysticism, put little faith in a meaningful immortality for the human personality."

"So you don't believe in God?"

"For far too long mankind has groaned under the weight of the constant and confusing redefinition of such religious terms as *God* and *immortality*," replied Vaughn vehemently. "It's time for a new age. It's time, Miss McDaniel, for society to make amends to all those it has historically persecuted for openly espousing humanist philosophy."

"Persecuted? What are you talking about?" *And how does he know who I am?* she wondered, suddenly very interested in finding out more about this alluring man. *I did not give him my name, nor did I tell him I am the artist.*

"The ancient Athenians, normally extremely tolerant people, accused Protagoras of impiety. They banished him and burned his works in the marketplace after collecting copies from all who had them in their possession. Voltaire, arguably the most influential humanist during the French Enlightenment, was forced to leave his native France because of his unceasing and effective attacks against the Catholic Church. He lived in exile for most of his life. The list goes on and on."

Gabriella was stunned. She realized she'd struck a chord that lay tautly strung at the core of this hypnotically eloquent stranger's soul. "If you feel that way, then you undoubtedly find the New Testament incompatible with your philosophy."

Vaughn shrugged. "Its theology, taken literally, is totally alien to the humanist viewpoint. About the best I can say is that Jesus was a great and good man. He might have been the greatest free-speech victim in the history of religion — a martyr for the cause of humanity, if you will. But he was no god."

He paused, then added, "In spite of Benjamin Disraeli's popularization of the quip 'All wise men have the same religion, but wise men never tell,' the truth of the matter is that the worldly discretion of the sophisticated concerning the supernatural is due not so much to fear as to the dogged persistence of the

Machiavellian myth that religious superstition is a necessary restraint upon the masses."

Gabriella was finding it increasingly difficult to keep her composure. Vaughn's words both intrigued and disturbed her. His views about God and religion were diametrically opposed to her own; yet there was something almost magnetic about his personality that made it hard not to agree with his viewpoint. She found herself drawn to him, yet unsettled by his words.

"You're beginning to sound more like a politician and less like a philosopher with each breath, Mr. Aurochs," she said and stepped back a few feet, as if by putting some distance between them she could free herself from the verbal web he seemed to be weaving.

Vaughn's demeanor changed again in chameleon-like fashion. He smiled disarmingly. "Please . . . call me Vaughn. And please accept my apology if I've offended you." He winked, then added, "As for politics . . . I leave the reformation of ideological thought to men like your father."

Gabriella suddenly felt weak. She took several deep breaths, hoping to diminish the reaction that was turning her legs to rubber. "You know my father?"

Before Vaughn could reply Antonio appeared. "Ah ha . . . I see you two have already met," he said, smiling effusively. He looked at Gabriella and added, "What's wrong, my dear? You look a bit pale."

"It's nothing, Antonio. I'm just a little tired. You know, the excitement of my first show and all that."

"I'm afraid Miss McDaniel and I don't see eye to eye on some things," Vaughn added.

"Oh?"

"But it doesn't matter, Antonio. She's everything you said she was . . . And more."

Gabriella stared at Vaughn. Sudden understanding flooded her eyes. She glanced at Antonio.

"Well, I'll leave you two alone," Antonio said conspiratorially.

His eyes twinkled. "I'm sure you'll work things out," he added and disappeared into the crowd.

After he'd left Gabriella said, "I'm afraid I owe you an apology, Mr.— uh, Vaughn."

"Not at all, Miss McDaniel. I have a tendency to be rather abrupt."

"Gabriella."

"OK . . . Gabriella."

She eyed him speculatively and remembered her first conversation with Paul. However, her feelings tonight were quite different. "You are the one who sponsored my show, aren't you?"

He nodded.

"Why?"

Vaughn shrugged. "Let's just say that I'm a patron of the arts and I like beautiful things."

"But why *me?*"

"How about having dinner with me and I'll tell you?"

Gabriella was thoughtful for a moment. Something inside was telling her that going to dinner with this man was a mistake, but she ignored the warning. She was not particularly attracted to Vaughn, in spite of his stunning good looks. But she was curious. Not so much about why he sponsored her show as what his relationship was to her father. She glanced at her watch again, then took a last look at the front door and thought, *Paul Kingman, you blew it.*

"I suppose that's the least I can do," she replied and wondered how she was going to get rid of the butterflies in her stomach. They seemed to be constant companions these days.

"Splendid. My limousine is outside."

Gabriella raised her eyebrows. "That overly long, dove-gray car parked in front of the gallery?"

He nodded.

They walked outside, and Gabriella, eyeing the logo on the limo, said, "A unicorn? You don't seem the type."

Vaughn laughed good-naturedly, and that startled Gabriella. For some reason she didn't think him capable of the emotion.

"I assure you it's more than a simplistic fascination."

"Oh?"

"My father spent the majority of his adult life in China," he continued, "and my mother was a Chinese orphan, raised by a Tibetan people, the Tangut. According to the *Chinese Book of Rites*, the *Li Ki*, there are four benevolent or spiritual animals: the phoenix, *feng-huang*; the tortoise, *kuei*; the dragon, *ling*; and the unicorn, *ch'i lin*. *Ch'i* represents the male aspect, *lin* the female. Their unison represents perfect harmony.

"Legend has it that a unicorn appeared to the mother of Confucius before his birth, and just before he died a charioteer injured one, foretelling the imminence of his death."

Gabriella studied Vaughn as he spoke, again curious as to why his words seemed to have such a magnetic quality. The more she heard, the more she decided that a better word would be *hypnotic.*

"Why is there a peach tree alongside the unicorn in the logo?" she asked, intrigued by his explanations.

"In China the *p'an t'ao* is the symbol of longevity. It is said that one of these trees grew near the palace of Hsi Wang Mu, and that its fruit ripened only once in three thousand years. Mingled with mulberry trees, it could cure disease and confer immortality."

Vaughn's eyes continued to appraise her. "Since you seem to be fascinated with trees yourself," he added, indicating her paintings, "it might interest you to know that I have a unique garden of lotus, date, and pomegranate trees. Each has a symbolic meaning attached to it, a result of the rise of Taoism as an organized religion."

"No doubt Taoism did for Confucianism what humanism did for Catholicism," she retorted, feeling suddenly sarcastic.

Vaughn looked at her strangely. "An astute observation . . . although I don't believe I've ever heard anyone characterize it quite that way before. Now, shall we go to dinner?"

Gabriella wasn't at all sure, in spite of her earlier agreement, that she wanted to be alone with this unsettling, fascinating man. However, since he'd mentioned her father's name, she had the nagging feeling he knew more about the Senator than he was letting on. And the only way she was going to find out just how much he knew was to have dinner with him.

Antonio watched the two of them from inside the gallery, wondering if he'd done the right thing in telling Vaughn Aurochs about Gabriella McDaniel. He knew Vaughn's penchant for collecting was not limited to works of art.

Paul sat back in his chair and put his feet up on the desk. His office was cluttered with papers, and several books on archaeology and Greek mythology lay open on the couch.

In spite of the twinkling lights of the city and a full moon, the night seemed especially dark.

He rubbed the tiredness from his eyes, then placed his arms behind his head and stared at the monochrome monitor sitting on top of Sam. He reread what he'd written.

After a few moments of contemplation he sat forward and erased two hours worth of work, unhappy with what he'd written. "It has to be right," he muttered as he picked up his father's journal, knowing he was going to have to read the account again before he was convinced.

October 20, 1948
Jerusalem

I am stunned! What I've just finished translating is beyond belief. May God have mercy on us if it is true. And at this point I have no reason to believe it is not.

I am also tired. More tired than I can ever remember being. There have been many days in the last week when I have doubted. Tonight I have begun to believe.

Enough of my editorializing. I must commit the translation of the sixth document to paper while it is fresh in my mind:

I, Uriel, have been entrusted with the task of finding the one whom He has ordained. He, not I, shall deliver the message. What follows was penned before the parchments were given to me for safekeeping. I am merely a Watcher.

(trans. note: Here the handwriting changes. It is evident, not only from the cryptic comment, but from the style as well, that the author and the commentator are different. Am still unclear as to what a Watcher is and who the author is.)

Beneath the plain of abomination lie the graves of giants. The offspring of the fallen ones, the Reph___ (unreadable). Though the *Nephilim* are bound, their offspring flourished. The how of it all remains unknown, but the results are devastating.

It began in ___rden (unreadable).

(trans. note: several lines unreadable at this point. Even though the parchments are amazingly well preserved, there is still decay. Fortunately, the documents seem to be a highly advanced type of parchment. The air does not affect them as one would expect.)

_____ (unreadable) cursed because of their lust for the flesh of men they perished in the Great Deluge. But do not think it is over, remember ____dom (unreadable) and Go___ (unreadable). The remnant are still active. They seek the life of the flesh. The blood.

Paul looked up from his reading and sighed. He set the journal down and turned off Sam, then looked at his watch. It was nearly 9 o'clock, and he wasn't getting anywhere. His father's legacy was astounding, if what the journal said was true. And he'd only finished reading half of the translations.

He reached into his pocket and toyed with the key he'd carried with him for several days now. Why he hadn't gone to his father's bank and used the key yet was a mystery to him. For some odd reason, every time he thought about going there and opening the safe-deposit box, something distracting always seemed to come up.

Although he was certain he knew what was in the box, he just didn't feel the time was right. But something inside told him it wouldn't be long before it was.

Suddenly he slapped his forehead and swore. "I can't believe I forgot!" he said as he turned off the light, locked the door behind him, and rushed out of the office. By the time the elevator finally came, he had whipped himself mentally at least a dozen times for forgetting that he'd promised to attend the opening of Gabriella's show. "Great way to start a romantic entanglement," he muttered as he ran past the bronze lions, hoping he could get a cab quickly.

Just as he was about to step off the curb, a black stretch limousine stopped directly in front of him. The tinted window on the right rear passenger side slowly rolled down. Startled, he watched it disappear into the door frame. The inside of the limo seemed darker than the night.

"Mr. Kingman," said the disembodied voice from the midst of the darkness, "I think it's time you and I had a heart to heart talk."

XIV

It was almost midnight by the time Gabriella and Vaughn finished dinner. Vaughn suggested they go to his office for a night-cap. Gabriella said she wasn't interested in a drink, but would like to see the trees he'd talked about earlier.

When they arrived at the penthouse suite, she was surprised to learn that the office was on the twenty-second floor of a skyscraper that Vaughn not only owned, but worked and lived in.

The thick oak door leading into the office was emblazoned with large gold lettering: SOLOMON BULL-OX ENTERPRISES.

"Another play on words?" asked Gabriella as they entered the office. Vaughn had told her about the origin of his last name over dinner and explained that the European wild ox had been hunted by the great Assyrian conqueror Tiglath-pileser.

"That was my father's idea," Vaughn answered perfunctorily as he ushered Gabriella into his dominion. "He formed the company in 1950, just after we returned from China. Although he'd gone to China as a missionary, he gave that up and became a coppersmith after his first wife died in a flash flood.

"He named the company after King Solomon because of the wealth he intended to acquire and because Solomon made a fortune mining copper in the *Arabah* and smelting it at Ezion-Geber."

"That was a refining port built for him on the edge of the Red Sea by the Phoenicians, was it not?"

Vaughn stared at Gabriella, pleasantly surprised by her depth of knowledge.

Gabriella grew contemplative as she followed him into the

outer office. "*Arabah* is the Hebrew name of the valley lying between Mount Hermon and the Red Sea, isn't it?"

Vaughn nodded as he switched on the lights. "Literally translated the word means 'desert.' Even though there is a measure of fertility in the area, there are vast stretches of sour soil and ever-obtrusive pockets of marl. Most of the hillsides in the area remain parched year-round because they are out of reach of the streams that dot the landscape."

"You seem to know an awful lot about that area. Do you go there often?"

"Occasionally my financial interests take me to the Middle East. It pays to be knowledgeable about the areas in which I transact business. Now, why don't we change the subject?"

"OK. You told me you were born in a small Chinese village at the edge of a desert, but you didn't tell me where in China."

Vaughn stopped what he was doing. "Why are you so interested in my past? You've been quizzing me all night."

"It pays to know about those you do business with. Isn't that what you just said?"

Vaughn chuckled. "Remind me never to underestimate you."

"Oh, I don't think you need reminding."

"Are you always so persistent . . . and so direct?"

"Only when I want answers to my questions."

"OK. I concede . . . For now. I was born in Bashan. My father settled there after Deborah — my father's first wife — died. It was an area particularly rich in copper deposits. My grandfather had been a blacksmith in Germany — before he came to America and started investing in real estate. My father learned how to work molten metal from him."

"What about you? Did your father pass on the tradition?"

"My father and I were never close. We had different interests," Vaughn replied cryptically.

Something tugged at Gabriella's memory. She remembered reading about another Bashan, but it wasn't a city. It was an area in Palestine that extended from Gilead to Hermon. What was nagging her, however, was that she was almost certain the inhabitants were called Rephaim. And that was the word Paul had muttered before he'd told her about their fathers knowing one another. What was the connection?

She made a mental note to ask Paul about it when she saw him tomorrow . . . After she'd introduced him to her brother.

She sensed it was time to stop probing. She had seen a strange look in Vaughn's eyes when she'd asked him about his birthplace and his father and realized that in both instances she had touched a sore spot. "Well, where are all the trees I've been hearing about?" she asked, skeptical that Vaughn could have a garden in the sky.

Vaughn motioned for his guest to follow him into the next room. An exquisitely carved solid mahogany desk and a seven-foot-tall grandfather clock carved out of wood from the Black Forest in Germany awaited them behind a second, less massive oak door. Also, behind and to the right of the magnificently crafted desk, was a six-foot-high bookcase filled to overflowing.

Gabriella quickly scanned some of the unfamiliar titles: *Time Frames* by Niles Eldridge; *The Emerging Order* by Jeremy Rifkin and Ted Howard; *Algeny*, also by Jeremy Rifkin; *The Evolutionary Journey* by Barbara Marx Hubbard; *The New Evolutionary Timetable* by Stephen Stanley.

She thought that seemed rather peculiar reading material for a businessman. But then, nothing so far this evening had been ordinary about Vaughn Aurochs.

The rich, deep reddish-brown coloring of the handcrafted desk provided a striking contrast to the thick, slate-gray carpeting and the dark ebony wood of the grandfather clock.

What really caught her eye, however, was the framed photograph of a large silver-gray wolf. The shot had obviously been taken from very close up. The wolf was standing on what appeared to be snow-covered tundra, and he was looking straight into the camera. For a moment she almost believed that the look in those yellow eyes reminded her of the look she'd seen in Vaughn's eyes during dinner — when he'd been telling her more about the "new age" he'd spoken about at the gallery.

"I took this shot in Alaska," said Vaughn as he picked up the photograph from his desk, "from about ten feet away."

"Ten feet! How did you get so close?"

"I guess I have a way with animals."

Gabriella stared at him, amazed and more than a little skeptical. He might have a way with *tamed* animals, but from what Paul told her, not even the Eskimos ever got that close to a wild wolf. The more she discovered about Vaughn Aurochs, the more she began to wonder about what kind of man she was really dealing with.

"How come there aren't any windows?" she asked, glancing around the room in an effort to change the subject. She found it odd that a man of Vaughn's obvious wealth would have a penthouse office without them.

Vaughn smiled and sat down behind his desk. "Turn around and watch," he said as he fiddled with something underneath the lip of the desktop. Silently the east wall of the room began to slide back into itself.

Gabriella gasped. The view was stunning. The night sky was exceptionally clear for early April and shimmered with an unusual abundance of stars. Along with the twinkling lights of the city below, it formed the backdrop for a hexagonal-shaped garden filled with a variety of trees and shrubs: fig, pomegranate, lotus, palm, and many others Gabriella did not recognize.

Vaughn fiddled with another invisible switch, and several soft-colored lights came on, positioned so as not to detract from the natural splendor of the nighttime view. The lights in the office dimmed automatically.

Gabriella walked over to the glass-enclosed portico. Her eyes grew wide as she scanned the beautifully manicured scenery. "What kind of birds are those?" she asked pointing to several small- to medium-sized birds with long, graduated tails moving among the branches of one of the palms.

"Turtledoves," replied Vaughn laconically, as though he expected her to understand the significance of their presence. "I collect them."

Gabriella stared through the glass for several minutes, watching the birds flutter from branch to branch. She turned abruptly, feeling Vaughn's penetrating gaze on her back. She walked over to where he sat and stood transfixed, marveling at the solitary painting on the wall behind the mahogany desk. She hadn't paid attention to it earlier because of the photograph of the wolf.

It was huge, perhaps six feet by six feet, and though it was obviously the work of a Chinese artist, it was unusual in that it was in color and not at all like the black-and-white Chinese landscapes she'd seen the other day when she and Paul had gone to the city museum to see an exhibit of Chinese art. She'd wanted to go because trees are predominant in many Chinese works and because she was fascinated with the oriental mastery of working in monochrome. She remembered her on-the-spot teaching as they perused the various schools of painting represented.

"The Chinese envision man's importance in the universe as being of far less importance than we in the West," she'd said enthusiastically. "Also, the Chinese painter rarely, if ever, works directly from nature with his canvas before him; yet the Chinese artist studies the intricacies of nature with a comprehensively discerning eye, associating himself with the naturalistic state of being in a much more intimate fashion than his western counterpart.

"The artist may spend years of his life traveling and observing nature. Eventually, after long contemplation, he produces his work of art in the stillness of a studio. Because the materials he uses allow for few alterations, the artist's ideas must be clear, his technique sure, and his execution spontaneous. The final representation may be executed rapidly, using but a few splashes and lines, or it may be tediously built up from miniature brushstrokes. In either case, the result is an immediate expression of the artist's personality."

Paul admitted to her afterwards that he'd marveled at the ease with which she had moved from one landscape to another, pointing out the different techniques used by the various artists, and how she was able to communicate her knowledge of the subject without being intimidating or boring. He'd also told her that for the first time in his life he felt very relaxed with the fact that it was not he who was doing the talking. That was yet another indication to her that something very special was developing between them. That kind of honesty was rare.

Gabriella snapped back to the present. The two-day-old conversation died inside her head as she assessed the work hanging on the wall in front of her. Like Vaughn, there was something both alluring and unsettling about the piece.

An enormous, turquoise-green tortoise and an equally gargantuan coppery-red and black snake were engaged in a violent confrontation. After several moments, she realized it was a battle to the death. The artist had captured the struggle so magnificently that she felt the battle was taking place inside her own soul.

After scrutinizing the painting for several more minutes, she realized the tortoise was winning the battle.

Sitting in his chair, Vaughn watched Gabriella intently, a shimmering glint of amusement — and something almost sinister — in his eyes.

She was so captivated by the artwork that when he spoke, his deep, melodious voice startled her. "The tortoise represents righteousness . . . The snake symbolizes the power of evil," he explained and leaned forward, his eyes narrowing. "Most people decide that the tortoise is the winner. That is certainly what the artist intended his patrons to think. However, I see something else. Something far more subtle and evocative."

"Oh?"

Vaughn rose and came around to stand beside her, as he had done at the gallery, fastening his gaze upon the magnificent work of art. His eyes took on a glazed, distant look that reminded Gabriella of the translucent membrane which protects the eyes of snakes.

"The head of the tortoise is green, a color that became the symbol of the outcast class in China. The Chinese called them *lo hu*. They had no legal status and were obliged during the T'ang dynasty to wear a strip of green cloth tied around their heads. The degenerate males of this class lived off the earnings from the prostitution of their wives and daughters. To the Chinese they represented the very lowest depths of immorality; calling a person a tortoise meant to put him in the vilest class of human beings. It identified him as illegitimate. In fact, the abuse of the word, which generally had an honorable meaning, is similar to the use in western countries of the name of Deity in swearing."

Gabriella sensed there was something deeply personal about what Vaughn was telling her, just as she had sensed there was more to what Paul had been saying when he'd told her about his father's death.

"You seem to know an awful lot about China," she interrupted, "especially for one who only lived there the first six years of his life."

He shrugged. "As I told you at dinner, I have some very profound memories." His voice was thick with emotion as he continued telling her about the painting. "For me, the tortoise in this particular painting has a dual meaning. First, it represents righteousness corrupted by ignorance. And second, it depicts the result of the frustration borne of that corruption. The snake, on the other hand, although it traditionally symbolizes the absolute power of evil, can be interpreted as the evil that is in the world which must be eradicated."

"And what would that evil be?" asked Gabriella, suddenly suspicious of where the conversation was going.

"The intolerance of the blind," he replied, his voice taking on the same icy quality as when he had been talking to her about humanism in Antonio's gallery. He let the rest of the thought hang in the air like an unfinished rebuke. "My father never married my mother," he continued after a moment's hesitation, as if he were deciding whether or not to tell her about his past. "When I was five, nine months before my mother died, several of the children began to taunt me, calling me a tortoise.

"One of the teenage thugs in the village forced me to wear a green strip of cloth tied around my forehead whenever I saw him on the street and to do menial tasks for him and the other children. My mother discovered the brutality. A week before she died the boy was found dead, his neck broken, a green strip of cloth tied around his throat."

"You never told me your mother's name."

Vaughn looked at her strangely, then replied, "Chi Lin."

The room was suddenly quiet, and it seemed to Gabriella that a chill had fallen on them, like the first light coating of an early, unexpected snowfall. In spite of the heaviness in the room, her mind was racing. *Chi Lin.* Hadn't he told her that in Chinese that meant unicorn? And that was the logo she'd seen on his limo. What did it all mean? And why did she suddenly feel so uneasy? She should have listened to the voice.

Vaughn returned to his chair and sat down. As if suddenly conscious of what he'd been saying and to whom he'd been speaking, he changed the subject. "The anthropomorphizing of animals was quite common among the scholars of the T'ang and Sung dynasties," he quipped, adjusting something that hung around his neck, beneath his shirt. "It was said that the rabbit lives in the moon, where it pounds out the drugs from which the elixir of life is made; the monkey is in control of witches and hobgoblins; the fox represents cunning; the lion is a symbol for the teacher; the eagle represents prayer."

He sighed heavily, as if he were more than just physically tired. "It seems that mankind is forever trying to conjure up some sort of mystical or supernatural philosophy to explain the unexplainable."

Abruptly a Scripture popped into Gabriella's head: . . . *for Satan himself masquerades as an angel of light. It is not surprising then, if his servants masquerade as servants of righteousness.* The thought startled her, not so much because of the abruptness of it, but because of its intensity and clarity. *What is going on?*

She shook her head to clear it, wondering what had come over her, and really began to listen to what Vaughn was saying. He seemed to have forgotten that she was even there.

He paused, then pointed at the framed words from *Paradise*

Lost sitting on his desk, quoting them verbatim, closing his eyes as he did so:

> *"To suffer woes which Hope thinks infinite;*
> *To forgive wrongs darker than death or night;*
>   *To defy Power, which seems omnipotent;*
> *To love and bear; to Hope till Hope creates*
>   *From its own wreck the thing it contemplates;*
> *Neither to change, nor falter, nor repent;*
> *This, like thy glory, Titan, is to be*
>   *Good, great and joyous, beautiful and free;*
> *This is alone Life, Joy, Empire, and Victory."*

When he was finished, Gabriella, who'd been resisting a rising urgency to leave, said, "It's getting late. I think it's time for me to go."

In the space of several hours, and particularly during the last few moments, Vaughn's demeanor had changed abruptly several times, thoroughly confusing her. Odd as it seemed, she'd had the feeling several times tonight that she'd been talking to two distinctly different personalities.

Moreover, Vaughn had never really explained what his relationship to her father was, nor had he given her a satisfactory answer as to why he'd sponsored her art show. Whenever she'd tried to bring the conversation around to either of those topics, he'd skillfully changed the subject.

Her host stood up abruptly. "It's been a most enlightening evening, Miss McDaniel," he said, and his voice sounded strange, distant. It was almost as if he were *dismissing* her. "I look forward to our next meeting."

XV

After Gabriella had gone, Vaughn sat at his desk and stared out into the night. He thought about all he had accomplished in two short decades.

His father had died prematurely at the age of fifty-six, in 1965, just six years after the company he'd founded entered the ranks of the Fortune 200.

When Vaughn had first noticed the butterfly discolorations on his father's face, he'd thought it was the result of Franklin's excessive drinking. He realized later that his father drank because of the lupus . . . And because of the memories he could never seem to bury. Ironically, as a result of those memories Franklin had created the beginnings of the empire Vaughn now presided over.

Suddenly Vaughn experienced a vivid recollection.

Damascus. Late February, 1949.

The countryside of Syria was alive with almond blossoms. Beautiful pearl-white blossoms tinged with pink. Vaughn had never seen such a profusion of color. Life at the edge of the Ordos Desert, in northern China, had been drab. It was there his father had developed the habit of walking long distances whenever he had a problem to solve.

One day, shortly after he and his father had arrived in the city the ancient Egyptians called *Timasqu*, Franklin had taken him along on one of his walks. On the outskirts of the city there was a vast field of almond trees, some as high as twelve to fourteen feet. Vaughn had seen such trees in the Orient, but they didn't flourish there like they did here. Seeing so many of the plants blossoming in profusion overwhelmed him. "Vaughn, these are almond trees," his father said as he hoisted him upon his shoulders so he could be closer to the blossoms. "They are native to western India and Persia, but spread westward from there to where we are now, possibly as long ago as thirty-five hundred years."

"Is that a long time, Daddy?"

His father laughed. "Yes, son, it's a very long time. To the ancient Jews the almond was a welcome harbinger of spring," he continued, "a reminder that winter was passing away, flowers would soon appear on the earth again, the time of the singing of the birds had arrived, and the voice of the turtledove would soon be heard again throughout the land." His father had also told him the Hebrews referred to the almond as "the waker," and that because it symbolized the speedy and powerful result of light, the Israelites had used it as the pattern for the bowls of the golden candlesticks in the Holy of Holies.

"What's a turtledove?"

"One of the best-known birds of the Holy Land. It was often used by the poor for sacrifices . . ." His father paused and grew suddenly pensive. After a moment's hesitation he finished his answer. "The turtledove's peculiar note and its gentle disposition made it a type of Christ."

"What's a Christ, Daddy?"

"Not what, son, who. He was a man who lived and died a long time ago."

"Like Mommy?"

Franklin lowered his son to the ground, then sighed and said, "Not exactly."

"Oh . . ." he'd replied, knowing immediately from the look on his father's weather-beaten, deeply lined face that he'd asked one of those questions that always seemed to upset his father.

"The almond tree is considered by many people to be a very special kind of tree," his father continued as they resumed their walk, now hand in hand. "There was a great French king named Charlemagne who became Emperor of the Holy Roman Empire over eleven hundred years ago. Once, while on a long march, he and his army made a camp. His soldiers thrust their spears, which were made from almond branches, into the ground before they went to sleep. In the morning they discovered the spears had sprouted large blossoms, just like these, during the night. Thus the army had shade for their tents during the heat of the day."

"You mean a dead branch came to life overnight . . . just like that?" he'd asked, skeptical that such a miracle could happen.

His father laughed again and shook his head in amazement. "Yes, Vaughn. Just like that . . ."

After they returned to America, later that same year, his father became a major force in the very lucrative and rapidly expanding liquor industry, virtually overnight, by distilling almonds into a liqueur.

Franklin packaged the golden-brown liquid in an amber-colored bottle designed in an oblong-oval shape, mimicking the shape of the nut that was the source of his steadily growing fortune. And he named his elixir Angelica, after the name he'd posthumously given the child who died in Deborah's womb. Two weeks after he'd buried her, he had a vivid dream in which a young girl cried out to him, begging to be named so her soul would be set free. He later told Vaughn he was certain it was his unborn daughter calling to him from the grave.

Franklin died in June 1965, just one month before his fifty-seventh birthday. Vaughn did not shed any tears at his father's passing. By that time the earlier bond of closeness had dissolved, a victim of his father's obsession with the accumulation of money and power. Vaughn had vowed to build Solomon Bull-Ox into the most formidable multinational corporation in the world, and it had only taken him two decades to accomplish that goal.

Last September, on his forty-second birthday, the twentieth anniversary of his assuming control of his father's company, he had given himself a birthday present no one could have ever purchased for him in any store in the world. On that day he, Vaughn Aurochs, illegitimate son of an ex-missionary turned coppersmith turned entrepreneur, had signed the papers merging Solomon Bull-Ox Enterprises with the Kronos Corporation.

As a result of that merger, the new company, Rainbow International, was now a vast consortium — a multilayered, multipurpose corporate entity that spanned all seven continents. There was nowhere Rainbow International didn't reach. The deal had been kept secret because of international antitrust restrictions. Only a few people knew that he now ruled the largest, most comprehensive, privately-owned corporation in the history of the world.

Vaughn chuckled at the thought.

The irony of the whole situation was that he and his father had returned from China in 1949. The father had started Solomon Bull-Ox a year later at age forty-two, and the son had insured its virtual immortality by the same age. Perhaps more intriguing was the fact that it had been David McDaniel who had been instrumental in securing the necessary international trade agreements for Solomon Bull-Ox, back in the sixties, when he was still practicing law.

This evening Vaughn had finally met the daughter of the man who had become his partner, the man who would almost assuredly become the next President of the United States. Fate had also dealt one further very interesting card to Vaughn Aurochs.

Paul Kingman.

Vaughn's thoughts were interrupted as the Gustav Becker Adam and Eve grandfather clock chimed twice — the end of the second evening watch as the ancient Romans reckoned time. *The dog barks*, he thought. Darkness would be at its apex soon.

He reached inside his shirt and pulled out the amulet, then began to chant the liturgy he knew by heart — the one that always entered his mind unbidden. He was vaguely aware that the amulet had begun to heat up, as it did every night at this time.

The ritual had started just over seven months ago, on the night of his forty-second birthday. The amulet had been an anonymous gift he'd received in the mail. The only indication of its origin was a postmark indicating it had been mailed from Damascus.

When he'd first opened the package he examined the box, looking for a card, thinking perhaps one of his Arab intermediaries had sent him the silver-and-gold trinket as a joke; some of his business associates, particularly in the Middle East, had strange senses of humor. There was only a small, white, rectangular card with a single word stenciled in red on it: AZAZEL.

Later that evening, as he dressed for dinner, he'd felt a strong urge to reexamine the amulet. He took it out of its box and, as he stood bare-chested, hung the amulet around his neck. An immediate sensation of well-being washed over him, as if a long-lost family heirloom had been returned unexpectedly to its rightful owner.

He decided to wear the amulet for the evening, thinking it would be an interesting conversation piece. Several people commented on the unique piece of jewelry, but other than a few lewd remarks about its odd phallic shape, no one seemed to think it unusual.

He had gone to sleep around 1 A.M. that night. Barely forty-five minutes later he awakened from a strange, dark dream in which he had been walking aimlessly through the desert. The sun beat down upon him mercilessly, and it was burning a sickle-shaped scar into his forehead.

Without thinking, he grasped the amulet and clutched it in his right hand. It felt hot, as did the area just above his heart. And his body was drenched with sweat, despite the fact that he'd set the thermostat for 65 degrees.

He was about to take off the source of his discomfort when he sensed rather than heard a voice inside his head say, "The world is yours for the taking. You were mine from the womb. I am the Prince of Light. The kingdoms of this world are mine alone to give. Serve me, and I will make you the possessor of heaven and earth . . . for all eternity."

Then the chanting started inside his head.

At first it was slow and rhythmic. However, it quickly accelerated, not only becoming faster but more guttural. Before long he found himself moving his lips in unison.

He'd worn the amulet ever since, never taking it off.

Vaughn leaned back in the huge black leather chair and closed his eyes. He thought of a quote he'd read in the *Kebra Nagast, The Glory of Kings*, a fourteenth-century Ethiopian tract attributing the words to the Queen of Sheba:

> Through wisdom I have dived down into the great sea, and have seized in the place of her depths a pearl whereby I am rich. I went down like the great iron anchor, whereby men anchor ships for the night on the high seas, and I received a lamp which lighteth me, and I came up by the ropes of the boat of understanding.

The chant on his lips began to rise in pitch. His throat became dry, his voice raspy with the guttural incantation. The noise reached a fevered pitch, and the room was filled with what sounded like a dozen barking dogs. Vaughn's face was flushed red with blood, and he began to perspire.

The silver ram's-head amulet — two gold horns protruding out of the goat's head attached to the body and tail of a fish — was suddenly infused with a life of its own. Out of its two ruby-red eyes shone an eerie, viscous light that wrapped itself around the darkness, becoming one with the suddenly undulating, coffee-colored blackness.

Abruptly Vaughn stood up.

In a stupor he walked to the glass enclosure, opened the door, and stepped inside. He searched the small aviary with dull, bloodshot, sunken eyes until he finally found one of the smaller turtledoves. In one swift motion he grabbed the docile bird with his left hand, grasped its tiny head in his right, and twisted his powerful hands in different directions simultaneously. The bird's neck snapped with a soft *crack!*

He knelt to the imported stone floor, raised the sacrifice to his lips, and began to drink the still-warm blood as it gushed from the neck wound.

After a time he stood, tossed the bird to the back of the aviary, and wiped his hands and face on the small towel he kept for this purpose just inside the door. When his face and hands were again unstained, he stepped out of the enclosure and began to chant once again. Vaughn had no control over himself during these interludes, as he thought of them, and lately he'd had the inexplicable feeling that whatever force he had yielded himself to was growing stronger — not just in him, but in the world. It was almost as if he were beginning to see in the terrestrial world around him the physical manifestation of the celestial presence that was with him so tangibly in the room each night. A presence that was infinitely old, infinitely wise, infinitely powerful.

Oddly, he had no fear of it. Something inside him knew that soon, very soon, his own power would be such that no one on earth would be able to deny him anything. If they did, they would perish at his command.

The chanting stopped.

He was exhausted, his body sapped of vitality, as if he'd been leached by a medieval barber. He knew it would be several hours before he felt himself again.

As the first yellow-white rays of dawn began to push back the gray-black of night, Vaughn fell into a fitful sleep and immediately began to dream about the desert.

On the other side of the city, in the penthouse suite of the Halcyon Building, Yuri ben Raphah watched the sun rise majestically over the city. The white-hot warmth of its light splashed across the cloudless cerulean sky, giving the canvas of dawn a golden patina.

The silver-haired man smiled appreciatively as he remembered a day from his past when, during his sojourn in the desert not far from another capital city, he'd watched the same sun rise, only with different eyes. Then he'd been walking barefoot along the marl and the pulverized limestone beach, and the light had reflected off a shimmering green expanse of water instead of glass, steel, and concrete.

Standing only inches from the plate-glass window, he placed both palms spread-eagle on the tinted glass. He stood that way for several minutes, as if his hands were able to absorb the light and convert it to food, just as cells in the body absorb nutrients from the blood converting them to energy.

He'd been up all night praying intensely. And even though he never had need of food or sleep and never tired from the tasks he'd been created to perform, on this morning he had the look of one who had been engaged in a protracted battle that had drained him.

Gradually he began a liturgy of praise and worship, speaking in what sounded like a variety of different languages. After a time he turned from the window, knelt down on one of the Persian rugs, raised his hands to Heaven, and began to sing in a loud voice.

At first his mouth only produced fragments of sound. After about an hour, however, the staccato liturgy metamorphosed into a delightful symphony, filling the room with a wondrous melody and harmony. Even the walls seemed to vibrate with the musical hum. The sun raced over the lip of the windowpane as it marched into morning and inundated the room with its golden brilliance. When Yuri felt the light wash over his back, he jumped up and began to dance fervently and sing loudly.

There was light and sound everywhere. Not all of the light was from the sun, and not all of the sound was from his mouth. Had anyone been watching, they would have been dazzled by the brilliance of the light and overcome by the soul-shaking power of the music.

Yuri ran back and forth, praising and singing. His hands were raised above his head, and the long white robe he wore flapped wildly about his body. His silver-gray hair swished over the top of his scalp as if he were caught in the middle of a whirlwind.

Oddly, the sun seemed to pause, as if it had become an enchanted spectator, distracted from its original purpose. It hung in the stunningly bright blue sky, a huge, burning, yellow-white globe.

Yuri stopped dancing abruptly. He stood still in the middle of the room for several seconds, then turned to face the sun. His singing slowly slipped into a melodious humming. The soft, sweet sounds slid off his vocal chords and finally came to rest in the quiet stillness of silent prayer.

Slowly, almost reluctantly, the sun moved upward and westward, leaving Yuri standing silently alone — but not alone — in the room. He stayed that way for perhaps another hour, communing with the Lord God Most High, Creator of Heaven and Earth.

In the aftermath a soft white haze permeated every nook and cranny of the room. And the smell of frankincense was overwhelming.

Had Paul Kingman or Gabriella McDaniel been present to witness the spectacle, they would both have been startled — not so much by Yuri ben Raphah's behavior as by the fact that the same translucent haze which filled the now deceased Joel Goldman's penthouse apartment had also at one time filled each of their residences. And the heavenly aroma that now flooded his nostrils had also been smelled by both of them.

XVI

Nathan sat in one of his old haunts, Saturnalia's, remembering. He grimaced, thinking of how his father's rhetoric nauseated him and yet teased his intellect at the same time. *How I've changed in two years*, he thought and realized with painful insight that what gnawed at his insides was that deep down he didn't want to believe he had no hope. Yet everything he saw happening around him told him otherwise.

He looked up from his musings and saw his sister enter the club. She was not alone. He smiled and stood up, then motioned so she would see him.

When Gabriella saw her brother, she waved and returned the smile. "Nathan!" she called out. "I thought for sure we'd beat you here."

"I got tired of the Library of Congress. Thought I'd come early and reflect upon some of my more pagan undertakings in this establishment," he said, grinning. He offered his hand in greeting and added, "You must be Paul."

Paul nodded and returned the handshake. "Library of Congress, eh? What were you doing there?"

Nathan shrugged, and before he could answer Gabriella replied, "Research. And you *are* going to tell us all about it today, aren't you?"

Nathan chuckled. "You must have been reading my mind, little sister."

"You too, huh!" chimed in Paul as he sat down in the booth across from Nathan and next to Gabriella. "I'm glad to hear that I'm not the only one who feels that way."

"Now, boys," said Gabriella playfully, "it's not nice to make fun of the gifts God gave us women. We use them to keep you headstrong types out of trouble, you know."

"And to manipulate us into doing whatever *you* want," chided Nathan.

"How would you know, dear brother? You let the last woman I recommended you marry slip through your fingers."

"Whoa," said Paul. "There's just some things they never told me about this job."

Gabriella and Nathan stopped their bantering and looked at Paul quizzically. "What?" they said in unison, then laughed at their timing.

Paul shrugged. "I saw a poster once of a cowboy. He was standing in front of a barbed-wire fence, with a bunch of cattle behind him." His eyes sparkled as he talked. He knew he was a good storyteller, and it always pleased him when he involved his audience so completely that they forgot about themselves and became involved with his characters, real or imagined. Nathan and Gabriella were listening intently, and he could tell by the look on their faces that he'd done it again.

"The cowboy was covered with dust, and he sported a five-day growth of beard. He looked like he'd just finished the longest cattle drive of his career. Everything about him said that he was bone-tired. Except for his eyes. They gleamed with accomplishment. The caption underneath the photograph read: 'There's just some things they never told me about this job.'"

Nathan and Gabriella laughed, and Paul joined in.

"Welcome to the family," said Nathan as his sister shot him a look that said, Not quite so fast, please!

"Thanks," replied Paul, casting a quick look at Gabriella. "But if I've learned anything about your sister in the past couple of weeks, it's that she undoubtedly will have something to say about that."

Knowing they were teasing her, Gabriella grimaced coyly and said, "No comment at this time. Isn't that what the politicians say when they don't want to divulge something important? Or to keep the public guessing about their real feelings?"

Nathan and Paul eyed each other speculatively as the waitress arrived to take their orders.

Paul noticed the half-empty drink sitting on the table in front of Nathan, and his eyes were drawn to the mosaic of bright colors that highlighted the coaster beneath it. The image was disturbing and alluring at the same time. A sensuously beautiful, coppery-redheaded woman sat naked in a erotic pose upon a huge, male lion. The golden-colored cat sported a prominent, vibrant yellow-orange mane. In the woman's left hand was an iris with pink-purple and blackish-violet flowers. Intertwined around her right forearm, its head rising above her right hand as if poised to strike, was a red-and-gold serpent with a copper-colored neck. Behind the woman and the lion, in the background, was a half-rainbow surrounded by ten six-pointed stars, each a different color.

Gabriella's brother said, "I've been sitting here for over two hours and have barely managed to get halfway through my first drink. Would you two care to join me?"

Paul smiled and said, "Not for me, thanks. It's too early in the day." He continued to appraise the coaster.

Gabriella looked at him in surprise, then echoed his denial. "Coffee for me, big brother."

"That's right . . . I'd forgotten you quit drinking just before I left for Europe." He gave the waitress their order, then studied his sister appreciatively. Although she had changed little physically during his time away — she was still stunning — there was a new air of confidence about her. He'd seen it in her eyes at breakfast the other morning, and now he noticed it again in the way she talked.

It wasn't the harsh, arrogant attitude he was used to seeing in people who had "tumbled from the womb with the gift," as his father used to say. *No, it's not at all the same as the Senator's attitude*, he thought.

Paul spoke abruptly, as if out of a dream. The sight of the

coaster had brought to mind something he'd been wrestling with. "Something unusual happened last night that might be of interest to both of you."

Inexplicably Nathan suddenly felt a tingling in his spine, like he always felt just before getting a sudden insight. He wasn't sure what it was about Paul's statement that snared his attention, but he had the strangest feeling that whatever Paul had to say was going to turn out to be important to him. He sat forward and leaned against the edge of the table expectantly.

Gabriella moved her coffee cup and turned sideways so she could see Paul better. The butterflies were back.

"Last night Senator David McDaniel picked me up in his limousine, just outside my office."

Gabriella was shocked. "What! I thought you told me the two of you had never met."

"We hadn't . . . until last night."

"But how —"

"Let him finish, sis," Nathan told her, suddenly extremely curious because of her surprise at the news.

"We had a very interesting conversation. He offered me one million dollars for the parchments."

"What parchments?" asked Gabriella and Nathan simultaneously.

Paul shook his head. "I'm sorry, Gabriella. I thought you knew about them, because of the journal."

"Maybe you'd better start at the beginning and tell us everything," she said. "I have a feeling that what my brother has been 'researching' might just tie in with some of the strange things you've been telling me. And before I forget, I want you to tell me about the Rephaim when you're finished."

Nathan was amazed at the way his sister had put things together so quickly. He felt more encouraged than he had in two years. Maybe she would be his ally after all.

"The Rephaim!" exclaimed Paul. "Why did you bring them up?"

"I'll tell you when you finish."

Paul brought Nathan up to date on what he'd read in his father's journal and added a few things Gabriella was unaware of. Then he said, "I left my office shortly after 9. That's when your father showed up." He glanced at Gabriella and added apologetically, "And that's why I never made it to your opening. I'm really sorry."

"Never mind about that. What did my father have to say? And how does he know about the parchments?"

"Well, I haven't pieced it all together yet, but apparently he was acting on behalf of a man by the name of Vaughn Aurochs, who by the way came to see me in my office the other day and also offered to purchase the parchments for an unspecified sum. Your father told me I should reconsider Aurochs's offer."

Gabriella chewed on her lower lip.

Nathan asked, "What is it, sis?"

"Later . . . I'll tell you both later. Go on, Paul."

"Before I gave him my answer, I asked him about my father. And that seemed to shake him up. He said he didn't want to discuss the past."

"Did you tell him about us?" asked Gabriella, suddenly pensive.

"No. And that's the strange part. I started to several times and for some reason it just never came out."

"I may be a little dense," said Nathan, "but I'm not sure I understand why you two are acting the way you are."

"Not here," replied Paul mysteriously. "Let's go to my office in the Kronos Building."

Gabriella couldn't keep from speaking. "I still don't understand. Why is my father so interested in some ancient parchments? And how is he connected to Vaughn Aurochs?" she asked.

"Did you say the *Kronos* Building?" interrupted Nathan before Paul could answer his sister.

"Yes. It's the twenty-story building across from the park."

Nathan's spine was tingling again. His expression was glum as he said, "Did you know that the Senator owns not only the building in which you have your office, but the corporation from which the building takes its name?"

"No, I didn't," replied Paul, his demeanor abruptly subdued as he contemplated the importance of this new bit of information.

"Then you're probably also not aware that the Kronos Corporation, during the last six years, has become the second largest multinational corporation in the world," Nathan added, watching his sister's reactions carefully out of the corner of his eye. He was treading on thin ice again, but he couldn't let that keep him from speaking what was in his heart.

Gabriella stared at her brother, but said nothing.

Nathan continued. "I knew the corporation was big, but I never really understood just how big until I'd been in Europe for about six months. Everywhere I went I saw evidence of the Kronos Corporation's involvement in business, finance, and politics.

"Intrigued, I began to inquire about the corporation's holdings and was stunned to discover that not only has the corporation become involved with the European Common Market, but it has substantial influence on virtually every international economic market, including Russia, the Middle East, and Third-World countries. There are sixty-six corporate offices worldwide."

Paul had been nodding as Nathan talked. His journalist's antennae were vibrating as more pieces of the puzzle were fitting together. "Then the brain behind the corporate facade is none other than your father, Senator David McDaniel."

Nathan shook his head. "Not exactly. I thought so, at first," he continued hurriedly, "but now I believe there is much more involved than I ever imagined."

Gabriella bristled. "You two mental giants have left me dizzy. I haven't the faintest idea what you've been babbling about. And I'm not at all pleased with what I think I hear you saying about Father," she added, staring at Nathan accusingly.

"Maybe I can help," interjected Paul. It was obvious that the Senator's siblings had very different views of their father and equally obvious that if anyone was going to defuse the suddenly tense situation it would have to be him. And he had a pretty good idea how to do it. "*Kronos* is another name for the Greek mythological character Cronus," he said matter-of-factly, as though that were a piece of information people kept readily available in their heads.

Gabriella marveled at the store of knowledge in Paul's brain and at his ability to call it forth at a moment's notice. *I wonder if he has any idea how God plans to use his mind*, she thought, suddenly distracted from her anger at Nathan.

"Cronus was a Titan . . . one of six children of Uranus and Gaia," continued Paul, hoping he could subdue Gabriella's anger and give Nathan some additional information at the same time. "In classical mythology Uranus was the personification of Heaven and the ruler of the world. Gaia was the ancient Greek goddess of the earth. Besides being the mother of the Titans, she was also the mother of the mountains, the Cyclops, and the Erinyes."

"Erinyes?" Nathan asked.

"The Romans called them the *Dirae*; in Greek mythology they were known as the Furies. Cronus dethroned his father, at the instigation of his mother, and was in turn dethroned by his son, Zeus."

"He was identified by the Romans with the god Saturn, wasn't he?" questioned Nathan, becoming inexplicably agitated as Paul spoke.

Paul nodded.

"Do you realize where this is leading?" murmured Nathan.

Paul's expression was grim, but Gabriella only looked confused. "Please, spare me the suspense. You two might have figured out why this is so important, but I sure haven't."

Paul continued his recitation. "Saturn was an ancient agricultural divinity of Latin and Roman origin. He was comparable in rank with Janus, the old Roman god of beginnings and of the rising and setting of the sun. Janus is usually represented as having one head with two bearded faces back to back, looking in opposite directions."

"In other words, sis, Janus represents deceitfulness," interjected Nathan dryly.

"Saturn is also synonymous with abundance; he is supposed to have been King of Italy during the Golden Age — the time when, as one historian puts it, 'the baleful love of lucre did not poison the blood of the hard-working, contented peasantry.'"

Gabriella smiled and said, "Very poetic. Whoever penned those words probably had the soul of an artist."

"Undoubtedly," chimed Nathan. "Plus a vision of how to 'keep 'em down on the farm.'"

Paul was anxious to make his point, and he was glad he'd forestalled the argument between brother and sister. "Slavery and private property were unknown during the Golden Age; all men shared things in common," he explained, stressing the last two words. "It was Saturn's reign that brought prosperity and abundance. The Saturnalia, a Roman holiday honoring the god for which it was named, was celebrated on the seventeenth of December. It originally consisted of a series of rural festivals which were nothing less than a period of unrestrained, bacchanalian festivities lasting seven days, until the twenty-third of December. There are those today who insist that Christmas is really a pagan holiday derived from this carnival of debauchery and merrymaking."

"I just read something along those lines at the Library of Congress," chimed in Nathan. "A few Biblical scholars have argued that Jesus was not born in December, but in April. And that Easter, supposedly a time set aside to commemorate His resurrection, was in fact an ancient Assyrian holiday to pay homage to Ishtar, the goddess of love and war. I think the book said the ancient Hebrews called her Ashtoreth."

"I'm with you now," said Gabriella, getting excited as she looked back and forth between her brother and Paul. She finally had something she could relate to her experiences. "In ancient art, including several paintings that were recovered from Pompeii, Saturn was depicted as a man standing with his chest bare, a sickle in his hand." Suddenly she gasped and felt sick to her stomach. "It can't be!" she moaned, almost wailing.

Paul and Nathan stared at her, startled by her outburst.

"What can't be?" asked Paul.

"Several years ago Father asked me to paint a logo for his corporation. He told me he wanted people to identify his corporation with abundance and prosperity for every race and nationality. He suggested that I draw a man with a sickle in his hand standing behind a woman seated atop a cornucopia overflowing with meats and fruits. Behind them was a rainbow. Circling the logo he had me draw seven six-pointed stars, with the names of each of the seven continents printed inside them."

Nathan grunted with sudden insight. *Lord, help us*, he thought, *the man is not only after the Presidency . . . he's after control of the whole world.* "I overheard Father talking with someone the other night who apparently owns a company called Rainbow International. The man was trying to convince Father to join forces with him."

Gabriella's whole body seemed to be on fire. "And I was with Vaughn Aurochs last night. We had dinner together. He made an offhand comment about Father, and although I can't remember exactly what he said, I do remember I had the distinct impression he and Father were more than mere acquaintances. But his company is called Solomon Bull-Ox, not Rainbow International."

Paul glanced back and forth between Gabriella and her brother, stupefied. The information was coming too fast for him, and he was having trouble putting it all together. He sat back in his seat, suddenly feeling exhausted.

It was becoming more and more obvious that he had not met Gabriella McDaniel, or her brother, by accident. There were just too many *coincidences* for that to be the case. The question was, who was orchestrating the whole thing? He wasn't sure he was ready for the answer. Not to mention the fact that he still hadn't disclosed the fact that his father was a thief.

After a few minutes of silence, Gabriella said, "Do you realize we're sitting in a club called Saturnalia's?"

Nathan groaned with understanding. "And the logo for this club is very similar to the one you just described," he added, holding up his sodden coaster for them to see.

All three were again silent. The afternoon had slipped by them as they talked. The sun had set, and the darkening sky outside the club looked ominous and foreboding.

Gabriella looked out the window. The clouds were heavy and black with moisture. "It looks like we might get a few snow flurries tonight. We better be going if we want to make it to your office before the weather turns nasty."

Nathan signaled the waitress and paid the tab.

As the three of them stood up to leave, a glint of light caught Gabriella's eye, just as the light reflecting off a spider's web draws sudden attention to what previously was invisible. She glanced toward the main bar area and frowned.

Standing in front of the bar was a tall, thin, extremely pale man. Although he was wearing different clothes, Gabriella was certain he was the same man who'd confronted her in the art appreciation class. She would have recognized the snakeskin boots anywhere.

As she passed by him, she had an overwhelming feeling of *strangeness*. Even more so than the first time she'd seen him. She also realized it was the light reflecting off the silver chain around his neck that had captured her attention. She cut her eyes sideways and noticed he was wearing the same ram's-head he'd worn in class; only today there was something different about the unusual piece of jewelry.

It seemed to her that the twin, dull-red rubies of the goat's eyes glowed with an internal fire of their own. She wasn't positive, but she was fairly certain that the eyes had not glowed like that the first time she'd seen it. She shook her head and blinked and started to ask Paul if he remembered the man, but was distracted by what her brother was saying.

". . . mythology provides us ample opportunity for speculation about the origins of man and the universe. It seems that every religion has its own creation and fall of man theory." He began putting on his overcoat. "The one thing that stands out most about all of them is that they are so very similar, almost to the point of simply being variations on the theme. One has to wonder if indeed there was one, true, absolute beginning orchestrated by God." He finished buttoning up the heavy coat. "If that is the case, then all the other theories *are* simply theories — proposed explanations of phenomena that are entirely conjectural, standing in opposition to the certainty of absolute truth."

"What's even more important," interjected Gabriella, excited by what she heard in her brother's voice, "is to ask why there are so many diverse yet subtly similar accounts of creation. Most people who wonder about the glaring inconsistencies in the theory of evolution are willing to accept the possibility of a benevolent and infallible God creating offspring who because of and not in spite of their perfection fell from grace.

"But they are unwilling to accept the possibility that there is a malevolent evil force operating in the world. An evil entity who has as much substance in his realm as we do in ours. An incarnate force that has, from before the beginning of time, purposed in his heart and soul to usurp authority and Deity from God Almighty. The prophet Isaiah said it best: 'How are you fallen from heaven, O Lucifer, son of the morning! How are you cast down to the ground, which did weaken the nations! For you have said in your heart, "I will ascend into heaven. I will exalt my throne above the stars of God; I will also sit on the mount of the congregation on the farthest sides of the north. I will ascend above the heights of the clouds; I will be like the Most High." Yet you shall be brought down to Sheol, to the lowest depths of the pit.'"

Paul and Nathan stared at Gabriella, who blinked as if she were only just now hearing herself.

"Let's get to my office," said Paul abruptly as he urged his two friends toward the exit. He hoped they hadn't seen the shock in his eyes. Their comments had hit very close to home.

The pale man at the bar turned from his companion and stared intently at the backs of the three as they left. His glassy blue eyes sparkled with a malevolent glint as he raised his left hand and began to stroke the silver ram's-head with the glowing red eyes.

XVII

Paul turned the light on in his office and stood stunned.

The room looked as if it had been hit by a cyclone. Papers littered the floor, and all the furniture had been shoved around or knocked over.

"What in the name of . . ." he said as he crossed the room and paused at his desk. The drawers had been pried open, the locks snapped. Every file had been rifled and every drawer ransacked.

"It appears you need a maid," said Nathan, trying to swallow the taste of fear.

"My father's journal has been stolen," said Paul, working at his computer as he spoke. He was angry and frustrated, and he felt violated.

"Maybe you'd better call the police," suggested Gabriella.

"No police."

Gabriella frowned and looked at Nathan, who just shrugged.

"Aha. Just as I thought."

"What?"

"Whoever was here was also interested in whatever I'd stored in Sam."

Gabriella had a hollow feeling in the pit of her stomach. She walked over to the balcony and looked out at the darkening sky, praying silently. A light snow was falling, and a few of the large, thick flakes were sticking to the glass door.

Someone coughed at the doorway.

She turned at the sound and stared open-mouthed.

Nathan and Paul looked up from where they were watching data scroll over the computer screen.

In the doorway stood an unusually tall man. A soft, shimmering light appeared to encase his whole body, like a cocoon. It made it seem as if he were standing in a haze.

"I'm sorry if I caught you by surprise," said the stranger in a voice that sounded musical.

"You didn't surprise us at all. Please come in," said Gabriella calmly, the nauseous feeling disappearing.

Paul glanced at Gabriella, then quickly looked back at the stranger. He didn't know why, but he knew they had nothing to fear from this man.

Nathan's eyes never left the stranger. He couldn't quite put his finger on what it was, but there was something very odd about him.

The stranger smiled warmly and replied, "Thank you very much. I was beginning to feel rude."

"Do you know this man, Gabriella?" asked Paul.

"Not exactly —"

"Please don't be alarmed," interrupted the stranger, picking up one of two heavy, large wingback chairs with one hand, effortlessly setting it upright on its four legs. "My name is Yuri ben Raphah."

After a moment's hesitation Paul replied, "I'm Paul Kingman, and this is my office. These are my friends Gabriella and Nathan."

Yuri nodded knowingly. "It's a pleasure to meet all of you," he said. "It seems your office is in a bit of disarray, Mr. Kingman."

"Normally the place is organized in a disorganized fashion, if you know what I mean. Tonight, however —" Paul just shrugged.

"We arrived just before you and discovered that someone broke in to steal something," explained Nathan, eyeing the stranger, wondering how he just happened to be on the tenth floor at the same time they were.

"Did they get what they were after?"

Gabriella couldn't take her eyes off the man. He looked familiar, yet she knew they'd never met. And then it came to her. She remembered her dream.

"Do you work in the Kronos Building, Mr. Raphah?" asked Nathan, cutting off Paul's response.

Yuri smiled. "No, young man, I do not."

Nathan was surprised that the stranger referred to him as "young man." The silver-haired man himself didn't look much older than fifty.

Gabriella frowned at her brother and said, "To answer your question, Mr. Raphah, we're not completely sure yet. What my brother meant to ask, I'm sure, is, What brings you here tonight?" Yuri looked at Gabriella, and his crystalline-clear gaze penetrated all the way to her heart. "I came here to speak with Paul . . . About his father."

"You knew my father?"

"Not exactly. I knew of his work."

"At the university?"

"No. Earlier . . . when he was in Canaan."

Paul sighed. "My father's dead. I buried him three weeks ago."

"I know. That's why I'm here."

"Where is Canaan?" asked Nathan, hoping to redirect the very confusing conversation.

Paul picked up the other overturned wingback, straining to do so, and sat down opposite the stranger, then motioned for Gabriella and Nathan to make themselves comfortable. Gabriella sank onto the couch, and Nathan sat on the edge of Paul's desk.

"Canaan is the ancient term for the land of Palestine, west of the Jordan," explained Paul. "The Canaanites were a talented race of people who were highly developed in both the arts and sciences. Their major drawback was that the people had become decadent, even vile. Excavation of places such as Jericho, Bethel, Megiddo, and Ras Shamra have revealed that the Canaanite people had become degenerate. Their fertility rites and their worship of the mother goddesses were particularly debilitating. Homosexuality was rampant."

"But I thought most of those cities were in Israel," said Nathan.

"They are today," said Gabriella, remembering her brief visit.

"That's right," said Paul.

"The Canaanite pantheon of gods was an abomination unto Jehovah . . . the basest, most vile perversions of worship in the ancient world," interjected Yuri, his voice heavy with sadness.

Nathan had the uncanny feeling that Yuri was speaking from personal knowledge. *Crazy!* he told himself. *That would make the guy over three thousand years old!*

Paul noted that the stranger didn't sound condemning, merely concerned . . . And disappointed. He continued his explanation, not knowing why he felt compelled to speak. "The monotheistic faith of my ancestors was constantly in peril of contamination from the Canaanites' nature worship to immoral gods, prostitute goddesses, serpents, cultic doves . . . and bulls. The head of the pantheon, El, was a bloody tyrant who dethroned his own father and decapitated his own daughter. The Canaanites referred to him as 'father bull,' *abu adami*, the progenitor of the gods."

"A charming little deity," commented Nathan dryly.

Yuri stared at Paul intently with eyes that seemed to be on fire. "Your ancestors began their conquest in earnest," he added, "after victories by Joshua over the King of the Amorites and Og, King of Bashan. Unfortunately, as men are wont to do, they did not do exactly as God had instructed. As a result, they suffered unnecessarily."

The small office grew suddenly quiet. The snow had stopped falling, and because the heavy cloud cover was clearing, the temperature outside had started to drop dramatically. The window was now slick with ice. In the silence the four could hear the wind whipping at the glass; it reverberated in its frame, producing an odd, wailing sound.

"What happened after that?" asked Gabriella.

Paul shrugged. "Only another thirty-four hundred years of struggle," he replied flippantly, hoping to alleviate the chill that had settled upon the group.

No one laughed.

"In modern history the Jews never truly possessed the land promised to Abraham by God until May 14th, 1948," said Nathan, surprising everyone. "That was the day the British finally sailed out of Haifa, and Erez Israel became a reality."

"My father returned from Syria to Jerusalem three months later," muttered Paul, remembering the earlier conversation at Saturnalia's.

"A beautiful city," said Yuri appreciatively.

"You've been there?" asked Gabriella.

The man, aglow with light, sighed. There was a wistful look in his sparkling eyes. "Many times. It is a city that never changes . . . and yet it is one in which many things have changed."

"That's very poetic, Mr. Raphah."

"Truth has that quality, Miss McDaniel."

Paul's antennae started to twitch. He hadn't given Nathan and Gabriella's last name when he'd introduced them. How did this stranger know . . . ? "You said you knew of my father's work?"

"Yes. At the time he was in the desert, near *Bahr Lût*."

Paul, Nathan, and Gabriella each looked confused.

"Forgive me," said Yuri, genuinely apologetic. "I keep using outdated terminology. Your father found some rather unique documents in a cave along the shores of what is now referred to as the Dead Sea."

As Yuri talked, Paul was thinking about all the sudden interest in the parchments.

"I happened to read in the paper about your father's death. The obituary indicated he was survived by a son," continued Yuri. "After making a few inquiries I discovered you had an office here in this building. I have information that might be of some help to you," he finished.

"Oh?"

"The people who broke into your office and vandalized it were after those parchments."

Paul snapped his fingers as realization flooded over him. "Of course! Not just the journal, but the parchments. Then they *are* authentic?"

Yuri nodded. "I knew the author."

"That's impossible!" exclaimed Paul. "The parchments were written almost two thousand years ago, during the time of the Roman occupation of Palestine."

Nathan said, "What the man means, Paul, is that he knows who wrote the documents. Isn't that right, Mr. Raphah?"

The silver-haired man smiled, but made no reply.

"Will you two *please* be quiet and let Yuri finish," wailed Gabriella.

"I know things are happening a bit fast for you," said Yuri soothingly, "but you must understand that there are millions of lives at stake."

"Millions of lives?" interrupted Nathan. "What's he talking about, Paul?"

"That's what Paul brought us up here to tell us," said Gabriella, looking at him, her eyes sparkling with anticipation. "Isn't it?"

Paul sighed. "I'm not sure any more *what* I'm doing," he said, exasperated. "So much has happened lately. I need time —"

Yuri eyed Paul thoughtfully and said gently, "There isn't much time left, Paul. I take it you haven't explained the whole story to your two friends."

Paul shook his head.

Yuri stood up abruptly. "I'm staying across the plaza, in the penthouse apartment of the Halcyon Building. I'm not there very much, but if you need me, you can reach me by leaving a message."

Without a further word, he was gone — so rapidly that it was almost as if he'd never been there.

"Whew," said Nathan, sliding off Paul's desk, staring after Yuri. "That guy was something else. You know . . . the whole time he was talking I had the strangest feeling that he wasn't *real*." He shook his head. "I know that sounds weird," he added hastily, "but that's how I felt. Like he was a holographic image of a real person." He turned to his sister and said, "*You* know what I'm talking about, sis, don't you?"

Gabriella stared past her brother and nodded. "Just like the time you took me to the laser light exhibition at the museum, when I was seventeen."

Nathan nodded rapidly. "Yeah. Now they use holograms at Disney World. The images are so real — they even talk to you."

Paul remained silent, contemplative.

Nathan glanced at him and said, "What do you think, Paul?"

He looked up and replied, "I think I'd better tell you two what I brought you here to tell you . . . and then you can tell me if you still think Mr. Raphah was a hologram come to life."

"What does 'halcyon' mean?" asked Gabriella abruptly.

"It was a mythical bird," replied Paul with his usual encyclopedic aplomb, "usually identified with the kingfisher. It was said to have the power of calming winds and waves at sea."

Gabriella frowned thoughtfully. "Paul, why didn't you want us to call the police?"

Paul said heavily, "Because the information contained in my father's journal could ruin everything I've worked for all my life . . . unless I find a way to fix what happened forty years ago."

Once again the room was suffocatingly silent.

"How about some coffee?" suggested Nathan.

"Great," said Paul as he got up from the chair and went over to Sam. "I've got a long night ahead of me, and I can use all the help I can get. You two want to stay?"

Gabriella nodded her head. "Why don't you bring us all back a cup, Nathan? I think we're going to need it."

"You're *sure* it was his son?" hissed Vaughn. "Absolutely sure it was Nathan McDaniel you saw?"

The man with the snakeskin boots nodded.

"Well, well, well," said the billionaire, toying with the amulet around his neck. He stared across the room at the garden aviary and smiled a smile that looked more like the snarl of a wolf than an expression of happiness. But he was indeed happy. "That explains why the door was ajar when I left Senator McDaniel's office. I knew I'd closed it behind me."

The pale man said nothing. He knew better than to comment.

Vaughn stood up and walked over to the glass enclosure. He didn't pay attention to anything inside, but rather focused on the night outside the building. "It seems the Senator has been holding back on us. I think it's time we show him what kind of behavior is expected of one destined for greatness, don't you?"

The pale man grinned and stroked his own amulet.

Yuri ben Raphah paced the apartment, thinking. It was not going to be easy to keep from interfering this time. So much was at stake. Yet disobedience was unthinkable. However, things were going to get rough. He could feel it in his spirit.

He'd barely gotten to Paul's in time the other night. On his way there he'd encountered Rephaim. There had been a battle, and he'd realized immediately that the soldiers of darkness were there to distract him and keep him from getting to Paul's house. He'd been able to defeat them without difficulty, but it had taken time. He arrived just as one of the enchanter's minions had begun to manifest itself in Paul's room. Again the battle had been fierce, and he knew he'd won only because of Gabriella's prayers. Praise the Holy One that she was obedient.

Yuri sighed. He was worried about all of them, but he was especially concerned about Paul. His *soul* was at stake. And with it, much more.

Events were definitely accelerating. He was going to have to be constantly alert. He couldn't afford to let the Rephaim overwhelm his charges. The consequences were too devastating to think about.

XVIII

Gabriella shivered. After a few moments she said, "I wish Nathan would hurry up and get back with that coffee."

"Are you cold?" asked Paul.

She nodded and wrapped her arms around herself.

"I have a spare jacket, if I can find it in this mess," he told her as he rummaged through the debris. "Here . . ." he said when he'd found it, draping it over her shoulders. "This should keep you warm. They turn down the heat in the building at night to conserve energy."

"Thanks," she said distractedly, "but I'm not sure it's the weather that's making me cold." She walked over and stood in front of the door leading to the balcony and stared out at the icy darkness.

Tentatively Paul came up behind her and put his arms around her. "You know, I've wanted to hold you like this since I first laid eyes on you," he said. "We've only known each other three weeks, but it feels like much longer. There are times when I feel like I've known you all my life."

Gabriella sighed and leaned against him. "I feel the same way. I haven't been able to get you out of my mind since I had dinner at your house." She was exhausted, and Paul felt warm and comfortable. It was good to be held by a man again. It had been a long time. Too long. "There's a part of me that I want to share with you," she continued after a few moments, "but I'm not sure how to tell you. And I have so many conflicting emotions rolling around inside me, I'm not certain if what I feel is real."

Paul turned her around so she was looking into his eyes. "I

want to know everything about you," he said, opening himself up. "The good, the bad . . . all of it. Since you came into my life I'm beginning to feel things I thought I'd go a lifetime without experiencing. And I don't mind telling you, it's got me a little frightened."

"Me too, on both accounts," she said, sighing.

"Well?"

Gabriella frowned, then closed her eyes momentarily. The soft light of the office reflected off the thick ebony strands of her hair and brought out the same burgundy highlights Paul recalled seeing at the university as the sun had slipped below the windowsill.

He marveled at the effect she had on him. All evening he'd been suppressing an urge to take hold of this subtly alluring woman. And now that he had, he wanted to hold her even closer; close enough to soak up the amber softness of her skin, the warm musk of her breath, the sweet, pristine fragrance he imagined he would smell if he nuzzled his head gently against the inviting curve of her neck.

Entranced by her quiet strength, he thought of the opening lines of one of his favorite poems. On impulse he recited:

> *"She walks in beauty, like the night*
> *of cloudless climes and starry skies;*
> *And all that's best of dark and bright*
> *Meet in her aspect and her eyes:*
> *Thus mellow'd to that tender light*
> *Which heaven to gaudy day denies."'*

Gabriella opened her eyes and stared into the deep blue ocean of his gaze. "First you tell me I glow, and now you quote me beautiful poetry. I don't know what to say," she whispered. "Most men don't know poetry beyond what they read in Hallmark cards." Her throat was dry, and it felt like her tongue was tangled in her teeth.

Paul eased forward and kissed her. Slowly, without hesitancy.

Gabriella felt passion surge. She wanted to abandon herself to the heat, but something stopped her. She pulled back from Paul's inviting yet undemanding embrace. "Oh boy," she said, putting a distance between them with words because her body refused to respond to her mind's command to walk over and sit down on the couch. "I'm not sure I'm ready for this."

"That's okay. Lord Byron has had that effect on more than one woman," Paul replied carelessly, shaken himself by the intensity of the feeling.

Gabriella felt suddenly indignant because of his offhanded tone. "Oh, I see . . . you've used the quote before." She closed her eyes again, tightly this time, as though she could stop her thoughts with a physical act. "Many times no doubt," she added, suddenly feeling foolish and frustrated. Why did communication always have to be so difficult between men and women?

"No . . . That's not what I meant at all," Paul said hastily and reached over to stroke her cheek. Her eyes fluttered open at his touch. "I shared the opening lines of that poem with you because you remind me of all that is pure, sweet and . . ." He paused, searching for the right word. ". . . innocent."

"Innocent?"

"Yes. You seem to me to be a woman who, in spite of having lived in the world, remains untouched by it."

Gabriella was rocked by Paul's insight. It was exactly how she felt about herself. She'd always believed she was *different*; but she hadn't, until recently, been able to verbalize that belief in a way that communicated something other than adolescent conceit.

Throughout her childhood she'd sensed there was something that set her apart — not only from her older brother, but from the other children at the Catholic schools her father had enrolled her in as well. It wasn't that she considered herself better than her classmates, but rather that she could see and feel things they couldn't.

In fact, they always laughed at her when she tried to explain about *knowing*. So she'd learned at a young age to keep quiet about the voice that never lied to her. When she was sixteen, she'd mustered up the courage to ask Sister Martha, her favorite teacher, about the voice.

The sister had listened patiently, then smiled and said, "Gabriella, my dear, that's the Holy Spirit within you, guiding you and protecting you from harm. He will never leave you or forsake you. When you draw close to Him, He will draw close to you. And if you search Him out with all that is within you, He will give you the desires of your heart."

"He will?"

The sister nodded.

"Why?"

"Because He loves you . . . and because *He* put those desires in your heart."

It was nearly ten years before she began to understand fully what Sister Martha was saying, and it was only just recently, after two years of diligent study of the Holy Scriptures, that she'd realized just how important it was that she speak up and share the gift of the voice with anyone who would listen.

When she'd caught her breath she said, "I'm flattered, Paul. Please forgive me. It's been a long time . . ." She fidgeted with the sleeve of the jacket. How should she begin?

Paul waited patiently.

"There have been times over the past two years when I've wondered what I'd do when — and if — I found myself in these circumstances." She glanced up shyly. "You know . . . really attracted to a man. I've been lost in my work these past few years, so romance . . ." She let the sentence trail.

"And?" he asked, curious about what had caused this exceedingly beautiful woman to abstain from romantic interludes for the last two years.

Gabriella looked away from the warm sea of passion she saw in Paul's eyes. "I'm not sure, even now," she replied softly.

Paul sighed and stepped back. "You know, it's funny . . . I knew the moment I saw you there was something extraordinarily different about you. But I had no idea what it was. I've been so caught up in my own work the past ten years that I've thought of little else but becoming a success. I've won several major awards for the type of writing I do, but none of those accolades has ever made me feel successful — or happy."

Gabriella knew instinctively that Paul was opening himself up to her in a way he hadn't with a woman before. And he wasn't making fun of what she'd told him. It reminded her about how her brother hadn't laughed at her when she told him about the voice. On more than one occasion he had supported her when she'd done something the adults in her world considered reckless — many times just to spite their father's contention that she was letting her "femaleness" get in the way of her brain. That was why she and Nathan were much closer than a brother and sister separated by ten years would normally be.

That this man she'd only met three weeks ago should have as much insight into who she was and what she felt as her brother Nathan did after twenty-eight years startled and invigorated her. She told herself not to get too excited; she would not repeat the mistakes of the past. She touched his arm. "I'm listening."

"Well, I can't explain it, but ever since I saw you 'glowing' at the university I've had the feeling that my life is going to change immeasurably . . . and that you're going to be the catalyst."

A subtle chill of confirmation coursed up and down Gabriella's spine. "I feel the chemistry too, Paul. When I saw you sitting there in the classroom, your baby-blues staring at me with unabashed curiosity, my heart skipped. It actually skipped several beats," she added, her voice light.

Paul nodded, surprised that Gabriella was using the same words he would use had he been the one recounting the experience.

She continued, "When you followed me and stopped me beside the dogwood, I knew we were going to be close friends."

"Just friends?"

She shrugged her shoulders, but said nothing, suddenly pensive.

Paul, surprised by her sudden change of demeanor, studied her, perplexed. It looked like she was standing in the midst of a shimmering, silken haze. He wondered if the fluorescent lighting was acting up.

Gabriella's voice pulled his eyes to hers. "You asked me earlier if I knew the stranger that was here tonight."

He nodded.

"Well . . . I believe he's an angel." She stared at him intently, looking for some sign of disapproval. She needed to be sure about so many things. "I know you probably think I'm nuts," she added hastily, "but please hear me out before you judge."

Her comment left him speechless. Although what she was telling him seemed totally absurd, something deep down inside him urged him to listen with an open mind. Not to mention that the whole time he'd been talking to the silver-haired stranger, he'd had the feeling he'd seen him somewhere before.

Gabriella told him about her brother's conversation with the priest at Chartres Cathedral and of his startling experience afterwards, in his hotel room in Paris, then said, "On the same night that happened to Nathan — the night after I had dinner at your house — I had a similar experience."

"What are you telling me?"

She frowned again. "I'm not sure exactly. I had a dream, not a vision like Nathan. In it I was talking to a tall man with silver-gray hair. The man I saw and heard in my dream was the same man who was here in your office tonight."

"You're absolutely positive?"

"Yes."

"What did he say?"

"'Do not forget the word of God to the Hebrews.'"

"That's all?"

She nodded. "It wasn't until after my conversation with Nathan that I realized what the man in my dream was telling me." She paused and chewed her lip.

"Go on."

"It's rather complicated."

"Try me."

"Well, it has to do with what we were talking about the other day in your office."

"About my dream? About Cain and Abel and the blood sacrifice you were telling me about?"

Gabriella nodded, then plunged ahead. "When I began to study the Bible in earnest two years ago, I discovered a richness contained within its pages that goes far beyond any theological or religious considerations. From your own studies in preparation for your *Bar Mitzvah* you are no doubt aware that the Old Testament Scriptures are not only a historical account of events spanning several thousand years, but are prophetic and allegorical as well."

Paul nodded as she talked.

"Because of this, the historical account functions as a kind of Rosetta stone and makes it possible for the serious student of the textual record to learn not only about temporal happenings which have significance in a rather limited context, but also to gain an understanding of spiritual matters which transcend time and have a far more universal application. You might say that the historical record is *terrestrial*, while the spiritual record is *celestial*."

"I'm not sure I follow you."

Gabriella paused and collected her thoughts, then tried a different approach. She realized she needed to talk to Paul in terms of events he could relate to as a Jew, because that was really what this discussion was about — his heritage and how it tied in with *her* heritage.

"The first Jew, Abram, was a native of Chaldea, born in the pagan city of Ur, in southern Babylonia. Although he was a descendant in the ninth generation from Shem, the son of Noah, he was a man who came from a family of idol-worshipers who lived almost twenty-two hundred years before Christ. Nevertheless, in spite of his pagan background, Abram was chosen by God to become the progenitor of God's chosen people, because of his obedience to the voice of God. Thus Abram became the first man *after the Flood* to enter into a blood covenant with God."

"Are you referring to circumcision?" Paul interrupted.

"That, and much more."

Paul was overwhelmed at the depth of Gabriella's knowledge. She must have spent a great deal of time studying the Old Testament to have such insights. "I'm with you so far," he said. "But how does this relate to my dream?"

"God's relationship with His creations has always been defined in terms of covenants: the Adamic, the Noahic, the Abrahamic, the Davidic, and the New Covenant of His Son, Jesus Christ. All of these covenants have one thing in common — a *bloodline*."

Gabriella stopped talking abruptly and looked around the office, then walked over to where a pile of books was lying on the floor. "It will be easier if I show you what I'm talking about," she said as she sifted through the pile. "Do you happen to have a Bible handy?"

"In the drawer of my desk," replied Paul. He walked over and retrieved it, then handed it to Gabriella. "It's one of the few things whoever was here earlier didn't mess with."

"Great, it's a *King James*," said Gabriella. She flipped it open to the New Testament. "The Book of Hebrews explains the importance of the blood."

"What blood?"

"Not *what* . . . whose."

"OK, whose?"

"Jesus of Nazareth's."

"Oh boy," said Paul as he walked over and sat down on the couch. "I have a feeling we're about to go off the deep end."

Gabriella noted the pained look on his face. She said, "Not if you're patient . . . And not if you'll trust me."

He stared at her with clouded eyes.

Silently Gabriella said a quick prayer, then pressed on. "In the Book of Leviticus Moses recounts God's words to His people: 'For the life of the flesh is in the blood; and I have given it to you upon the altar to make an atonement for your souls: for it is the blood that maketh an atonement for the soul.' And the author of the letter to the Hebrews writes at length about the blood of Jesus."

"I don't see the correlation."

"Just listen for a moment and you will." Gabriella paused and prayed silently a second time while she turned to the passage she wanted. When she found it, she began reading out loud: "'For when Moses had spoken every precept to all the people according to the law, he took the blood of calves and of goats, with water, and scarlet wool, and hyssop, and sprinkled both the book, and all the people, saying, This is is the blood of the testament which God hath enjoined unto you.

"'Moreover he sprinkled with blood both the tabernacle, and all the vessels of ministry. And almost all things are by the law purged with blood; and without shedding of blood is no remission.

"'It was therefore necessary that the patterns of things in the heavens should be purified with these; but the heavenly things themselves with better sacrifices than these. For Christ is not entered into the holy places made with hands, which are the figures of the true; but into heaven itself, now to appear in the presence of God for us:

"'Nor yet that he should offer himself often, as the high priest entereth into the holy place every year with the blood of others; for then must he often have suffered since the foundation of the world: but now once in the end of the world hath he appeared to put away sin by the sacrifice of himself.

"'And as it is appointed unto man once to die, but after this the judgment: so Christ was once offered to bear the sins of many; and unto them that look for him shall he appear the second time without sin unto salvation.'"

When Gabriella finished, Paul stared at her, but said nothing. She closed the Bible and sat down next to him on the couch, then put her hand on his arm. "Didn't you tell me that you read something intriguing about blood in your father's journal?"

Paul frowned. He hadn't had time to study the entire contents before they'd been stolen. "I can't remember." He stood up and began to pace the room. "Why would someone steal my father's journal?" he asked abruptly, suddenly frustrated.

Gabriella realized that by changing the subject Paul had effectively told her he didn't want to discuss any of this any further. She knew she was pushing him hard, but she also knew there was too much at stake to let him off the hook so easily.

"Because there was something very important written on those pages," she replied. "And we've got to figure out what." She stared at him intently, then indicated she wanted him to sit back down beside her. When he did, she said, "I'm going to share something with you, and I want you to try and forget all your religious upbringing."

"That's like asking a blind man to describe a color."

Gabriella squeezed his arm hard.

"OK, OK, I'm listening."

"Because of Adam's sin God — specifically, the Son of God, one member of the Trinity — took on a human body. As Jesus, the Anointed One, He lived among us as a man. He was crucified, died, and was resurrected so we could be reconciled to God the Father. Even though Jesus was born of a woman, He remained God. He was perfect man, perfect Deity."

"That's what Elizabeth used to tell me," Paul said thickly.

"Elizabeth?"

"My mother."

Gabriella's heart went out to him. She knew how difficult this was for him, and she wanted to say something to comfort him. Suddenly she had it. "Paul," she said softly, "did your mother also tell you what her name meant?"

"The Hebrew means, 'God her oath.'"

"Do you know that the Biblical Elizabeth was a descendant of Aaron?"

"Moses' brother? The first High Priest?"

Gabriella nodded. "She was also the wife of Zacharias and the mother of John the Baptist."

Paul chuckled. "Wasn't he the guy who lived in the wilderness and ate grasshoppers?"

"Yes, he was. His mother was Mary's cousin. John was the man who heralded and baptized the Messiah . . . his cousin Jesus."

Paul absorbed the information, fascinated. The frustration he'd felt just a moment ago had suddenly vanished. Suddenly he remembered where he'd seen Yuri ben Raphah! And the memory caused him to wonder, *Could there be a connection? Yuri. Uriel. Incredible!*

When he'd turned on the lamp beside his bed the night he'd awakened from his nightmare in a cold sweat, the night he felt he was battling an unseen enemy, he'd seen a silver-haired man standing in his doorway. That man *could* have been Yuri, he realized. He knew that in Hebrew Raphah meant "God has healed," and Uriel meant "God is light." But it just didn't make sense. It was too much for his mind to grasp.

"Let's assume for a moment that what you've been telling me is true — that Jesus was, and is, the Messiah. Why, then, has an angel of God suddenly appeared to *us*?"

"I don't know. Maybe because of the parchments."

Paul was thoughtful. "Maybe he's trying to tell us something."

"Like what?"

Paul shrugged. An idea had been forming in his head, but he was reluctant to share it with her because it involved her father. "I'm not sure you'd believe me."

"That sounds familiar."

"OK . . . You asked for it. I've been asking myself why all of a sudden there is such tremendous interest in some ancient manuscripts that supposedly no one but my father knew about for forty years."

"And?"

"In the space of one week two men, one of them your father, have tried to buy the parchments, sight unseen, for an exorbitant sum of money."

"Just what are you implying?"

Paul realized he was treading on thin ice, but he felt compelled to say what he'd been thinking. "Your father has Presidential aspirations, doesn't he?"

"So?" snipped Gabriella, remembering Nathan's words: *I believe father is involved in something horrendous . . . something so diabolical that even though it appears to be good, it will ultimately enslave every person who believes in and supports him.*

"Well, I did some checking on this fellow Vaughn Aurochs. He's an extremely rich and very powerful man. In fact, when I called a couple of my sources, they told me to back off, saying I didn't want to mess with him . . . that I'd be playing with fire."

Gabriella lashed out at him. "Do you think my father is up to something illegal? Something sinister?"

"I didn't say that."

"No, you didn't. But my brother did."

XIX

Nathan appeared in the doorway, three cups of coffee in his hands. He looked at Paul, who seemed to be in a daze, and then at his sister, who looked angry and hurt. Something had happened while he was gone, but he knew better than to pry. "I had to go down the street to get these," he explained and handed them each a cup.

Gabriella glared at her brother and said, "Why don't you tell us about what you've been researching. It might help to clear the air."

Nathan peered at his sister, wondering what had gotten into her. He set down his cup, reached into the inside pocket of his jacket, and pulled out the newspaper clipping he'd been carrying with him for months, ever since Paris. "Before I say anything, you both need to read this." He spread out the full-page advertisement on Paul's desk.

When they'd finished reading, Nathan said, "I know this might sound like I have an overactive imagination, but I believe it's worth thinking about. And remember, it's not the wording of the advertisement that's important. It's what's being said between the lines that is so dramatic."

"We're all ears," said Paul as he glanced sideways at Gabriella. She had moved away from him, and the distance suddenly seemed unbreachable.

"Charles Darwin wrote *On the Origin of the Species* in 1859," Nathan began, making a concerted effort not to be pedantic, yet knowing that this basic information was critical in order for them to see the same connection he did. "In that book he stated his theory of natural selection or the 'survival of the fittest.' However, Darwin realized there were serious shortcomings with his theory. Most importantly, he recognized there was a problem with the fossil record — or rather the lack of it. His hope was that one day science would discover fossils that would support his theory. It's been over 125 years, and those fossils still haven't been discovered!"

"What are you getting at?" asked Gabriella.

"Let me finish and I think you'll understand. In the early seventies an idea called 'punctuated equilibrium' began to gain prominence over Darwin's theory in scientific circles."

"I've heard of that," interrupted Paul. "Basically it's the idea that instead of a steady, perpetual process of evolution, evolutionary changes in species occur in rapid, periodic bursts."

Nathan nodded. "There are large spans of time in between those periodic bursts during which the *new* species adjusts and adapts to its environment. The salient point is that not all members of a particular species survive these so-called 'quantum jumps' of evolution."

"And which species do survive?" his sister asked.

"Only those members which have the requisite genetic makeup that allows them to adapt to *global* transformations remain to perpetuate the species."

"So you're saying that 'periodic global realignment' is the latest scientific theory?"

"That's right. Interestingly, about this same time, in the early seventies, the 'New Age' movement came along."

"You mean the Age of Aquarius idea?" Gabriella inquired.

Nathan nodded. "Something like that, sis. Actually we talked about it at Saturnalia's."

"When?" interrupted Paul, furrowing his brow.

"Remember when you were telling us about the mother goddess, Gaia?"

"Yes."

"Well, the New Agers believe the earth itself is a living organism that is part of a cosmic consciousness. Man is merely one of millions of life-forms integrally related via the Gaia principle to the larger concept of a universal entity or consciousness." Nathan used his hands to draw a circle in the air. "They contend that unless man undergoes a radical change in consciousness, the living organism — the earth, the mother goddess Gaia — is doomed to die. Some of the more zealous — one might even say the more radical — adherents to the concept actually argue that in the near future there will be a 'cleansing' of all the negative energies of the planet."

"Negative energies?" Paul interrupted.

"Yeah. All those who are unable to make the transition to the so-called *higher consciousness*."

"For instance?"

Nathan shrugged. "People incapable of subordinating individual desires and tuning in to the cosmic mind. According to these more radical New Agers such individuals must be sacrificed — in love and with respect for their eternal soulish existence, of course — for the survival of the larger organism."

"Whew!" breathed Gabriella. "That's pretty disgusting, Nathan."

Paul was frowning. "It sounds to me like a modified form of what Hitler preached."

"According to the New Agers, it's more like a consciousness transfusion," said Nathan. "Out with the old, in with the new."

"But how do they justify this so-called *cleansing*?" asked Paul, his stomach feeling queasy over what he was hearing.

"Reincarnation."

"What!" Gabriella was flabbergasted.

Nathan sat on the edge of Paul's desk. "The New Agers have adopted and radically modified the karmic doctrine of eastern mysticism, giving it a kind of Hollywood aura. No one ever comes back as a cow or a dog or a monkey, according to modified reincarnation. You might have lived as a prostitute or a bag lady in a past life, and you might be an Albert Schweitzer or a famous movie star in a future or present life, but you will always be human."

"That's preposterous," said Gabriella. She might have laughed if it weren't so deadly serious.

"An awful lot of people *do* believe it," said Paul thoughtfully. "Including some notable movie stars."

He started thinking about the project that, until three weeks ago, had consumed most of his time. The article he'd begun working on was one he'd promised himself he'd write before he was thirty. Now, less than a week before his self-imposed deadline, he was still struggling with his theme.

What he needed was a source of material that would elevate what his editor had called "a dead horse topic" out of the ordinary and into the extraordinary.

His desire was to awaken people who looked to "government" as the means to cure the ills of society, who had made the government a god. A government which, because of its advocates' idolatry, had declared itself to be the instrument of their salvation.

People the world over had anthropomorphized the concept of the Sovereign into a *golem*. In Jewish folklore the *golem* was a man-made figure constructed in the form of a human being and endowed with life.

There were moments, in his nightmares, when he imagined that the various heads of state were all clones of Dr. Frankenstein. Like Mary Shelley's misguided doctor, who nightly robbed graves seeking the body parts he needed to create his perfect man, they'd been robbing the graves of the politically naive, fashioning a "monster" out of diverse ideologies, surreptitiously sewing together their respective doctrines of "world harmony" under the cover of darkness.

All that was required now was a source of power to animate the corpse. Paul's own private theory was that the brain of the monster was a world government — singularly and ostensibly benevolent. However, like Mary Shelley's tragic character, the power that would eventually bring life to the perfect creation of man would also prove to be the source of its destruction.

Nathan's comments on the New Agers had revived Paul's journalistic instinct for the "ultimate" story.

"We need to tie all of this together," Gabriella said crisply. "I guess your story has a punch line?"

Nathan returned his sister's gaze and replied, "You're not going to like it, sis."

"I don't doubt that. But before you shake us up any more, I want to ask Paul a question."

"What's that?" Paul turned toward the sofa where she was sitting.

"Will you tell us about the Rephaim?"

"Now?"

Gabriella pressed her temples with her fingertips. "I've got a hunch that *now* is the perfect time."

Paul waited a thoughtful moment, then said, "Remember when I was talking about the gods El and Baal, and Yuri was talking about the perversions in Canaan?"

Nathan and Gabriella nodded in unison.

"Well, I've been boning up on archaeology — especially in reference to Mesopotamia."

"The ancient area between the Tigris and Euphrates Rivers that's now part of Iraq," interjected Nathan. "Where Babylon was located."

"Exactly. During the late twenties through the mid-thirties the French excavated a site known as Ras Shamra, located on the north Syrian coast, opposite the peninsula of Cyprus. They found clay tablets written in a dialect similar to the Hebrew spoken at the time of Moses. In those texts El was represented as the 'Supreme Being.' He inhabited a place called the 'Mount of the North,' the Ugaritic equivalent of Olympus. One of the religious dramas tells us that El sired progeny from two human wives, one of whom was called Asherah, the mother goddess."

"So how does this relate to the Rephaim?" Gabriella asked somewhat sharply.

"Patience, sis," said Nathan, realizing that what Paul was saying paralleled his own discoveries, only in the spiritual realm. "I think Paul is clueing us in to something on a much different scale."

"What's most important," continued Paul, "is that the Ras Shamra tablets uncovered an impressive body of mythology comparable to that of the Greeks." He stared at his two friends. "What if all the stories about creation in all the different religions are more than just myth? What if they're *true*?"

"They'd all have to have a common source," answered Nathan with a shrug of his shoulders.

"Precisely. Now, keeping that thought in mind, let me answer Gabriella's question."

"Thank you." She flashed him a quick smile which warmed him. He was glad the earlier tension between them had abated.

"According to the parchments my father translated in his journal, the Rephaim are demonic spirits— literally *spirits of the deceased*. They are the offspring of a group of angels, called the *Nephilim* — 'the fallen ones' — and human women."

"You said *are*, Paul."

"That's right, Nathan. Although these giants, as they are called in the Old Testament, were destroyed in the Noahic Flood, they are also spiritual beings and therefore they never die."

"I knew it!" exclaimed Gabriella. She picked up the advertisement Nathan had brought with him and jabbed the paper with her finger. "We're talking about the Antichrist!"

"The Antichrist!" Nathan felt as if the wind had been knocked out of him. He hadn't even considered such a possibility. It was mind-boggling . . . and frightening. Oddly, even as fear tried to overcome him, he felt exhilarated.

The strangeness of the whole situation brought to mind something he'd told an old college chum one night after they'd consumed a great deal of beer. "I was born old, and I'm going to die an 'old, young man,'" he'd drunkenly prophesied that evening in the Rathskeller. His friend had laughed and replied, "Nathan, you're the only person I know who is so serious about life that you aren't afraid to mock it with the total abandon and ambivalence of a true Stoic." The contradiction in terms hadn't been lost on him.

His whole life had been one continual effort to balance the conflicting emotions that constantly whirled around inside his head, like a dust devil scourging the plains of Kansas. There were moments when he felt as if he'd spent a lifetime desperately searching for the Holy Grail, even though by the time he'd turned twenty-five he'd all but decided the Holy Grail wasn't all that holy. And there were other times when he thought of himself as the character from *Scaramouche* who had been born with the gift of laughter and the sense that the world was mad. Unfortunately, the older he got, the more the gift of laughter that he'd indeed been born with had been overwhelmed by a growing sense of unease that the world was in fact truly mad.

Before his encounter with the priest at Chartres, he'd spent many a night in introspective analysis, trying to find the gift he was certain he'd lost somewhere along the Yellow Brick Road of his life. Like Dorothy after she'd fallen asleep in the poppy field, forgetting where she was and what it was she was looking for, he had been fearful he was living in a dreamworld and that there was no "good witch of the North" to rescue him from his deadly slumber.

Nevertheless, something rooted deep down in the depths of his soul wouldn't let him give up his quest. And it was his conversation with the priest that had finally enabled him to identify the "something" as his search for a truth on which he could rest his soul.

"Pay attention, big brother," chided Gabriella. "We're getting some heavy-duty revelation here."

"Sorry, sis."

"As I was saying, the Old Testament is full of types," Gabriella explained once again, this time for Nathan's benefit. "Either Christ or Antichrist. Perhaps the most blatant example of an individual who foreshadowed the Antichrist was Nimrod."

"The rebel," muttered Paul.

"He was responsible for establishing a great confederacy in revolt against God," she continued. "Don't you see?"

"No," Nathan admitted, "I don't. Why does this guy Nimrod foreshadow the Antichrist?"

"Some archaeologists believe Nimrod was the founder of Babylon," Paul explained. "Others associate him with the legendary Gilgamesh. When he convinced the people they should build a ziggurat whose top would reach to Heaven, he was trying to create a center of unity from which he could establish a world empire — an earthly empire that would stand in opposition to the spiritual authority of God. The symbol of his rebellion was the Tower of Babel."

"So Satan was attempting even then to raise up a universal ruler of men," Nathan concluded, the sudden understanding slamming against his psyche. For he realized something neither Paul nor Gabriella had seen yet. However, he had one more bit of information to uncover before he could tell them the real reason he'd shown them the advertisement. If he was right, the information was going to devastate his sister. It was going to change all their lives.

"We've got a lot of work to do," he said, standing quickly, drawing back into himself lest they see too much in his eyes.

XX

The hallway of the Halcyon Building seemed deathly quiet to Nathan. It was just after midnight, the first minutes of Monday morning. He'd chosen this time to steal into the building because he was fairly certain everyone would be asleep, including Benny, the doorman.

Nathan smiled as he crept by the old man's office and heard him snoring. When he'd discovered that the old man ordered out coffee and donuts every night at 11 from the all-night deli down the street, he'd given the delivery boy a five-dollar bill and told him he was an old friend of Benny's who hadn't seen him in a long time. The kid shrugged his shoulders and handed over the bag. Then he'd slipped a sleeping pill into the coffee, so Benny would be out only a couple of hours. When he awoke, he'd be so embarrassed he fell asleep, he wouldn't tell anybody.

Nathan was sweating as he stepped into the elevator. He'd never broken into someone's home before. But this wasn't really like breaking in, he kept telling himself. Joel Goldman, the former tenant, had been dead almost a month, according to what he'd discovered at the County Records Building. And there was no new tenant by the name of Yuri ben Raphah listed. The clincher, however, came when the girl at County Records told him the apartment had *always* been leased in the name of a corporation — Rainbow International. And that was the name of the corporation he'd heard mentioned in his father's office by the man he now knew to be Vaughn Aurochs.

On a hunch, he'd called information and discovered that there was still a phone connected in Goldman's apartment. Just before he left Gabriella's, he'd dialed the number and let it ring for a full minute before hanging up. He didn't want any surprises when he arrived.

Everything was finally coming together. A year and a half of tracking down leads in Europe, and six months of research in three of the world's biggest libraries, coupled with what he'd learned from Paul Kingman, was about to pay off. Only he wasn't so sure he was happy about it, because the information he'd uncovered was going to ruin his father.

And that was why he hadn't told Paul and Gabriella everything he knew.

He'd purposely folded the newspaper clipping so they wouldn't see that the advertisement had been placed by Rainbow International. He wanted to have all the facts straight before he dropped the bombshell in his sister's lap.

He was also curious as to why the enigmatic silver-haired stranger who called himself Yuri ben Raphah was staying in an apartment owned by Rainbow Internationl. If Yuri was indeed trying to help Paul, why was he living in the enemy camp? And how did he have such detailed knowledge of events that had taken place over three millennia ago? None of it made any sense.

Not to mention that Paul's cryptic words kept swirling through his mind: *". . . then you can tell me if you think Mr. Raphah was a hologram come to life."* What the heck had he meant by that?

The elevator stopped, and the door opened onto the small anteroom of the penthouse suite. Nathan stepped out and wiped his sweating palms on his pants, then reached into his pocket for the key. He still had a few favors owed him from his days as Senator McDaniel's political advisor, and he'd been using them up rapidly this past week.

His hands were trembling as he put the key in the door.

He stepped into the apartment quickly and quietly closed the door behind, then expelled a deep breath. No one would hear him. He was at the top of the building, and this was the only apartment on the floor.

Surprisingly the apartment wasn't as dark as he'd expected it to be. The sky was cloudless, and the curtains were pulled back from a large plate-glass window. The nearly full moon filled the living room with a soft, translucent light, reminding him of a huge, flawed pearl.

Although he felt certain no one had any idea he was here, he didn't want to take a chance of being discovered by turning on the lights. He removed a flashlight from his hip pocket and played the tiny beam of light over the room. When it landed on an obsidian table, he walked forward to get a closer look.

He whistled when he saw the first-edition Gutenberg. Even though it was only half of the Bible, the Old Testament, it was easily worth several million dollars. He wondered why such a valuable object was not better protected.

He muttered sudden profanity, feeling nauseous. "How could I be so stupid?"

He raced to the front door, his heart beating furiously, and played the light over the frame. More curses came from his mouth when he saw it — there was an alarm. Hurriedly he used the flashlight to trace the wires to the small plate on the wall, then sagged against it and breathed a sigh of relief. The tiny lights in the panel were dark. The alarm was not armed. Evidently Yuri ben Raphah, whoever he was, was not afraid of burglars. Nathan chuckled at the thought sourly. *He* was a burglar now.

He walked back to the table and picked up a newspaper lying folded next to the Gutenberg Bible. He shined the light on it and frowned. It was an obituary, and the photograph was circled in red. He read it rapidly, then muttered, "Gotcha!" At the bottom, also in red lettering, were scribbled the cryptic words: *"Must tell the sons about the fathers."*

Paul stared at the Monday morning traffic through the window of the cab, then looked at his watch. It was 9:45. *Perfect,* he thought. *I'll get there just as the bank opens.*

At two minutes to 10 he stepped out of the cab onto the curb in front of his father's bank. He paid the cabby, giving him a healthy tip. The warm sunshine felt refreshing on his back, and he stared at his reflection mirrored in the glass façade. "Not bad for almost thirty," he muttered, straightening the wrinkles out of his gray pinstripe suit as he strolled over to a newspaper stand.

He had a few minutes before the bank opened, so he bought a copy of the *Post* and scanned the front page. His eyes stopped stark-still on an item at the bottom.

COUNCIL ON ORGANIZED RELIGION
ANNOUNCES JUNE MEETING

Bishop Andrew McCarthy, Archbishop of the Catholic Diocese for the District of Columbia, announced today that the Council on Organized Religion has chosen the Day of Pentecost to hold its first meeting. "We intend to bring together leaders from as many religions in America as possible," McCarthy said when reached by telephone at his office, "in the interest of fostering a more unified attitude toward organized religion." Attending will be representatives from some two hundred different religious organizations, including many that more traditional denominations label cults. McCarthy, one of the chief organizers of the June conference, added, "If we are to achieve our vision for the twenty-first century, that of a global community, then we here in America must immediately begin to develop a religious orientation that focuses on love rather than theological differences."

Paul stopped reading and looked up. An idea had suddenly come to him. The security guard inside the bank changed the "Closed" sign to "Open" and unlocked the door. Paul looked at his watch. It was exactly 10 o'clock. Bankers were nothing if not punctual. He folded the paper and tucked it under his arm, smiling. He knew now how he was going bring the existence of the parchments to light and keep his father's name untarnished.

"Beautiful morning, isn't it," he said as he passed the security guard.

"That it is, sir," the older man replied, returning Paul's smile.

Paul strode to the desk labeled Information and asked the girl for the location of the safe-deposit boxes.

"Do you have a box with us, Mr. —"

"Kingman. No, but my father did. He died three weeks ago, and I'm just now getting around to putting everything in order."

"Oh, I see. Just a moment please." She picked up the phone and dialed an extension. After a brief conversation she said, "Mr. Hillary will be with you in a moment."

Paul waited impatiently, anxious to see what was in his father's box.

"Mr. Kingman?"

Paul turned. "Yes."

The man stuck out his hand. "I'm Mr. Hillary. I understand your father had a safe-deposit box with us. And he passed away?"

Paul nodded. "That's correct."

"Well, if you'll just follow me, you can fill out the necessary paperwork."

Twenty minutes later they were standing inside the vault holding the safe-deposit boxes. "Someone will be outside when you're finished," said Mr. Hillary. "Just let them know if you wish to continue the rental."

"Thank you. I will."

Paul stared at the locked box, his heart beating rapidly. It looked awfully small. He ran his hands over the smooth metal. It felt cold and made him shudder. "I'll bring you some cherry blossoms," he mumbled, suddenly remembering his father loved the pink-and-white flowers.

He pulled out the key his father had left him and inserted it into the lock. "Well, here goes," he muttered. He opened the lid and stared dumbfoundedly at a perfectly empty box.

"I need to see him, Sarah," said Nathan adamantly, "and I need to see him *now*." He was standing in the outer office of his father's Senate chambers. It was just after 8 A.M., and the Senate building was relatively quiet. But he knew his father had been up and hard at work since before dawn. That was his style.

Sarah stared up at him with a bemused look on her face. "You know, Nathan, you two are very much alike," she said as she scanned the Senator's daily schedule. "You both demand things when you should ask for them and ask for things you should demand. It must be something in the McDaniel bloodline."

Nathan managed a half-smile. "I'm sorry, Sarah. It's just that I have something important to discuss with him, and it can't wait."

"That's what everybody says."

"I know, but I'm his *son*."

Sarah shook her head and chuckled. "Now that's a first. The way you two went at it the last time you were here, I thought it would be another two years before I saw you again."

Nathan grimaced. "I guess I had that coming, didn't I?"

Sarah nodded and smiled, then winked. "But you're too good-looking for me to hold a grudge. Now, go on in before I change my mind and start acting like a woman who's the secretary to one of the most important men on the Hill. And when the Senator asks you why I didn't buzz him, tell him you asked me to get you some coffee."

Nathan looked perplexed. "I did?"

Sarah stood up and replied, "Yes, you did. And I'm on my way to get it for you right now. You've only got about twenty minutes before your father has to be on the floor. They're voting on one of his bills today, and he wants to be there to make sure nothing goes wrong. So make the time count."

Nathan smiled and said, "Thanks, Sarah, I will. And I don't care what they say about you, you're still the best in my book." He gave her a wink of his own just before he stepped into his father's inner sanctum.

Senator David McDaniel was sitting in the leather chair behind his massive desk and had his back turned to the door. He was so immersed in what he was reading that he didn't hear the door open and close and wasn't aware that anyone else was in the room with him until he heard his son's voice behind him.

"Father, we have to talk," said Nathan, trying to muster the courage of Joshua at the battle of Jericho.

Startled by the unexpected intrusion on his privacy, the Senator swiveled in his chair and glared at his son. Without taking his eyes off his visitor, he casually opened the drawer in front of him and placed the papers he was reading inside, then closed the drawer. "Why didn't Sarah let me know you were here? No, never mind. You don't have to answer that. She's probably off getting you coffee, right?"

Nathan nodded and tried to keep the surprise off his face.

"Don't look so shocked. Sarah uses that ploy whenever someone I should speak to but probably would put off arrives without an appointment. She knows it's the best way to circumvent my rules without making me angry at her."

"I guess she knows you pretty well after fifteen years."

The Senator grunted. "That's more than I can say for you, unfortunately."

Nathan sat down in the chair across from his father and matched the infamous penetrating gaze some said reminded them of the look in an adder's eyes just before it struck its prey. "I didn't come here to argue with you, Father."

"No? Then what did you come here for?"

Nathan sighed. "To try one final time to reason with you."

McDaniel sat back in the chair and appraised his son with unforgiving eyes. "Oh, really . . . What exactly is it that you think I'm being unreasonable about? And don't tell me it's about the Kronos Corporation, because I no longer have any interest in that company. You can verify that by checking the public record."

"We both know that wouldn't matter anyway, don't we? And besides, that's not the real issue."

"Oh? Tell me, what is, then?"

"What's your relationship with Vaughn Aurochs . . . and with Rainbow International?"

"Before I answer that, you tell me why my business affairs are suddenly so important to you. You left here in a huff two years ago, after making some wild accusations about me at a very important luncheon. One that I arranged for you to speak at — acting as my proxy, I might add — so that you could begin laying the foundation for my Presidential aspirations, not to disparage and humiliate me. Since then I haven't heard a peep out of you . . . Until now." The Senator's eyes sparkled with indignation. "Out of the blue you show up, unannounced, twice in one week, and demand information about matters that don't concern you any longer . . . and you expect *me* to be *reasonable!*"

His father had not raised his voice one bit, but Nathan knew he was being raked over the coals. No, a better analogy was that of being expertly flayed by a razor-sharp, double-edged sword. The victim didn't feel the pain until it was too late to do anything about it.

The Senator was not only well-known for his polemic oratorical skills, but for his stinging rebukes as well. Many who'd experienced them firsthand said it felt like David McDaniel used words the same way the ancient Romans used the scourge. Now Nathan understood their analogy. Even though this wasn't the first time he'd been on the receiving end of his father's verbal punishment, he'd never felt the full force and effect until today.

Nonetheless, he was determined not to respond to his father's demagoguery. If he did, he would have no chance at all to break through the barrier that separated them. As it was, it was going to be very difficult, considering what he had come to say. "I was in your office the night you and Vaughn Aurochs had your little *tete-a-tete*, and I overheard you discussing his plans for Rainbow International. I've been doing quite a bit of research since I left the States, and now it's all starting to come together."

Anger flared in the Senator's eyes. "You spied on me! Who do you think you are?"

"Your former campaign manager and right-hand man . . . and your son. In both capacities I have always had a great deal of interest and concern for what you are doing . . . Especially since you are an elected representative who is supposed to be serving his constituency and not his own financial and political interests."

"How dare you judge me."

"I'm not judging you, Father. I am merely expressing my belief that I think there are times when your judgment is clouded by your political aspirations. When Mother died in the accident, something inside you changed dramatically. You withdrew from all emotional attachments, including those with Gabriella and me. All of your energy and time went into your work. You became obsessed with power, and for nearly twenty-five years you've had no compunction about manipulating those around you to achieve your goals." Nathan paused, then added softly, "It was almost as if you didn't want to acknowledge or accept Mother's death."

McDaniel was incredulous. "You have no idea what you're talking about, Nathan. I loved your mother deeply. Her death devastated me. And for your information, I am not obsessed with power." The Senator sat forward and gave his son a penetrating, caustic look. "Why is it you have such disdain for anyone who sets lofty goals and achieves them? What is so offensive to you about wanting to be the best?"

"That's not the issue, Father, and you know it."

"What *is* the issue then? Altruism?"

"In a way, yes."

"Wake up and read the handwriting on the wall, Nathan," the Senator said scornfully. "If anyone has lost something, it's your whole generation. Collectively you've lost the drive to excel, to overcome all odds in order to succeed. That's what made this country great. And, I might add, that's what is making Japan a nation to be reckoned with. Unfortunately, you and others like you consider ambition a filthy word instead of an admirable character trait."

His father paused, then added, "Besides, in spite of what you might think, the truth is, the majority of humanity are like sheep — they need shepherds to watch over them and make sure they don't get devoured by wolves. Fifteen years as a Senator has taught me that, if nothing else."

"Well, at least we agree on something. The problem is, a number of wolves have crept into the flock disguised as sheep . . . and the shepherds are like greedy dogs that never have enough. They are shepherds who look to their own way — every one for his own gain."

Nathan paused momentarily, suddenly overcome by a strange sensation. His whole body was tingling. He felt like he was on fire — on the inside. And somehow he knew it wasn't simply adrenaline.

Before his father could respond with a rebuttal, a veritable fountain of words gushed forth from Nathan's lips like a geyser. "Woe to the shepherds who feed themselves! Shouldn't the shepherds feed the flock? You eat the fat of the land and clothe yourselves with wool — you slaughter the fatling, but you don't feed the flock. You have failed to strengthen the weak, and the sick you have failed to heal. You neglect to bring those back who are driven away, nor have you sought out those who are lost. You have ruled them with force and cruelty, so that they have become scattered and have become food for the beasts of the land. Because of this, it is time for judgment between sheep and sheep and rams and goats, between the fat and lean sheep. The flock shall be delivered from the mouths of the shepherds; they shall no longer be food for the wicked."

Nathan stopped speaking as abruptly as he'd started. The silence in the room was as thick and heavy as the Persian carpets he'd seen last night in Joel Goldman's apartment. *What in the world was that all about?* he wondered as he stared at his father in amazement.

Maybe it had something to with what Gabriella had shared with him the other night when he'd asked her if there was anyone of importance in the Bible with the same name as his. She'd smiled and told him about his namesake, the prophet in the Old Testament who was King David's trusted adviser. The Lord had revealed to the prophet in a dream that He didn't want the Temple built by David, but by his son Solomon. And later, when David sent Uriah the Hittite to his death in battle so he could marry Uriah's wife, Bathsheba, it was Nathan who admonished the King for his indiscretion by telling the King a parable. Perhaps there really was something to all this stuff about a person's name being God-given and indicative of character.

Finally, after what seemed like an eternity, but was actually only a couple of minutes, his father spoke. "Whatever happened to you in Europe has affected your ability to think and speak rationally. I suggest you seek professional help."

Nathan suddenly felt exhausted. He'd been up all night studying his Bible and the information he'd been collecting. He'd come here today not sure of what he was going to say, but certain he had to make a final, all-out effort to get through to his father. It was obvious he hadn't succeeded. Nevertheless, as much as he wanted to simply get up and leave, he couldn't. He'd done that two years ago, but he was a different person today. He felt compelled to make one last attempt before he acknowledged defeat. He decided to try something that was still new to him, something he had to believe by faith might work. "I'm not sure what just happened myself, Father," he said haltingly. "But I do know this — I believe God is trying to use me to get through to you."

His father's eyes lost their accusatory luster, and the scowl slowly disappeared from his face.

"I'm not sure why, but I feel strongly that I need to tell you a brief story. Maybe it will help you understand what I've been trying to say."

McDaniel glanced at his watch. "Make it quick. In ten minutes I have to be on the Senate floor."

Nathan plunged ahead, inexplicably feeling a sudden sense of hope there just might be a chance for him to breach the chasm that had grown between the two of them over the years. "Thirteen hundred years before the birth of Christ a Mesopotamian soothsayer by the name of Balaam was riding on his donkey through a vineyard when the animal abruptly balked and refused to go on. The animal balked two more succeeding times, and each time Balaam struck the donkey to turn her back onto the road. After the third time, however, the Lord opened the mouth of the animal and she said, 'What have I done to you that you have struck me these three times?'"

Nathan could tell by the sudden change in his father's expression that he had the Senator's attention. It was obvious he'd caught his father completely off guard. And that realization fueled his resolve.

"Balaam held a brief conversation with his mount and then, finally, discovered the reason for the donkey's extraordinary behavior."

"What was it?" whispered McDaniel in an uncharacteristic display of curiosity.

"The Lord opened Balaam's eyes, and he saw the Angel of the Lord standing in his way with a drawn sword in his hand. Balaam immediately fell on his face, and the Angel of the Lord spoke to him and said, 'Why have you struck your donkey these three times? Behold, I have come out to stand against you because your way is perverse before me. The donkey saw me and turned aside from me these three times. If she had not turned aside from me, surely I would also have killed you by now and let her live.'"

The Senator's eyes were hooded as he asked, "What does this have to do with you and me?"

Nathan sat forward and replied, "You're going to have to do some reading to get the complete answer to that question, but I will tell you this much: Balaam was a hireling prophet. His desire was to create a market for the gift God had given him. According to Biblical scholars, this is what is meant by the phrase 'the way of Balaam' or 'Balaam's error.' The attitude is the chief characteristic of one who is a false teacher, a wolf in sheep's clothing, if you will."

"You're talking gibberish again, Nathan. Religious mumbo jumbo. Just like you did last week. What's gotten into you?"

Nathan chuckled. "I'm not sure you're ready for the answer to that just yet."

McDaniel looked at his watch a final time. "Fine," he said dismissively. "Make your point. We're out of time."

"Not quite."

"What?"

"Never mind. My point is this: Balaam's error was that he could only see the *natural*, what Gabriella calls the *terrestrial*, morality. Like all false prophets — men and women who secretly initiate and promulgate destructive heresies — he was ignorant of the higher — Gabriella calls this the *celestial* — morality of vicarious atonement."

"Leave your sister out of this. She's not the one who's gone off the deep end."

"You have no idea."

"What's that supposed to mean?"

Nathan stood up to leave. "It means, Father, that you've never really taken the time to discover what Gabriella and I are all about because you've been too busy building your political empire. It also means that I regret allowing you to manipulate me for so long and using me to further your own ends, even to the point of convincing me that lying to my sister was in her best interests."

McDaniel stood up and started to say something, but Nathan cut him off. "Don't bother giving me one of your practiced retorts, Father. It won't work anymore. I know better now. God help me, it's taken me two years to come to grips with myself, but I do know better now, and nothing you can say will change that."

He opened the door just as Sarah began speaking on the intercom: "Senator, it's time—" When she saw Nathan standing in the doorway and the look on the Senator's face behind him, she stopped abruptly.

Nathan turned and added, "Think about Balaam, Father. You and he have a lot in common. Oh, and by the way, there's one thing I forgot to mention. Balaam's name in Hebrew literally means 'a thing swallowed' or 'ruin.' However, the Greek translation is more appropriate. It means 'subverter or devourer of the people.'"

XXI

Gabriella was working in her studio when she heard someone pounding on her front door. She frowned and looked at her watch. It was just after 11, and she wasn't expecting anyone. Reluctantly — she was in the middle of a creative burst of energy — she headed downstairs, casting a furtive glance at the easel as she went out the door. This was going to be one of her best works.

"Paul!" she said when she opened the door. "What are you doing here?"

"Can I come in?"

"Of course." Gabriella closed the door behind them. "This is a surprise."

"It's a surprise for me too."

"How about some coffee? I was just about to make some," she lied, realizing he was extremely upset and needed to talk.

He nodded, then looked around at the living room. It was spacious and uncluttered. The floors were polished hardwood, just like in his father's house, only there were no rugs. A couch and love seat dominated the center of the room. In front of them was a small coffee table on top of which sat a bronze sculpture. There were also several magazines dedicated to art and design. And a Bible. An enormous stone fireplace dominated the far wall, and bookshelves banked either side. Against another wall stood a large, antique armoire with a stained-glass front. Inside were numerous miniature porcelain figurines.

"What do you collect?" he asked, gesturing to the armoire while following Gabriella into the kitchen.

"Angels." She opened the refrigerator and pulled out a bag of fresh Java coffee beans, which she poured into a coffee grinder.

Paul sat at the oak dining table and watched her work. He shook his head in amazement. "Angels?"

"Uh huh. I've been collecting them since I was sixteen. I have one from almost every country in the world. "

"That's a lot of angels."

"Not as many as there are in Heaven."

Paul released a weary sigh. "No, I guess not." He stared into space.

Gabriella busied herself before turning and asking, "How do you like it?"

"Huh?"

"Your coffee."

"Oh. Lots of cream, no sugar."

Gabriella wanted desperately to ask him what was wrong, but she knew it would be better to let him tell her in his own time. "I take mine the same way."

Paul looked at her as if he hadn't heard her. "They weren't there," he said woodenly.

"What?"

"The parchments. I went to my father's bank this morning and opened his safe-deposit box. It was empty."

Gabriella frowned. "I don't understand."

"My father left me a key along with his journal. The key was to a safe-deposit box. After I read the journal I was certain that's where he'd stored the parchments for safekeeping."

"Oh, I see." Gabriella placed the ground coffee in a filter, then turned on the coffeemaker and filled it with water. As the coffee started to brew, she sat down across from Paul. "Where else could they be?"

Paul shrugged. "I have no idea."

"Well, at least you have the translation stored in Sam, don't you?"

Paul nodded. "But that's not enough."

"Why?"

He sighed. "Because the Council on Organized Religion will want proof . . . hard evidence that the translations in my father's journal are not just something he concocted to make a name for himself."

Gabriella blinked. "The Council on Organized Religion? You've lost me."

Paul reached inside his coat pocket, pulled out a folded section of newspaper, and handed it to her. She read the clipping, then asked, "What does this meeting have to do with the parchments?"

Paul sniffed. The aroma from the brewing coffee was reviving him. "I interviewed Bishop McCarthy, the man mentioned in that news release, last fall for an article I was writing on AIDS, and we hit it off pretty well. He'd read a number of my previous articles and liked them. When I saw that announcement in this morning's paper, I hoped I might have an opportunity to present my father's find before the Council . . . and to protect his name. But now . . ." He shrugged, letting the sentence hang.

Gabriella poured them each a cup of coffee, adding generous amounts of cream to both. She handed Paul his cup, then sat down again with hers and took a sip. She smiled when Paul said, "Hey, there's cinnamon in this!"

"Like it?"

"It's great. And here I've been drinking plain old instant all these years. I didn't know what I was missing."

Gabriella felt immediately satisfied with herself over pleasing him with such a small thing. "A woman's touch adds spice to a lot of things," she said wryly, surprised at the implication of her words.

Paul stared into her eyes intently, then put his cup aside and took her hand. "I think I'm falling in love with you," he said abruptly.

Gabriella felt her face flush. She leaned back in her chair and took a deep breath to calm the ever-present butterflies.

"You probably think I'm crazy," he continued softly, "but I wasn't kidding the other night when I said that I felt like I've always known you . . . like you've always been with me inside here," he added, tapping the side of his head. "Now the imagined has become the reality . . . And reality is much better than the image ever was." He paused, then added, "I've been waiting my entire adult life to meet a woman like you."

His eyes were looking straight inside her. What should she say? She swallowed several times because her mouth had suddenly gone dry, then said, "Paul, I need to tell you about Robert."

"Robert?" He rested his elbows on the tabletop and took a sip of coffee. It was lukewarm, and the flavor had suddenly gone flat.

Gabriella fidgeted. "Two years after I returned from Europe, a week after my twenty-first birthday, I met Robert and fell in love. One night we went to dinner to celebrate the sale of one of my paintings." She looked out the window and stared at the cherry trees. The blossoms, so full and colorful just last week, were already wilting and falling off the trees. "We both drank too much. Afterwards we came back here for a nightcap and ended up in my studio, upstairs, on the couch. Nathan's been sleeping there now — until he finds his own place."

Paul listened, intensely interested in Gabriella's story. He realized he was hearing the answer to the unspoken question that had remained in his mind — and in his heart — since he'd kissed her in his office.

"One thing led to another," she continued, her voice distant, as if she were talking about someone else, someone who was only a memory. "And before I knew it we were about to make love — my first time, I might add — when suddenly a light exploded inside my head." She leveled her gaze at Paul, searching for the right explanation, wanting desperately for him to understand what Robert hadn't. "It was like someone had pointed one of those huge spotlights used to advertise grand openings of K-Marts and Wal-Marts at my brain.

"I was suddenly sober . . . completely and absolutely sober! When I realized what I'd almost done, I jumped up and ran into the bathroom. Robert was taken completely by surprise. He was still drunk and therefore found it very difficult to understand my explanation of instant sobriety."

Paul suppressed a smile. He bet it had been hard on old Robert.

"I wrapped myself up in a towel and came out of the bathroom. I was shaking all over. I wasn't quite sure what was happening. Nevertheless, I tried to explain to Robert that although I didn't consider myself a prude, my virginity was, and always has been, very important to me." She stared at Paul, searching his eyes for any hint that he found what she was saying ludicrous. She was relieved to see only genuine curiosity . . . And compassion.

"Robert asked me what on earth I was talking about, and the harder I tried to tell him how I felt, the more difficult it became. After about twenty minutes of shouting, Robert left."

"What happened after he sobered up?"

Gabriella shrugged. "He wouldn't return my phone calls. After a week of trying to contact him at both his work and his home, I gave up. Needless to say, I was devastated." Her voice was full of emotion. "You see, I really thought we were in love."

"And that's why you keep your guard up — why you always pull back from me whenever I try to get close to you?"

She nodded. "I made a decision then and there that until God spoke to me and told me differently, I wasn't going to get involved. Not with anyone. At the time the prospect of remaining single indefinitely didn't exactly appeal to me, but I got used to it. After a year or so I didn't even think about it anymore. My work — and my relationship with the Lord — were about all I could handle."

"You mean you haven't been out with anyone in nearly seven years? Not even *one* date?"

"That's right. For almost four years I threw myself into my work and developed a very disciplined lifestyle. I'd get up before sunrise, pray for an hour, then run a couple of miles before having breakfast. By the time the sun came up, I was at my easel. Most of what I sold at Antonio's came from the time period in my life that I now call 'my time in the wilderness of doubt.' You probably think it odd that a Senator's daughter behaved that way. But it's the truth."

Paul didn't reply. He was overwhelmed by her explanation.

She toyed with the handle of her cup. Sunlight pooled on the table and turned her skin the color of warm honey. "I've relived that night in my mind a thousand times. And I always end up trying to figure out how I could have gone from inebriation to stone-cold sober in the blink of an eye."

"And?"

"And I tried to paint my answers. Nothing else seemed to work for me."

Paul smiled reassuringly. "It may surprise you, but I think I understand."

"You do?" Her pulse quickened.

"In a way I made a similar decision. I just didn't go about it the way you did."

"What do you mean?"

"Well, writing has been everything to me. I live for the next story. And in each article I've ever written there is a piece of me. I guess you might say that I've been working out who I am by writing about people and circumstances that mirror my own quest for the Holy Grail."

"Working out your salvation . . ." mumbled Gabriella, getting sudden insight into what the Scripture meant.

"What?"

"It's from Philippians. The Scripture says: '. . . work out your own salvation with fear and trembling, for it is God who works in you both to will and to do of His good pleasure.'"

"What made you think of that particular Scripture?"

"I never got my answer by painting. It wasn't until I began to study the Bible in earnest that I finally realized it was the Holy Spirit who had touched me that night and kept me from doing something I'm sure I would have regretted."

"Oh, I see . . . I think."

"Can I get you some fresh coffee?" she asked, not sure she wanted to have this discussion right now.

"No thanks. And don't change the subject. It's out of character." He studied her reaction, wondering why she was suddenly so nervous. "Explain what you mean by this Holy Spirit stuff and tell me how you *did* get your answer."

"I-cried-out-to-God-with-all-my-heart." She blurted the words so rapidly that it sounded like one long word. "And I begged Him to reveal Himself to me," she added, slowing, catching her breath.

"Well, tell me the rest," Paul urged, half wondering why he kept pushing her to tell him something he knew was going to stir up feelings he'd buried a long time ago.

She stood up. "I need some more coffee, even if you don't."

"Since you're up . . ." He lifted his cup toward her.

Gabriella refilled both their cups. She wrapped her hands around her mug, not sure why she was suddenly chilled despite all the sunlight splashing around the room. "Two years ago I was working on a particularly difficult piece. I'd been painting for several hours, and it was late at night. I was physically exhausted, but my mind was running a marathon. I couldn't unwind in the studio, so I went for a walk."

The memory was as real as if it had happened only last night. "It was June, and as you well know, normally the air would be filthy, gritty —"

"And it probably stank," interrupted Paul.

Gabriella nodded. "But on this particular night it was unusually cool. There were about a million stars in the sky. I was wearing jeans and a cotton top. There was a light breeze, but I wasn't the least bit chilly. As I walked, all my tension dissolved. When I'd started out, I had no particular direction; however, my legs seemed to have a will of their own and they carried me to the park."

"You mean the one across from my office?"

"Quite a coincidence, huh?"

"That's a long way to be walking at night, alone, in Death City."

"I know. I was startled when I realized what I'd done."

"Were you frightened?"

"That's the odd part. I wasn't. In fact, my first thought was how peaceful I felt, and my second was, What am I going to do now?"

"Well?" prodded Paul, intensely interested in the outcome of her story.

"The weather made the decision for me."

"How's that?"

"It started to rain. Not a downpour, mind you, but enough so that I had to run and stand under the trees at the edge of the park. While I was waiting for the rain to stop so I could flag down a cab, something unusual happened."

Paul leaned forward, his coffee forgotten again. The hairs on the back of his neck were standing straight up, and he felt an odd tingling sensation along his spine.

"Remember the night you cooked dinner for me and I told you about the cedars in Israel?"

He nodded.

"Well, standing there in the rain I was suddenly overcome by the distinct, pungent smell of those cedars."

"But there are no cedars in the park."

"I know. But I swear I was . . . *enveloped* is the only word I can think of . . . with the overwhelming fragrance. I closed my eyes, just like I'd done in Israel, so I could concentrate on the aroma. Immediately the same voice that had spoken to me in Israel spoke to me again."

Paul let out the breath he'd been holding. It came out sounding as if he'd been punched in the chest. "What did the voice say this time?"

"'I am the Great I Am. I have heard your prayers, and I shall guide you in the paths I have set before you. Do not be afraid, for there are none who can stand against Me.'"

"What happened after that?"

"I realized who was talking to me."

"Who?"

"When I was sixteen I asked one of the nuns at the Catholic school I attended about a voice that I'd always heard inside my head whenever I had difficult decisions to make. She quoted a Scripture to me, and that same Scripture flooded my mind that night in the park."

"Tell me."

"'For it is written: Who shall ascend into the hill of the Lord? Or who shall stand in His holy place? He that has clean hands and a pure heart; who has not lifted up his soul into vanity, nor sworn deceitfully. He shall receive the blessing from the Lord, and righteousness from the God of his salvation. This is the generation of them that seek Him, that seek His face.'"

"And you believe the voice that spoke to you in Israel, as well as the voice in the park, was the voice of God?"

Gabriella nodded, chewing her lip.

"But it just doesn't make any *sense*," he ventured, almost as if he were arguing with himself. "None of this makes any sense. My father's crime forty years ago, his connection with your father, our meeting, the missing parchments —"

"Paul," interrupted Gabriella softly. He stared at her with troubled eyes, and her heart went out to him. "Let me finish, and maybe it will make a little more sense."

"OK . . . I'm listening."

"I felt invigorated and full of peace simultaneously. I had my answer. When the rain stopped, I found a cab, and after I got home I took a steaming hot shower and made a large pot of coffee. Then I sat down on the divan with the Bible that had been Mother's and searched for about half an hour until I found the Scripture Sister Martha had quoted to me.

"I read it with new understanding and continued reading other Scriptures until just before dawn. The last one I read before falling asleep was the 22nd Psalm." She leapt to her feet, asking, "Would you like me to read it to you?"

Without waiting for his answer she ran and got the well-worn

Bible. Coming back into the kitchen she read aloud: "'I was cast upon you from the womb: you are my God from my mother's belly. Be not far from me; for trouble is near; for there is none to help. Many bulls have compassed me: strong bulls of Bashan have beset me around. They gaped upon me with their mouths, as a ravening and a roaring lion —'"

Paul interrupted her and finished the Scripture: "'I am poured out like water, and all my bones are out of joint: my heart is like wax; it is melted in the midst of my bowels. My strength is dried up like potsherd; and my tongue cleaves to my jaws; and you have brought me into the dust of death. For dogs have compassed me: the assembly of the wicked have enclosed me: they pierced my hands and my feet. I may tell all my bones: they look and stare upon me. They part my garments among them, and cast lots upon my vesture. But be you not far from me, O Lord: O my strength, hasten you to help me. Deliver my soul from the sword; my darling from the power of the dog. Save me from the lion's mouth: for you have heard me from the horn of the unicorn.'"

Gabriella listened, stunned that he knew it verbatim. "You know that Scripture by heart!"

There was a glazed look in Paul's normally sparkling eyes. "I spent eight years studying for my *Bar Mitzvah*. My father took charge of teaching me at home, supplementing what Rabbi Silverman taught me at school. He used to read to me every night from the *Torah*.

"After my *Bar Mitzvah* I never studied the *Torah* again." He felt tears in his eyes. "On my fifteenth birthday, the second anniversary of my *Bar Mitzvah*, my mother came into my room just before I went to sleep and read to me from the 22nd Psalm. She made it come alive as my father never had. And she told me that it had been sung by David after he'd had a vision of the Messiah hanging, torn and bleeding, on the cross.

"I was confused because we Jews believe that the coming of the *mashiyach* is future. When I asked her about it, she just smiled and said, 'Someday, Paul, you will understand that Jesus *was* and *is* the Messiah — past, present, and future tense.' When she leaned over and kissed me on the forehead, I felt her tears on my cheek." Paul wiped the wetness from his face with the back of his hand. "Two weeks later she was dead. I still miss her."

Gabriella went to him and slipped her arm around his neck. "I'm so sorry, Paul." She stroked his hair. "I never really knew my mother. Yet somehow I feel that had our mothers lived, they would be good friends."

Paul touched her arm. Her skin felt soft and warm, and her scent was cinnamon. "Thanks, Gabriella. That means a lot to me." He looked up into her sparkling eyes. "Now finish your story. I have a feeling there's a point to all this."

Gabriella stepped back and went over to the window, then picked up where she'd left off. "I fell asleep reading, but I only rested a few hours. When I woke up, just before sunrise, I rolled off the divan and knelt on the floor with my face on the rug and my arms outstretched. I prayed out loud with a joy in my heart that I'd never felt before. I even recall the exact words: 'I confess my sins and give my life to You, Lord . . . spirit, soul, and body. I pray earnestly that You will guide me in all things and that You will keep me safe in Your arms until I am able to walk in the fullness of what You have called me to do. Thank You for revealing Yourself to me.'"

Paul sat silent for several minutes, knowing something extraordinary had happened between him and Gabriella. He stood up, walked over to her, and put his arms around her. At his touch Gabriella turned to face him and nestled into his embrace. "I can't seem to get enough of this," he said, feeling like he didn't want to let go . . . ever.

"I know what you mean. When I'm with you, nothing else seems to matter. Yet, it's been so long since I've allowed myself to really *feel* that I'm not sure just what to do with the feelings." She tilted her head upward. "Does that make any sense?"

Paul responded by kissing her . . . deeply, passionately. Even though Gabriella did not resist this time, she did not let go completely. As always, something inside held back. This time, however, it was Paul who broke the contact.

"Gabriella," he said when he'd regained his breath, "I want you so bad that I ache. But I also want this relationship to be unique." He stared into the jade-green depths of her eyes. He was caught in a whirlpool of emotion.

"Unlike you, I *haven't* abstained for the past few years," he continued, holding nothing back. "But something is always missing. I meet a woman that I'm attracted to, we have dinner several times, maybe see a show or go to the theater. And then we end up in bed. It's fun, it's acceptable in our society, perhaps even *expected*. In spite of that, I always feel even more empty when it's over than before."

"Paul —"

"Shhh. Let me finish. This isn't easy for me."

Gabriella's eyes glistened.

"I don't mean to imply that I'm some kind of lady-killer. I'm not. I can count on one hand the number of women I've been with in the past ten years. What I'm trying to say is that I'm a little frightened of how I feel too. I want to love you, but I'm not sure I know *how* to love. I don't have much of a track record in that area."

"Neither do I."

Paul stepped back and stared out the window at the cherry trees. It was several minutes before he spoke. "I'd like to see your studio," he said abruptly.

"And I'd like to show it to you."

She took his hand as they climbed the stairs. She felt light-headed, almost giddy. "You know, you're only the third man I've allowed to see my studio."

"Oh? Besides Robert and —"

"Nathan."

"I'm flattered."

"You should be."

When Paul stepped into the room, he was hit full force by the abundance of light. The room was alive with color so vibrant he imagined he could *feel* the different pigments. He released a low

257

whistle. "This is incredible! And it's so different from downstairs
. . . Like night and day."

Gabriella laughed musically. "Light is the essence — the master — of art, and color is its servant. Now you know why I gave
the lecture I did the day we met. Without light we are nothing."

Paul was rocked with insight. The words his mother had said
about what she'd inscribed on the back of her picture flooded
back to him: "Without love we are nothing." Light . . . Life . . .
Love. Incredible!

He turned to face Gabriella and took her by the shoulders. "I
know what I have to do now," he said.

"What?" She was dazed by his sudden change of demeanor,
yet excited by what she heard in his voice.

"I'll tell you Friday."

"Friday?"

Paul grinned. "It's my thirtieth birthday *and* Passover. I want
you and Nathan to share it with me. I have something very special in mind."

Across the street, in a red convertible, sat the pale man with
snakeskin boots. It was early afternoon now, and he was
extremely uncomfortable. The bright daylight irritated him.
However, he knew better than to disobey. His master did not tol-
erate failure.

Paul came out of the house, but the pale man didn't move. It
was the Senator's son he was interested in. He'd been following
Nathan for several days, but had lost him late last night on the
other side of town, near the park.

He watched the cab pick up Paul, then stared at the second
story of Gabriella's house with cold, malevolent eyes. He kept
waiting.

After Paul left, Gabriella wandered around, cleaning coffee
cups and thinking. So much had happened in such a short time

that she felt as if she were caught up in a whirlwind. She'd successfully doused the fiery emotions she'd experienced in her late teens and early twenties after her disastrous encounter with Robert. Now those embers had been rekindled, and she wasn't at all sure what she was going to do about it.

Work and God had taken the place of the men in her life for over seven years. Oh, there had been men who'd tried to pierce the veil she'd covered herself with, but none had been successful. Until now. Still, she couldn't quite put her finger on just what was so special about Paul Kingman . . . or why he made her feel the way she did.

Another thought nagged at her and intruded forcefully into her musings. Something had clicked in her mind when she and Paul read/recited Psalm 22. "Strong bulls of Bashan have beset me around . . . save me from the lion's mouth: for you have heard me from the horns of the unicorn."

Vaughn had told her he was born in China — in a village called Bashan. And the logo for his company was a unicorn. Not to mention that the translation of his mother's name meant the same thing. Coincidence? she wondered, the rational part of her mind rebelling at the possibility.

Abruptly she went to the bookshelves in the living room and searched for the book she wanted. "Aha!" She pulled the heavy book out and flipped it open, turning the pages rapidly until she found what she needed. She read several lines before mumbling, "It can't be! It can't be!"

She slammed the book shut, tucked it under her arm, and headed for the stairs. Nathan had told her that morning he was going out of town for a couple of days, but when she'd asked where he was going and why, all he would tell her was, "I'm tracking down some information on the elusive Vaughn Aurochs."

She'd felt uneasy, but he patted her hand and said, "Don't worry — it's no big deal. I just want to know more about the guy who sponsored my little sister's first one-woman show."

"Nathan McDaniel —"

"Gotta run, sis. See you Friday morning."

"At least tell me where I can reach you."

"You can't. But I'll give you the number where I'll be until 1 o'clock today."

Gabriella eyed a wall clock as she ran up to her studio. It was five till 1. She found the number she'd scribbled on the pad beside the phone.

"Please, God, let him still be there," she prayed as she dialed frantically.

XXII

Paul looked up into the clear night sky and sighed.

It was Passover. *Leil shimmurim.* The oldest of the Jewish festivals and the first of the seven major Hebraic yearly festivals, which also included Unleavened Bread, Firstfruits, Pentecost, Trumpets, Atonements, and finally Tabernacles.

The night of watching.

The time when Jews recall the birth of Israel's nationhood and the long years of travail which preceded it.

Pesach.

The night of the tenth plague of Pharaoh. The night on which the Lord smote all the firstborn of man and cattle in the land of Egypt at midnight.

It was also Paul's thirtieth birthday. "Joseph and David each began their reign at age thirty," he told the stars. "And Christ began His short but extremely fruitful ministry at the same age."

Paul blinked several times at the overwhelming thought. He was standing so close to the window in his living room that his breath left an indistinct, smoky-colored smudge on the otherwise clear pane of class.

He studied the heavens intently, focusing on the shimmering stars, as if they held the answer to his unspoken questions. The first full moon following the Spring Equinox had risen early, big and round. A soft red haze obscured the gray-black pockmarks, making it seem like a flawed celestial pearl.

Gabriella had told him Vaughn Aurochs had told her that according to Chinese lore, the rabbit lives in the moon and pounds out the elixir of life in its bowels. He'd looked at her skeptically as she'd added, "There are even some who believe the moon is the habitation of Satan."

A muffled knock at the door behind him made him pull his eyes and thoughts away from the blood-red moon. He squared his shoulders, then turned and walked across the living room to the front door. "Welcome to my *Seder*," he said as he opened it and ushered his two guests inside.

The park was deathly quiet.

Across the street, the red-tinged yellow-white light of the full moon reflected off the bronze skins of the two lions at the entrance to the Kronos Building, giving them an illusion of life. However, in the heart of the miniature forest the darkness was thick as day-old coffee.

Two men were busy with their preparations, oblivious to the deepening chill of the night. They both knew they had plenty of time. They didn't need to be ready until just before the stroke of 12.

The face of the man on the right, normally pale and gaunt, looked even more so in the strange moonlight. He was dressed in black. Had he not been moving, it would have been easy to think he was an escapee from a wax museum. As he wrestled with the makeshift wooden structure he was assembling, he spoke authoritatively to the man working with him. "Bring me the she-goat, Antonio . . . and make sure no one sees you."

Antonio glanced ruefully at his companion and nervously rubbed the ram's-head ring on his wedding finger. "Why tonight of all nights? And why here? We've never been this exposed before."

The man with the snakeskin boots stopped what he was doing for a moment and appraised the short, heavy-set Italian. "You know as well as I that we must never question the master's decisions. The lord of light has his reasons." He grasped the amulet hanging around his neck and held it in his left hand, adding forcefully, "And you are well aware of the consequences of disobedience."

Antonio shivered. "I'll get the goat."

Releasing the amulet, the man reached down into the shadows and picked up the first of two bundles he'd brought with him. He opened up the stained cloth covering and stared appreciatively at its contents. The light from the moon glinted off the sickle-shaped steel *khadga*, the ritual knife used in the sacrificial rites of the Hindu goddess Kali, consort of Siva.

He grasped the delicately crafted wooden handle, inlaid with gold and gemstones, and held the perfectly balanced knife up to the moonlight for scrutiny. He admired the long, gracefully curved blade, eyeing appreciatively the beautifully forged cutting edge of the ancient weapon. *Yes*, he thought, *tonight's ritual will be very special indeed*.

He smiled and licked his pale lips in anticipation, then replaced the ceremonial knife in its leather sheath, ignoring the indistinct whimper from the second bundle.

Gabriella laughed musically. "I'm so excited. This is going to be a birthday to remember," she said, studying the dining-room table. Paul had covered it with a bleached white tablecloth. There were four place settings, each with its own wine glass. He sat at the end next to the kitchen, and Gabriella sat on his right, Nathan on his left. In the center was a large pitcher of grape juice.

The chair at the other end, the head of the table, remained vacant. Paul's guests eyed it expectantly.

"I can't remember when I've seen my sister so enthused," said Nathan. "You'd think it was *her* birthday."

"Now, now . . . Be nice. You're not out of the doghouse yet," Gabriella responded.

"Did I miss something?" asked Paul.

"My sister is very upset with me for not telling her where I've been since Monday. She thinks I might be in some kind of danger."

Paul turned toward Gabriella. "Oh?"

"We'll talk about it later."

Paul shrugged, but made a mental note to follow up on her comment. "Tonight you're both in for a big surprise." His eyes mimicked the light from the fire burning brightly in the living-room hearth.

"I've never been to a Passover *Seder* before, traditional or otherwise," said Gabriella, eyeing her brother. "Have you, Nathan?"

Nathan chuckled. "No, I can't say that I have."

"In that case, let's begin," said Paul dramatically, rubbing his hands together.

The inside of the Kronos Building was dark when the Senator arrived. The limousine he'd taken dropped him off at the front entrance and sped off into the night.

The exterior of the twenty-story building was bathed in the soft, hazy, yellow-white light of the moon. Although the sky was clear and the moon full, the light reflecting off the windows seemed to be swallowed up by the surrounding darkness.

McDaniel scanned the façade of the building, not looking for anything in particular, simply admiring the eye-pleasing scene. The physical structure had been designed around the windows rather than vice versa. As a result every office had a panoramic view of the park. According to the *Washington Post*, the magnificent granite waterfall surrounded by the plethora of dwarf oak trees that lined the plaza in front of the brass lions qualified the imposing and subtly hypnotic structure as an "artistic compliment to the sometimes dry sterility of modernistic architectural design."

How far I've come in such a short time, thought McDaniel. *Vashti, my love, you would be proud.*

"Over here, Senator . . ." said a sepulchral voice from the shadows behind the waterfall, near the front entrance. Startled, the Senator searched the darkened area next to the bronze lions.

Vaughn stepped from the shadows as if he'd been part of the

darkness and had then taken on physical form before McDaniel's eyes. "You made good time," he said, glancing cursorily at his watch. "We have almost forty-five minutes to spare."

The Senator glared at him and replied brusquely, "You did say it was *urgent*."

Vaughn turned, saying, "So I did. Shall we go inside?"

The Senator was suddenly chilled. He wished now that he'd remembered to bring his overcoat. "Yes . . . I think that would be wise. We don't need to be calling attention to ourselves."

Vaughn remained silent.

"What do you mean we have forty-five minutes to spare?" asked McDaniel as an afterthought, looking at his own watch. "What's so special about midnight?"

"I have a surprise for you, Senator . . . One I think you'll find most interesting."

The slowly dwindling fire crackled softly as Paul cleared the table. When he was finished, all that remained were four glasses of grape juice — one at the empty head of the table — and three pieces of *matzoh*, the unleavened bread of the ritual.

Gabriella and Nathan watched him work.

He had taken care of the entire meal and had not allowed them to do a single thing except to sit back and enjoy.

"Paul, this is *your* birthday — we should be waiting on you hand and foot," Gabriella told him.

"Yeah . . . why the special treatment?" chimed in Nathan, pushing his seat back so he could stretch his legs.

Paul dismissed them with a wave of his hand. "Tonight I have chosen to take the place of a servant . . . and to honor the memory of someone very dear to me." He gestured at the empty chair, where the untouched cup of grape juice had remained all evening, and added, "The place you see with the empty chair and the special cup has been considered the place of Elijah. It was prophesied that Elijah would return to prepare the way of Messiah. It is therefore customary to open the door and invite the spirit of Elijah to come inside in preparation for the coming of Messiah, which is the great hope.

"My mother believed that Yeshua was Messiah, that He occupied this place during His *Seder* and that there was no empty seat. She said we should think of this as a symbolic place for His presence. According to her, although John the Baptist came in the spirit of Elijah and was the forerunner as Yeshua taught, some still see evidence Elijah will literally come again before Messiah's second coming.

"Therefore, perhaps we can also open the door to invite Elijah, the spirit of repentance, and to say 'even so, come, Lord Yeshua,' recognizing that the exact details of the future are things about which we must not be dogmatic."

Paul left his place at the table and went to the front door. As he opened it he said, "O Lord God, we invite the spirit of Elijah tonight, in anticipation of the return of Lord Yeshua, Messiah. We pray for justice and goodness to come upon the earth. We pray that all men may come to love You and to know the blessing of the freedom You have offered, and the greater freedom and salvation that shall be manifested at Your return. We ask these things in the name of Messiah. Amen."

Gabriella and Nathan glanced at the front door expectantly. Paul stared into the darkness for several minutes, then closed the door and walked into the living room. He pulled out his mother's Bible from the small bookcase next to the couch and returned with it to the dining-room table, where he opened it to Psalm 116 and began to read quietly.

He finished reading and closed the Bible. No one spoke. The fire crackled in the grate, and there seemed to be a haze in the room. Also, there was an almost imperceptible smell in the room that wasn't from the food or the cedar.

Finally Gabriella broke the silence. "That was beautiful, Paul. I'll always remember this *Seder.*" Her eyes were full of emotion. She said a silent prayer of thanks to the Lord as she realized God had given her a sign — and an answer. It was clear from Paul's last comments that the Lord was speaking to his heart and that he was beginning to respond to the Holy Spirit, even if he didn't realize it. "How long has it been since you've celebrated Passover like this?"

"Fifteen years to the day."

Nathan watched Paul intently, as though he saw something in Paul invisible to the natural eye. After a few moments he realized what it was.

In the past few weeks it was as if Nathan had become as a man blind from birth who'd abruptly had his vision miraculously restored. He'd begun to see things about himself he'd never known were there. Most importantly, he'd come to understand that he was a man who had for most of his life carried on a love-hate relationship with the world around him. He had always seen tremendous potential for humanity, yet he hated the fact that most people were willing to settle for mediocrity.

Now it dawned on him that he saw that same love-hate mentality mirrored in Paul's eyes.

"On my fifteenth birthday my mother told me that five is the Biblical number of grace," Paul was saying, "and three is the number of divine perfection. 'Fifteen is special, Paul,' she said, 'because it refers to acts wrought by the energy of divine grace. The two Hebrew letters which express it, *Yod*, ten, and *Hey*, five, spell the name *Jah*, who is the foundation of all grace.'" He paused and focused on the fire.

"Why wait so long?" asked Nathan.

"My mother died two weeks later. Things were never quite the same after that."

"Did you know that fifteen also refers to resurrection, Paul?" asked Gabriella softly.

"No, I didn't."

"Remember when you told me that *my* birthday fell on the Feast of Tabernacles, the *fifteenth* day of the seventh month?" continued Gabriella.

Paul nodded.

"Well, I was curious about it, so I looked it up."

"What did you find?" interrupted Nathan, suddenly intrigued by the conversation.

"There are some who believe the final trumpet will sound on the Feast of Tabernacles."

Paul frowned. "Final trumpet?"

"The Second Coming of Jesus," supplied Nathan in a hushed voice.

Four men encircled the makeshift wooden altar, silent and unmoving. Each stood on one of the points of the pentagram drawn with white spray paint on the dark black earth. Two were wearing suits, and two were dressed casually. Two wore ram's-head rings on their wedding fingers, and two wore amulets around their necks.

The altar that rested in the center of the pentagram faced east and pointed toward the unoccupied spot of the five-pointed star. The temporary sacrificial stand was four feet high, three wide, and three long. Thirty-six cubic feet. Six times six. The Biblical number of man multiplied by itself.

David McDaniel could not take his eyes off the altar. More importantly, he couldn't believe he was standing in a park, at midnight, with three other men, waiting to participate in a ritual that he thought should be reserved for madmen or late-night B-grade horror flicks.

The top of the altar had a rising at each corner, which continued square to a point about one half its height, gradually sloping off to an edge or point. Each rising looked like a horn. The entire section rested upon a hollow wooden box, which formed the body of the altar. It was supported by six small wooden legs, two on each side and one on each end.

On each of the four sides of the hollow box was written a different name: Baal-berith, Dagon, Chiun, Ashtoreth.

The moon hung almost directly overhead, its reddish-pink haze more pronounced than it had been all night, giving the pockmarked surface an almost blood-red color.

Vaughn had told McDaniel earlier that tonight he would be initiated. "You have served the master well," the billionaire said once they'd arrived at David's old office. "But now it is time for you to enter a new realm of understanding . . . time for you to formally dedicate yourself to his service." When the Senator had asked for an explanation, he'd been brought here to the wooden altar where two others were waiting.

Vaughn, dressed in a black satin hooded monk's robe, stood to the left of the altar, facing it, on the southeast point of the pentagram. A strange-looking amulet hung from his neck. Across from him stood an anonymous long-haired man, holding a rope attached to a black goat.

The man Vaughn had introduced as Antonio stood on the point diagonally across from Vaughn and opposite the stranger, on one of what could be considered the two base points of the star. The short, heavy-set Italian was wearing a white-gold ram's-head ring that was almost identical to his; however, the eyes of Antonio's ram were sapphire blue instead of red.

McDaniel occupied the other base point, on the same side as Vaughn, diagonally opposite the pale stranger. His own ring had arrived in the mail on his forty-second birthday, not quite two years after Vashti had been killed. To this day he had no idea where it came from. The postmark had been blurred. The only identification in the box it came in was a small white card with a single word printed in red: AZAZEL.

From the moment he'd laid eyes on the unusual piece of jewelry he'd felt compelled to wear it. Now the cold metal on his wedding finger was warming rapidly.

He rubbed his hand against his trousers — swallowing hard, trying futilely to generate saliva — and focused on the altar. Abruptly he realized why it looked so familiar. He and Vashti had traveled to Greece and Italy on their way home from Palestine in order to see some of the ancient ruins there. He'd felt compelled to visit Herculaneum, an ancient city on the Bay of Naples, just as he'd been drawn to Beersheba and Kadesh-Barnea. Herculaneum had been buried, along with Pompeii, by the eruption of Mount Vesuvius and had been partially excavated before the War.

At one of the sites was a temple dedicated to the goddess Isis, also known as Ishtar. The sanctuary consisted of a rectangular area surrounded by a peristyle of twenty-five columns. Inside was a temple with six altars. Adjoining the temple were two large *ecclesiasterion*, rooms for the mysteries, and five small *sacrarium*, rooms for the rites of initiation.

That's where he'd seen the fresco that now flashed upon his brain in a frightening moment of *deja vu*.

In the center and to the back of the fresco, a shaven priest, flanked on either side by sphinxes, stood before the shrine holding a red vase for the veneration of the worshipers. No one had been able to tell McDaniel for certain what was in the vase, although several of the archaeologists suggested it was most likely sacred Nile water. To the right of the High Priest stood a priestess, and on his left a Nubian priest holding a *sistrum*. On each side of the priests were several rows of chanting worshipers watched by four *ibises*, the beautiful black-and-white birds sacred to the goddess.

In the center foreground a fire burned upon an altar with four horns. An altar that was identical — except for the engraved names — to the one he was staring at now.

A nagging thought unsettled him. Something was missing.

Of course. The *anclabris*! A smaller, different kind of altar, a sort of table upon which the entrails of the victims were placed. Also, the *mensa sacra*, the table on which incense was presented, along with offerings not intended to be burned. Beads of perspiration broke out on his forehead.

The hypnotic character of Vaughn's voice pulled all thoughts from his mind, leaving him drained and empty. ". . . *Accesi confinium mortis et calcato Proserpinae limine per omnia vectus elementa remeavi, nocte media vidi solem candido corus-cantem lumine, deos inferos et deos superos accessi coram et adoravi de proxumo.*"

The billionaire seemed to be bathed in an eerie, pulsing white light. When he finished, the pale stranger translated: "I approached the very gates of death and set one foot on Proserpine's threshold, yet was permitted to return, rapt through all the elements. At midnight I saw the sun shining as if it were noon; I entered the presence of the gods of the underworld and the gods of the upperworld, stood near and worshiped them." Vaughn's eyes remained closed, as did the stranger's.

McDaniel cast a furtive glance at Antonio and discovered he was equally entranced by the altar.

He heard his name spoken, as if from a great distance. "David McDaniel . . ." said the unfamiliar guttural voice now issuing forth from Vaughn's mouth. "It is time for you to dedicate yourself in the service of the *deus deum magnorum potior et potiorum summus et summorum maximus et maximorum regnator* — the god more powerful than the great gods, and chief of the more powerful gods, and greatest of the chief gods, and ruler of the greatest gods. It is time for you to become one of us, a member of the *collegium of the pastophori.*

"You who stand before me as initiates are to become the shrine-bearers of my light. You have been chosen to proclaim my coming. It was I who spoke to you in the desert. Serve me, and the kingdoms of this world are yours. Serve me, and you shall not see death. Serve me, and I will make you a god."

McDaniel felt drugged. He also felt extremely vulnerable . . . more vulnerable than he'd ever felt in his life. It was as if his soul had suddenly been illuminated by the invisible light of an X-ray machine. He imagined that Vaughn's eyes were the source of that light, and they were probing the very essence of his being. He began to tremble, and he felt nauseous. But any skepticism was quickly replaced by anticipation.

"What say you, David McDaniel?"

McDaniel hoped he wasn't gaping, but he knew his mouth must be hanging open. Now was the moment of decision. "I accept," he heard himself say. "What must I do?"

The light around Vaughn became brighter. It took on a jade-green tint, like the color of the stones in McDaniel's ring.

Vaughn opened his eyes, then turned to face the waxen-faced man. "Bring forth the she-goat, and place the sacrifice upon the altar."

The man obeyed.

Once the goat was bound to the altar by the four leather straps attached to the four horns, the man stepped over to the bushes behind Vaughn and picked up a small bundle. He unwrapped the cloth reverently and held up the long, shiny, sickle-shaped knife, then handed the *khadga* to Vaughn.

Vaughn stepped up to the altar and grasped the amulet hanging around his neck with his left hand. He began to chant with what sounded like a multitude of voices. The pale man, having resumed his place, immediately joined in. Then Antonio added his voice.

McDaniel was overwhelmed. He could not stop himself from adding his voice to the unintelligible liturgy. He too began to chant. He was frightened and exhilarated at the same time. Power, raw and electric, surged through him. His entire body cried out for more, like an addict needing another fix to maintain the high even while his mind screams for release from the ecstasy of the seduction. He was no longer trembling, immersed in the sensuality of the moment.

Abruptly all four men stopped chanting, like a quartet under the control of a single maestro.

Vaughn turned from the altar and stared at Antonio. "Come forward, initiate." His voice had gone hollow, raspy.

Antonio stepped forward and stood swaying in front of the altar. Vaughn handed him the dagger, then stepped back to his place on the pentagram and said, "The life of the flesh is in the blood. We offer up this blood sacrifice to you, Lucifer, the light-bearer, in recognition of our covenant. We lift up the heart of this animal as an offering to the one who will usher in the New Age."

Vaughn stared at Antonio and said, "Now, Antonio, in the name of Natas, Apollyon, Abaddon, Baal, and Marduk, release the blood of the goat and offer up your heart to the master. With this sacrifice you will become one of his chosen."

Antonio raised the *khadga* and with a deftly executed motion, as if this ritual were one he'd performed many times, plunged the point into the chest of the goat.

The animal shrieked.

Antonio moved at blinding speed, using the outer edge of the knife to slice through its throat, neatly severing its jugular vein, silencing the sacrifice.

There was much blood, and McDaniel suddenly realized why the box supporting the altar was hollow.

The waxen man stepped forward and took the knife from Antonio. The sapphire eyes on his ring had changed color. They were now ruby-red.

The nameless man made several quick incisions in the chest of the goat, then reached inside the cavity and pulled out the heart, holding it up in bloodied hands for Vaughn to see. Finally he removed the goat from the altar and threw the carcass into the bushes after placing the heart within the lower box.

When that was done, he picked up the second bundle hidden in the bushes and placed it upon the altar, but did not unwrap it.

Vaughn again stepped forward and grabbed the *khadga*, grasping the amulet about his neck. "O Lucifer, god of light, we welcome you in our presence," he said. "We beseech you to manifest yourself that we might gaze upon your radiant beauty and be magnified in the light of your magnificence. We again offer up a blood sacrifice that is worthy of you." He motioned for David to step forward.

McDaniel's mind was crystal-clear. He felt peaceful and detached, as if he were merely an observer. He knew without a doubt that if he were truly to achieve the pinnacle of power he would have to participate.

He stepped forward slowly.

Vaughn gave him the knife and retreated to his place on the pentagram. The pale man remained standing beside McDaniel, holding the bundle of cloth.

This time Vaughn began to chant alone.

McDaniel raised up the knife automatically as Vaughn's

chanting increased in pitch and tone. At its peak it sounded like a pack of dogs barking and howling.

"Now, David," said a deep-throated, hollow voice in his ear. "Make the blood sacrifice now!"

McDaniel raised the knife higher still. Once again his whole body felt energized, as if it were coming to life for the first time. He *felt* light envelop him, lift him above the mundane, deposit him at the apex of understanding.

He started to bring the knife down in the same precise arc that Antonio had used. Just before the point of the *khadga* reached the bundle, the nameless man pulled back the folds of the cloth, revealing a baby. Horrified at what he was doing, unable to stop, Senator David McDaniel stared into the baby's eyes.

Time accelerated.

After what seemed like an eternity, but was only minutes, the Senator looked down and moaned. Then, realizing what he'd done, he dropped the knife. He stumbled backward a few steps, hoping against hope that all this wasn't real.

The waxen man stepped forward and guided him to his place on the pentagram.

Vaughn nodded his approval and said in a monotone, "Angel of light, we ask that you protect us from our enemies . . . those who would try to prevent us from accomplishing your purpose on the earth. Send forth your angels to deal with all who would stand against us."

The pale man wrapped the dead child in the brown cloth and placed the tiny body inside the box alongside the heart of the goat. He grabbed McDaniel, who was standing dazedly a few feet from the front of the altar, staring at his hands, and again guided him to his place on the pentagram.

Before the virgin blood could be used to complete the ritual, it would have to be desecrated. But that would come later.

Vaughn began to chant a final liturgy.

The pale man, then Antonio joined in.

McDaniel was the last to add his voice. *This is all a dream*, he thought. *I'll wake up tomorrow, and none of this will have happened.*

As the chanting grew louder, a greenish white light began to take form at the eastern point of the pentagram. The unnatural brilliance etched itself upon the indigo darkness.

Vaughn threw his head back and laughed. The sickle-shaped scar at the edge of his hairline pulsed with the same color as the light. In a loud voice he said, "Welcome, Lucifer, angel of light! Come and take your rightful place as our lord and master. We, the elect who serve you faithfully, receive you on Earth."

XXIII

Inside Paul's house the fire once again burned brightly. It made a loud crackling sound as added dry wood caught fire. The smell of cedar permeated the air.

Nathan sat on the floor, in front of the fireplace, gazing intently into the depths of the flames. Gabriella and Paul shared the couch. Paul was talking, but Nathan only half heard him. ". . . so now you know what I've been thinking about for the past week. Last summer I finished an article on AIDS. During my research I interviewed five highly respected men from a variety of religious backgrounds, including Archbishop Andrew McCarthy. As it turns out they are all involved in a unique project. They've been organizing a very special meeting to be held here in the city, in June, seven weeks from today."

Gabriella did a quick mental calculation. "On the Day of Pentecost?" she asked.

Paul nodded.

"Why is that date so significant?" asked Nathan as he pulled his eyes reluctantly from the yellow, blue, and red flames. He found the fire a welcome distraction from the thoughts that kept running around in his head.

"It's significant because of what Pentecost represents," answered Paul. "And because several leading Jewish Rabbis are attending the meeting."

"Jews refer to Pentecost as the Feast of Weeks or Firstfruits, don't they?" offered Gabriella.

Paul nodded. "The days preceding the festival are called 'the three days of separation and sanctification.' It's a time when Jews commemorate the giving of the Law, because God commanded Moses to set bounds about the mountain of God and to tell the people to separate and sanctify themselves." He paused and glanced at Gabriella, then added, "You probably realize what I have in mind."

"I think so."

"Well, will somebody let *me* in on the secret?" Nathan asked.

Paul chuckled. "Pentecost symbolizes a day of revelation in both Judaism and Christianity. For Jews, it commemorates the giving of the Law by God to His people."

"Christians, on the other hand," chimed in Gabriella, "look to Pentecost as the beginning of church history. The day when the Holy Spirit in-filled the Apostles, and several thousand others, giving them power to accomplish what Jesus had commanded them to do. Because Jesus is the firstborn of many, and because all power was given unto Him, in Heaven and on Earth, through His death and resurrection that power is transferred to any who willingly accept Him as their Lord and Savior."

She paused for a moment, and the fire crackled, punctuating the silence. Suddenly a sharp, piercing sound sliced through the quiet. Several dogs began to howl outside the house. Then, as abruptly as the howling had started, it stopped.

Nathan rubbed the back of his neck, massaging away a sudden prickly feeling, and Gabriella rubbed her arms to smooth away the goose bumps that caused her to shiver.

Paul looked at his watch and frowned. It was shortly after midnight. Oddly, he remembered the night he'd wrestled with the darkness in his bedroom — the night he thought he'd seen Yuri ben Raphah standing at the foot of his bed. The dogs had barked then too. He shook his head, clearing it of the memory, and said, "The meeting will bring together men and women from virtually every Christian denomination in the United States."

"What do they hope to accomplish?" Nathan wanted to know.

"An agreement on religious doctrinal principles."

"To what end?" prodded Gabriella, intrigued.

"More uniformity in religion."

"You mean a world religion, don't you, Paul." Nathan's words were a statement, not a question.

"Yes. I believe that's why they invited three of the country's most prominent Rabbis to participate." He paused, then added, "I was able to persuade them to allow me to speak as well."

"How did you accomplish that?"

"I told Archbishop McCarthy about the parchments."

"But you don't have the parchments."

"No, but I do have the text of my father's journal stored in Sam. That will have to be enough."

"You know there's going to be a great deal of controversy over this, don't you?" Nathan ran his hand through his hair wearily. He felt tired, worn-out. He wasn't sure he was up to what he knew he had to do.

Paul nodded. "But I do have an ace in the hole, so to speak."

"Oh?" Gabriella arched her eyebrow.

Paul stood and went over to the desk in the far corner of the room. He pulled out a single piece of parchment encased in plastic, along with several worn typewritten pieces of paper. "After I left you the other day, I went back to my father's house on impulse and began searching his files. I found this."

"What is it?" Nathan took the parchment from Paul and studied the writing on it. "It looks like Greek."

"It is. Apparently the person who originally possessed the parchments was a Roman citizen. A Praetorian in fact."

"A Praetorian?" asked Gabriella.

"One of an elite group of Roman soldiers. He was Pontius Pilate's Commander of the Garrison."

"Why do you think this particular document will help?" asked Nathan.

"Because the man who wrote it was the man who pierced Jesus' side with a spear as He hung on the cross. Three days later he was present at the tomb when Jesus rose from the dead. The account he gives of both events is so precise and detailed, it could not have been forged."

Nathan whistled softly and handed the document to his sister. It was an extraordinary piece of history.

Gabriella grasped it reverently and let out the breath she'd been holding in a long, soft sigh. "Your father discovered *this* along with the parchments?" she asked.

"That's right. The Archbishop agreed to allow me to speak to the delegates about what is contained in the parchments my father discovered, contingent upon verification of the authenticity of this document."

"Paul," she said softly, "are you *sure* you want to do this?"

"Absolutely."

Nathan probed the depths of the fire with tired eyes. He watched the blue, red, and yellow colors dance on the burning logs and thought about what he was going to tell his sister about their father. Abruptly he realized that the fire had stopped crackling and was burning silently. After several more minutes he stood up and said, "Thanks for this evening, Paul. I really enjoyed myself. It will be a long time before I forget about the *Seder*."

Gabriella stared at her brother. "You're leaving?"

He nodded.

"You promised to tell me — us — about what you've uncovered. You said it related to all this."

Nathan grimaced. "I know I promised, sis. I need one more day though. There's still a few loose ends I have to tie up. I want to be absolutely certain that everything I've discovered isn't simply the outgrowth of an overactive imagination. There's too much at stake for me to be careless."

"Okay, but that's it — one more day."

"Thanks. I won't let you down." He headed for the front door, grabbing his sweater on the way. He was halfway out when he turned and added, "Maybe you should tell Paul what you told me on the way over here . . . about Bashan and the Rephaim. Especially in light of tonight."

Paul eyed Gabriella narrowly after Nathan had gone. "What was *that* all about?"

279

"Vaughn Aurochs . . . and my father," she replied, biting her lip.

"Oh?"

She got up from the couch and walked over to the fireplace, then turned and faced Paul. The heat felt good on her back. She hoped it would keep the chill she'd experienced earlier when she shared her information with Nathan from stealing over her again. "Remember on Monday, when I told you what happened to me in the park and we talked about Psalm 22?"

"Yes."

"Well, after you left I decided to look up a couple of things in my *Unger's*."

"Your what?"

"It's a Bible dictionary. Anyway, I looked up the word *Bashan*."

"Why?"

"Remember me telling you about Vaughn Aurochs taking me to dinner, and later to his office, after my one-woman show?"

Paul nodded.

"What I didn't tell you was that Vaughn told me that he'd been born in a Chinese town called Bashan."

"So?"

"Several thousand years ago there was also an area in Palestine known as Bashan. It extended from Gilead in the south to Hermon on the north and from the Jordan River to Salcah. During the time of Moses it was inhabited by a race of giants known as the Rephaim. We talked about these beings earlier, but now I think I understand more about them."

"I still wonder about these *giants*," Paul chuckled. "I mean, were they men with pituitary problems?"

Gabriella didn't laugh. Instead her demeanor changed abruptly. "Nathan told me that Father is Vaughn Aurochs's business associate, then suggested that I read the Book of Revelation."

"Why the Book of Revelation?"

"Because it talks about the Antichrist and his prophet," she whispered, unable any longer to keep back the tears. Several large drops trickled down her suddenly flushed face.

Paul went to her and wrapped his arms around her. She wept against his shoulder. "Oh, Paul, I'm so scared. There are moments when I feel like the nice, neat, orderly world I've constructed for myself over the past seven years is starting to crack at the seams. I feel like I have no control over what's happening to me."

"I know what you mean."

Gabriella cast a furtive glance up at him. "You do?"

He nodded, then asked, "What's Vaughn Aurochs got to do with all this?"

"Nathan hasn't told me in so many words, but I'm sure he believes that Vaughn Aurochs is the Antichrist."

Paul held her more tightly to him and gazed out the window, frowning. That sounded a bit far out for Nathan. True, he'd only known Gabriella's brother a short time, but the older man certainly didn't seem like the type of person to conjure up wild stories out of his imagination. Maybe that's what he was talking about when he said he had a few loose ends to tie up.

XXIV

Nathan walked down the darkened street, his mind in turmoil. The cold air made him shiver. Events were definitely escalating. He knew now that he was right about Rainbow International and the Kronos Corporation. He just needed time to figure out how to tell his sister about their father . . . And the truth about who Vaughn Aurochs really was.

The abrupt roar of an engine and the sudden sound of screeching tires startled him out of his reverie. He looked up only to be blinded by a pair of dazzling lights racing straight at him. The sudden light piercing the darkness seemed to catch and hold him, trapping him like a moth who has flown too close to the flame. "What the . . ." he muttered as his reflexes took over. He lurched backwards, landing on his rear in the middle of the street, and felt a *whoosh* of wind as the car sped over the place he'd stood moments before. He jumped up and yelled at the taillights, "Hey, you idiot, watch where you're driving!"

The car's brakes squealed loudly, and Nathan watched as the automobile turned on a dime and headed back in his direction. He was suddenly sick to his stomach. Whoever was behind the wheel intended to run him down! He turned to run, but slipped and fell to his knees on the cold, hard asphalt. His whole body trembled as his adrenal glands went into overdrive.

Struggling to stand, he winced. The palms of his hands were scraped and bleeding. Pain, like a jolt of high-voltage electricity, shot up through him, causing him to gag. In spite of the fact that he felt like his body had suddenly been zapped with a surge of power, he couldn't get his legs to respond.

The deafening roar of the accelerating engine and the smell of burning rubber blotted out all thoughts of pain. He managed to get halfway to his feet just as the two headlights became one bright, burning light bearing down on him. He turned and screamed, "O God! — N-o-o-o-o . . ."

The driver of the shiny red '68 Shelby Mustang ignored the man's scream and the subsequent sickening sound of metal impacting upon flesh and bone. Dark circles shadowed his vacant eyes. The smile on his waxen face was an evil grin of satisfaction as he shifted into fourth gear and sped off into the night, leaving Nathan's broken and bleeding body crumpled on the dark street.

XXV

Just when Gabriella thought she was all cried out, she had to work hard at keeping fresh tears from flowing.

"So how was Colorado?" asked her father after taking a long pull on his third scotch. "I haven't heard a word from you since the funeral."

Gabriella watched her father consume the scotch like it was water. She was still trying to adjust to the fact that he was drinking liquor again. He'd shocked her by ordering a double scotch on the rocks immediately after they sat down. When she asked him what he was doing, he replied, "What any red-blooded American father would do in my circumstances. Mourning." From his tone, she knew better than to press the issue.

The June sunshine cascaded through the large plate-glass windows of the fancy Georgetown restaurant, inundating the half-filled room with a golden-yellow light. It was not quite noon, and yet in ten minutes the place would be packed. And noisy. She'd hoped they would be able to share a moment of intimacy without feeling like they were in a fishbowl.

"Grand Lake was beautiful, Father. As always. The snow was just starting to melt, and a few flowers were even beginning to bloom. And of course the cabin was cozy. I made a fire every night."

Senator McDaniel nodded his head imperceptibly as his daughter talked, as if he were involved in a separate conversation inside his head while he was listening to Gabriella.

"Am I boring you?"

"What?" The Senator took another long pull on his scotch, looked around, and caught the waiter's attention.

Gabriella frowned and bit her lip. It was difficult for her not to say anything as the tuxedoed man scurried off to the bar to fetch his well-known customer another double Glennfiddich on the rocks. In all the years they had been coming here together for lunch, her father had never touched a drop of liquor.

"I'm sorry, muffin. I was thinking about your brother."

Gabriella's stomach felt as if it were filled with lead. "Why did he have to die that way?" she asked, blinking repeatedly to stem the tears. "Run down by a hit-and-run driver and left like a dog in the street to die. It's not fair." She paused and looked hard at her father. "We never even got to see his body."

"Let's not argue about that again." He waved his hand in dismissal. "I told you, Vaughn took care of all the details. Nathan's body was so mangled, they had to identify him by his dental records."

Gabriella again bit her bottom lip, fighting to keep her control. She'd had over a month to think about what she was going to say to her father when she saw him again, and she wasn't about to give him an excuse to ignore her. One of the things she'd finally come to grips with during her time away was that her father had been ignoring her for far too long. Now, more than ever, it was important that they start interacting as a father and daughter should.

The waiter arrived with the Senator's scotch, and Gabriella requested, "Coffee please . . . with lots of cream." She stared past her father, thinking about the information she'd found in Nathan's suitcase and the implications of what he'd uncovered.

At first she'd been overwhelmed. However, after a month of going over and over the material, she was simply astonished. It was incredible what he'd accomplished in such a short time.

"Have you seen Paul Kingman since you've been back?" the Senator inquired.

"Huh? I mean, what did you say?"

"Now you're the one who's not listening," McDaniel said, studying his daughter.

"It seems to run in the family." The waiter returned with her coffee, and she sipped it slowly, relishing the warmth because, even though it was a warm day, she felt chilled. Almost as if part of her insides had frozen solid when Nathan died.

"Never mind . . . it wasn't important." McDaniel focused on the glass of scotch. The condensation coating the outside had gotten so dense it ran down the sides and soaked the napkin beneath. The large, silver drops reminded him of tears. Tears he'd been unable to shed when his only son had died. Tears unshed since Vashti died. With effort he pulled his eyes from the glass and stared into the sparkling jade-green gaze of his daughter.

"What's happened to us?" he asked in a rare moment of uncontrolled frustration. "Why is it we don't seem to communicate anymore?"

Gabriella avoided the penetrating look and the questions, and instead let her gaze sweep the room. It was filling rapidly. Suddenly she tensed. By the podium, talking to the *maitre d'*, was the pale man she'd first seen at the college, then later at Saturnalia's. Only now he was dressed impeccably in a charcoal-gray suit with a burgundy-red tie. Oddly, from this distance it almost looked like it was the color of blood. And his hair was much shorter. She glanced at his feet to see if he was still wearing snakeskin boots, but there were too many people between them for her to see clearly.

She looked back at her father, then reached across the table and touched his arm. "Do you know that man standing at the podium?" She gestured as unobtrusively as she could.

Her father glanced over his right shoulder. "Which one? There are at least half a dozen men standing there."

Gabriella searched the front of the room. The man had melted into the crowd. "He's gone."

"Who was it?"

"I thought I saw someone I knew. I wondered if you knew him too."

"This is Washington. I know a lot of people."

Gabriella frowned. She was certain her father had seen the man she was talking about. How could he have missed him? "Let's order lunch. You know how I get when I haven't eaten."

McDaniel shook his head. "And they say *politicians* make strange bedfellows."

It was Friday, so the Senator ordered the Dover Sole special. In spite of his failure to live the kind of life he believed a faithful Catholic should lead, he did not consider himself lapsed in all areas. Gabriella, not wanting to offend her father, and not really hungry, ordered the same. Although they rarely discussed religion, he'd made it clear he would never accept her "conversion," as he referred to it. As far as he was concerned, once a Catholic, always a Catholic.

Both of them picked at their food. Gabriella used the time to gather her thoughts. She realized, however, that the longer she remained silent, the harder it would be to break through the barrier growing between her and her father.

Finally the waiter cleared the table and brought McDaniel an aftermeal drink. Angelica, straight up.

Gabriella ordered a cappuccino, took a deep breath, and said, "There's something I have to talk to you about, Father." She felt strange inside, almost giddy. At the same time a heaviness seemed to hover over her words. "It's about the Kronos Corporation."

Her father raised his eyebrows, lifted the snifter of Angelica, and swirled the glass, watching the light filter through the amber liquid, then brought the snifter under his nose and inhaled, closing his eyes.

Gabriella watched the ritual, nonplussed. It was like she wasn't even present. Her father took a sip of the liqueur and swirled it in his mouth, finally swallowing. Only then did he open his eyes. "What about the Kronos Corporation?"

"Is it true that you merged the company with Vaughn Aurochs and that now he's your business partner? That the two of you have been masterminding some significant global business transactions?"

McDaniel studied his daughter, seeing something in her he'd never seen before. And it unnerved him. There was an intensity about her that Vashti had never possessed. It was the same intensity he'd felt when he first decided to run for Senator. And yet, it was somehow different. Less harsh and unyielding, but without any diminishment of fervor. "Who gave you that bit of information?"

"Does it matter?"

"It does if you expect me to answer you."

Gabriella returned her father's icy stare, suddenly resolved not to give in to his intimidation. She refused to allow him to treat her as if she were a disgruntled constituent or lobbyist. "Nathan," she replied defiantly.

"I see. And when did he tell you this?"

"He didn't. I read it in a journal he started writing two years ago, just after he arrived in Europe. He kept extensive notes on a variety of interesting topics."

"What else does the journal tell you?"

Gabriella knew she was being baited, but she didn't care. "That you sold the Kronos Corporation to Vaughn Aurochs for what might be considered a meager sum considering its true value — that you're now a major stockholder in Rainbow International — and that Vaughn Aurochs is the man who intends to insure that you become the next President of the United States."

"Assuming that your facts are correct —"

"They're not *my* facts, Father."

McDaniel shrugged and took another sip of Angelica. "Okay. Assuming then that *Nathan's* facts are correct, why are you so disturbed? You've known for some time that I've been planning to run for President. We discussed the possibility fifteen years ago. And you, as well as anybody, know that it takes vast sums of money to run a campaign."

"That's true — we did talk about the *possibility*. What we didn't discuss was the how and when."

"I beg your pardon?"

Gabriella pushed her half-finished cappuccino to the side and leaned forward so she wouldn't have to raise her voice. "You intend running next year, don't you? And don't give me the kind of answer you'd reserve for an inquisitive news hound. This is too important for you to play the engaging Senator who is very circumspect about his public pronouncements."

"My running depends."

"On what?"

"On whether or not I decide it would be opportune for me to do so, among other things."

"You . . . or Vaughn Aurochs?"

Her father grew suddenly indignant. "What's gotten into you, young lady? You're starting to sound like your brother." His eyes became dark and angry.

Gabriella sat back abruptly, feeling like she'd just been punched in the chest. She was having trouble getting her breath. She reached for her water glass, trying to calm her fluttering stomach.

McDaniel set down the nearly empty snifter. "Forgive me, muffin. I'm under a lot of pressure right now. And your brother's death hasn't helped matters." His smile looked forced and much too contrived.

"I don't know who you are anymore, Father," said Gabriella, wondering what had happened to the man she'd admired for so long. "You're like a chameleon. One minute you appear to be a caring, warmhearted man, concerned about the needs of others; the next, you're cold and calculating, the consummate judge, jury and executioner." She tried to keep the edge out of her voice, but couldn't. "The son who at one time worshiped the ground you walked on lies dead in his grave barely a month, and already you talk about him as if his death were an *inconvenience*. A liability that distracts you from achieving your grand vision."

"That's a lie, and you know it," the Senator snapped, a pained look on his face. "I loved your brother as much as I love you. True, he disappointed me, but I certainly don't think of his death as a 'liability.'" His face was flushed, and he was shaking. "My goodness, Gabriella, what do you take me for?"

Gabriella closed her eyes momentarily, trying to get a grip on her emotions. This conversation wasn't going at all like she'd planned. The whole idea was crazy! Vaughn Aurochs the Antichrist and her father his prophet? There was no way she could even begin to think about discussing such an implausible possibility with her father. At best he'd laugh at her. At worst he'd have serious doubts about her sanity. But what if it were true? What then?

She opened her eyes. "I'm sorry I brought the issue up. I guess I need more than a month in Colorado to heal the wounds."

"Well, we've both had a rough month," suggested McDaniel placatingly. "Let's consider the matter dropped, okay?"

She nodded her assent.

"Fine." He looked at his watch and stood up. "It's time I got back to the salt mines. I'm going to be late for my appointment with the Secretary of State." A hint of a smile flickered across his lips.

Gabriella stared at him for a moment with sad eyes, then mumbled, "Watch out for the women."

McDaniel flashed his best "everything is going to be alright" smile and motioned for the waiter to bring the check. "I'll see you soon, muffin," he said, giving her a quick hug before he departed, "and we'll do something fun together."

"Like what?"

"I don't know. Something different. Something we haven't done together in a long time. You decide and give me a call when you have." He flashed her a final smile, then turned and walked away.

As her father passed the next table, he smiled and waved, and Gabriella heard him say, "Hello, Dave, good to see you. Give Sarah a call tomorrow and set up an appointment. We need to talk about that bill of yours."

She watched him exit the room, a man totally in his element, and muttered under her breath, "I'll settle for the hug, Father. Save the rhetoric for the Secretary of State."

When Gabriella left the restaurant, she had the uncanny feeling that someone was watching her. She stopped just outside the front door and turned, looking through the plate-glass entrance toward the podium.

The chill she'd felt earlier returned, only much more intensely, sending a shiver down her spine. The pale man in the charcoal-gray suit was standing only a few feet away . . . And he was staring at her! Even though the man's eyes were vacuous, something in them, something sinister, something black and cold and malevolent, reached out and tried to touch her.

Sheer old-fashioned fright seized her, and she couldn't stop trembling. *Is this how the cornered prey of a snake feels the instant before it gets devoured?* she wondered.

Abruptly she was jostled by someone hurrying along the sidewalk. The moment of dread passed as the cabby waiting by the curb opened the rear door of his car and asked, "Where to, miss?"

She glanced at the cabby, then back inside the restaurant. The pale man was gone again . . . as if he'd evaporated in the warm sunshine. She needed to talk to Paul. He would know what to do.

"The Kronos Building," she replied, stepping into the cab, grateful for the security.

"I assume you're in possession of the original parchment," said Archbishop McCarthy as he scrutinized the photocopy Paul handed to him.

Paul nodded.

The Archbishop was thoughtful. "And you're certain the document is authentic? It wouldn't do at all if the thing is a forgery. We both have reputations to protect."

"My father had all the requisite tests done at the university.

He left behind a variety of notarized affidavits from some very distinguished colleagues."

"Extraordinary that a find this monumental has remained unknown all these years. It never ceases to amaze me when things like this happen."

"Apparently my father didn't realize what he'd discovered until just before he died," Paul lied. "By then he was too sick to do anything about his discovery. He left the document to me in his will, with a partial translation. I had to get a friend in the language department to finish translating the Greek."

Archbishop McCarthy stood up and walked to the window of his office. He focused on the Washington Monument a mile away. "I knew of your father's work. He was a well-respected scholar."

Paul was stunned. "In Palestine?"

"What?"

"You knew of his work in Israel, just after the War?"

"No . . . I didn't know he was in Israel in '67. I'm talking about the article he published in the late sixties . . . the one that caused such a stir in academic circles."

Paul swallowed hard, fighting to keep his stomach from doing cartwheels. He and the Archbishop weren't communicating, thank God. He couldn't believe he'd let the comment about Palestine slip out. "You mean his defiant answer to Albert Schweitzer?" he asked, glad the Archbishop hadn't realized what he was talking about.

Andrew McCarthy turned to face his guest, and for some strange reason Paul found himself staring at the Archbishop's hands. They were not the hands of a man unaccustomed to physical labor. This man was no paper-pusher.

"I must admit that the title threw me at first," continued the most powerful Catholic in Washington.

"'The Historical Jesus Isn't Lost, Nor Was He the Son of God,'" mumbled Paul.

McCarthy nodded. "You see, I'd never read *The Quest for the Historical Jesus* . . . until I read your father's article. I was a young and naive priest in those days," he added wistfully.

Paul frowned. "I've never read Schweitzer's work."

The Archbishop clasped his hands together and asked, "What did you think of your father's article?"

Paul shrugged. "I was fifteen, and my mother had just died. My father and I started drifting apart after that. I never really paid much attention to his work."

"I see." McCarthy walked over to his bookshelf and pulled Schweitzer's 1906 work from the shelf. As he flipped to the back of the thin book he said, "Your father used the next to last paragraph of Schweitzer's work as the opening paragraph of his article. He argued, rather persuasively I might add, that Jesus was not the Messiah, but simply a Jew whom Christians stripped of Hebrew heritage and deified." He paused and gave a shrewd look at his guest. "Shall I read you the opening words?"

Paul nodded, not trusting himself to speak.

"'The Jesus of Nazareth who came forward publicly as the Messiah, who preached the ethic of the Kingdom of Heaven upon earth, and died to give His work its final consecration never had any existence. He is a figure designed by rationalism, endowed with life by liberalism, and clothed by modern technology in historical garb.'" The Archbishop stopped reading and set the book down on his desk, leaving it open.

"I'm not sure I understand your point."

McCarthy's eyes became hooded, and Paul felt as if he were being measured and weighed. It was an odd sensation.

"Your father was obviously a man of acute sensitivity to the tension between Judaism and Christianity. He was also a man of impeccable credentials. No doubt a document purportedly written by the centurion who pierced Jesus' side and who later witnessed the miracle at the tomb would shatter the belief he so eloquently defended twenty years ago."

Paul was suddenly wary. "My father died before he completed work on the document. I told you, he was a very sick man."

"So you said."

Paul changed the subject abruptly. "When I talked to you on the phone, you agreed to allow me to speak to the delegates attending the Council on Organized Religion on Wednesday, provided I could prove the authenticity of the document. Are you satisfied that I have met your requirement?" he asked, standing.

"For now," replied the Archbishop, turning again to gaze out the window.

Paul stepped into the bright sunshine and hailed a cab. As the cabby wove his way through the Friday afternoon traffic, toward the Kronos Building, Paul thought about what the Archbishop had inferred about his father . . . and about the last paragraph of Schweitzer's work.

The Archbishop had left him alone momentarily, and he'd picked the book up off the desk and read the passage for himself. "And to those who obey Him, whether they be wise or simple, He will reveal Himself in the toils, the conflicts, the sufferings which they shall pass through in His fellowship, and, as an ineffable mystery, they shall learn in their own experience Who He is."

Why had his father ignored the obvious?

XXVI

"Don't be ridiculous, Senator," snarled Vaughn. "I'm not about to let the meddling of a young woman — even if she is your daughter — interfere with my plans." His ebony eyes seethed. "There is far too much at stake."

David McDaniel shivered and pulled his eyes from Vaughn's. He was sweating, even though he knew Vaughn kept his office air-conditioning set at 65. The billionaire had called him shortly before 5 and said it was imperative they meet. It was now after 9 P.M.

The Senator shifted uncomfortably in his chair. "What are you talking about?" he asked, nonplussed by what he'd seen in those cold, malevolent eyes. No other human being he'd ever met had been able to unnerve him the way Vaughn did just by looking at him.

"You know very well what I'm talking about. Your conversation this afternoon with Gabriella . . . At your favorite restaurant in Georgetown."

"I don't see —"

"That's right, you *don't see*," interrupted Vaughn, leaning forward abruptly. His amulet hung like a pendulum just above the polished surface of the mahogany desk. In the soft light the ruddy stain in the wood looked like dried blood. "Your son meddled into affairs he had no business in . . . and it cost him his life."

McDaniel was shocked. "Nathan's death was an accident. I saw the report."

"You are now a member of the inner sanctum, Senator. The lord of light is a hard taskmaster, but the rewards of serving him faithfully are immeasurable. The penalty for interference, on the other hand . . ." Vaughn shrugged and let the threat hang.

"What are you saying?"

"Surely you realize that your life, and the lives of your children, now belong to the master to do with as he pleases."

"But —"

"I've had enough of your protestations of innocence. Your destiny and mine are now intertwined, Senator," Vaughn said emphatically as he stood up. He pressed a concealed button to the right of the bookcase, and a rectangular panel slid back, revealing a hidden bar. He poured some Angelica for them both. "You've sought power your whole life, and I've shown you the way to possess what you've asked for beyond your wildest imaginations." He handed McDaniel a half-full snifter. "There is no turning back now. Your fate was sealed that night in the park."

His tone became less harsh as he swirled the glass underneath his nose, savoring the sweet aroma. "The blood you willingly shed now binds you not only to the master, but to me as well. And we are both bound — by blood covenant — to serve the lord of light . . . Lucifer." He took a stiff drink of the amber-colored liquid, then cupped the snifter in his hands, warming it.

McDaniel set his snifter down on the desk and jumped to his feet, suddenly angry. "Leave my children out of this! Nathan's death was an accident, nothing more. And Gabriella is *not* meddling. She's merely concerned about some things her brother said shortly before he died. As for the lunch meeting you're so concerned about, I used the time to convince her to forget about what Nathan told her."

"I suppose that's why she went straight to the Kronos Building to see Paul Kingman as soon as you left," Vaughn remarked snidely.

"Curse Benjamin Kingman. He mocks me from the grave." The Senator eyed his business partner speculatively. "You're still worried about those parchments, aren't you? What's so important about them anyway?"

Vaughn's eyes became hooded. "Genealogy, Senator . . . Genealogy."

"What?"

"Do you know who Herod the Great was?"

McDaniel looked at him blankly.

"No, I don't suppose you would." Vaughn leaned against the bookcase and gestured for McDaniel to sit back down.

The Senator complied, sidetracked by this sudden change of direction in their conversation. He had the feeling he was about to hear something significant . . . something few people knew. He himself knew so little about the enigmatic billionaire that he craved *any* information that might give him a foothold in his dealings with this man who wielded power on a scale few men had ever dreamed possible. Any glimpse he could get of the reasoning behind Vaughn's motives was bound to be enlightening . . . and beneficial later.

"Herod was of Idumean blood," continued Vaughn, "a descendant of Esau. Over two thousand years ago the Edomites lived in the southern district of Palestine." He paused for emphasis. "In the area known as the Negeb."

McDaniel's heart began to pound at the mention of the Negeb. *There's no way he could know*, he told himself. *No one knows except Gabriella.*

"It was the Edomites who joined Nebuchadnezzar when he besieged Jerusalem . . . and the Edomites who took an active role in the plunder of the city and the slaughter of other Jews. Later, during the rule of the Maccabees, the Hasmonean family from which Herod the Great is also descended, the Edomites were subdued and incorporated within the Jewish nation in an area often referred to by Greek and Roman writers of the period as Idumea.

"Mark Antony gave Herod a tetrarchy and persuaded the Roman Senate to make him King over Palestine. Although Herod was a Jew, he exploited his people unmercifully. The dynasty he founded, with the help of nine or ten wives, was characterized by a passionate desire for immortality — in the form of ostentatious architectural display."

He took a sip of Angelica, then continued, "Herod's crowning achievement was convincing the Jews it was essential that he rebuild the ancient Temple which Solomon had originally built and Zerubbabel had restored upon Israel's return from the captivity of Babylon. It was a masterstroke of genius."

"Why is that?"

"Because, Senator, Herod's plan was twofold. His avowed purpose was to conciliate the Jews who'd been alienated by his excessive cruelties. His real purpose, however, was far more subtle . . . and far more dramatic."

"Go on."

"Herod intended to possess the public genealogies stored in the Temple, especially those relating to the priestly families."

"I don't understand."

"The genealogies allegedly set forth the ancestry of the expected Messiah. Herod was determined to destroy the lineage, lest the Messiah come and usurp his kingdom."

"What does that have to do with what we've been talking about?"

Vaughn sighed, as if the Senator were an errant child who had failed to do his homework. "The parchments Benjamin Kingman discovered on the shores of the Dead Sea chronicle the genealogy of another exalted ruler."

"Oh?"

"The Prince of Tyre."

"Who?"

"The man who is going to restore the splendor of Babylon."

"And who is that man?"

Vaughn's smile chilled McDaniel to the bone. "I am."

"You're mad," grunted McDaniel.

"Well, Senator," said Vaughn, his face a harsh mask, "if that's the case, then what are you?"

McDaniel ran his hand through his graying hair. All resistance seemed to drain from him. "I can't believe I let you lead me into that madness in the park." He picked up the snifter and took a large gulp. It burned all the way down. "A blood sacrifice . . ."

Vaughn's demeanor changed suddenly, just as a chameleon's color changes when it wants to hide. "It's done, David," he said placatingly. "And you made the right decision. Now that we've become one in spirit, no one can stand in our way . . . *No one*. I am the deliverer, and you are my prophet." He finished off the Angelica that remained in his snifter and poured himself another.

David stared at Vaughn momentarily, then finished off his own drink and held up his glass for more. "This stuff is addictive," he said, managing a weak half-smile. Oddly, he suddenly felt relaxed. The tingling sensation that always came when he drank the expensive liqueur was spreading outward from the base of his neck, and as it reached his extremities he added, "I used to be an Amaretto drinker twenty-five years ago. And I gave it up without a second thought after Vashti died. But this Angelica," he eyed Vaughn appraisingly, "there's something unusual about it."

"My father came up with the idea shortly after we arrived in America from China."

"What made him choose the almond?"

"My mother. She was an orphan. The only thing she knew about her parents was that her mother died in childbirth and her father was an American whose last name was Tannin."

"Unusual name."

Vaughn's eyes glazed over as he stared past McDaniel at the colorful oil painting hanging behind his desk. "It means wolf in Hebrew."

McDaniel started to say something, then thought better of it. He was glad the conversation had changed direction. He was worried about Gabriella, and he knew that if Vaughn realized it, the billionaire would use it against him.

"At any rate, Chi Lin was raised by the Tangut, a nomadic people who lived and traded along the silk road. They taught her how to distill a potent liqueur from ripe almonds. She used to make it for my father."

"There's a strange kind of aftertaste that leaves me feeling not quite satisfied, thirsty for more."

Vaughn pulled his eyes from the painting and chuckled sardonically. "That's my father's special touch."

"Oh?"

"His recipe calls for blending in caperberry."

"Caperberry?"

"The immature fruit of *Capparis spinosa*, a plant that grows in the clefts of rocks and walls." He handed David his refilled snifter. "It's a stimulant . . . and an aphrodisiac."

Paul listened to the light rain that was falling outside his office as he stared at the green letters on the monitor slowly scrolling down the screen. He might not have his father's journal, but he did have the parts he'd transcribed into Sam.

However, his mind was only half on what he was doing. He'd found a note from Gabriella attached to his office door when he arrived about 2 o'clock and realized that he'd just missed her. He was excited she was back from Colorado, and he couldn't wait to see her. He'd called her house immediately, but had only gotten her answering machine, so he left a message inviting her to dinner at his house tomorrow night. He had much to tell her.

After a month of reading and rereading, he had a pretty good idea what his father had done with the parchments. He had to make sure, however, that he wasn't off on some wild-goose chase before he went after them.

He was also certain that someone was trying very hard to make sure he didn't discover whatever was contained in the parchments — whatever it was had caused his father to steal them and cover up his theft for nearly forty years. A crime that by its very nature had violated everything Benjamin Kingman believed in.

He was convinced there was more to his father's strange behavior than his fear of being caught for absconding with a national treasure. Much more. And he was equally certain that Senator David McDaniel and Vaughn Aurochs were deeply involved.

There were two other things on his mind as well.

The other night he'd been reading through some of the reference material he'd collected as part of his research for his as yet unwritten book, and he'd stumbled across some interesting ideas Karl Jung had about archetypal consciousness, the collective unconscious, and genetic memory. Jung described archetypes as universal patterns expressed in behavior and images. Archetypes, according to the famous Swiss psychiatrist, along with instincts, make up the collective unconscious mind, which some researchers referred to as racial memory. The really fascinating concept, however, was that Jung conceived the idea that Christianity was a part of the historical process *necessary for the development of consciousness*.

Paul was certain that somehow this tied into what Nathan had uncovered and what Gabriella had been trying to tell him these past few weeks. However, he couldn't seem to put it all together in a way that made sense. Not now, anyway. Because lately what continued to drive all other thoughts from his mind was the increasingly uneasy feeling that Nathan's death had not been an accident. Before he could be positive, however, he needed to ask Gabriella some questions. And he wasn't quite sure he felt comfortable bringing up the subject. She'd been devastated after Nathan's funeral.

Paul sighed, sat back, and put his feet up. He rubbed his eyes and stretched. The rain fell harder, and he watched the drops sliding down the glass. He thought about his father's funeral . . . and the tears he'd shed. "Why didn't you share your life with me, Father?" he muttered, wishing Benjamin was alive so he could ask him in person. "And why didn't I share mine with you?"

The phone rang, startling him.

"Hello."

"Paul?"

"Gabriella! It's good to hear your voice. I've missed you."

"Me too. And the answer is yes."

"What?"

"Dinner, silly."

"Great."

"I wish tomorrow was tonight. I have so much I need to talk to you about."

"I'm all ears."

"Not on the phone."

"I could come over."

"No . . . I need the time to pull myself together."

"I thought you did that in Colorado."

"So did I."

"I see. Well, it's pretty nasty out anyway."

"Raining there too, huh?"

"Yeah."

"What are you doing at your office at this hour?'

"Working."

"Dumb question, I guess."

"Not really. I don't even know what time it is."

"Nearly midnight. I tried your house, and when there was no answer I got worried. I don't know what I'd have done if you hadn't answered."

"Thanks," Paul told her, smiling as he visualized her captivating green eyes and soft, sensuous lips.

"For what?"

"For being you. And for your trust. It means a lot to me."

"And to me."

"I'm glad. Gabriella?"

"Yes?"

Paul sighed. "Never mind. I'll tell you tomorrow."

"See you at 8 then. G'bye."

Paul stared at the phone for several minutes after he hung up. Something in Gabriella's voice had touched him deeply. She sounded vulnerable, and that was something he'd never heard in her voice before. Probably only because she'd been careful not to let him see that side of her.

"Gabriella McDaniel," he said out loud to the rain, "I'm definitely in love with you, and I hope you feel the same way about me." He stood up, walked over to the window, and stared down at the park below, then back up at the heavens. "Now if I can only find a way to tell you everything I have to without destroying you," he added, absently scanning the darkness for the moon.

It had been just over a month since Passover. He wondered idly if the red moon on his birthday had been a fluke or a portent of things to come. He hoped the answer was the former, but something inside told him it was the latter.

Vaughn stood swaying inside his glass menagerie. It was just after 2 A.M. His lips were covered with blood, and he held the broken body of a limp turtledove in his right hand. His eyes were closed, and the chanting he'd begun earlier had stopped.

After several minutes he opened his eyes. There were dark circles under them, making them look even blacker than normal. The sickle-shaped scar on his head was pulsing.

He listened intently for a few seconds, and when he finally heard the soft rustling of the snake, he smiled. He discarded the drained body of the bird, then turned and opened the door separating the garden aviary from his office. The huge snake slithered silently across the floor, its hooded eyes focused on one of the remaining live turtledoves.

The pale man in the snakeskin boots had watched the whole ritual. Now, as the giant boa constrictor slithered toward its meal, he smiled humorlessly.

"Kill the girl," said Vaughn in a muted, guttural voice. "And make it soon. We need the Senator with us 100 percent."

The waxen man nodded, never taking his eyes off the snake. He watched mesmerized as the reptile struck in the blink of an eye. Unhinged jaws, stretched to twice their normal size, snatched the unsuspecting bird from its perch, killing and consuming it in one fluid motion.

XXVII

Yuri watched the sunset from the penthouse suite in the Halcyon Building and marveled at the diverse colors parading across the twilight sky. It was Saturday, just four days before Pentecost. The tall, silver-haired man sighed as he thought about coming events. "There is so little time left," he mumbled, then closed his eyes and began to pray.

He was still confused about why he hadn't been allowed to help Nathan. He had power to prevent Nathan's death, but not permission. And because he'd failed to intervene, the Rephaim had claimed yet another victim in a war that was older than time. Now he knew the enemy was planning a vicious assault on both Paul and Gabriella. However, he still had not been given release to act. "Why?" he cried out in his prayers.

The Father remained silent.

"That was wonderful," said Gabriella, smiling contentedly. "It's the best meal I've eaten in over a month." She relaxed in her chair and watched while Paul cleared the table.

He returned her smile and replied, "Good. I'm glad you like my cooking. They say the third time is the charm."

"Who are *they*?"

Paul shrugged. "The sages of antiquity."

"Well, far be it from me to argue with sages."

Paul finished clearing the table. "Coffee?"

"You bet. Here or by the fire?"

"Need you ask?"

"By the fire it is."

Gabriella went over to the couch and snuggled into the corner of it, feeling like she *belonged* here in Paul's home at this particular moment. It was an odd feeling, but one which comforted her in a way she'd have been hard pressed to describe. She watched the fire dancing in the hearth and remembered their first dinner together. So much had happened over the last three months, she sometimes wondered if it weren't all a dream.

"I've turned into quite the coffee connoisseur since I met you," said Paul as he handed Gabriella a steaming mug, then joined her on the couch. "I thought we'd try some Swiss mocha tonight."

Gabriella took a sip and beamed. "You're a fast learner."

"At some things anyway."

Gabriella glanced sideways at him, but said nothing.

They both sat staring at the fire for several minutes, each lost in their own thoughts. Finally Gabriella said, "I know I have to let Nathan go, but I miss him so much. Sometimes, first thing in the morning, when I wake up and realize I'll never hear his laughter or see his smile on earth again, the ache nearly overwhelms me. Strangely, however, there have been days when I thought I actually could hear him calling my name, and I've had to think twice about answering him." She chewed on her lower lip. "Does that make any sense?"

Paul nodded. "For nearly three years after my mother died, there were times when I would wake up and get out of bed and go into the kitchen and stand staring at the refrigerator. She used to get up late at night, after everyone had gone to bed, and make herself chocolate milk. She said it kept her feeling like a kid." He chuckled, remembering. "Whenever I'd wake up and surprise her, she'd laugh and make me a glass too. Then she'd make me promise not to tell anyone. 'It's our secret, Paul,' she'd say conspiratorially. 'And if anyone asks where the chocolate went, we'll tell them that ants have been known to carry off whole candy bars while people were asleep.'"

"Is that how long it took for the pain to go away? Three years?"

"I don't think the pain ever really goes away. It just mellows into a dull ache you grow accustomed to." Paul sighed. "And for what it's worth, time indeed does heal all wounds."

"All?"

He shrugged.

Gabriella set down her mug. She got up, went over to the front door, and picked up the small blue backpack she'd brought with her. "When I went through Nathan's belongings, I found three file folders full of this," she said as she sat back down and began pulling out newspaper clippings, photographs, and notes scribbled on yellow legal pads. "Nathan was very thorough when it came to gathering information. He also had an uncanny sense of timing. As a matter of fact, those are two reasons why Father got elected to the Senate."

"Oh?"

"Nathan discovered that Father's opponent, the incumbent, had ties to organized crime. Instead of jumping the gun and confronting him prematurely, Nathan, at some personal risk, meticulously gathered enough information so the FBI could indict. The information was made public on the eve of the election. And the rest, as they say, is history."

"Sounds like some pretty good detective work to me."

"The media thought so too. One journalist labeled the campaign the one that 'knocked the professional pollsters out of their proverbial political pulpits.'"

"I take it your father was the underdog."

Gabriella nodded, then frowned. "Two days before Nathan died, he and I had breakfast together. He told me that in retrospect if he'd known the outcome of his actions at the time, he would not have 'unleashed a wolf in sheep's clothing on an unsuspecting populace.'"

"You've lost me."

"It's all here," replied Gabriella, a dour look on her face. She indicated the pile of papers she'd spread between them. "My brother spent the last two years of his life gathering damaging information about my father, just like he did against my father's opponent fifteen years ago."

Paul's antennae were vibrating. "What kind of damaging information?"

"It may take a while."

"So?"

Gabriella was pensive. "And I'm not sure I believe everything I'm about to tell you."

"Well, two heads are better than one," prodded Paul, feeling a sudden surge of excitement. "Tell me what Nathan uncovered and I'll give you my honest, unbiased opinion. Fair enough?"

"I guess so. But it all just seems so —"

"Crazy?"

"Yeah. *Crazy* is the perfect word."

"I know how you feel. I've read some things in my father's journal that have challenged *my* perspective of reality on more than one occasion this past month."

"But I thought —"

"Later. You first."

"Does the name Joel Goldman mean anything to you?"

"No. Should it?"

"Two years ago, just before Nathan left for Europe, there was a bit of an uproar at the university. It involved a special exhibition of art and a lecture on the famous 'black paintings.'"

Paul nodded. "The art faculty members were quite embarrassed by the whole thing, but I can't remember why."

"An anonymous donor gave the university some very valuable works done by Francisco Goya —"

"Late eighteenth-, early nineteenth-century Spanish artist, right? I saw *The Naked Maja* at the Prado when I was in Madrid several years ago on assignment and learned that he actually painted two — one nude and one fully clothed. My guide told me his model was the Duchess of Alba, with whom Goya supposedly had a rather torrid affair."

"That's right. Goya was a first-rate rococo decorator who initially gained notoriety in 1796 when he produced a series of eighty etchings called *Los Caprichos*, a fantastic medley of one man's startling vision of universal greed, vanity, superstition and cruelty."

"I remember reading that he was a very controversial artist in his time — that the aristocracy of eighteenth-century Spain, deeply influenced by their fundamentally Catholic society, were not quite ready for his boldness."

"He's still controversial." Gabriella moved closer to Paul and handed him several photographs, along with half a dozen legal pages of notes. "Goya purchased a villa in 1819 near Madrid, the *Quinta del Sordo*, or 'deaf man's house,' when he was seventy-three. There, over the next three years, he painted what were, if not his greatest paintings, at least his most deeply personal ones. Nathan's investigations took him to Spain, where he photographed the 'black paintings.'"

She took the 8 x 10 photographs from Paul and arranged them in order on the couch between them. "Take a look at these. A series of huge oil murals, done in grays and gray ochers. For his eyes only." The collection of photographs she displayed produced a stunning collage. "As you can see, they are relentlessly black in spirit — hence the name."

Paul felt overwhelmed by the vivid images of witches, skeletons, violent gods, hysterics, monsters, lunatics . . . all of them howling, struggling, dancing, and devouring one another. Gabriella watched Paul study them and felt her pulse quicken. "All told, Goya completed fourteen murals. He painted them directly onto the plaster walls of the largest rooms in the *del Sordo*. They're nothing less than the artistic rendering of the genesis of evil out of primordial chaos. A graphic depiction of evil's ultimate, triumphant universality."

Paul was disturbed by what he heard in Gabriella's voice. "Surely *you* don't believe that?"

"Let me finish," she snapped, immediately regretting her tone. "I'm sorry. I didn't mean to sound like a shrew. I just have to get the whole thing out. Okay?"

He nodded.

"What makes *Los Caprichos* so remarkably original is that while all artists tend to live intensely *with* their work, Goya tried to live *in* his work," she continued, drawing upon the reservoir of information she'd accumulated over a decade of study. "Goya attempted to materialize the ethereal world that existed inside his mind so the images he meticulously wedded to canvas would form a total environment. He painted both aggressively and polemically. His work is extremely visceral because the images he painted beckon our souls to enter into the works." She paused, choosing her words carefully.

"Goya's work assaults our *emotions* as well as our senses. His paintings *demand* involvement. And maybe, just maybe, he was trying to tell the world something important . . . Something so incredible it borders on the lunatic."

"How does Goldman fit in to all this?"

"The art department thought it would be a good idea to publicize the donation by bringing in someone of international repute to lecture on the works. They chose Goldman, a renowned art collector and recognized authority on the works of Goya. And that's where the story really gets interesting." Her eyes glittered as she handed him the first page from the pile of legal pads. "Look what Nathan wrote."

Paul read quickly.

Goldman's contention is that Goya was not simply painting the substance of his nightmares, thereby giving reality to the demons that plagued his dreams. According to him, although he never said exactly where he unearthed the information, what Goya was painting was the *reality* of evil. Goldman insisted that the murals were a final testament to the *incarnate existence* of evil. He believed that the black paintings were a warning to mankind that demons are real. He also contended that although they live in the spiritual realm, they can — and do — manifest in the natural realm on a regular basis.

They feed off man's misfortunes like horses feed at a salt lick. Moreover, they are not passive; they inaugurate strife in order to generate spiritual energy to feed on. Once there is sufficient pain and suffering, they go into a kind of feeding frenzy. They can't help themselves.

(see clippings, file #3. Italics mine.)

"I see what you mean about Nathan being thorough," he told her when he was finished. "But I still don't understand how all of this fits together."

Gabriella rustled through the pile of papers and pulled out the folded advertisement she'd found, along with another clipping. "Read these and you will."

Paul was shocked to see his father's obituary among Nathan's possessions, but he was even more surprised when he reread the advertisement entitled *Open Letter to 144,000 Rainbow People*.

"Rainbow International!" he muttered when he saw who placed the ad. "Where did Nathan get these?"

"Joel Goldman's penthouse apartment . . . In the Halcyon Building." Gabriella looked suddenly drained. "According to Nathan's files, Goldman died under mysterious circumstances a week before your father." She paused, then groaned. "Oh, Paul, don't you see why I'm so confused? And scared?"

Paul was suddenly confused himself. "Is there more?" he asked.

"Turn over the advertisement."

"'Must tell the sons about the fathers,'" he read.

"You told me that my father met your father in Palestine. Apparently Joel Goldman intended to contact you and Nathan and tell you both something important about the two of them." Her tone was almost hysterical. "Now he's dead . . . Your father's dead . . . And Nathan is dead!" She could no longer hold back the tears. "What — is — going — on?"

Paul pulled her toward him and held her close. His arms felt safe and secure. She needed so very much to be told everything was going to be all right.

"Gabriella, listen to me," he said when her weeping abated. "I know you've been through a lot, but there's something I have to tell you."

Uncertain why, Gabriella stiffened and pulled back. She pushed the long black strands of her hair off her face and wiped the tears from her cheeks with the back of her hand.

Paul took a deep breath. "I don't think Nathan's death was an accident. And before you say anything, hear me out."

Gabriella felt nauseous as he spoke.

"I'm not *certain* yet," he continued rapidly. "It's just that for the past two weeks some things have been rolling around inside my head, and when you started telling me about what Nathan had uncovered, it was like pieces of a puzzle coming together."

Gabriella's fists were clenched, and her knuckles were white. "But who would want to kill my brother?"

Paul shook his head. "I can't prove it yet, but my gut instincts — what my editor calls my journalist's antennae — tell me that Vaughn Aurochs is involved. And my antennae are rarely wrong."

"Vaughn Aurochs? Why?"

"I can't answer that just yet either."

"Well, what *do* your antennae tell you?" She could hear the day-old conversation with her father inside her head: "I told you, Vaughn took care of all the details. Nathan's body was so mangled, they had to identify him by his dental records."

Paul sighed heavily. "Nathan's death is somehow tied in with the theft of my father's journal, the missing parchments, and *your* father's involvement with Rainbow International."

"Oh no, you don't," she said, suddenly angry. "First Nathan and now you. I don't know what you hope to gain by dragging my father into this, but I don't like it."

Her words slapped Paul in the face. "What are you talking about?"

Gabriella stood up, ready for a fight. Nevertheless, her legs were trembling. "Just because I told you Nathan believed Vaughn Aurochs is the Antichrist, and he and my father are business associates, doesn't mean that *I* believe it." She wrapped her arms around herself, suddenly chilled. "And this business about Nathan's death not being an accident . . . I don't buy that either."

"Then why are you so angry?"

"Don't wax Socratic on me now, Paul Kingman. I'm angry because you told me once that no matter what happened you'd protect me." She brushed by him and headed for the door. "And if attacking the integrity of my father is your idea of protecting me, I don't want your protection." She grabbed her purse.

Paul stood up. "Gabriella, please, you're overreacting. Let's talk this out."

"I've heard enough talk," she replied, slamming the door on her way out.

Paul ran to the front door and opened it. "Gabriella, I'm sorry. Please . . . come back." But she had disappeared around the corner. He muttered a curse as he headed after her.

He got to the corner in time to see her jump into a cab. He was angry with himself for the way he'd handled the evening. And he was so lost in thought that he didn't pay any attention to the red Mustang that pulled out from the curb and began following the cab.

Gabriella's whole body was trembling. It was all she could do to keep from breaking down and weeping.

The cabby kept staring at her in his rearview mirror. "Everything OK, lady?"

"No, everything's *not* OK," she retorted, angry with herself for taking out her frustrations on Paul. He was only trying to help. And he really hadn't said anything she hadn't already thought about at least a dozen times . . . except the part about Nathan's death not being an accident.

She gave the cabby her address, then began thinking about how she would apologize. She realized that she loved Paul and that she wanted more than anything for it to be *right* this time. The voice inside her told her it was.

The cab came to a stop in front of her house, and she got out.

She paid the cabby and stood for a minute in the street, watching him drive off, wondering if he thought she was crazy. "Well, who cares?" she mumbled.

She turned toward the sidewalk, deep in thought, and yet something caused her to pause. She looked up momentarily, and a scream died on her lips as 4,200 pounds of rubber, metal, and chrome slammed into her at nearly forty miles an hour. Gabriella bounced off the shiny red hood of the Shelby Mustang like a toy doll. Somehow her body missed the windshield and was thrown free of the wheels. Otherwise she would have been crushed.

It was over in seconds.

The crumpled, twisted body lying in the middle of the street looked like an abused Raggedy Ann doll. And the broken doll bled and bled and bled.

No one had seen the actual accident. But Gabriella's neighbor across the street, Mrs. Johnson-Davies, who always left her windows open at night in the summer, rushed to her living-room window at the first sound of impact.

Her scream picked up where Gabriella's had ended.

She saw the taillights of the car speeding off and got a quick glimpse of the license plate. Shaking, she ran to the phone and dialed 911.

After the paramedics had taken Gabriella to the hospital, a detective asked Mrs. Johnson-Davies what she'd seen. When she got to the description of the car, she remembered that the vehicle had been red and that the license plate seemed odd to her.

"What do you mean by odd?"

"I think it said Azalea, or something like that."

"You mean like the flower?" The detective wrote as the lady talked, making sure to get the details correct. It wasn't every day that a Senator's daughter was run down in front of her home, on the outskirts of the nation's capital, barely a month after her brother had been killed the same way.

It would be national news within the hour.

"I'm not sure. I just caught a quick glimpse. And I remember thinking that the spelling was odd."

"OK. We'll check it out," he said, hoping the victim didn't die before he could tell his partner, who'd gone ahead to the hospital, something more concrete.

He glanced at the chalk marks on the street, outlining the woman's form, and headed for his car, thinking, "There's no way that woman is going to be telling anybody anything — ever — not with all that blood lost."

XXVIII

Paul stared out the tenth-floor plate-glass window of Mount Sinai Hospital through tired, reddened eyes, barely seeing the sprawling city below. The first orange-yellow tentacles of the sun were reaching up from the dark perimeter of night, grasping hold of the dawn.

This Wednesday morning was very possibly the worst morning of his life. About the only morning he could remember being worse was the day of his father's funeral, three months ago. It had been raining then.

Benjamin had died in this same hospital, nine floors below this one, just as winter died in this part of the earth, quietly and without fanfare. Now the woman Paul loved lay comatose in the Intensive Care Unit of the hospital, as his father had done in the last hours of his life. Paul had been by her side since shortly after she'd been admitted, except during her surgery to relieve inner-cranial bleeding.

Had he tears to cry, he would still be crying.

Summer is supposed to be a time of life, not death, he thought, watching the steady caterpillar progress of the first light of day. *Funny how moments like these are lost amidst the clutter of our social rituals. Each day the sun births its life-giving presence into the world. Each day we have an opportunity to begin our lives anew and to wrest from the implacable scribe of our lives — time — the right to make every minute count for something more than simply existing. Yet how casually we treat that opportunity.*

"You must stop blaming yourself," came Yuri's soft voice from behind him. "More importantly . . . you must stop blaming God."

Paul turned from his perusal of the city and stared hard at Yuri. His sunken eyes cried out for help. "You show up at the strangest times," he said woodenly.

"How is she?"

"You mean, 'What did the doctor say?'" Paul's tone was sarcastic. "The same thing he said three hours ago. Gabriella's condition is extremely critical but stable. They've done all they can. She suffered numerous internal injuries, and they're still unable to determine the extent of brain damage. They had to suction a clot from one of the major arteries leading to the brain."

Yuri sighed. "I guess in situations like this all we can do is wait, hope for the best . . . and pray."

Paul rubbed his aching eyes repeatedly. He was bone-tired. He hadn't slept, except for brief catnaps, in over seventy-two hours. "She might come out of her coma at any moment, or she might linger . . . indefinitely." The word tasted bitter.

"Is there anything I can do?"

"Do! Ha, that's a good one." He leaned against the window, ignoring the warmth from the sun on his back, which did little to ease the chill in his gut. "You know, Gabriella believes you're an angel. Can you imagine that?"

Yuri said nothing.

"Tell me something, Mr. Angel. If God is so wonderful, why has He taken everything good in my life from me?"

Yuri's voice was soft, soothing, almost musical. "Sometimes God takes away so He can give back."

"What?"

"Man's ways are not the ways of the Great I Am."

"How philosophic." Paul turned his back on Yuri, leaned his head against the window, and closed his eyes. "This is all just a horrible dream," he muttered. "I keep telling myself that I'll wake up any minute and the nightmare will be over. But it doesn't work."

Yuri's soft but forceful words prodded him. "You *must* speak before the Council, Paul. It's more important now than ever before."

"Leave me alone. I don't care about the Council meeting . . . or about people I don't even know and who don't know me."

"What about Gabriella? And Nathan? I know you care about what happened to them."

"So?"

"Have you asked yourself why Vaughn Aurochs wanted the parchments your father discovered so badly? And why he and Senator McDaniel became business associates last September?"

Paul whirled. "What do you know about that?" Something Gabriella had said the night she'd been struck down suddenly clicked inside his head. "Wait a minute! The Halcyon Building. Joel Goldman. You're living in Goldman's penthouse, aren't you?"

Yuri nodded.

"You've known from the beginning what this is all about, haven't you?"

"That's an interesting choice of words, my young friend. *'From the beginning . . .'*"

"Well?"

"I'd like to share a Scripture with you. It's from the book of Hosea: 'My people are destroyed for lack of knowledge: because you have rejected knowledge, I will also reject you, that you shall not be a priest to me: seeing that you have forgotten the law of your God, I will also forget your children.'"

Paul remained pensive.

"There are answers at the Council meeting, and there are things you need to say. Millions of lives are at stake."

"That's what you said the night you showed up in my office. I'm tired of riddles. Why won't you give me a straight answer?"

"Because I don't have permission."

"Permission?" Paul shook his head. The man was inscrutable. He loved to talk in riddles. He should have been born Chinese. "I can't believe I'm having this conversation."

Yuri smiled enigmatically. "One day you will. Now you have just enough time to go home, change clothes, and organize your thoughts. The first session begins at 9, and you're the second speaker, correct?"

"How did you know?"

Yuri smiled. "We angels know quite a bit."

Paul chuckled without humor. "I bet."

Yuri stared at him for a moment, as if he were trying to reach a decision about something. Abruptly he asked Paul an odd question. "Are you familiar with the Tabernacle of Moses?"

"From the Old Testament?"

Yuri nodded.

"Somewhat. Why?"

"Because I have something to tell you about it that might help you better understand what's been happening to you and Gabriella . . . and Nathan . . . And why it's so important for you to be at that meeting today."

Paul listened intently, his anger — and his pain — momentarily forgotten. There was something about the glint in Yuri's eyes and the tone in his voice that he couldn't resist.

"Shortly after Moses, under God's command and authority, rescued the Israelites from Egypt and led them through the Red Sea into the wilderness, the Lord commanded him to build a Tabernacle — according to exact specifications. It took exactly *nine months* for the people to construct a temporary, earthly habitation for the presence of Jehovah Elohim, the Creator of Heaven and Earth."

"The same time it takes for a baby to grow in its mother's womb," mumbled Paul, awed by the amazing parallel.

Yuri nodded. "As you probably know, the Tabernacle was divided into three parts: the Outer Court, the Inner Court, and the Holy of Holies. Inside the Holy of Holies was the Ark of the Covenant. The Ark was cut from acacia, or *shit'tim* wood, and plated inside and out with pure gold. It was magnificent."

Yuri paused and closed his eyes, remembering. Even now he could hear the Seraphim singing around the Throne. The music was like nothing that had ever been heard on Earth. Reluctantly he opened his eyes and continued.

"The lid was called the Mercy Seat. It was the same size as the Ark and was also made of acacia overlaid with gold. Upon this lid, at both ends of the Ark, were two pure gold Cherubim the size of men. They were constantly maintained in an upright position and faced one another, looking down upon the Mercy Seat.

"Between the Cherubim was the *Shekinah*, the cloud of glory in which Jehovah Elohim, the manifest presence of God Himself, appeared as He hovered above the Mercy Seat. And it was upon the Mercy Seat that the blood of a slain bullock was sprinkled as atonement for the sin of the nation of Israel. The High Priest could never enter the Most Holy Place without the blood."

Something snapped inside Paul. "Gabriella used to talk about blood in the same way," he said. "But she was referring to the blood of Jesus. Is there a connection?"

"That's what I've been trying to tell you, my young friend. *The blood is the key.* And you will find the answer to many of your questions in the parchments your father discovered. However, there are those who would take the truth written there and pervert it. You must not let that happen."

"I don't understand. What can I do?"

Yuri stepped forward and put his arm around Paul. "Don't give in now. The enemy desires to sift you as wheat. Resist him and he must flee. I'll stay and watch over Gabriella for you. You needn't worry about her safety. If there's any change in her condition, I'll notify you immediately."

Paul stared into Yuri's hazel-green eyes. He felt as if he were floating. Renewed strength suffused his body as all his anger drained from him. Hope flickered and caught. Once again he had an anchor for his soul.

He glanced at his watch. It was nearly 7. He knew he needed to be at the morning session in order to get a feel for the tone of the meeting. There was no time for sleep.

"I'm going to look in on Gabriella one last time." Paul turned once again and stared at the rising sun. The fine, fibrous filaments of dawn had woven themselves together into a brilliant, crystalline tapestry of light.

Inside Gabriella's room, Paul approached her bedside. She was hooked up to tubes and wires, including a ventilator. Her normally healthy looking, honey-colored face was pale, and her head was still covered by a swath of bandages. Paul knew that all of her once abundant black hair had been shaved off in the emergency room. Her left leg was held rigid in a cast that went from her ankle to her hip. Her right forearm also wore a cast, from just above the elbow to the wrist. He also knew, from what the doctor had told him, that she'd required over one hundred internal stitches.

He knelt beside the bed, oblivious to the other patients in the Intensive Care Unit, and laid his right hand on her bound forearm. He felt like crying and yelling at God simultaneously. Abruptly Yuri's words intruded. *". . . all we can do is wait, hope for the best and pray."* He began to pray quietly, knowing it was all that was left for him to do.

He wasn't sure who needed prayer more — himself or Gabriella. He felt burned-out inside, like someone had turned a flamethrower on him, scorching his emotions into ashes. Yet, deep within him anger flickered. And he was rapidly coming to the point where he was able to focus that anger on one individual. A man he'd only met once, but who had left an indelible impression on him. Vaughn Aurochs.

He opened his eyes and stared at Gabriella. Her once-bright and inquisitive eyes were heavily shadowed by dark bruises. A plastic tube protruded from and was taped to the side of the mouth which had, on more than one occasion, laughed musically at his offbeat sense of humor.

After several minutes he stood up and sighed, then bent over and kissed her on the cheek. Reaching down, he grasped her right hand just below the cast and said, "I'm sorry, Gabriella, for the other night. I hate arguing. I'm sorry that I never got to say I'm sorry. Most of all, I regret never telling you that I love you." He stared at her battered body, seeing something beyond her physical presence, and stroked the small section of exposed flesh on her arm tenderly. "Will you marry me, my love?" The mechanical *whoosh* of the ventilator sounded harsh in his ears . . . like the raspy, wheezing sound an old man makes as he desperately tries to fill emphysematic lungs with oxygen. He gazed down at Gabriella for a few more minutes, thinking about the last words he'd said to his comatose father: *"Death always wins . . ."*

Finally he released her hand and vowed, "Not this time — not this time." Then he turned quietly and left the room.

XXIX

Senator David McDaniel sat on the stage behind Archbishop Andrew McCarthy and scanned the faces of the audience waiting expectantly in Fisher Auditorium. The room was packed with almost two thousand people. His mind was in turmoil as Archbishop McCarthy began his opening speech from the podium.

McDaniel had spent the past four days at the cabin in Grand Lake, preparing for this morning, and had cut himself off from the outside world.

No phone.

No television.

Nothing but the mountains and fresh air.

That's why he'd only just heard about Gabriella's accident. His aide had told him about it just after his private jet landed at Dulles. Unfortunately, he didn't have time to get to the hospital to see how she was doing. This meeting was an important part of his and Vaughn's timetable. He'd fended off the rapid-fire questions from a small crowd of reporters with terse replies of "No comment."

Once they were in the limo, on the way to the meeting, his aide told him Gabriella was in a coma and the doctors had done all they could for her to this point. Nothing would be gained by his going to the hospital, and a great deal would be lost if he failed to appear at the meeting.

He pulled a sigh from his innermost being. It was one of the very few moments during his political career when he truly had no comment. How could he make a statement about something he knew nothing about? Now the Archbishop's words intruded into his musings.

". . . as far as religion or theology is concerned, we are at a significant crossroads. Either we, and I mean Western theologians and religious leaders in general, learn to cooperate or we shall find ourselves out of a job." He paused for emphasis. "If art was the keynote of the Renaissance, religion the soul of the Reformation, and science and philosophy the gods of the Enlightenment, as Will Durant suggests in his *magnum opus* of history, then what we theologians face today is the refinement of two millennia of debate over the role of the church in secular affairs into a serious threat. A threat that combines all three of the perspectives developed in those time periods into a single, formidable enemy.

"Indeed, the power of technology combined with man's insatiable quest for answers to unanswerable questions may very well have given life to a *golem* that can only be destroyed by exorcising the root of its power: man's preoccupation with self."

The audience has become his servant, thought McDaniel appreciatively, listening to an expectant silence settle silkily over the crowd. *He has them right where he wants them.*

"Outside of religion, mankind's ability to create solutions for perceived problems, both current and potential, is limited by technology," continued the Archbishop eloquently. "Religion, on the other hand, offers humanity hope that transcends man's ability to create. It is a tether that, like a baby's umbilical cord, keeps man in contact with the source of nourishment which feeds the hunger technology cannot satiate.

"That is why we have come together . . . to reach agreement on how best to restore the luster to the tarnished image of the only vehicle capable of transporting a hurting and disconsolate world from the edge of the dark abyss of Hell to the gates of Heaven itself."

The sound of applause filled McDaniel's ears. He suddenly felt charged with energy. All thoughts of Gabriella fled from his mind. The excitement in the auditorium was palpable. It was a golden opportunity for him to do what he did best . . . to reach down deep and touch souls. Archbishop McCarthy had primed them well.

"Our first speaker this morning," continued the Archbishop as the applause subsided, "is a man with whom many of you in this room are no doubt familiar. If you do not recognize his face, you have probably at least heard his name. In fact, he spoke here on this campus a year ago and shared his exciting vision for a renewed, revitalized America."

McCarthy turned his head, looked back over his shoulder, and stared at David. "He is here today to share with you a different kind of vision." He nodded imperceptibly, and David stood up. "The man whom I believe should be the next President of the United States . . . Senator David McDaniel."

Gabriella dreamed.

She was standing on a small, rocky island. She could see the salt-white crags of the shoreline where the crystal-clear, blue-green sea met the gray and black volcanic rocks that comprised lethal jetties.

There was bright white light everywhere. Oddly, there was an even brighter white light within the light. Gradually the light within the light began to take on form and substance.

Gabriella stared at the Light and saw seven golden candlesticks. In the midst of the seven candlesticks stood a tall man clothed with a pure white garment flowing to His feet. Around His chest was a golden girdle. His head and hair were white like wool, as white as snow, and His eyes were as a flame of fire. And His feet were like brass, as if they burned in a furnace. In His right hand He held seven stars, and out of His mouth went a sharp two-edged sword. His countenance was as the sun shining in strength.

Then the Light spoke, and the voice was as the sound of many waters. "I am Alpha and Omega, the First and the Last. I have called you from the womb to speak forth truth and righteousness and to proclaim the acceptable day of the Lord. Go into all the earth and tell those whom you shall see that I am alive . . . forevermore."

Paul shifted uncomfortably in his seat. His first shock had come when he'd seen Senator David McDaniel on the stage. His second came when the Archbishop turned and motioned for McDaniel to come forward.

Because he was sitting in the front row of the auditorium, and because he'd been staring at the Senator intently, wondering if he knew about Gabriella, Paul noticed the almost imperceptible signal that had passed between the two men. They obviously knew each other quite well. And there was something else. It was almost as if the Archbishop were conducting an orchestra and McDaniel was his star pupil, coming forward to perform.

Paul suddenly felt as if he'd been cast into a den of lions. An odd thought ran through his mind. He hoped that when it came time for him to speak, he would not be labeled a heretic, cast from the auditorium, and stoned as Stephen had been.

He also wondered how Gabriella was doing.

Yuri sat in the waiting room with his eyes closed when Gabriella's EKG monitor went off with a high-pitched, droning *Beeeeep!*

The duty nurse called for the resident and consulted her chart to verify that the attending physician had left a *Do Not Resuscitate* order for the patient because of the flat-line EEG.

Yuri's eyes snapped open.

Even though he had heard nothing, he knew.

He stood up and slowly walked to the doorway of the ICU where he stood listening to the EKG. "Brady down," one doctor said to indicate the heart was slowing to inactivity. There were now two residents and three nurses standing around Gabriella, talking among themselves and watching the monitors.

Abruptly all activity around Gabriella ceased.

The noise from the ventilator sounded strange and artificial in Yuri's ears. One of the nurses reached over and shut the mechanical breather off. One resident noted the time on her chart. 10:22 A.M.

Yuri watched impassively as the other resident pulled the sheet over Gabriella's face. Finally the Watcher turned and left the ICU, knowing he must be the one to tell Paul.

David McDaniel was thinking as he talked. Vaughn had assured him that he was indeed going to become President of the United States, but that he would have to wait five more years before achieving his goal. He had argued vehemently that he wanted to make a serious run for the White House in '88, but Vaughn had convinced him that it was better to wait until '92.

Instead, the two of them had decided they would let everyone think he was running; then at the last possible moment he would announce that he was not in fact a candidate. Vaughn had also promised him that as a result of this strategy, he would be appointed Secretary of State, a position that would serve him well for the '92 election.

He and Vaughn would use the next five years to lay the groundwork, so that shortly after he was elected President in November 1992 Congress would pass a resolution calling for America to support the ten-nation coalition government which even now was preparing to make its presence known to the world. Then, when the time was ripe, he would be nominated by someone not even remotely connected to him for the position of head of the New World Government.

He would ascend to the pinnacle of world power. An achievement that went far beyond anything he'd believed possible for himself. And in the midst of his triumph the lord of light would return in glory and manifest himself.

McDaniel glanced at his watch. 10:20.

He'd been talking twenty minutes. Time to wrap things up in a nice neat package.

"The time has come when not only politicians but theologians as well must put aside doctrinal differences," he said to his rapt audience. "We must all realize it is time for a New Age to unfold — an age in which neither politics nor religion is supreme."

There was scattered applause.

"Forty years ago," he continued, "when I was living in the desert, chronicling the madness we labeled World War II, the lord of light spoke to me and revealed himself to me in a blaze of light. I felt like Saul on the road to Damascus . . . and I was humbled beyond what mere words can express. It was then that I received the vision I've shared with you today.

"I urge you to reach out and grasp the hand of the god I serve and to walk with him into the future — a future where a New Heaven and a New Earth await those of us who will humbly submit ourselves to him."

There was more applause, and this time it was more intense and prolonged. The crescendo built like a wave rushing to the shore but did not crest. McDaniel knew he'd branded his vision into their hearts.

Dazed by the intensity of the response, Paul stared at his watch. It had taken exactly twenty-two minutes for the Senator to turn deception into truth, evil into good, sheep into goats.

He stood up as the Senator left the podium, feeling defeated even before he spoke. Archbishop McCarthy stepped forward and indicated for him to come up on stage. He motioned that he had to speak to the Senator momentarily. McCarthy frowned and shrugged. "We'll take a ten-minute break before our next speaker," the Archbishop said into the microphone. "Please remain in the auditorium."

McDaniel was in the middle of a group of reporters. Paul started in his direction, but stopped when a strong hand took hold of his arm. He turned and gazed into Yuri's glistening eyes.

"I'm sorry, Paul," the silver-haired man said softly. "Gabriella is dead. There was nothing I could do to intervene."

Paul stared at Yuri for several seconds, in a stupor, as if he hadn't heard correctly, fighting back tears. *What does Yuri mean there was nothing he could do to intervene?*

"No!" he moaned.

Yuri's voice was gentle and soothing. "You mustn't give up, Paul . . . no matter what. Remember, the enemy wants you to believe he's won. He only wins if you quit."

Paul was devastated. Suddenly nothing mattered except that Gabriella was dead. There was no point in speaking before the Council. God had failed him.

He watched the crowd gather around the Senator. The flicker of anger he'd felt earlier at Gabriella's bedside ignited. Even though he couldn't prove it, he knew that somehow the Senator and Vaughn Aurochs were responsible for her death. "There's something I have to do," he told Yuri.

Yuri followed his seething gaze. "I'll go with you."

McDaniel looked up and saw Paul headed in his direction. "Excuse me, gentlemen," he said to the reporters. "I've got some personal business to attend to. My aide will inform you about my press conference next week." He pushed his way through the group of reporters and left his aide to deal with their questions about his formal announcement of candidacy.

"Mr. Kingman, this is quite a surprise," said the Senator as Paul and Yuri reached him.

Paul pinned him with cold eyes. How had people as wonderful as Nathan and Gabriella come from the loins of this man? "That was quite a speech, Senator. I thought the applause was going to bring down the house."

The Senator eyed Paul speculatively, not quite sure he was being paid a compliment. "It's a beginning."

"So was the Tower of Babel."

McDaniel's stomach did a somersault. "I beg your pardon . . ." he stammered.

"'Come, let us build ourselves a city, and a tower whose top may reach to heaven; and let us make a name for ourselves . . .'"

"You're talking gibberish, Mr. Kingman."

"Am I?" Paul's eyes were daggers.

The Senator studied Paul briefly, then said, "If you'll excuse me I —"

Paul was livid. "Did you know that Gabriella was in the hospital?" he blurted out. "That she was run down in front of her house by a hit-and-run driver Saturday night?"

The Senator grimaced. "I heard about it this morning from my aide, on the way here from the airport."

Paul was incredulous. "And you didn't even bother coming to the hospital?"

McDaniel sighed heavily. "I was told she was in a coma and the doctors had done all they could do. If you'll excuse me, I'm on my way there now."

"It's too late, Senator."

"What?"

"Gabriella's dead."

McDaniel went ashen. "First Nathan and now Gabriella. How much is enough?" he muttered.

"You've brought this upon yourself, Senator," said Yuri dispassionately. "And your association with Vaughn Aurochs will continue to bring destruction upon you."

"Who are *you*?" scowled McDaniel, noticing Yuri for the first time.

"He's a friend," Paul answered.

"Well, your friend is pretty outspoken."

"Are you familiar with the Azazel sacrifice, Senator?" pressed Yuri, his eyes penetrating and hard.

"I beg your pardon?"

Paul stared at Yuri, wondering what he was talking about. Was there no end to his riddles?

"In the Book of Leviticus, Moses recounts the ceremony the High Priests of Israel performed as a sin offering to God, atoning for the people's sins. Two unblemished goats were selected by Aaron, the High Priest, and presented before the Lord at the door of the Tabernacle. One goat was for the Lord, the other was a scapegoat. Azazel in Hebrew."

"Why are you telling me this?" asked McDaniel, scowling.

"I think you know the answer to that, Senator."

"This is nonsense," muttered McDaniel. "I don't have to stand here and listen to some religious fanatic talking to me about blood sacrifices."

Yuri watched him intently. "I didn't say anything about *blood*, Senator."

McDaniel ignored the silver-haired man and focused on Paul. "What exactly are you doing here today?"

Paul looked at Yuri, then back at McDaniel. "I came to talk about the parchments, Senator."

McDaniel arched his brow. "Oh? And what do they have to do with this meeting?"

Before Paul could reply, the Senator's aide walked up. "Senator, there's an important call for you in the lobby," he said.

McDaniel nodded. "Must be the hospital . . . about Gabriella," he told Paul. "I'll have to go there and make arrangements for my daughter's body." He paused, then added, "I expect you'll be at the funeral?"

Paul wanted to punch him.

"Senator . . ." said Yuri.

McDaniel looked at him warily.

"Remember well the words of the prophet Daniel: 'And the king shall do according to his will, and he shall exalt himself and magnify himself above every god, and shall speak marvelous things against the God of gods, and shall prosper until the indignation be accomplished: for that is determined shall be done. Neither shall he regard the God of his fathers, nor the desire of women, nor regard any god: for he shall magnify himself above all.'"

McDaniel stared into the depths of Yuri's hazel-green eyes for several moments before he turned his back on the two men and left the auditorium without uttering another word.

Paul watched him go, then looked at Yuri. "What was that all about?"

"The Senator serves a different god than you or I," replied

Yuri cryptically. "And he has no idea of the true cost of his misguided discipleship."

"He looked shaken by what you said."

Yuri shrugged. "For the moment perhaps. But his lust for power will burn the fear from him. And his own hunger will drive him like a rancher drives cattle — to the slaughterhouse."

Paul studied Yuri with sudden insight. Maybe Gabriella was right after all. He decided to ask Yuri if he *had* been in his room the night he'd wrestled with the darkness. "There's something I need to —"

"Ladies and gentlemen, please take your seats," came Archbishop McCarthy's booming voice.

"You're on," said Yuri, winking.

"But —"

Yuri shook his head. "We'll talk later." He turned to leave.

"Yuri . . ."

The older man turned. "Yes?"

"I need to see her before they —"

"I understand. The doctor said they were going to perform the autopsy at 1 o'clock."

"Where are you going?"

Yuri arched his brow, but said nothing.

"I'll be at the hospital later."

Yuri turned and walked up the aisle.

"Mr. Kingman," pressed Archbishop McCarthy from the stage. "It's time."

Paul watched Yuri leave the auditorium, then headed for the podium, not sure what he was going to say. "If you are an angel, Yuri ben Raphah," he muttered under his breath, "I could certainly use your help right now."

XXX

Paul looked out over the packed auditorium and took a deep breath. There had been a brief, polite round of applause when he was introduced by Archbishop McCarthy. Although he was a well-known journalist, he'd never written anything that would have necessarily caught the attention of any of the delegates to this convention.

He didn't mind. It was what he was about to say today that mattered.

He knew he wasn't going to make a lot of new friends here today, but regardless of what might happen as a result of his speech, he hoped they would remember his words for a long time. He hoped they would hear the truth of what he said . . . before it was too late.

In spite of his earlier resolve, he was nervous. He was having a hard time shaking the ominous sense of heaviness that had settled upon him like a heavy cloak while he was talking to the Senator. First Nathan had been run down and killed, and now Gabriella was dead. *Was he next?*

"Ladies and gentlemen, delegates, members of the press," said Paul solemnly, "I want to thank you in advance for your patience and attention. Although I'm accustomed to writing words that paint pictures in people's minds, I am considerably less acquainted with the art of public speaking."

He scanned the audience and was relieved to see several smiles of encouragement from both delegates and the general public. Maybe this wasn't going to be so bad after all.

"On a hot summer day in June, some thirty-three hundred

and fifty years ago," he began, "an eighty-year-old man came down from the Mountain of God in the Sinai desert. He had been praying and fasting for forty days and nights, taking neither food nor water. Much to his dismay, he discovered that in that short space of time his people had been deceived and corrupted because of their lack of faith.

"During the forty days he'd been seeking God's face, the men and women he'd led from bondage to freedom, under the guidance of the Lord God Almighty, had decided they were going to create a golden calf they would worship as the source of their deliverance. When the old man discovered what his people had done, he rebuked them in the name of the Lord, took the molten calf which they had made, and burned it in a fire. Then he ground it to powder and scattered the golden dust upon the waters of a nearby stream, which turned the color of blood.

"The great patriarch then stood at the entrance to the camp and commanded that all who served the Lord should come and stand beside him and openly acknowledge their faithfulness to their true Deliverer. Most of the people did so. But three thousand refused to consecrate themselves to God. They were all put to death."

Paul paused and looked out over the auditorium. He definitely had everyone's attention. He was glad for that. It made it easier to say what he had come to tell them.

"The old man, of course, was Moses. The people he led were Jews," he continued, giving the Rabbis in the front row a furtive glance. "Jews who were accustomed to persecution and slaughter because of who they were. But this was different. This was *their* God passing judgment on them because of apostasy and unbelief. This was their God dealing with sin.

"Interestingly enough, the number of people killed that day was prophetic. The number who died on the day Moses brought the Law down from Mount Sinai was the exact number of people who on the Day of Pentecost received the baptism of the Holy Spirit after hearing the Apostle Peter speak — a man who just seven weeks before denied, not once but three times, that he knew the Lord Jesus Christ."

The crowd began to come alive with a subtle but distinct murmuring. Paul pressed on, ignoring the rippling hum. He doubted they had any idea where he was leading them.

"I share this slice of Jewish history with you because it demonstrates, rather vividly, that God has always had a plan for mankind. He was, is, and always will be in control of what happens here on this planet. His sovereignty remains unquestioned — if not unchallenged — no matter what anyone might say or think.

"During the forty days Moses was on Mount Sinai, God revealed to him not only the Law that was designed to protect the Jews from sin, but a minutely detailed plan for a Tabernacle. A holy place He would inhabit and thereby fellowship with His fallen creation.

"You see, it was God's original plan to live *inside* man . . . not in some earthly structure. But because Eve was deceived and disobeyed God, and because Adam loved his wife more than truth and disobeyed God, man willfully separated himself from the gift of intimate communion with his Creator.

"It took the Israelites exactly nine months to build the Tabernacle as God commanded . . . the same length of time it takes for a baby growing inside its mother to become complete enough to survive outside her womb. On the day God's earthly habitation was finished, the Lord manifested Himself to His people in the form of a cloud of glory. This manifestation of His presence was so powerful that no one, not even the priests, were able to stand before Him.

"Later God spoke to His people through Moses, telling them He had given them a choice: life or death. And He admonished them to choose life . . . His life . . . life everlasting. What the Greeks would later call *zoe*."

Paul stared pointedly at the faces of the people before him. "Ladies and gentlemen," he said dramatically, "all of us on the earth today have that same choice to make. We must choose whom we are going to serve. Are we going to serve a counterfeit god who duplicates all that is pure and holy, turning it into death and destruction? Or are we going to serve the one true God, who freely gives His everlasting life without demanding the payment of our souls?"

The hum in the audience grew into a buzz of discomfort. Paul realized his words were having their desired effect.

"Forty years ago a young American archaeologist, who also happened to be a Jew, discovered a leather-bound bundle of parchments in a cave on the shores of the Dead Sea. His discovery was made shortly after the discovery of the Dead Sea Scrolls. Until now, what Benjamin Kingman found in the desert has never been publicly announced."

The audience waited with hushed expectancy. Three Rabbis sitting in the front row were conferring anxiously with one another. This was not at all what they had been expecting when they'd agreed to attend the conference.

"My father died exactly three months ago today," continued Paul in a hushed voice. "Part of the legacy he left to me were those parchments, along with his journal containing his translation. Shortly after I came into possession of my father's journal, it was stolen from my office. All I have by way of proof of what I'm about to tell you is that portion of my father's journal that I managed to store on computer disk before the theft."

Paul's eyes were drawn to the back of the auditorium. There, standing by the door, was a pale man wearing snakeskin boots. Something pricked his memory. Something Gabriella had said their last night together? No! It was something he'd *read* to her from Nathan's notes: *"Goldman insisted that the murals were a final testament to the incarnate existence of evil. He believed that the black paintings were a warning to mankind that demons are real. He also contended that although they live in the spiritual realm, they can — and do — manifest in the natural realm."*

They locked eyes momentarily, and Paul felt a shudder promenade up and down his spine. The man's eyes seemed vacant . . . soulless. Paul's fear was replaced by anger. Maybe the waxen man knew something about Gabriella's death. Instantaneously Paul decided to confront the stranger after he finished his talk.

But first things first.

He told the audience what was in the parchments. When he'd finished telling them all that he knew, and how he believed Vaughn Aurochs and Senator David McDaniel fit into the picture, he added, "The Word of God tells us that many will come claiming to be Christ. Indeed, Jesus said that '. . . there shall arise false Christs, and false prophets, and shall show great signs and wonders; insomuch that, if it were possible, they shall deceive the very elect. Behold, I have told you before. Wherefore if they shall say unto you, Behold, he is in the desert; go not forth: behold, he is in the secret chambers, believe it not. For as the lightning comes out of the east, and shines even unto the west; so shall the coming of the Son of man be.'"

An explosion of sound erupted.

The steering committee members were staring at one another like men who'd seen a ghost. Archbishop McCarthy stood up hurriedly and rushed to the podium. He raised his hands, indicating he wanted silence.

Gradually the noise subsided.

The Archbishop glanced furtively at Paul and then, visibly struggling to keep calm, made a decision. "Ladies and gentlemen . . . please . . . restrain yourselves from such outbursts," he said forcefully, maintaining his control. "We have come here in a spirit of conciliation, and in spite of the fact that we might not agree with everything that is said, we must hear this man out."

As Archbishop McCarthy spoke, he was looking down at the Rabbis. It was obvious they were among those who were the most agitated. He turned to Paul and whispered, "Because it was I who recommended that you be one of our speakers, I shall allow you to continue. But I insist that you finish what you have to say immediately and step down."

Paul nodded perfunctorily. "Let me bring the concept into perspective in terms of what is happening in the world today," he continued as the muttering subsided, "not only in terms of politics, but of religion as well. When man fell and was cast from the Garden, God sent angels to help him survive on a cursed planet. These angels in turn succumbed to the sin that was in the world and mated with daughters of men. Their offspring were spiritually illegitimate — half-human . . . half-angelic. Their father, indirectly, was Satan.

"The *Nephilim*, or fallen ones, died along with the rest of apostate humanity in the Great Noahic Flood. However, only their physical bodies perished."

Paul was amazed at the effect his words were having. Some people were visibly angry. Others were simply overwhelmed. Still others looked confused and uncomfortable.

"The demonic spirits of the fallen ones, the offspring of angels and man, are real. They have power. And, most importantly, they feed off the perversions of the flesh that mankind indulges in."

Skeptical looks from the audience did not deter Paul. He was determined to tell them what he knew, no matter what the cost.

"You see, ladies and gentlemen, what Scripture says is true: 'For the life of the flesh is *in the blood*.' If an individual gives in to demonic forces by engaging in activities that produce spiritual death — regardless of whether or not they are conscious they are doing so — the demonic spirits, like vampires, feed on that sin."

Paul felt the hostility and anger brewing. Yet he could also tell that some members of the assembly had *heard*. Most were simply outraged at what they perceived to be a presumptuous and perhaps even blasphemous attitude.

He finished by admonishing them with a quote from Joshua: "'Now, therefore, fear the Lord and serve Him in sincerity and truth: and put away the gods which your fathers served on the other side of the flood, and in Egypt; and serve you the Lord. And if it seems evil unto you to serve the Lord, choose you this day whom you will serve; whether the gods which your fathers served that were on the other side of the flood, or the gods of the Amorites, in whose land you dwell: but as for me and my house, we will serve the Lord.'"

The audience could not contain itself any longer, and hundreds of yelling and shouting people jumped to their feet to protest Paul's words.

Paul stepped back from the podium and from the hostility rising before him like a wall.

The three Rabbis were on their feet, shaking their fists angrily, trying to be heard above the noise.

Archbishop McCarthy again rushed to the podium and tried to bring some order to the auditorium, but he couldn't get the crowd to calm down. When he turned to demand that Paul leave immediately, he found Paul had already left the stage and was making his way up the aisle, walking slowly and with determination to the back of the auditorium.

Paul stared straight ahead, as if he were completely oblivious to the controversy raging around him like a wildfire out of control. People were shouting at him as he walked up the aisle, but he ignored them. Several tried to grab him, but for some reason they never even touched him. The last thing he heard as he left the auditorium was Archbishop McCarthy's voice screaming for order over the microphone.

XXXI

Paul searched the lobby, frowning. He was looking for the waxen man with the snakeskin boots. But the stranger had disappeared. He was about to give up and head for the hospital when he heard a guttural voice behind him.

"Mr. Kingman . . ."

Paul whirled, recognizing the scratchy oral signature of Vaughn Aurochs. "You!" he shouted and moved in Vaughn's direction.

Seemingly out of thin air, the pale man was between them, and his eyes were like Arctic ice — soul-piercing shards of steel-blue coldness.

Paul hesitated, overwhelmed by the intensity of the man's gaze and the raw power emanating from it. He felt as if he'd been stalked and entrapped in the blink of an eye by a wild animal.

"You haven't any idea what you're dealing with, do you, Mr. Kingman?"

"I know that you're responsible for Nathan and Gabriella's deaths, even if I can't prove it — yet."

Vaughn's cold, harsh sneer of a laugh slapped Paul in the face. "Your naiveté amazes me, Mr. Kingman. But then, it's to be expected from one such as yourself."

Vaughn's insolent demeanor had an unusual effect on Paul. Instead of infuriating him further, he found that the billionaire's attitude evoked a sense of pity, and he was momentarily taken aback. Vaughn appraised him, while the waxen man stood stoic, his penetrating gaze unwavering.

"'Skin for skin, yes, all that a man has will he give for his soul . . .'" chortled Vaughn.

"What?"

"You should spend more time reading your Holy Scriptures, Mr. Kingman. Perhaps then you might garner a glimmer of understanding." Vaughn smiled snidely. "I'll give you a hint, however — one that will make the contest all the more interesting. The man referred to in those words was the third son of Issachar, and in Hebrew his name means 'he returns.'"

Paul felt confused . . . dizzy . . . almost hypnotized. He shook his head to clear it. "I know why you want the parchments," he said, trying to regain ground he sensed that he'd lost.

"Is that so?"

"You're a fraud and a counterfeit. Once I make the parchments my father discovered public, and once I'm able to prove your complicity in the deaths of Senator McDaniel's son and daughter, you'll be finished."

"Do you really think so, Mr. Kingman?"

"I know it."

"Well then, how do you explain what just happened in there?" asked Vaughn, inclining his head.

The question hit Paul hard, and doubt swelled inside him.

Vaughn, sensing Paul's uncertainty, pressed his advantage. "You don't have anything to substantiate your fanciful imaginings, Mr. Kingman. And as for the parchments . . ." He shrugged. "You and I both know that your father stole a national treasure. I hardly think you want that made public."

Paul looked back and forth between Vaughn and the pale man, feeling overwhelmed. He made one last effort at a show of strength. "Even though I can't prove it yet, I know you were responsible for the disappearance of my father's journal. I believe you want those parchments very badly, Mr. Aurochs . . . bad enough to kill for them. I also believe that Senator McDaniel is involved with you somehow, although I can't imagine why he'd sanction the murder of his two children. Nothing can be that valuable."

"As I said a moment ago, Mr. Kingman, you have no idea."

Abruptly Paul felt an urgency to return to the hospital. He wasn't sure why, but it was suddenly extremely important that he see Gabriella. An odd thought flashed through his mind. *This conversation is not making any sense because it's not supposed to. It's a delay tactic.*

"I don't know how," Paul said defiantly, "but I am going to expose you. And I am going to use the parchments to do it. You can be sure of that." With that he turned to leave.

"Good-bye, Mr. Kingman," came the hollow voice behind him, sending a shiver up and down his spine.

As Paul exited the lobby, Vaughn faced the waxen man. "He still has the parchments," the man said, a trace of fear in his voice.

"He can't expose anything he can't find," Vaughn told him. His eyes were glazed, almost opaque. "It seems that Mr. Kingman has ignored the obvious and intends to stand against us. The master grows weary of this cat and mouse game. Take care of the matter. Now."

Paul stepped into the bright sunshine feeling as if he'd just emerged out of a deep, dark pit. He blinked while his eyes adjusted. He was sweating, and his stomach felt queasy. He glanced at his watch. It was almost noon. He had to get to the hospital. But first he had a stop to make. If he hurried he'd have just enough time . . .

He hailed a cab.

A moment later the waxen man emerged from the building, then watched Paul get into the taxi and disappear around the corner of the building. Minutes later he was following his quarry. He was driving the bright red Shelby Mustang with the custom license plate that read AZAZEL.

Paul asked the cabby to wait, got out, and walked through the iron gates at the entrance of the cemetery. It took him several minutes to locate his father's burial site. The grass surrounding the concrete marker was green and plush. *How much difference a few months makes*, thought Paul, remembering how wet and gray the March morning had been when he buried Benjamin Kingman. He stood and stared at the tombstone for several minutes, not sure why he had come.

BENJAMIN
KINGMAN

May he dwell
in the bright
Garden of Eden

Without warning, the hairs on the back of his neck stood up. He looked up and frowned. Then the nauseous feeling he'd experienced outside Fisher Auditorium returned with a vengeance.

He saw the pale man in the snakeskin boots coming toward him.

Paul shivered, shoved balled fists into his pockets, and turned his face upward. "What the —" he muttered. Great black clouds had replaced the cotton-ball puffs that had been floating lazily in the sky just moments before. And the heavens had changed from a crystalline blue to an ominous-looking slate-gray and ocher. The temperature had also dropped abruptly.

When the waxen man was about ten feet away, he spoke, the deep baritone sound of his voice chilling Paul to the bone. "You are mine to do with as I please."

The pale stranger seemed to transform before Paul's eyes. Paul stared openmouthed, swearing that the man had taken on the appearance of one of the creatures he'd seen in the photographs of Goya's "black paintings."

The fight went out of him, and he had the urge to run, but he couldn't move. The waxen man chortled. "'Skin for skin . . . yes, all that a man has . . .'" He screeched and lunged for Paul.

Suddenly there was a brilliant flash of light, followed by what sounded like a crack of thunder. Paul's eyes stung with tears. His skin felt scorched, as if he'd been blasted by a searing wind. He thought of the summer *sirocco* his father had written about in his journal.

A strange afterimage was etched upon his retinas. Black was white, and white was black — like a photo-negative — just as on the day of his father's funeral when the lightning bolt had burned the sky.

He blanched and gasped.

Yuri ben Raphah stood between him and the waxen man. The silver-haired man was now clad in a robe so white, it hurt Paul to look at it. And he was carrying a huge, shining sword.

"You must leave immediately, Paul. There's no time left."

"But —"

"Now!" boomed Yuri. "Do as I say. This one leads the Rephaim. You are no match for him."

"The Rephaim!"

"Go!" pressed Yuri. "Before it's too late."

Suddenly Paul was running across the cemetery. The wind howled about him, and the black sky seemed to be racing toward the earth. Great bolts of lightning crisscrossed the sky. The unexpected fury of the sudden storm was much worse than on the day he'd buried his father.

Rain fell.

Hard.

And an odd wailing sounded in the air.

Paul knew this was no ordinary storm. In a burst of emotion he called out, "O Holy One of Israel, protect me. I give myself to You wholly and without reservation. Yeshua Hamashiach, save me from the Abyss of Hell."

When he reached the entrance, Paul stopped underneath the overhang and turned, panting for breath. His whole body was trembling. Water ran down his face — both celestial and terrestrial tears.

The sky had become so black he could only barely make out Yuri and the waxen man. They seemed to be enveloped in an odd, smoky haze. He squinted, but it was raining too hard for him to see clearly.

Paul jumped inside the cab. "Mount Sinai," he said, his blood pounding in his ears. "And hurry."

Yuri glared at his age-old enemy. They had met in battle many times before. The last time had been in the distant past . . . at the Vale of Siddim, when Chedorlaomer and his allies had fought the five confederate kings who ruled Sodom, Gomorrah, Admah, Zeboiim, and Zoar. The Lord had not given him permission then to dispatch the Rephaim. But today would be different. Today he would have his victory.

"You have no authority here now," he said in a loud voice that sounded like a freight train roaring down a mountainous incline at top speed. "And by the blood of the Lamb I command you into the dry places of the earth."

"It's not time," hissed the Rephaim. He drew himself up to his full stature, even though his expression now showed fear, not confidence.

Yuri raised his sword that shone with a light brighter than that of the sun. "Oh, but it *is* time." He pointed the magnificent weapon at the Rephaim's chest. Light flashed again — like a thousand bolts of lightning striking simultaneously.

For a moment the air was fouled by a stench that smelled as if a thousand matches had been ignited at the same time, only to be extinguished in the blink of an eye. And then it was gone, replaced by the smell of frankincense.

The rain stopped abruptly.

The sky cleared.

The cemetery was empty.

XXXII

The solitary wall clock in the basement of Mount Sinai Hospital read 12:55. Paul stared at it morosely, wishing he could turn back the hands of time to four days ago.

He stood in front of the door marked PATHOLOGY, trying to ignore the smell of formaldehyde. The odor permeated the hallway with the distinct stink of death.

He took a deep breath, expecting the influx of oxygen into his lungs, however tainted, to help steel him for what he knew he was about to see. He was not at all sure he could emotionally deal with seeing Gabriella's lifeless body lying on a metal gurney.

It's the cheapness and finality of death that I hate, he thought as he opened the door and stepped inside, remembering the funeral of a ten-year-old hemophiliac who had contracted the AIDS virus and died the previous summer. It had been part of the research for the article he'd written. He remembered the boy's mother staring at the face of her son in the open casket and the words she'd spoken.

"That's not my son," she'd remarked severely, as if her petulant words could bring back the life which death had stolen. "My boy never looked like this . . ." she continued, mechanically fixing the crooked tie the undertaker had provided to go with the suit her son was wearing. "No sir, he was always laughing and smiling and telling me, 'It's OK, Mama, I'm not afraid to die because I know God loves me and He'll take good care of me.'" When she finished straightening his suit she sighed heavily, fighting tears, and said, "This here ain't my boy, no sir. It's just a cheap imitation of the real thing."

345

Paul reflected on the moment, etched into his memory because of its poignancy, and it occurred to him that the woman had verbalized exactly how he'd felt his whole life about death.

It was cheap.

What was left behind in its aftermath was a fake — a sordid imitation of what was real. He realized now, less than a year later, that when he'd looked into his father's casket he knew what he'd see there: a cheap parody of life.

He closed the door behind him, pushing the disconcerting thoughts out of his mind. The young intern sitting behind the desk blocking his way asked him if he'd come to view a particular body. He said thickly, "Gabriella McDaniel."

The intern searched the typewritten sheet before him, then directed Paul to the rear of the room. He walked mechanically to where he saw a body covered with a white sheet.

He pulled up a chair, feeling very peculiar about the whole thing, but also feeling he wanted to be near Gabriella for a final few minutes. He wanted to believe that only Gabriella's *physical* body had ceased to function. That her spirit was alive and in the presence of the Lord — rejoicing. But his grief made that extremely difficult.

Hesitantly he tugged at the sheet and looked down at Gabriella's face. It was blue, like her fingernails, especially around her lips, which were a dark violet color. Several tubes were still stuck in her, and they gave her once beautiful body a cluttered appearance.

He moved, dragging the chair with him, so he could grasp the hand not sealed in a cast. He sat, then closed his eyes and bowed his head.

The lifeless appendage felt cold. There was also a stiffness about it that he realized must be the onset of *rigor mortis*.

Not quite sure why he was doing it, he began to pray silently. He lifted up his pain, placed it on the altar of sacrifice as Abraham had done with Isaac, and asked for mercy and understanding.

His whole body felt hot. Not just warm like a person with a

fever. He was burning with a consuming, fiery heat, as if he were sitting in the midst of a blast furnace.

Yet, he was not consumed.

And there was no pain.

Instead, he felt as though he were a conduit through which the most awesome power in the universe was flowing. His skin tingled with what felt like electricity.

Disoriented, he opened his eyes and discovered that he was immersed in a thick cloud — like the haze he'd seen in his bedroom three days after he buried his father. Only now the haze was much thicker. Immediately he thought of the Tabernacle, on the day Moses dedicated it to the Lord, when the *Shekinah* glory of the Holy One of Israel, the Lord God Almighty, had manifested in the form of a cloud.

He felt languid, almost drugged; yet every sense seemed heightened, even acute. Suddenly he sensed rather than heard a soft, strong voice speaking inside his head: "Fear not, for the Great I Am is with you. Even as Solomon did not ask Me for long life, nor riches, nor for the life of his enemies, so too, My son, you have not asked for these things. Because you have asked, as Solomon did, for an understanding heart that you might discern between good and evil, I shall give you all these things and more.

"I have done according to your words and have given you that which you have not asked for. Both riches and honor are yours, and if you will walk in My ways and keep My statutes and follow the way of the path My beloved Son has shown you, I will lengthen your days until He returns in glory.

"Also, as a sign to those who do not believe that I am, I shall raise My daughter from the dead that she might go forth as a helpmate to you. Go forth into all the earth and proclaim the glory of My precious Son, Jesus.

"Open your eyes and behold that My Word does not return unto Me void."

Paul did as he'd been commanded. He opened his eyes and stared at Gabriella. Her face was no longer blue!

The dark circles and puffy swelling around her eyes were also gone. And her skin was once again the color of honey.

Her fingers twitched in his hand, warm and soft. And her fingernails were once again a healthy pink color.

Overcome, Paul could not move or speak.

Gabriella's eyelids fluttered open.

She touched her tongue to her lips several times. Her mouth felt desert-dry, and her tongue tasted metallic. Her whole body ached. However, these were the only two discomforts she felt. Otherwise, she felt refreshed, as if she'd awakened from a much-needed, overnight sleep.

She raised herself up on her elbows and realized that her left leg and right arm were in casts. Paul was holding her left hand, staring at her, stupefied.

"Paul . . ." she said in a raspy but calm voice, "I will."

Paul tried to speak, failed, then tried again. "You will . . . what?"

Gabriella smiled. "You just asked me if I'd marry you and I said, 'Yes . . . I will.' I love you, and I'm certainly not going to risk losing you by saying no."

Paul wondered whether he should laugh or cry.

"Now that we've established that," she added, gathering the sheet about her body modestly, "please get hold of a doctor so he can remove these tubes and casts. I'm feeling much better, and I hardly think these are necessary."

Paul stood, knocking over the chair. Tears ran down his face. He hugged Gabriella. "I want to shout!"

Gabriella shrugged, wide-eyed, not sure what all the fuss was about. "Go ahead . . . shout."

He stepped back and whooped.

The young intern came running around the corner. When he saw Gabriella sitting up on the gurney with the sheet wrapped around her, and Paul laughing, crying, and praising the Lord with his hands raised high above his head, he grabbed the wall for support. "I don't believe it," he muttered, suddenly weak in the knees. "Those idiots on the tenth floor sent me a woman to be autopsied who was still alive! But that's impossible . . . I checked the body myself an hour ago."

He took several deep breaths, then walked over to the gurney. "What in the name of Heaven is going on here?"

Paul stopped shouting and turned. He sobered when he saw the ashen-faced intern.

Gabriella glanced first at Paul, then back at the intern. "What are you staring at?" she asked, suddenly feeling odd. And where was she? This wasn't like any hospital room she'd ever been in before.

"You, you . . ." was all the intern managed.

"I beg your pardon?"

The man glanced at Paul, who was grinning broadly.

"Haven't you ever witnessed a miracle before?" Paul asked.

"Miracle?" asked Gabriella. "What are you talking about, Paul?"

"You died over two hours ago," mumbled the intern.

"Died?"

The man nodded.

"Maybe you should call her doctor," interrupted Paul. "I think he might be very interested in what's happened here."

The intern looked at Paul, then back at Gabriella. "But what am I going to put in my report?" he muttered as he headed for his desk.

Paul looked at Gabriella, suddenly somber, and said, "Your heart stopped beating over two hours ago. The doctor had left a 'do not resuscitate' order because you suffered excessive brain damage in the accident."

At the mention of the accident Gabriella became pensive. She pondered what Paul had told her, then said, "I'm starved. You think a girl could get something to eat in this place?"

Paul laughed and shook his head. "You're really something else, you know that?"

"I guess that's why you decided to marry me, huh?"

Paul's eyes were sparkling. "It's not over, you know. They're never going to believe. And we still have to contend with Vaughn

Aurochs." He didn't have the heart to tell her about her father just yet. That would come later.

"You're absolutely right, darling," replied Gabriella solemnly as she used her thumb to wipe away the tears that lingered on his cheek. "But what a glorious beginning, don't you think?"

EPILOGUE

Horeb. Hebrew for dryness or desert. The old man smiled at the thought, then sighed and looked out the window of the monastery, admiring the aftermath of sunset.

The deep blue, cloudless sky was tinged with crimson as the last yellow-orange rays of daylight slowly dissolved with the onset of twilight. Even though the day had been especially hot, the temperature had already started to drop dramatically. Before long, it would actually be cold. Such was the way of the desert.

The man, who'd been a monk at this place, located at the foot of Jebel Musa, since he was fifteen, felt more than the change of weather in his bones. "It won't be long now," he muttered. Then, almost as an afterthought, he added, "Father, have mercy on the lost."

He sighed again, then reluctantly pulled his eyes from the breathtaking view outside. He stared at the bundle of parchments on the desk before him and thought about things he'd learned long ago.

Jebel Musa. The mountain of Moses.

The monastery had been constructed by the Emperor Justinian at the base of Mount Sinai, where Moses twice received the Books of the Law from God. It was situated southwest of the ancient city of Rephidim, in the heart of the Wilderness of Sin. Rephidim was the site where the children of Israel murmured against God because of lack of water. God provided a miracle, but Moses disobeyed and struck the rock one time too many, causing the Holy One to deny the Patriarch the right to enter the Promised Land.

The old man tugged absently at his gray-white beard, realizing the Biblical account had special meaning for him now. The bundle of parchments had arrived from America six months ago, addressed to the head librarian at St. Catherine's.

The instructions had been explicit. He was to hold them for safekeeping. Under no circumstances was he to read them.

But like Moses he had disobeyed.

Blinking, he realized that the small room had grown dark. Twilight had given way to the onset of night. He shivered and lit a candle, then sat in the flickering light, staring at the walls. He couldn't explain it, but he was certain that someday soon someone was going to come for the parchments.

He thought about the Rephaim and shuddered.

He prayed he would still be alive.